HAZEL & HOLLY

Also by Sara C. Snider

The Tree and Tower Series:
The Thirteenth Tower
A Shadowed Spirit

The Forgotten Web: A Novella

HAZEL

&

HOLLY

Sara C. Snider

DOUBLE BEAST PUBLISHING
Stockholm, Sweden

For Lori
Jennifer
and Melissa
Sisters extraordinaire

Death Before Dawn

Hazel peered at the twilit sky as she hurried along the wooded path. The lantern she clutched in a tight fist swung to and fro, casting erratic shadows though the way had begun to lighten with the approaching dawn. Her visit would be brief this time. She'd been too liberal with the valerian tea. Hazel wasn't one to oversleep, but restfulness had eluded her lately.

The skirts of her dress rustled against the brush and bushes, a rasping whisper as if the woods themselves hushed her ungainly approach.

"I won't be long," she said. No one was there, but one never knew when out in the woods.

She passed through a wrought iron gate set within a crumbling stone wall and came to a single-room stone cottage nearly overtaken with ivy and brambles of sweet briar. The water-warped door stood propped against the door frame into which it no longer fit. Hazel slipped past it and stepped inside.

The wavering light of her lamp failed to push back the deep gloom within the cottage. She fetched a handful of sticks from a corner, placed them in the hearth, and used her lantern to ignite them. She blew on the gentle flames until the cold coals flared alight.

Hazel lingered by the fire. It was always so damp in this place, as if the chill seeped into her bones as soon as she stepped over the threshold. But she was late, and it wouldn't do to tarry too long.

She walked to a table upon which sat an ewer and basin. Water dripping from a hole in the roof had filled the ewer, and Hazel poured some of the water into the bowl. From her pocket, she pulled out a piece of honey cake wrapped in cloth and crumbled the cake into the water.

She looked out the window at the lightening sky, but the sun still hadn't risen.

"You are late."

Hazel turned and found Willow warming her pale hands by the feeble fire. "I overslept."

Willow smiled, turned her back on the hearth, and sauntered over to Hazel. She reached out to touch Hazel's hair, but Hazel moved away. "Still frightened, daughter?"

"I'm not afraid," Hazel said. "I just prefer not to be touched by the dead."

Willow waved a hand, then leaned over the bowl. She took a deep breath, opening her mouth as she lingered over the water. She straightened. "Honey cake." Then she smiled. "What did you used to call it? Sunny cake?" Willow laughed. "You always thought it made the day brighter."

"That was a long time ago."

"Not that long."

"We don't have much time. The sun will soon be up."

Willow sighed. "Very well." She put on a serious expression, clasped her hands together, and in a stern voice said, "What is your progress?"

Hazel frowned. "I'm doing this for your benefit, you know. I'm not the one with her soul trapped in a geas. One would think you'd care more about your own well-being."

Willow gave a short laugh. "Well-being? My dear, I am dead. I am not a being at all, well or otherwise."

"So you're happy then? Is that it? You're happy to haunt this decrepit, rotting heap, waiting with each new moon for me to come by with a crumb of cake and to stir the fire? Because that's all you'll ever have, and when I'm gone, you won't have even that. That doesn't concern you?"

Willow tightened her jaw and closed her eyes. "Leave it alone, Hazel."

"I will not leave it alone! He did this to you—your own husband. My father. Was this part of your arrangement? Is this what you bargained for? What was it you used to tell me? He'll come when needed? Well, where is he now?!"

Willow stood there, her body trembling and her eyes clenched shut, but she said nothing.

"Answer me!"

A cold wind gusted through the room, extinguishing the fire and knocking the air from Hazel's lungs.

Willow bared her teeth and grabbed Hazel's chin in an icy grip. "The geas cannot be undone, whatever you might think. It is done, and I will *not* give him the satisfaction of my misery!" She let go of Hazel's chin and put her hand over her eyes.

Hazel rubbed her jaw, working warmth back into her chilled skin. "There is a way, Mother. I will find it. I will find Father and make him undo what he's done."

Willow gave a mirthless laugh. "And what *is* your progress, daughter? What have you found so far?"

"I *will* find him."

Willow walked to a window with ivy growing through the glassless panes. "The sun is rising, Hazel. Give Holly my love."

"Mother..."

"Do not bring honey cake next time." She slipped out the door just as sunlight streamed through the shattered windows.

Hazel watched as the dawn chased away the gloom, lessening the damp that hung in the air. Outside, birds began to chirp, but their melody did nothing to soothe the sorrow that had settled in her heart. She picked up the basin and threw the water and cake crumbs out a window. Then, casting a single look behind her, Hazel slipped out the door.

Seamless Dreams

Hazel followed the wooded path back to the cottage she shared with her sister. The sun was well up by the time she returned, and the new warmth pulled the heady scent of honeysuckle into the air. She eyed the herb patch as she passed through the garden, noted a number of red mites on the hyssop and lemon balm, and made a mental note to return later with a bowl of soapy water to wash the pests away.

She rounded a corner and found a young man standing near the front door, his back against the wall as Holly, with a broom in hand, stood too close to him than was proper or polite.

"What's going on?" Hazel said.

Holly turned, and the young man slumped as he let out a heavy breath. Her sister grinned, and her round cheeks flushed like apple blossoms. "We have a visitor!" she said, brushing away a few wisps of honey-golden hair that had escaped from her kerchief.

"I can see that," Hazel said. "Why is he here?"

Holly blinked. "I... I don't know." She turned to the young man, and he cringed back against the wall. "Why are you here?"

The young man held up an envelope sealed with a glob of purple wax. "Delivery for the Witch Hazel sisters," he said in a feeble voice.

Holly squealed and snatched the envelope from his hand. Dropping the broom, she broke the seal and opened the letter. The young man slinked away and ran out of sight.

Hazel picked up the broom and propped it against the wall. "What does it say?"

Holly held the letter in a white-knuckled grip, her lips moving as she silently read to herself. Then she looked up and beamed at Hazel. "It's an invitation!"

"To what?"

But Holly just dropped the letter and ran into the house.

Hazel sighed. The girl was exhausting. She picked up the letter and peered at an elaborate, scrolling hand adorned with motifs of rabbits, acorns, birds, and trees. It was ridiculously lavish, which made the reading laborious at best. Hazel was tempted to throw it on the trash heap but didn't for fear of not being able to get an answer out of Holly. Ignoring the ornamentation as best she could, she made out the following message:

To the most excellent Sisters of Witchery, Hazel and Holly,

You are cordially invited to the estate of Hawthorn and Hemlock, Brothers Extraordinaire of Warlockery, Sorcery, and Intrigue, for a night of Magic, Enchantment, and Fabulous Feasting. Present yourselves in your finest attire, along with this invitation, at the Brothers' estate at eight o'clock on the 23rd night of Ascending Midren, and brace yourselves for what is surely to be the most ineffable event of your entire lives.

As always: Punctuality is of the essence; lollygaggers will be turned away at the gate.

Respectfully and Eagerly,
Hawthorn and Hemlock

Hazel wrinkled her nose. What utter nonsense. Warlockery? That wasn't even a word. She walked inside the cottage and found Holly in her room, rummaging through a chest of clothes.

"I haven't anything to wear!"

Hazel waved the letter. "Don't tell me you want to go to this thing."

Holly poked her head out of the chest and screwed up her face at

Hazel. "You mean you *don't*? They said it's going to be ineffable, Hazel. *Ineffable*. We *have* to go!"

"We don't *have* to do anything other than use our good sense. That party is bound to be nothing more than a ridiculous charade."

"But I love charades!"

"We're not going."

Holly's face fell as if she had just heard the most devastating news of her life. Then she drew herself up and said, "Fine. I'll go by myself."

"What?"

"If you don't want to go, then don't go. But *I'm* going."

"You most certainly are not. You don't know these warlocks or what they'll be doing."

"They'll be throwing an amazing party. And I'll be there. I *am* a woman grown now, Hazel."

"You're seventeen." At twenty-three, Hazel was hardly an old woman. But sometimes her younger sister made her feel ancient.

Holly nodded. "Exactly." She returned to rummaging through her chest of clothes and didn't notice Hazel's glare.

"And what will you do if you're taken advantage of and thrown in a ditch?"

"Nobody in the Grove has ever been thrown in a ditch."

"What about Redwood?"

"Everyone knows he got drunk and *fell* in the ditch."

"Well, what if you get taken advantage of then?"

"Then that will be *your* fault for not coming with me. Honestly, Hazel, you're the older sister. You're supposed to be looking out for me."

Hazel's mouth fell open. She was about to tell Holly off when her younger sister smiled in that way she did whenever she succeeded in goading Hazel. Then she turned serious. "Please, Hazel. We never go anywhere or do anything. Just this once?"

Hazel clenched her jaw. Then she closed her eyes and sighed. "You have a festival dress. You can wear that."

"Oh no, I can't wear that."

"Why not?"

"It's rustic!"

Hazel folded her arms. "What's wrong with rustic?"

"Nothing, it's just…" Holly peered at Hazel with dewy, hopeful eyes. "It's going to be ineffable, Hazel. *Ineffable.*"

"I'm really starting to hate that word."

"I can't go dressed as a rustic to something like that!"

Hazel rubbed her eyes. "Fine. If you want something nicer to wear, then you'll be the one to make it. I'll not be burdened with being your seamstress, you hear me?"

A broad smile split across Holly's face, and she nodded and headed for the door.

"You'd best hurry," Hazel called after her. "The twenty-third Ascending is less than ten days away."

Later, Hazel stood in the kitchen, pounding a particularly stubborn rump of mutton into submission with a mallet when Holly stumbled through the front door. Her entrance was like a cascade of dried leaves, all rustling and crackling as she held in her arms a heap of shiny, blue-black material. Holly had draped part of the fabric around her body and over her head, forming a hood. The rest she clutched in a haphazard bundle.

"What on earth is that?" Hazel said.

Holly beamed. "Oh, Hazel, have you ever seen such material? The merchant called it taffeta. Have you ever heard such a delicious word? It sounds like candy."

"A dress made of candy? Don't be ridiculous."

"It's not *really* candy. It just sounds like it. Look, touch it. It's so shiny and… and smooth." She presented the heap of fabric to Hazel.

Hazel pursed her lips. She didn't want to touch it, but Holly might not leave her alone otherwise. She rubbed a piece of fabric between her fingers. It felt coarser than it looked. Not all that wonderful, in her estimation. "How much did this cost?"

"It's my money, so don't you worry about it."

"You paid too much, in other words."

"It wasn't too much; it was worth it. Occasions like this don't come along every day, you know."

"You're right. Mid-Ascension festivals only come four times a year. That's not counting the Declension festivals, which, of course, last for three days and nights."

"You know what I mean. Stop being sour."

"Fine. Go make your dress. Revel in sewing and clipping and trimming."

"I will." Holly drew herself up, clutched the fabric to her chest, and swished out of the room.

Hazel remained still, watching the door where Holly had disappeared. Then, tightening her jaw, she followed.

She opened the door, finding the tiny bedroom draped with the taffeta. It hung from the rafters along with wooden charms and bundles of dried herbs and flowers. Holly pushed one of the drapes aside and scowled at Hazel. "Now what?"

"You never asked about my visit with Mother."

Holly deflated as she looked down. "How did it go?"

"Terribly. We had an argument. She's unconcerned with trying to find a way to undo the geas. She says it can't be done."

Holly wrung her hands, her gaze darting off to the side. "Maybe she's right. Mother always did know best."

Hazel glowered at her. "Mother never knew best. Ever. Her current situation proves that."

Holly straightened, her eyes turning misty. "Do not speak ill of the dead."

Hazel closed her eyes and rubbed her forehead. "I'm sorry. It's just... I'm at my wit's end trying to figure out how to fix this, and yet no one else seems to care."

"I care," Holly said in a small voice.

They watched each other. Then, letting out a breath, Hazel waved towards the reams of fabric. "You'll not get this fabric worked into a dress with it draped around like this."

Holly smiled. "I know, but it's just so sumptuous I couldn't resist. I hope I have some left over for curtains."

"You have everything you need? Thread? Buttons?"

Holly opened her mouth but hesitated. Then she said, "Mostly."

"Mostly?"

She cringed. "I was hoping Chester would have renewed his stash, and he has... partially. But it's not enough." She went to a corner of her room and, from a hole in the wall, pulled out a mouse the color of chestnuts.

Hazel backed out of the room "No."

Holly followed her. "Please, Hazel."

"If you think I'll have anything to do with that filthy little beast, then you'll be sorely disappointed."

Holly gasped. "He's not filthy! I bathe him twice a week."

Hazel gave a disgusted grunt. "Of course you do."

"Please. I'd do it myself, but I need all the time I can get to make this dress before the twenty-third." Holly's clear blue eyes turned liquidy as she stared at Hazel.

Hazel sighed. "Fine." When Holly squeaked, she added, "But just this once! You'll not ask me to do anything like this ever again."

Holly clamped her mouth shut and nodded. Hazel waited as Holly returned to her room and rummaged around. After a few minutes, she walked back out, mouse in hand, who was now equipped with what looked to be an oversized vest with pockets.

"What on earth is he wearing?"

Holly beamed. "It's his fetching vest. It's got deep pockets so he has a place to stash his spoils. I made it myself."

Hazel tried to keep the horror from showing on her face, but she suspected she failed miserably. "And what is it I'm supposed to do with him?"

"I need you to take him to Zinnia's place and... well... let him loose."

"You want me to set that filthy creature loose in a fellow witch's house? You've gone mad!"

"He's not filthy!" Holly took deep breath. "Zinnia's house might as well be a museum, what with all the junk she has stashed there. She keeps *everything*. We're doing her a favor by relieving her of some of the clutter." She petted the mouse on his tiny head. "Chester will do all the work. You just set him loose and wait for him to return, empty his pockets, and send him back until you have enough supplies. He's very polite and well trained, never leaves behind any droppings, and he *never* chews on anything. She'll not even notice he was there."

"Except for her missing possessions."

Holly scoffed. "There's enough for everyone. Not my fault she doesn't know how to share."

"And how much is 'enough'?"

"Well," Holly began, looking thoughtful. "As much as you can carry, really."

Hazel's mouth hung open.

Holly beamed and offered the mouse on her outstretched hand.

Hazel backed away. "What are you doing?"

"You need to take Chester with you, silly. That's the whole point."

"I know, but... I'm not going to carry him... *like that.*"

"No, of course not. Chester usually likes to ride on top of my head, all nestled in my hair. Or on my shoulder. Or, when he's sleepy, in my pocket. He's very versatile."

Once again, Hazel's mouth fell open. This conversation with Holly was starting to make her feel like a lackwit. "You're joking, right? No, I know you're joking, because I will die a spectacular, frenzied death before I ever allow that to happen."

Holly emitted a guttural sigh. "*Fine.*" She returned to her room and, after a few minutes, came back and held out a little wicker cage, the lower portion of which had been woven with strips of colorful ribbons. Chester, still wearing his vest, sat inside, nibbling on a scattering of sunflower seeds.

Ignoring the sickening feeling settling in her stomach, Hazel took the cage. "How am I supposed to get in her house? I've not been invited. Unless, of course, you're going to suggest I wait until she leaves and then break inside."

"Of course not," Holly said. "You don't need to go in. Just let Chester loose outside and he'll find his own way. He's very resourceful."

"Clearly."

"And be sure to wait for him! Don't you dare leave him behind or smoosh him or whatever terrible things you're probably thinking right now. I'll never forgive you."

"Noted."

"Promise."

Hazel rolled her eyes. "I promise I won't hurt or abandon your trained rat."

Holly gasped. "He's a *mouse.* Rats are filthy."

An Unwelcome Visit

The day was waning by the time Hazel made it to Zinnia's house. Shadows had grown long, and the blue sky had shifted to pale gold. Hazel cursed herself for taking on this fool task, especially so late in the day.

Just outside Zinnia's garden, Hazel positioned herself behind a tree that would, she hoped, provide cover from unwanted eyes. She knelt and opened the door to the little wicker cage. Chester scampered out and sniffed the air, then started washing the backs of his ears with his paws.

"Go on, you foul little thing. Get." Hazel waved her hands at him, but Chester didn't move.

"Hazel? Is that you?"

Hazel turned and found Zinnia walking towards her with a basket hanging from her arm. "Zinnia... hello!"

Zinnia smiled, though the warmth never reached her eyes. Her gaze shifted to the ground. "Are you looking for something?"

Hazel's heart lurched into her throat, but when she looked down, Chester was gone. "Um... no. Everything's fine. I was just looking for some herbs. It seems I have a mite infestation that I'm not sure I'll recover from. I was looking for new cuttings for my garden."

"Shouldn't you get rid of the mites first?"

"What?"

"The mites, you'll need to rid them from your garden. Otherwise, your new plants will be infested as well." Zinnia screwed up her weathered face at Hazel.

Hazel forced a smile, her cheeks growing hot. "Of course. I know that. It doesn't hurt, though, to locate new cuttings now should they be needed."

Zinnia nodded, adjusting the basket on her arm while casting another glance at the ground. "What's the little cage for?"

Hazel winced inwardly. "Holly's lost her pet mouse. I bring the cage with me in case I find him while out looking for herbs."

"I see. Well, good evening to you then."

Hazel tensed. Zinnia's tone told her it was time to leave, but she dared not. She had promised Holly she wouldn't leave that miserable mouse behind. So she said, "Good evening," and continued her ridiculous charade of pretending to look for herbs.

Zinnia cleared her throat, so Hazel put on a smile and said, "I have a peppermint cordial that works wonders for coughs. I could give you some, if you'd like."

Zinnia's face reddened. "It's getting late, you know. Surely you can't search for herbs in the dark?"

Surely not, but she couldn't leave without a certain overdressed rodent. "Don't worry about me. I find that searching for herbs at night often gives one a new perspective on the world. You should try it sometime, Zinnia."

Zinnia scoffed and drew herself up. "I should think not, thank you very much." She pursed her lips, then said, "Well, at least come in for tea. It makes me nervous, having you out here skulking about. Come in for tea so you can't fault my hospitality, and then you'll search for your herbs elsewhere."

Hazel didn't want to have tea with Zinnia. The woman smelled of dirt and overly perfumed soap. Not to mention she was supposed to wait for Chester. Would he know where to find Hazel if she moved? It seemed unlikely that a rodent—bathed twice weekly though he was—would be self-possessed enough to think on his feet... or paws, as it were. But what else could she do? She couldn't refuse, not without going straight home. Anything else would be unforgivably rude. So Hazel clenched her jaw, put on the most gracious smile she could muster, and nodded.

The inside of Zinnia's home smelled like freshly turned earth and an overabundance of roses, lavender, and lilacs. It was both cloying and pleasant, unsettling as well as comforting. Hazel didn't at all care for the contradictory sensations.

Zinnia led her through a labyrinth of tall shelves littered with odds and ends before coming to a long, polished dark walnut table. "Please, have a seat."

There should have been eight chairs around the table, but in place of three of them stood three wooden statues nearly as tall as Hazel. One was carved into the shape of a bear, one a wolf, and the other a squirrel. Each wore a garland of dried flowers upon its polished head. The bear clutched a cane in its wooden paws.

"That's Grandfather Bear," Zinnia said. You can sit next to him, if you'd like. He's the most even-tempered out of the three. I'd stay clear of Sister Squirrel though. She's a bit of a trickster."

"Is that so?" Hazel said, but Zinnia had already disappeared among the stacks of shelves.

Taking Zinnia's advice, she sat down next to the bear. The chair creaked under her weight, the cushion exuding an aroma of musty rose. Holly had been right; the place was like a museum. Stacks of shelves filled the room, all cluttered with bones and feathers, colored glass bottles, and little jeweled boxes. There were tiny silver figurines shaped like men, birds, and fish. There were dusty books and yellowed scrolls, pearl-embroidered gloves, and bolts of cloth in countless colors and materials.

The shelves seemed to close in on Hazel. The smell of dirt thickened, as did the cloying scent of flowers that now held a hint of decay.

Something soft brushed against her hand, and Hazel cried out and jerked back. On the table sat Chester, the pockets on his vest bulging.

"Is everything all right?" Zinnia said, poking her head around a corner.

Hazel put her hands over the mouse, gritting her teeth at the way his whiskers tickled her palm. "Yes, quite all right. Just saw a strange shadow, is all. Perhaps Sister Squirrel is playing her tricks on me." Hazel forced a smile.

Zinnia lingered a moment, frowning at Hazel. Then she turned and disappeared.

Hazel let out a breath as she removed her hands from the mouse. Then, wrinkling her nose, she fished out the goods from Chester's pockets. Two buttons, three tiny beads, and a polished crystal that might have once been set in a ring. Hazel put the items in her own pocket as Chester scampered off. Holly had told her to bring as much as she could carry. At this rate, she'd be here all night.

Zinnia returned with a tray bearing a steaming teapot, two cups, and a plate of brown bread. "I trust you don't take sugar or cream in your tea. I never do. It's bad for the constitution."

"Plain is fine."

Zinnia poured the amber tea into the cups and handed one to Hazel. Hazel brought the tea to her nose. It smelled like dirt and flowers, just like the house. She put the cup back down. When Zinnia offered the plate of bread, Hazel took a slice. It was coarse and dense.

"Would you happen to have any butter or jam?" she said.

"Butter and jam are the quickest path to an early grave, mark my words. You'd do well to go without."

Zinnia's hospitality was wearing increasingly thin. Hazel gave a tight smile. "Of course," she said and nibbled on the dry bread.

They drank their tea in silence. Zinnia's gaze kept darting to the wolf statue and back to Hazel, then she'd narrow her eyes and sip her tea. It was terribly unsettling, though Hazel did her best to not let it show.

She waved to the surrounding shelves. "So, where did you find all this... treasure?"

"Here and there," Zinnia said.

They fell back into silence.

There was a scratching sound, then Chester scampered across the floor and under the table. Hazel's face grew hot, but Zinnia seemed not to have noticed the mouse. Her unwavering gaze remained fixed on Hazel.

"The bread is wonderful. I wonder if I could get the recipe."

"No."

Hazel blinked. Refusal to share a food recipe was considered rude. Given that all other types of recipes—be they for spells or potions—were closely guarded secrets, sharing recipes for meals was considered a show of good faith, a way to connect in an otherwise secretive world. "I beg your pardon?"

Zinnia narrowed her eyes. "You come to my home, tell me lies, and then expect me to share a recipe with you? I think not."

Hazel swallowed. "I don't know what you mean."

Zinnia slammed her cup onto the table, spilling tea onto the polished wood. "You think I don't see what goes on in here? Brother Wolf watches; he's seen what you've done." She got up from her chair. "Thief!"

Hazel also got up. "You're right, I shouldn't have come here." She fished out the trinkets Chester had procured and put them on the table. "I shouldn't have let Holly talk me into this foolish plan of hers. I apologize. Sincerely. I'll fetch the mouse and never bother you again. You have my word."

"The mouse stays."

Hazel frowned. "What would you want with that filthy creature?"

"Payment for your trespass."

"I can pay you with something else. I have a few gold coins, or I can pay you in herbs or food. Last year's mead turned out especially well. I can give you a crate."

"No. The mouse is the thief; the mouse will be payment."

"The mouse is not mine to give."

Zinnia narrowed her eyes. "Then neither of you will leave."

Hazel tensed. "Do not threaten me."

"You are in *my* home. I will do as I please."

The shelves behind Hazel ground along the floorboards as they closed the path to the door.

Hazel ran her hands along her skirts, feeling her pockets, but they were all empty. She was in another witch's home. Her magic would not work here. The only magic she would be able to do is whatever she could focus into an item that belonged to her. She had her dress, but that was big and unwieldy, not to mention on her body. She needed something smaller that she could manipulate.

The bear statue moved. The grooves in his carved coat rippled until the wood shivered away and was replaced with bristly fur. Grandfather Bear—a real bear now—turned towards her and hoisted himself up on his hind legs with the help of his cane.

Zinnia peeked from around him and grinned. "I don't think you realize what an honor this is. I could sic Brother Wolf on you. Trust me, you would not like that."

Hazel backed into a shelf as the bear shuffled towards her. She ran her hands along the dusty shelves as she looked for an item to defend herself. "What about the squirrel?" she said, struggling to keep her voice calm. "All things considered, I think I'd rather you sic the squirrel on me."

"Sister Squirrel would take far too long. Has a short attention span, that one. She's good for diversion, not apprehension."

Hazel's fingers brushed against a glass bottle, and she tried to grab it, but it toppled over and fell to the floor, shattering in a splash of crimson shards.

Zinnia's face twisted in anger. "Get her!"

Grandfather Bear drew himself up taller—if such a thing were possible—and roared. He lunged at her, but Hazel darted out of the way. She tried to run across the room, but something caught her foot and she fell. Pain seared through her hands as glass cut her skin. She grabbed hold of a shard and jabbed it at the bear as he came towards her. She got him in the arm, but he seemed to not have noticed. He brought up a great black paw and struck her head against the floor, and all else faded into darkness.

Water dripped onto Hazel's forehead as a little old man about as tall as her arm was long rifled through her pockets. Startled, she pushed herself up, scrabbling across the stone floor to get away.

The gnome gave a wry smile. "You don't got anything worth taking. No need to be overzealous about the matter." He picked up a lantern and started to walk away.

"Wait," Hazel said.

He turned around.

"Where are we?" Water dripped from a low, craggy ceiling that the gnome's lantern barely illuminated. All else was dark.

"Miss Zinnia's cellar. Well, part of it anyway." He started to walk away again.

"Wait," Hazel said.

The gnome sighed and turned back around.

"How do I get out?"

"Out?"

"Yes. Out. Where is the exit?"

The gnome screwed up his wrinkled face. "There isn't any out."

Hazel scoffed. "Don't be ridiculous." Her voice sounded dead and hollow in the dark, damp cellar.

He shrugged and walked away.

"Wait!" Hazel cried, but the gnome had gone, as had the light from his lantern.

She stared into the darkness where he had disappeared, willing the little man to come back, but he didn't. She sat there, listening to the racing of her heart, beating out of time to the drip-drops of the falling water from the ceiling.

"What have you gotten me into, Holly?"

But no one replied, not even an echo. She got to her feet and ran her hand along the wall as she walked. The stone was cool and damp. Every now and then her fingers would run over a patch of soft moss or a strand of slimy algae. When she came across an alcove in the wall, her heart jumped, thinking it a door. But it was only a deep impression, within which lay shards of bones and other items—some brittle, some sticky and soft. She jerked her hand away and moved on.

When Hazel at last felt the rough, splintered texture of wood, she let out a heavy, relieved breath. She ran her hands all along the door, looking for a handle, a keyhole, anything that might let her out or let her see. But nothing was there. Only a solid wall of rutted, heavy wood.

She continued to rove blindly with her hands. At the bottom was a narrow crack, no more than a finger's breadth. She wedged her fingers into the crevice, trying to find the other end of the door. Instead, she felt a tickling on her fingertips. Hazel cried out and yanked her hand back.

A soft scratching sound came from near the door, then a faint squeak. "Chester?"

Another squeak—louder, nearby. Hazel, hesitating a moment, gritted her teeth, then lowered her hand—palm up—to the floor. She ground her teeth harder as soft fur tickled her palm, and the tiny pricking on her skin from the mouse's claws. Hazel closed her eyes and shuddered, trying not to dwell on the way the creature's stiff, cord-like tail wrapped itself around one of her fingers.

Cringing, she reached with her other hand to the animal resting on her palm. It was Chester, all right; she could feel his vest with its bulging pockets. Yet the disgusting animal presented an opportunity.

Hazel needed a personal item into which she could focus her magic. The mouse, though he belonged to Holly, would probably work. They lived in the same house, after all.

Hazel set Chester back on the ground. Keeping a finger on him, she cast a spell of Transformation. Underneath her hand, the mouse grew. And grew. And grew some more.

The air in front of her warmed. Hazel put out her hands and met a wall of fur and rough fabric. She pulled her hands away and cleared her throat. "Chester?"

A resounding squeak came in reply that dwarfed her cautious voice. She grimaced, not wanting to dwell on the fact that a monstrous creature lurked next to her in the darkness.

"Could you take down the door?" She cleared her throat again. "Please."

Another deafening squeak came, along with a scratching sound. Chester's deep, heavy breaths quickened and then a splintering as the door began to crack. Hazel backed away and put her hands to her ears as the cracking grew louder, and then in a cloud of choking dust, the door broke from the hinges and fell.

Hazel coughed and waved at the air. Beyond the door was a hallway, dimly illuminated by a distant lamp. Chester's hulking form filled the doorway and blotted out the light. Taking a deep breath, she said, "Let's get out of here, Chester."

Chester squeezed through the doorway and charged down the hall. Hazel trailed after him, trying to figure out what she'd do if they ran into Zinnia and her guardian statues. From behind, came a light pattering of footsteps.

Hazel turned and found the little gnome trailing behind her.

"What do you want?" she said.

"I'm coming with you."

Hazel opened her mouth, but before she could reply, the gnome said, "You'd best hurry. Looks like your mouse is leaving without you."

Hazel turned to find Chester charging up a set of stairs. He came to another door that he pawed at and then knocked over. Hazel hurried after him into a room cluttered with junk. There were suits of armor and potted trees with wide, glossy leaves. Incense censers swung from the ceiling, and paintings covered every wall. There were massive wooden chests and piles of clothing, heaps of papers and books, and bundles of dried flowers tied together like sheaves of wheat.

Chester charged through all of it, toppling suits of armor and sending incense censers to clang together like disharmonious bells.

From behind one of the closed doors came Zinnia's voice. "What's all this then?" She opened the door and gawped when she saw the massive mouse hulking before her. She cried out, backing away. Chester leaped through the air and knocked her over.

"Get off me, you foul beast!"

Chester put his nose near her face, his long whiskers twitching as he sniffed at the witch. The gnome bolted through the clutter, knelt next to Zinnia, and rifled through her pockets.

Hazel grabbed a wooden box and stuffed it in one of Chester's pockets. "You should have taken the mead, Zinnia. I once felt bad about stealing from you. Not anymore." She finished stuffing Chester's pockets with anything she could get her hands on.

"Y-you..." Zinnia spluttered as her face purpled. But before she could finish the thought, Hazel ripped a strip of cloth from one of the clothing piles and stuffed it in Zinnia's mouth. Then she used another strip to tie Zinnia's hands together.

The gnome crawled up onto Chester's back, and with Hazel following close behind, they made their way out of the witch's home and into the night.

The sky had begun to lighten with dawn by the time they made it back to Hazel's cottage. The gnome slid off Chester's back, his weathered face splitting into a wide grin.

"Best bit of fun I've had in a long while," he said.

"What were you doing in her cellar?"

"We're both collectors, so it suited me fine to live under her house awhile. When it no longer suited me, well, it seemed I became another item for her to keep."

"That's terrible."

The gnome shrugged. "There're worse fates than being kept and cared for."

"What will you do now?"

"Find a new cellar that has need of a gnome." He peered up at her. "Say, what about you? I'll keep your preserves tidy and prevent your root vegetables from rotting. In return, I take some beer and some treasures that I can add to my collection."

"Uh... no. I don't think we need a cellar gnome, Mr.... ah..."

"Tum."

"Mr. Tum."

He nodded. "As you like. If you change your mind, though, just set some beer outside for me and I'll come right in. Think about it."

Stunned, Hazel could only nod. Tum smiled, gave her a wave, then ran off into the darkness.

Hazel turned to Chester and emptied out his pockets. She reversed her spell and returned him to his normal size, then she walked inside the house to wake up Holly.

Masked Revelry

Hazel tapped her foot as she waited in the main room of the cottage, tightening her clasped hands. "Are you ready yet?" she called to Holly. "Or am I to stand here the entire night, overdressed and with aching feet?" She smoothed the skirt of her dress—tea-dyed muslin embroidered with silk flowers and bees. She couldn't remember the last time she had worn it.

Holly's door opened, and she emerged in a flurry of rustling taffeta and streaming ribbons. Her golden hair had been piled atop her head, out of which sprouted three long peacock feathers. Holly must have used every scrap of fabric she had—the dress looked on the verge of swallowing her, as if it were some great blue-black beast, armored with gleaming scales of mismatched beads and crystals.

"Good grief, Holly. What's happened to you?"

Holly beamed, her rouged cheeks redder than usual. "Do you like it?" She twirled around, the ribbons on the dress streaming behind her.

Hazel most decidedly did not like it. Her sister looked like a swollen bruise, one that had apparently been adorned with every button and bauble in existence. She was about to tell her as much, but when she saw the hopeful, eager gleam in Holly's eyes, she cleared her throat instead. "It is... unique."

"Do you mean it? You don't think anyone will have a similar dress, do you? I want to stand out."

"You will most definitely stand out."

Holly giggled and clapped her hands. "Oh, Hazel, tonight is going to be so magical. I just know it."

"It will certainly be something."

They walked along the main road that wound through the Grove. A carriage hurtled past them in the same direction they walked. Otherwise, they saw no one. Eventually they came to a tall wrought iron fence that surrounded Hawthorn and Hemlock's home. The gate was flanked by two guards dressed in black-and-purple livery.

"You don't think we're late, do you?" Holly said as she eyed the guards.

"Of course I think we're late," Hazel said. "You took half the night putting on that dress of yours. I'll not be blamed if they turn us away."

Holly produced the rumpled invitation from her pocket and handed it to one of the guards. "We're the Witch Holly sisters. Invited. Says so right there." She pointed at the paper.

"Actually, it's the Witch Hazel sisters," Hazel said.

Holly glared at her. "Is not," she said under her breath.

"Don't be difficult. You're just going to confuse the poor man."

Holly opened her mouth, but the guard said, "Lollygaggers," and handed the invitation back to Holly. "Best be on your way."

"What?" Holly said.

"Did I stutter? Lolly. Gaggers. That's you. And this is you getting turned away at the gate. Says so right there." He tapped the invitation in Holly's hand.

"We're not late!"

"It's half past eight. So yes, actually, you are." He swept his arms towards the road. "Go on. Off with you now."

Holly straightened her back and pressed her lips into a fine line. "Listen, you. Do you know how much time I've spent on this dress? You need to let us in."

The guard looked her up and down. "Yes, I imagine you've put eternity into that dress, along with everything else. Doesn't make any difference though."

The other guard snickered.

Holly's face reddened.

"There will be other parties, Holly," Hazel said.

"Doesn't matter," Holly said. "We're getting in *this* one."

"No," the guard said, "you're not."

Holly glared at him, then she reached into her pocket and pulled out a pinecone the size of a robin's egg.

Hazel took a step back.

"Come on, miss," the guard said. "Run along home."

Holly flicked the cone and pelted him in the forehead.

"Ow!" the guard said as he put a hand to his head and bent over.

The other guard let out a short laugh before he remembered himself and put on a sober face. "You shouldn't have done that. Now we'll have to take you in. Let the brothers deal with you."

Holly flicked another cone and got him in an eye. The guard cried out and reeled back as he put his hands to his face. She walked up to the first guard, who stood doubled over while cradling his head in his hands.

"That pain you're feeling," Holly said, bending down next to him, "is from a tree getting ready to sprout from your head. Give me the keys to the gate, and I'll stop it from happening."

"What?" the guard said.

Holly made a disgusted sound and patted his pockets until she found a ring of keys. She tested several of them until she found the one that fit and opened the gate. She grinned. "Come on, Hazel!"

Hazel glanced at the guards and said, "You can't leave them like this, you know."

Holly rolled her eyes. "Fine. Come through the gate first though."

Once Hazel had followed Holly through the gate, Holly closed and locked it. Then, to the guards, she said, "You'll be fine. A tree isn't really going to sprout from your head." She paused. "Well, it *probably* won't. Human heads don't make good growing grounds. But"—she grinned—"you never know."

Hazel put a stern edge in her voice. "Holly..."

Holly's smile faded. "Just rub some salt or ash on your head, and that should get rid of the pain." She started to walk away but turned back around and added, "You're welcome."

They followed a road through Hawthorn and Hemlock's estate, past manicured lawns and hedges shaped into the likeness of woodland animals. They came to a great manor house, shrouded in curtains of ivy that twined up the grey stone walls. Holly bounced up the steps, took hold of the knocker at the door, and gave it three quick raps. A solemn butler in a starched suit answered the door.

As Holly opened her mouth, Hazel stepped forward and said, "We are the Witch Hazel sisters, here by invitation."

Holly slumped, her face crestfallen.

The butler sighed and said, "Follow me." He retreated into the house. Hazel and Holly trailed after him.

They walked down a wood-paneled hallway lined with painted portraits of frowning men. Some had dogs down by their feet, some held books. Others were cut off at the shoulders and were nothing more than disembodied heads of bushy-eyebrowed disapproval. Holly's mouth hung open as she gazed up at them. Hazel wore a frown of her own, keeping her gaze fixed on the butler's back. She felt as if the paintings watched her as she moved, and she did not care for being watched by the dead.

The butler came to a door, but instead of opening it, he turned towards the sisters and clasped his hands behind his back. "We see the mistresses' faces are exposed. Perhaps they would care for a covering provided by the house?" He waved towards an alcove, within which scores of masks hung upon the walls.

Holly squealed and ran over to peruse the selection. Hazel folded her arms. "I don't think so."

"We would insist," the butler said.

Hazel narrowed her eyes. "Who's this 'we' we're talking about? And why should they insist upon it?"

The butler drew himself up. "*We* are everyone, for whom few are trusted to speak."

Hazel opened her mouth, but Holly came over and thrust a mask into her hands. It was shaped in the likeness of a dragon, adorned with glittering crystals and sequins for scales.

Holly giggled. "That one's perfect for you." She tied a mask around her head, taking on the appearance of a cat with whiskers made of threads of finely spun glass.

The butler continued to look down his nose at Hazel while Holly bounced up and down.

"Come on, Hazel. We'll never get in otherwise."

Hazel let out a breath. "Fine," she said and tied the mask around her head.

The butler opened the door and, with a sweeping motion of his arm, ushered them inside.

Hazel and Holly walked into a grand ballroom with a painted ceiling that arced the height of two stories. Tall windows lined one end of the room, looking out onto a well-kept garden illuminated with candles in glass jars hanging in tree branches. And then, of course, there were the people.

The room hummed with movement and conversation, with rustling fabric of countless dresses. Hazel squinted. There were an awful lot of women. In fact, they were *all* women. The only men she could see was the butler that stood guard at the door, hands clasped behind his rigid back, and the musicians in a corner of the room.

Holly gasped as she walked inside, her head craned back as she took in the motifs above. One panel showed rabbits dining with foxes over tea and cakes, another showed a porcupine leading an army of armor-clad mice towards a distant city. There was even a painting of a witch stirring a cauldron from which a cloud of smoke rose and gave form to a surrounding forest.

Hazel bumped into a woman wearing a butterfly mask. "Pardon me."

The woman peered at Hazel through wings of stained glass. She huffed and moved on.

Holly disappeared into the crowd. Hazel tried to follow, but people closed in behind Holly and blocked her way. Gasps and tittering laughter rippled through the crowd. Hazel elbowed her way through—ignoring glares and sharp remarks—and eventually found Holly holding the hand of a man with wavy, shoulder-length auburn hair. He wore a burgundy waistcoat and breeches with bright white stockings. His face was covered with a mask of polished green ivy, with curling tendrils that coiled from his head like budding horns. Holly blushed, her neck reddening.

"My, what an enchanting dress," the man said, and he smiled, showing rows of pearly white teeth.

Holly giggled and put a hand to her cat-swathed cheek.

He turned towards the crowd. "There are so many fine witches here this evening I cannot possibly choose amongst you. So to help me decide,

I will hold a contest, the prize for which will be... me." He extended a leg, showing off a shapely calf. The surrounding women gasped and giggled.

Hazel frowned. "Ridiculous."

"It's a glamour, you know."

Hazel turned and found a man standing next to her. He wore an owl mask, built into which was a pair of round spectacles. He had a head of short brown hair, but that was all she could see of him.

"I beg your pardon?" Hazel said.

"My brother. That's not what he looks like."

"Your brother? You mean..."

The man gave a wry smile. "I'm Hemlock." He nodded towards the other man. "That's Hawthorn."

Hazel frowned again. "I don't understand. What does he mean by 'choosing amongst us'?"

Hemlock rubbed the back of his neck and twisted his mouth to the side. "Yes, well, it turns out he's looking for a wife."

"A wife? What on earth for?"

"What other reason is there for finding a mate? Love, companionship, extending one's legacy. That sort of thing."

"The invitation said nothing about this."

Hemlock winced. "Hawthorn thought it would be a 'nice' surprise." He glanced around the room and muttered, "He doesn't seem to be wrong."

"Well, in the case of my sister and me, he's dead wrong." She looked Hemlock up and down. "Are you in on this as well?"

He cleared his throat. "Ah, no. This was all Hawthorn's doing. I wanted nothing to do with it. I had planned on secluding myself through-out the spectacle, but I couldn't resist watching Hawthorn make a fool of himself."

A series of squeals rippled through the room as Hawthorn's hair fluttered as if caught in a breeze, and a pair of cream-colored bunnies hopped around his ankles.

A witch wearing a shimmering green dress and dragonfly mask fainted near Hawthorn's feet, and then a tussle broke out among the surrounding women. One woman reached for Hawthorn, but Holly—still at his side—planted a hand on her face and pushed her away.

"Ladies, please," Hawthorn said as a wide smile split across his face.

Another witch came up from behind Holly and pulled her by the hair. Holly cried out, her hands flailing as she stumbled backwards.

"Ridiculous," Hazel muttered again. She took a step forward, but then, from a corner of the room, music started to play, and the crowd pulled together in front of Hazel and cut her off from her sister.

Chaos erupted in the ballroom. Half the guests were dancing to a fervent tune, the other half were engaged in a petty brawl of hair pulling and dress snagging as each woman tried to reach Hawthorn. No one seemed to notice the man had retreated to a balcony, upon which he overlooked the scene with a smile wide enough to swallow the rising moon.

Scowling, Hazel rolled up her sleeves, cast a Dissolving spell, and clapped her hands together. Luckily, her magic had no constraints in warlocks' homes.

Hawthorn's glamour faded, revealing a middle-aged man with mousey-brown hair that had begun to silver at the temples. Ironically, he was still handsome in the dignified way reserved for older men. But he no longer had the smooth, flawless skin and the shiny, flowing hair that wafted around his face.

Hazel thought he looked better without the glamour, but she must have been the only one, for the music stopped and a hush fell over the room as everyone turned to look at him.

Hawthorn grinned at the attention. But then, looking at his hands, his face fell.

Murmurs rippled through the room. The guests started to shuffle out the door.

"Wait!" Hawthorn said, but no one paid him any mind. He gripped the balcony banister as his face reddened. "Merrick! Don't let them leave!"

The butler walked over to a gong sitting on a narrow table and struck it with a mallet.

Everyone froze, and the room quieted.

Merrick drew himself up tall and in a resounding voice said, "Dinner is served!"

A few women clapped their hands while others emitted various *oohs* and *aahs*. Everyone seemed to have forgotten about leaving and allowed Merrick to herd them through a door into a dining hall.

Hazel, however, hadn't forgotten a thing. She pushed her way through the crowd until she found Holly just as she was about to step into the dining room. Hazel grabbed her arm and yanked her back, and Holly emitted a startled yowl.

Holly pulled free and rubbed her arm. "That hurt, you know."

"We're leaving," Hazel said.

"But I don't want to leave." Holly's voice turned wistful. "Have you ever seen anything so grand? All the masks and the painted ceilings. Why don't we have painted ceilings?" She sighed. "When we get home, I'm going to paint them."

"You can't paint thatch," Hazel snapped, then clenched her jaw and took a breath. "Never mind. We need to leave. We shouldn't have come here. All this trickery. Should have expected as much from warlocks. Can't be trusted, the lot of them."

"But—" Holly began, though she was cut off again as Hazel grabbed her arm and pulled her into the hallway.

Hemlock stood in the little alcove with the masks. "Well done, dissolving Hawthorn's glamour. Always a pleasure to have a witch in the house." He smiled and gave a small bow.

Hazel glared at him. "I didn't do it for your amusement."

Hemlock smiled even more. "I know, which only makes it all the more amusing."

She made a disgusted sound, yanked her mask off along with Holly's, and pulled her sister to the door.

Holly sniffed as she gazed at her cat mask lying on the floor. "But... I don't want to leave."

"The night is still young," Hemlock said. "I hope you'll stay a little longer."

Hazel whirled around. "And why on earth would I do that? So you can make a mockery of me and my sister? So we can be fools for your amusement?"

"No," Hemlock said. "Because I knew your father, and word has it you've been looking for him."

Hazel narrowed her eyes. "I don't believe you."

"Your belief is not required, I'm afraid. It remains true, all the same."

"Then where is he? If you know him, tell me where he is."

He shook his head. "I said I knew Ash, not where he is. Yet knowing a man is a starting point, don't you think? I might know more of his habits and inclinations than you do. How much do you know of your father? The foods he likes to eat or the places he likes to frequent?"

Hazel tensed. Her father was little more than a vague memory—a hazy recollection of a man who had once been in her life but who now only lived in the shadows of her mind.

"I'll admit," Hemlock said, "that what I know of him is woefully inadequate. I haven't seen him since I was a very young man, and so what I do know of him perhaps is no longer true. But I'd like to think I can help you find the path. If you're interested, that is."

"Why would you help me? What do you want?"

Hemlock smiled and shook his head. "I don't want anything. I am embarrassed that my brother's antics have inconvenienced you, and this is my way of making amends."

"We weren't inconvenienced," Holly said but clamped her mouth shut when Hazel glared at her.

Hazel didn't want his help. This was a family matter, and she'd rather not enlist the help of a warlock she barely knew and didn't trust. And yet her refusal caught in her throat. So far, she hadn't been able to find her father on her own. Despite her determination to find a way to set her mother's soul free, Hazel didn't know what to do—she was out of options. So she just stood there, not wanting to accept yet unable to refuse.

Hemlock cleared his throat. "Such decisions need not be made at once. Perhaps we should join the others in the dining hall. A good meal always helps clear the thoughts, or so they say anyway."

Holly squeaked as she hopped up and down while clapping her hands. "Oh yes, please. That would be delightful. Right, Hazel?"

She might not be able to accept Hemlock's help, but she could, at least, accept an invitation to dinner. "Very well."

Dinnertime Drama

Red-faced servants carried massive bowls and platters of food into the
dining room through a swinging door. From beyond the door came
shouts and cries, the clanging of pots, then the brittle sound of shattering
glass. A few more servants bolted into the dining room, placed their trays
onto a sideboard, and hurried away in the opposite direction.

Hawthorn, once again glamoured, sat at the head of an impossibly
long table. There must have been nearly fifty women sitting around it.
He smiled at his guests. "Do forgive the ruckus, but I assure you the meal
will be worth it." He snapped his fingers.

When nothing happened, he turned to the butler standing near one
of the sideboards and raised his eyebrows.

Merrick coughed but remained still.

Hawthorn gave a nervous laugh. "That would be *now*, Merrick."
When the butler remained still, Hawthorn cast another worried glance
to his guests and then, to Merrick, hissed, "Please!"

"Very good, sir," Merrick said.

Hawthorn smoothed his hair and put on another smile. His gaze fell
on Hemlock, Hazel, and Holly lingering near the door, and he waved a

hand. "Come now, brother. We are not animals who eat our meals while standing. Come and sit, as is proper."

Hemlock muttered something under his breath. Then he turned towards Hazel and extended an arm. "Shall we?"

Hazel adjusted the dragon mask that once again covered her face. The thing was ridiculously heavy. But before she could answer, Holly bounced forward and said, "Yes, we shall!"

She scooted past Hazel and Hemlock to one of the chairs closest to Hawthorn. It was occupied by a woman in a purple dress wearing a parrot mask. Holly reached into her pocket and pulled out a little pinecone. She rolled it between her fingertips and lifted her hand.

"Holly, don't you dare!" Hazel said.

The room quieted as everyone turned to look at her, and Hazel's face flushed behind her mask. Judging by the color of Holly's neck, her sister did the same.

"But... Hazel!" Holly mewled.

Hazel marched to an empty seat at the other end of the table and sat down. Hemlock sat next to her, taking his position at the end of the table opposite Hawthorn. Holly, putting the pinecone back in her pocket, slumped into a chair across from Hazel.

Merrick and a few young men in black-and-purple livery made their way around the table, presenting various dishes to the guests. One tray held a collection of herring stuffed with pickled radishes and leeks. Hazel and Hemlock took one herring each, but Holly shook her head and waved the servant away.

Judging by the food, the theme of the evening was "stuffed." There were stuffed pheasants and stuffed parcels of ham, cakes filled with cream, and melons carved into jewelry boxes filled with an array of colorful fruits. There were stuffed gourds and stuffed lettuce leaves, walnut shells filled with tiny diced vegetables, and vegetables filled with finely chopped nuts.

Hazel tried to be polite and take a little of everything presented to her, but there seemed to be no end to the food and she refused to heap her plate like a glutton. Holly, however, had no such reservations. She took everything that she fancied, which was mostly the fruit, nut, and vegetable dishes. She seemed particularly fond of the mushrooms carved into the likeness of pinecones and grabbed hold of the servant's sleeve before he walked off so she could help herself to another serving.

Conversation around the table turned to a murmur as the guests tried to eat around their masks. Those with half masks that covered only their eyes carried on most of the dinnertime conversation. Those with full masks tried to gracefully navigate food behind their facial coverings and pretend they were making a good job of it.

It was all so ridiculous. Hazel wanted nothing to do with such folly and removed her mask. Gasps rippled around the room; several guests dropped their forks onto their plates with unceremonious clangs.

Hawthorn closed his eyes and covered his mouth with an embroidered linen napkin. "Merrick!" he cried.

Merrick hustled over to Hazel and grabbed her by the arm. "You will come with us," he said.

"What on earth for?"

"Propriety, madam, and your dismissal of it."

"Propriety can stuff it. I'm sure there's a cabbage leaf here somewhere for that."

Hawthorn covered his eyes while, with his other hand, he waved at the air. "Is she gone yet?"

"I'm right here, you perfumed oaf," Hazel said, not quite shouting but loud enough for her voice to carry across the sizeable table.

A few women covered their mouths as they gasped. The woman in the green dress and dragonfly mask fell out of her chair as she fainted.

Holly watched the whole affair while munching on a stuffed fig, dribbling crumbs of toasted bread and nuts.

Hemlock tried to hide a smile behind his wine glass.

"Does this amuse you?" Hazel said, annoyed.

"I am afraid that it does. Greatly."

She stood up. "I am not here for your amusement."

Merrick took the opportunity of her standing and pulled her towards the door.

A rage filled Hazel. She would not be silenced, not among these self-important buffoons. She yanked her arm out of Merrick's grasp and, before he could grab hold of her again, marched towards the table and pulled off the mask of the first woman she came to.

"Tansy, how nice to see you," Hazel said.

Tansy's cheeks bloomed red, and she reached for the mask. Hazel threw it across the room, sending Tansy to scuttle after it.

Hazel moved on to the next woman and yanked off her mask as well, and the next one. One masked woman got up and tried to run from the room, but Holly tackled her and pulled off her mask and held it up like a trophy.

The other women seemed frozen by Hazel's advance, blinking at each other from behind their masks before Hazel tore it off of them. No one seemed to know what to do in the face of such impropriety. Merrick remained by the door, his arms pulled close to his body as his features twisted in abject horror.

Hazel came to Hawthorn. "You," she growled.

"Merrick?" he said, still covering his eyes with his hand. "What's happening?"

Hazel pulled off his mask. He clutched at it, trying to bring it back to his face, but Hazel refused to let go. She rapped him on the skull with a knuckle, and Hawthorn cried out and let go of the mask as he put a hand to his head.

"You... you struck me," he said. "Am I bleeding? Merrick! Am I bleeding?" He pulled his hand away and blinked at his fingers, seemingly confused at the absence of blood. He returned his hand to his head and repeated the process.

"I barely touched you," Hazel said.

With his hand affixed to his head, Hawthorn rose from his chair and thrust a finger at her. "How dare you come here with your... your brutish ways. Merrick, escort her out." He checked his fingers again.

"I'll escort her," Hemlock said, rising from his chair.

Hazel glared at him, but her fury had faded, and she no longer wanted anything more to do with these people. "Come on, Holly."

Holly clutched the stolen mask to her chest and, walking to the table, grabbed a handful of figs and stuffed them into a pocket. Then she and Hazel followed Hemlock out.

Yet instead of leading them towards the hallway and to the front door, he crossed the ballroom and opened a different door that led into a library. He motioned for them to step inside. Hazel hesitated, but Holly, munching on a fig, walked right in.

Hemlock removed his mask, revealing a man roughly in his thirties.

His features were plain, lacking the refinement of his brother. Yet there was a strength in the lines of his jaw and a level clarity in his gaze that put Hazel at ease despite herself.

He removed the glasses from his mask and put them on. "Please, I only want to talk."

Hazel's mouth worked soundlessly as she tried to find the words to refuse him. But she couldn't. If he was telling the truth in knowing about her father, then she needed to find out what that was.

She let out a breath and followed Holly into the library.

Shelves of books lined the walls in a snug room furnished with a green upholstered sofa and matching armchair, which flanked a polished elm-wood tea table. Holly perused the books, running a finger along the spines as she munched on her figs. Hemlock cast her nervous glances, no doubt worried she might ruin the books with her sticky fingers, but he said nothing. Instead, he pulled on a tasseled cord dangling from the ceiling next to the fireplace. He motioned for Hazel to sit down. So, grabbing hold of her skirts, she settled into the armchair, and Hemlock sat on the sofa.

A young man in livery walked in.

"Ah, James," Hemlock said. "Could you bring us some tea?" He glanced at Holly, now rummaging through her pockets as she searched for more figs. "And perhaps some sandwiches or snacks of some sort. Whatever you can muster up is fine."

James glanced at Hazel and then Holly. Holly, seeing his attention on her, brightened and took a step towards him. He cleared his throat and said, "Very good, sir," then backed out the door. Holly, pouting, slumped onto the sofa next to Hemlock.

Hemlock adjusted his glasses. "I'm sure you have many questions."

Hazel did, but she wasn't sure where to start. "How do you know my father?"

"*Our* father," Holly said.

"Well," Hemlock began, sounding thoughtful, "we're warlocks. Much like witches, warlocks congregate from time to time. Perhaps even more so than witches do. Witches seem to be more forgiving of the solitaries, the ones that wish to practice their magic alone. Warlocks do as well but are... stricter in not wanting to let individuals remain solitary for too long. As such, your father's disappearance is a noticeable one among all of us."

"Where did he go?" Hazel said.

Hemlock shook his head. "As I said before, I don't know."

"Then why are we here?"

James walked into the room, carrying a tray, and Hazel leaned back into her chair and put a hand over her eyes. Remain calm, Hazel. All will become clear. James placed the tray on the table and left the room.

Hemlock poured amber-colored tea into the accompanying cups. There was also a plate heaped with dainty sandwiches. Holly took three, stuffing one into her mouth as she took the cup that Hemlock offered her.

"Good grief, Holly," Hazel said. "Try to show some restraint."

Holly screwed up her face as she chewed. "Why? The sandwiches are there to be eaten; it'd be rude not to have any. Right, Hemlock?"

Hemlock smiled. "Of course."

She flashed Hazel a smug grin before dipping one of her sandwiches into the tea and taking a bite.

Hazel swallowed a few sharp words along with some tea. It tasted bitter.

"Sugar?" Hemlock said, offering her a bowl of little white cubes.

Sugar would be nice, but she didn't want to be in any kind of agreement with Hemlock. "No, thank you."

He dropped a cube into his own tea and stirred with a little silver spoon. He seemed lost in thought, and so Hazel quietly sipped her tea as she waited for him to speak. Whatever she did, she shouldn't be the one to speak first.

"So how do you know our father?" Holly said, grabbing another sandwich. "You didn't really explain it all that well."

Hazel closed her eyes. Holly had the tact of a mud-covered dog.

Hemlock adjusted his glasses. "Ah, yes, of course. As I was saying, we warlocks gather somewhat regularly, and before he disappeared, Ash was a regular among our Conclaves."

Ash. Hazel knew it was her father's name, yet somehow it still seemed strange hearing it spoken like that. To Hemlock, Ash wasn't a father or a husband, he was just another man. To Hazel, her father was little more than a muffled voice behind a closed door or the immaculate handwriting of an old letter.

"Conclaves?" Holly said. "What are those like?"

Hemlock sipped some tea. "I imagine they are similar to your own meetings among witches."

"I doubt it. What are they like?"

Hemlock gave a tight smile. "We aren't really supposed to discuss it."

Holly slumped, her face crestfallen.

"As you were saying," Hazel said, annoyed at Holly's distraction.

Hemlock glanced between the two women, looking more and more like a trapped animal. "Ash had... ideas, some of which were less than... ah... popular among other warlocks."

"What kind of ideas?"

Hemlock remained silent, seemingly taking a great interest in stirring his tea. So much so that Holly leaned over and peered into his cup along with him.

"Is it the future?" she whispered.

Hazel set down her cup with a loud *clank*. "For all that is blessed, Holly, let the man speak!"

Holly pouted. "You'd be sorry if I was a diviner," she muttered, then slunk away to peruse the books.

"I apologize for my sister and for my outburst," Hazel said.

Hemlock shook his head. "Don't apologize. In fact, it's probably for the best."

"What do you mean?"

He leaned over to her and lowered his voice. "The truth is, your father is suspected of experimenting with... forbidden magic."

Hazel clenched her hands in an effort to keep her expression calm. "Necromancy, you mean."

Hemlock nodded.

"Yes, I suspected as much myself."

He blanched. "What has he done?"

She looked away. "Nothing that I am prepared to talk about."

"I want to help."

"You don't even know what the problem is."

"It doesn't matter. Necromancy..." Hemlock's voice had risen, and Holly peered at them over the top of a book she was pretending to read. He lowered his voice again. "Necromancy is a vile art, forbidden for good cause. As a fellow warlock, I can't help but feel partially responsible."

"Why on earth should you feel responsible?"

"Warlocks hold Conclaves for a reason. There must have been some indication in his behavior, an alluded reference that went unnoticed. We—I—should have been more vigilant."

"It wasn't anyone's fault but his."

They sat in silence for a while. Hazel wanted to tell him to not interfere, that this wasn't any of his concern, but once again she couldn't form the words. Was her reluctance really from a desire to keep the problem contained within the family, or was there another reason? She tried telling herself it was because he was a warlock and no warlocks were to be trusted. But that wasn't it. The truth of it was that her father's betrayal was like an open wound on her heart, and she didn't know if she could endure having her pain so exposed to the world.

Yet as much as Hazel hated to admit it, she might need him.

"How could you help?" she asked, unable to look at him.

"We have another Conclave coming up soon. I could make enquiries."

"Such as?"

"Such as finding any of his acquaintances, his haunts and habits. You might be surprised at the kind of information that is revealed during the banal chit-chat of warlocks' Conclaves. Most don't pay that much attention anymore. Conclaves have become more a formality than anything of substance. That is where we have gone wrong, and it is, I believe, where we must begin."

Hazel met his gaze. "Then let us begin."

Spoil Sport

Sunlight shone down on Holly as she sat outside the cottage. The air hummed with bees buzzing in and around the hive boxes Hazel kept. Nearby, a young doe grazed in the herb garden. "They're up to something," Holly said to the doe. She poked a needle into a skirt lying across her lap and pulled the thread through. "But they won't tell me what it is. I don't know why. Either they think I'm stupid, or... or I don't know what."

The doe poked her head up and peered at Holly, chewing on a mouthful of sage as her long ears twitched.

Holly waved a hand. "That's enough of the herbs. Go move on to the carrots or something."

The doe ambled over to where the vegetables grew.

Hazel came home along the woodland path, a basket slung over her arm. The doe bounded away and disappeared among the trees.

Hazel stopped, narrowing her eyes. "Was that deer grazing in the garden?"

Holly focused on her sewing. "No," she said, unable to keep herself from sounding sullen.

Hazel pressed her lips into a thin line.

"What?" Holly said, growing annoyed. "You think I'm hiding something from you? Bet you wouldn't like how that feels, would you?"

Hazel let out a heavy sigh. "Not now, Holly," she said and walked into the cottage.

Holly shook her head and continued sewing. Not now? Not ever, it seemed. What were Hazel and Hemlock doing anyway? They met from time to time, talking in hushed tones whenever they thought she couldn't hear. And then when she walked up to them, they'd put on those creepy fake smiles and talk about the weather or who might win the Honey Tankard for best mead during the Haernan Festival.

Of course Hawthorn never came by, much to Holly's disappointment. They'd had a real connection during the party, but then Hazel had been Hazel, and Holly hadn't seen him since. She sniffed. Hazel was always scaring the men away.

She finished the last stitch in her sewing, tied off the thread, and cut it with her teeth. Then she stood and held up the skirt to examine her work. She'd sewn the hem of the skirt together, turning the garment into a sack.

"Mighty fine work there, missy."

Holly spun around. A short little man about as tall as her knee grinned up at her.

"Who're you?" she asked.

The man bowed. "Name's Tum. Say, you going to do something with that bag of yours?"

Holly narrowed her eyes. "Why?"

"Bags are for keeping, and I've got bits that need to be kept."

"Oh? What kind of bits?"

Tum waved a hand. "A bit o' this and a bit o' that." He grinned.

Holly pursed her lips. "It's not for secrets! Well, not *your* secrets anyway." She raised her chin and said, "Good day." Then she walked off, heading towards the woods.

Tum scampered after her. "Where we going?"

"*I'm* going gathering. *You're* not invited."

"Don't be hasty, young miss. You'd do worse than having a cellar gnome help you gather."

"If you're a cellar gnome, why aren't you in a cellar?"

Tum grinned, showing rows of yellowed teeth. "Currently between jobs. Say, bet you can help me with that. I'd make it worth your while."

Holly stopped and peered down at him. "How so?"

"I seen you with your mouse, the one with the vest. I can fetch bits just as good as him, only the bits I fetch'll be bigger." He winked at her. "Bigger, right?" He cackled.

Holly frowned, not getting the joke. "And what do you get out of it?"

"I get a cut of the spoils, a spot in your cellar, and beer twice a week." He paused. "Three times a week. Plus I'll look after your underground space. Won't have rats causing any mischief without my say-so."

Holly gave it some thought. Rats were such filthy creatures, and they never listened to her, always doing as they pleased no matter what she said. "All right, Mr. Tum, you have a deal."

"Ho, ho, and off we go!" He held out his hands. "Gimme the bag."

Holly pursed her lips and clutched the bag against her chest.

Tum waggled his fingers. "Come on, now. Can't go gathering spoils without a spoils bag. Simple laws of nature and all that."

"That's true," Holly murmured. "But I'll make those same laws of nature turn you into a stunted little tree if you cross me!" She twisted her face into what she hoped was a frightful countenance and handed over the bag.

Tum chuckled, and Holly's heart sank.

"Fair enough," he said. He held up the bag as he looked at it and whistled. "Fine material, this. Where'd you get it?"

Holly drew herself up. "It's the skirt of my old festival dress. Got myself a new dress, so I don't need it anymore."

"Must be fine times you're living in if you've got no need of material like that. Fine times indeed." He lowered the bag and peered around. "Right, so where we spoiling?"

Holly scratched the back of her head. "Well, it's not really called *spoiling*, is it?"

Tum screwed up his face at her. "Gathering fish is fishing, gathering mushrooms is mushrooming, gathering spoils is spoiling. Pretty obvious, really."

"Fine, whatever." She also looked around. "Normally I'd head over to Zinnia's, but she's still pretty angry from last time."

Tum nodded sagely.

"Other than her," Holly continued, "I'm really not sure where to go."

"Well, if you could go anywhere in the world—anywhere in walking distance, that is—where would you go?"

Holly started to give it some thought when Tum leaped towards her.

"Answer quickly," he said, waving his arms. "No time to think. Quick! Quick!" He poked her in the leg with a stout finger until Holly, backing away while swatting at him, finally said, "Hawthorn's! I'd go to Hawthorn's house. Now leave me alone, you vile little beast!"

Tum stopped poking. "Well, all right then. Hawthorn's it is." Bag in hand, he headed off into the woods.

Holly squeaked and scampered after him. "No, no, no, no, I didn't mean we'd go to his house to go gathering. We can't do that!"

"Why not?"

"Well... because..."

"Because you're sweet on him?"

Holly's face turned hot. "What? No!" She tried to laugh but only managed to snort while inhaling a bit of spittle, which then sent her into a fit of coughing. She doubled over as she tried to catch her breath and managed to wheeze, "Not sweet."

"Right," Tum said flatly. When Holly had recovered, he said, "You know, it's a well-known fact that men love women with proper spoiling skills."

Holly wiped at her watering eyes with a sleeve. "Really?"

Tum gave another sage nod. "Oh yes. Has to do with providing for the home. Everyone knows that a woman who can gather her weight in spoils has the makings of a wondrous wife. A real *ünderwench*, as we gnomes like to call it."

Holly stared at him. "You have a name for it?"

Tum drew himself up as tall as his little frame would allow. "Of course. It's not proper unless it's got a proper name. Everyone knows that."

For someone that lurked in cellars, Tum seemed to know an awful lot of the world. Holly nodded, feeling ignorant and unable to argue against such sophisticated wisdom.

They headed over to Hawthorn and Hemlock's estate and came to the tall wrought iron fence.

"Well, now, that's a problem," Tum said.

"Can you squeeze through?" Holly picked up Tum by the collar of his shirt and thwacked him against the bars.

"Hey!" Tum said, flailing. "I'm not made of clay, you know. You can't just remold me however you like."

Holly dropped him on the ground and mumbled, "Sorry."

Tum glowered at her while straightening his shirt. He turned back towards the fence and kicked at it. "This thing got a door or something?"

"Down that way," Holly said, nodding to the left. "It's usually guarded though." In a whisper, she added, "Stupid guards."

Tum shook his head. "Nope, don't do guards. Next idea."

"What? Why not?"

"It's inefficient, and they got grabby hands." He wrinkled his nose. "I don't like grabby hands."

"Well, how else are we going to get in there?"

Tum gave it some thought, then stepped inside the bag and pulled it up around him.

"What are you doing?" Holly said.

"You're gonna have to fling me," Tum said.

"What?"

"That's right. I sit in the bag, and you fling the bag over the fence. Easy."

"But... you'll get hurt!"

Tum scoffed. "Hurt? I think not. Just dirt I'll be landing on, and no dirt ever hurt any cellar gnome, not ever. It's in our bones, you see. Now water..."—he clicked his tongue—"now that'd be a different story." He settled himself deeper within the bag. "Come on now. Time's wasting. Up and away."

When Holly hesitated, Tum waved his arms and shouted, "Away!"

He kept on shouting until Holly, fearful he'd attract the guards, said, "All right! Shoosh!" She grabbed the ends of the bag and lifted it up, bundling Tum inside.

"Now give it a good fling," Tum said, his voice muffled from the fabric. "Don't hold back."

Holly gently swung the bag from side to side, testing the weight.

"I said, give it a good fling!"

"All right," Holly shouted. To herself, she whispered, "Crabby monster."

"I heard that."

"Good!" Holly said though her cheeks warmed. She spun around with the bag, gathering speed until, fearful she'd lose control, she lobbed the bag over the fence and went tumbling backwards.

The bag arced over the iron bars and rustled through a patch of leaves from a low-hanging branch before landing on the grassy ground with a hollow thud.

Holly held her breath as the bag lay motionless. Then, after a moment, the fabric moved and Tum crawled out. He waved.

Holly waved back, but then her heart sank. How was he going to get out? She opened her mouth, about to shout her question, when Tum grabbed the bag and scampered out of sight.

Hawthorn's Help

Hazel sat at the kitchen table, sipping tea from a chipped ceramic cup as she peered out the window. Where had Holly run off to? Not that she should complain. Hemlock would be coming over soon, and it was growing increasingly difficult to talk to him without Holly coming by to see what they were doing.

A twinge of guilt gnawed at Hazel for excluding her sister, but it really was for the best. Holly had a simple, gentle soul, and this grisly business with their mother was upsetting—for both of them, yes, but perhaps even more so for Holly. She didn't need to be dragged into the details of finding their necromancer father. And who knew what awaited them when they did find him. Knowing Holly, she'd likely hug him and forgive him on the spot, conveniently forgetting everything he'd done. It would be easier for all of them to keep Holly ignorant of the matter and resolve it as quickly and quietly as possible.

If, of course, it was even possible at all. Hemlock's enquiries at the last warlock Conclave had failed to produce results, and the next one was weeks away. She and Hemlock had been meeting to discuss their options, but they seemed to be dwindling without much else in sight. It all might be a glorious waste of time, along with Hazel's efforts to protect Holly from any unsavory details.

Hazel continued to sip her tea, waiting and wondering, until Hemlock appeared on the woodland path. She got up and opened the door just as he was about to knock.

He blinked at her. "Ah, Hazel, hello. Fine day, isn't it?"

She pulled him inside and closed the door. "It's summer; the days are almost always fine and terribly boring to discuss. Let's just get to business, shall we?"

Hemlock adjusted his glasses and said, "Ah, yes. Of course." He cleared his throat. "I have sent letters to warlocks of acquaintance to make inquiries. They, ah, unfortunately have all gone unanswered." He blinked at her some more. "I will keep trying though."

Hazel sat down on the couch and shook her head. "I am beginning to think it's all quite pointless. No one seems to know anything, or if they do, they're not talking. I'm not any closer to finding my father than I was before our... partnership." She looked at him. "I'm afraid I've wasted your time."

"Don't be ridiculous. I..."

Hazel got up and opened the door. "Thank you, Hemlock, for everything you've done. But perhaps we should part ways now before wasting any more time and making utter fools of ourselves."

Hemlock's mouth worked soundlessly awhile and before he found his voice, Tum bolted through the open doorway, dragging behind him a bulging bag.

"Close the door!" he shouted. "Bar it, barricade it, whatever you need to do, just do it!"

"What—" Hazel began when Holly ran through the door after him. She darted into her bedroom and closed the door and didn't come back out.

"What on earth is happening?" Hazel said.

"Guards!" Tum said as he tried wedging himself under the couch, but he was too big. He burrowed under the cushions instead. "They got grabby hands, and I don't abide grabby hands." He pulled a cushion down on top of him and disappeared, visible only for the slight bulge on the seat of the couch.

"Watch out!" Hemlock said and pulled her away from the door as a pair of guards charged into her living room.

"Now see here!" Hazel said, but the guards paid her no mind. They walked up to the bag Tum had left lying on the floor, grabbed it, and up-ended the contents. Silver spoons and plates clanged to the floor, along with a teddy bear, a knitted striped scarf, and a few crumpled pieces of paper.

Holly poked her head out the door. "That doesn't belong to you!"

"It certainly doesn't belong to you!" one of the guards said as he turned towards her, and Holly squeaked and disappeared back into her room.

The other guard bent down and picked up the teddy bear. "Hey, Garret. Look." He held up the bear and in a high-pitched voice said, "I will love you forever."

Garret scowled at him. "Don't be an ass, Sid."

Sid sniggered and continued to wave the bear at Garret while making kissing sounds.

"I said knock it off." Garret swiped at the bear, but Sid yanked his hand back. Garret lunged towards him, and Sid laughed and threw the bear out the door, where it landed at the toes of Hawthorn's finely polished boots.

Both guards straightened, and Sid cleared his throat. "Didn't see you there, sir. We were just retrieving your things, as well as apprehending the thieves."

Hawthorn picked up the bear and gently dusted it off. He clutched it to his chest, his furrowed brow creasing his otherwise perfectly glamoured face as he eyed the guards, Hazel, and Hemlock.

"Hemlock, how could you?"

"I-I didn't...," Hemlock said.

Holly stepped out of her room. "It was me. I took them." She lifted her chin at the guards. "Do your worst!"

The guards moved towards her, but Hazel put herself between them and Holly.

"Nobody is doing anything in my house without my permission. Now, you two will tell me what's going on, or I'll turn the both of you into potted plants."

Holly gasped. "But that's what *I* do," she whispered.

Garret pointed a finger at her. "Your sister there is a thieving shrew. She needs to account for her crime."

"And just how, exactly, did she gain access to the house?" Hazel said. "You two stand guard at the gate, do you not?"

Sid shuffled his feet and cast Garret a nervous glance, but Garret just grew angry. He jabbed a finger towards Hazel. "I imagine with her witching ways."

"She turned herself into mist!" Sid said.

Garret closed his eyes and tightened his jaw. He turned towards Sid. "What mist?"

Sid shrank within himself a little. "I saw it... all pale and... misty."

Garret punched him in the shoulder, and Sid staggered back. "You're an idiot." To Hazel, he said, "She confessed to the crime; that's all we need to know."

Hazel scowled at the guards. "Am I the only one here who will acknowledge the gnome hiding under the couch cushions?"

"Hazel, no," Holly whispered.

"The same gnome that was carrying the bag of stolen goods that's still lying at your feet. Why doesn't he need to account for anything?"

Garret's sour expression faded, and he seemed less sure of himself. "She confessed," he murmured.

Hazel made a disgusted sound and walked over to the couch, threw off the cushions, and grabbed Tum by the collar of his shirt and lifted him up.

Tum screeched and howled as he flailed his arms and legs. "Hands off! Grabber!"

Hazel thrust Tum at Garret, and Tum grabbed hold of Garret's uniform and scrabbled up his chest and towards his head.

Garret cried out and backed away, swatting at Tum. "Get it off me!"

But Tum wouldn't budge. He planted a hand on Garret's nose and hoisted himself up. With his feet on Garret's shoulder, Tum hurled himself to the ground, grabbed a couple of spoons off the floor, then ran out the door.

Garret bent over and rested his hands on his knees as he caught his breath. Then, looking at Hazel, he said, "You'll pay for that."

Hemlock stepped forward. "My, what an exciting afternoon. Thankfully, it's all over and done with."

"But, sir—" Garret said.

Hemlock clapped him on the back and smiled. "Fine work today,

Garret. You too, Sid. Hawthorn and I can take over from here. You two return home. Can't leave the gate unattended too long, now can we?"

Garret squared his shoulders, his face impassive. "No, sir." To Sid, he said, "Come on," and then walked out the door.

Sid hesitated a moment as he glanced at Hawthorn. But the warlock just glowered and clutched the bear closer to his chest. Sid cleared his throat and followed Garret out.

After they had gone, Hazel slammed the door shut and locked it. She rounded on Holly. "What on earth were you thinking? Robbing Hemlock and Hawthorn? After they showed us hospitality? Have you no sense of decency?"

Holly wrung her fingers as she kept her gaze on the floor. "But Tum said..."

"And what exactly did that filthy little beast say to make you think it was a good idea? I'd love to know."

Holly looked up at her, at Hawthorn, then returned her gaze to the floor. "Nothing," she murmured. "It's not important."

Hazel put a hand over her eyes and let out a ragged sigh. "I swear, Holly, you'll be the death of me, and on days like today, I can't wait for that to happen."

Holly swallowed, but her gaze remained fixed downward.

Hemlock cleared his throat. "No harm done, really. I'm sure this has all just been a playful misunderstanding. Isn't that right, Hawthorn?"

Hawthorn continued to frown as he clutched the bear. He walked over to the remaining stolen goods scattered on the floor. He picked up the scarf, smelled it, then wrapped it around his neck. He moved his long fingers over the spoons and plates, picking up at last one of the crumpled pieces of paper. He smoothed it out, read it, and tossed it back onto the floor. "I suppose you're right," he said, straightening. "No harm done. What I don't understand, brother, is why you are here if you didn't have a hand in this... *playfulness.*"

Hemlock's cheeks reddened. "I am afraid that is a private matter between Hazel and me."

"No, it's not!" Holly cried. "I want to know why you're always here and what you two are always whispering about!" She folded her arms and gave them a defiant look.

Hawthorn stood next to her and folded his arms as well. "I'm afraid you'll have to come clean, brother."

Hazel closed her eyes. "Just tell them."

Hemlock adjusted his glasses and said, "Well, it's about your father, Holly."

Holly lifted her shoulders and shook her head. "What about him?"

Hemlock glanced at Hazel then said, "As you know, we've been trying to find him. What you might not know is we suspect he's been dealing in necromancy."

Both Hawthorn and Holly unfolded their arms. Hawthorn looked pale, but Holly looked confused and mildly disappointed. "Is that all? Why've you been keeping that a secret?"

Hemlock blinked a few times. "Well, we... uh..."

"We didn't want to upset you," Hazel said.

"And so you lurk around being all creepy and secretive? You thought that was a better idea?"

"Well," Hemlock said. "When you put it like that..."

"It doesn't matter," Hazel said. "All our efforts have turned up nothing, and so Hemlock won't be coming around anymore, so you have nothing to worry about."

"What do you mean you haven't had any luck?" Holly said. "Why not?"

"I'm afraid my contacts in the Conclave don't know anything," Hemlock said. "We've come to a dead end."

Silence hung in the room. Then Hawthorn walked over to the crumpled papers that had fallen from Tum's bag, picked them up, and with a flourish, handed them over to Hemlock.

Hemlock's brow furrowed as he took the papers. "What's this?"

"Your way forward, it would seem."

Hemlock read the papers and then, shaking his head, looked up at Hawthorn. "I don't understand. What is this?"

"It's a letter from an acquaintance of mine in the Conclave. An acquaintance that you do not share. He is one of the oldest members and, as such, is given more leeway for not attending than the other warlocks." He turned towards Holly. "If anyone knows how to find your father, it will be him."

Hazel said, "And why would he tell you anything at all?"

Hawthorn smiled, showing his perfect white teeth. "As it happens, he owes me a favor."

Pyrus and His Particular Price

The following day, Hazel, Holly, Hemlock, and Hawthorn sat in an ornate carriage as it rattled down the road. Holly stuck her head out the window, grinning as the wind buffeted her face.

"How is it that you know Pyrus?" Hemlock said. "Better yet, how is it that he owes you a favor?"

Hawthorn waved a bejeweled hand. "I know it's sometimes easy to forget, but I *am* older than you." He narrowed his eyes. "Honestly, Hemlock, would a simple glamour be too much to ask? People are bound to think you're my father rather than younger brother."

"Answer the question."

Hawthorn fiddled with the purple velvet curtain hanging from the window as he peered outside. "He is an old friend of Father's. As I am the eldest, Father introduced *me* and not *you*."

Hemlock tightened his jaw. "And the favor?"

Hawthorn chuckled. "Because of me, he has Shirley and Shiela."

"Who are they?"

"The two great loves of his life."

Hemlock frowned, looking puzzled, but he said nothing. Hawthorn smiled and returned his gaze towards the window.

The rest of the journey to Pyrus's home was spent largely in silence. On occasion, Hawthorn would break the quiet with a heavy sigh or with a comment on the beauty of the summertime woods, which he would then equate to a sunset or a still pond or a moonlit sky. Whenever he did, Hemlock would close his eyes and shake his head, seemingly putting great effort into keeping his breathing even.

When the carriage at last slowed, Hemlock opened the door and jumped out before it had a chance to stop. Holly squeaked and clamped her hands over her mouth, but when she saw he was all right, she smiled and giggled.

"Me too!" she said, and before Hazel could stop her, Holly threw herself out of the carriage after him. She landed in a cloud of dust, stirred up from the carriage and her own clumsy landing, but she seemed fine.

"Barbarians," Hawthorn murmured. Then, glancing at Hazel, he put on smile, showing his overly white teeth. "I mean that in the most affectionate way, of course."

Hazel ignored him. She had no desire to speak with Hawthorn and his affected buffoonery. Being alone with him in the carriage was almost enough to make Hazel pitch herself out the door after Holly, but then the carriage turned onto a manicured circular driveway and stopped at the steps of a great brick home.

Holly and Hemlock came strolling down the road to meet them. From within the house, dogs barked.

"No," Hemlock said to Holly as they approached, "I don't usually jump out of the coach like that. Certainly not while it's still moving. I..."—he cast a glance at Hawthorn—"just had an urge."

"If I had a coach," Holly said, "I'd make the driver drive me around every day, just so I could jump out of it like that. Bet I could get real good at it. Don't you think?"

Hemlock smiled. "I'm sure if you practiced, you'd become exceedingly talented in the art of jumping from speeding carriages."

Holly grinned.

The barking grew louder, and when the door opened, a pair of greyhounds raced out to greet Hawthorn. They jumped around him and *on* him and nearly knocked him over.

Hawthorn gave a nervous laugh and stiffly patted one on the head.

"There's a good girl, Shiela. Or is it Shirley?" He looked at a rumpled butler standing in the doorway, but the butler just shrugged.

Holly yelped and joined the dogs in jumping around Hawthorn. The dogs seemed to sense her enthusiasm and were soon jumping around her instead, tongues lolling like pink ribbons. One of the dogs barked, and Holly laughed and clapped her hands.

Hazel backed away. She'd rather not have a dog pouncing on her, thank you very much, and if it happened, she didn't know if she'd be able remove herself from the situation with any grace. The last thing she needed was to offend Pyrus by yelling at his two beloved dogs.

"Shiela! Shirley!" came a stern voice from within the house.

The dogs calmed and trotted back towards the door where they met a man in a long burgundy robe. The material was smooth and shiny, and it rustled when he moved. Holly sighed.

"Pyrus," Hawthorn said and smiled. He walked towards Pyrus and shook his hand. "It's been a long time."

"Not long enough," Pyrus said. "The girls still remember you. Fondly, it seems. You know I don't like competition."

Hawthorn smoothed his hair. "The ladies often find it difficult to forget me."

Pyrus smirked. "I imagine they do, though perhaps for different reasons than you think."

Hawthorn shrugged as if such differences were of no concern.

"Aren't you going to introduce us?" Hemlock said, his voice tight.

Hawthorn waved a limp hand. "This is Hemlock, my brother, as you undoubtedly know." Before Hemlock or Pyrus could say anything, Hawthorn rushed on, waggling his fingers towards the sisters. "And that's Hazel, and that's Holly. Two witch friends of Hemlock's." He sniffed.

Pyrus smiled and gave a slight bow to the women. "Charmed."

Holly put a hand to her cheek and giggled.

For a man that was supposedly one of the oldest warlocks alive, Pyrus looked deceptively young. His curly, shoulder-length hair was still mostly dark brown, showing only streaks of grey at the temples. Similarly, his beard bore a stripe of grey along his jaw, but the rest was dark. What was with these warlocks and their glamours? Hazel wondered if her father was the same way—projecting an illusion of vitality that hid a frail truth.

"And to what do I owe this pleasure?" Pyrus said.

"I'm told you know my father," Hazel said.

Pyrus's eyebrows arched upwards, and Hawthorn chuckled nervously. "There's a proper time and place for all things, Hazel, and this isn't it. We haven't even had tea yet."

Pyrus remained silent, watching Hazel with shrewd, grey eyes.

"Shall we go in?" Hawthorn said and, without waiting for a reply, walked into the house.

"The dogs certainly think so," Hemlock said as two wagging tails disappeared into the house behind Hawthorn.

"They're off!" Pyrus said and went into the house after them.

Hazel glanced at Hemlock, and he shrugged and gave a lopsided smile.

"Come on, Holly," she said. "Let's see what this warlock knows."

Pyrus's home looked much like Hemlock and Hawthorn's, with vast, dimly lit hallways of wood-paneled walls adorned with portraits. In the brothers' house, the portraits were of old men—possibly ancestors. But in Pyrus's home, all the portraits were of himself. Or of his dogs. Or both. Mostly both.

One painting depicted a striking landscape as the dogs ran over grass-covered hills beneath a sky of roiling clouds. Another painting depicted Pyrus carrying ropes of link sausages, leading the two dogs to a distant, sunlit land. Most disturbing of all was the painting of Pyrus wearing nothing but a torn white toga that barely covered his tan skin and bulging muscles while Shirley and Shiela flew around him on white, swanlike wings amid a flurry of colorful butterflies.

Hazel stopped to stare, but Hemlock nudged her and gave her a pleading look as he nodded towards the room into which the others had disappeared. Hazel followed and walked into a parlor with walls painted a burgundy color similar to Pyrus's robe. A great stone fireplace dominated one of the walls over which hung a trio of paintings: Pyrus in the middle, holding a thick book and wearing a black robe adorned with brightly colored gemstones, while the other two paintings featured Shiela and Shirley respectively, each sitting obediently while gazing towards the center portrait of Pyrus.

"You really like your dogs, don't you?" Holly said.

"They are my children," Pyrus said. "What father doesn't love his children?" He patted one of the dogs on its head, who lay upon a plush pillow in a corner of the room.

Holly's expression turned solemn, and she sat down on one of two chocolate-colored leather sofas, directly across from Hazel. The butler came in—his suit still rumpled and his hair in disarray—carrying a tea tray. When the dogs saw him, they ran towards him. The butler cried out and hurried to the table by the sofas and set down the tray as the dogs yipped and pranced around him, nipping at his coat-tails and at the cuffs of his pants.

Pyrus laughed. "They are such playful creatures, and they just love Cheswick. Isn't that right, Cheswick?"

"Y-yes, sir. Their uh... love... knows no bounds." Sweat ran down Cheswick's reddened face, and he gazed at the doorway as he wrung his hands. "Will there be anything else, sir?"

"No, thank you, Cheswick. That will be all."

Cheswick let out a ragged, heavy breath. "Very good, sir." He all but ran to the door, slamming it behind him before Shirley and Shiela could follow.

Holly helped herself to some tea before topping a biscuit with jam and stuffing it into her mouth.

"Good grief, Holly," Hazel said. "Can't you ever wait to be invited before you start gorging yourself?"

"What?" Holly said, biscuit crumbs tumbling from her mouth. "They put out the tray. That *is* being invited. Waiting for the words seems awfully repetitive." She ate another jam-topped biscuit, glowering at Hazel as she chewed.

Glaring back at her, Hazel said, "I apologize for my sister, Pyrus. Our mother died before Holly could be properly house-trained."

Pyrus nodded. "House-training is a tricky business. Not all animals are suited to the task. It requires a keen mind—of both the trainer and trainee—as well as mutual respect and a natural inclination towards cleanliness."

Holly licked her thumb and rubbed it on her skirt as she tried to remove a glob of jam. She looked up, finding everyone watching her. "What?"

Hemlock cleared his throat. "So, Pyrus, how long did you know our father?"

"I met Lupinus when he was a boy and I was a young man about to attend my first Conclave. My father and Lupinus's father—your grandfather—were friends, and so they thought it prudent their sons also become acquainted."

"But what about the dogs?" Holly said.

"I beg your pardon?"

"The dogs, where did you get them? That's what I want to know, not stuffy old warlock history."

Pyrus leaned back in his chair and rubbed his chin. "Well, the two stories are intertwined, in a way. Stuffy old warlocks like their customs, you see, and a custom was established when my father and Hawthorn and Hemlock's grandfather introduced their two eldest sons to each other. To keep up the custom, Lupinus introduced his eldest son to me, given I don't, nor will ever have, any sons of my own. Hawthorn, seeing I was childless, gave me a gift of two puppies, and my life has been blessed ever since."

"That's really nice," Holly said, gazing at Hawthorn.

Hawthorn smiled and smoothed his hair. "Yes, well, I do try."

"Though," Holly said, sounding thoughtful, "if introducing your sons is a custom, and your dogs are your children, does that mean Hawthorn will introduce his future son to your dog's eldest puppy?"

Hemlock choked on his tea. He set down his cup. "Excuse me," he wheezed.

"You all right?" Holly asked.

Hemlock removed his glasses and dabbed at his watering eyes with a napkin. He smiled. "I'm exceedingly well, thank you, Holly." He reached over and patted her on the hand. "You dear, dear girl."

Pyrus gave a wry smile. "I think it means that this particular custom has reached its end and that Hawthorn has paid proper respect to it with the gift of the dogs."

Holly slumped as her face fell. "Oh."

"Since we're on the subject of fathers," Hazel said, leaning forward. "I'm told you know ours."

Pyrus fixed her in a level gaze. "Yes. Ash. I remember when he first joined the Conclave. Curious fellow. Asked a lot of questions."

"What kinds of questions?"

"He mostly questioned our schools of magic, their uses and limitations. He didn't seem content to focus his efforts on one or two disciplines, as I'm sure you know is customary. He wanted to know everything about all of them. And yet even then he seemed discontented with what he found. Or, perhaps, with what he didn't find."

"Why? What was he looking for?"

Pyrus spread open his hands. "I couldn't say. All I can say is the man seemed restless, and that kind of restlessness can make a man unpredictable. Reckless, even."

Hazel studied him. "Do you know then? That he turned to necromancy?"

Pyrus chuckled. "Oh, yes. I knew Ash was headed towards necromancy almost as soon as I met him. I knew he would never be content with the permitted disciplines alone. Men like him never are."

"What? Why didn't you do something to stop him then?"

He laughed again. "My dear girl, you are talking to a warlock who has tried to convince the Conclave to allow necromancy as a permitted discipline."

The room grew silent as everyone stared at him. Even Hawthorn seemed uneasy as he shifted in his seat.

"You're a necromancer?" Holly asked.

"Hardly," Pyrus said. "As a young man, I focused on the Wyr discipline, like so many others. Now, though, I practice primarily Hearth. But whether we like it or not, necromantic magic exists, and I believe willfully ignoring it is a grave mistake." Pyrus chuckled. "*Grave.*" He rang a little bell, and Cheswick poked his head through the door. "Cheswick, I made a pun. And you said I lack a sense of humor."

"I'm sure I never said that, sir."

"Oh? Then who did?"

"I believe it was the witch Lobelia, sir."

"Well then, send her an invitation to tea. We'll straighten her out. Right, Cheswick?"

"Of course, sir." Cheswick disappeared again.

Pyrus tented his fingers as he stared off into the distance, his lips quirked into a small smile.

Hazel cleared her throat, and Pyrus refocused his attention on her. "What was I saying?"

"You wanted to make necromancy a permitted discipline."

"Ah, yes." He waved his hands. "As I was saying, necromancy exists, and as a result, there will always be those who practice it—with or without our approval. By making necromancy a permitted discipline, we can at least monitor its use, guide those practicing it in the hopes of keeping them from doing something too... *unsavory*."

The room grew quiet once again. Hazel wondered if Pyrus would consider trapping a person's soul in a geas unsavory. She was afraid to ask. Instead, she said, "He had to learn necromantic magic from someone. Where did he go?"

Pyrus rubbed his chin as his eyes took on a distant, unfocused look. "Trying to find teachers in necromancy is a line of questioning I've never dared undertake. I do, however, have my suspicions of whom Ash might have sought. But they are only that—suspicions."

"Who is it?"

Pyrus watched her a long while. "I think we need to have a word in private first."

A moment of silence passed, then Hemlock and Hawthorn got up and left the parlor. Holly, however, planted herself firmly on the sofa and folded her arms. "Why in private? I don't like all these secrets. I deserve to know too."

"I'm sure you do," Pyrus said. "But you are a Wild witch are you not? With a secondary in Hearth?"

"Yeah," Holly said, scowling. "So?"

"So, this is a matter of discipline, young lady. A discipline to which you do not belong."

"But Hazel does?"

Pyrus smiled. "That is what we must discuss."

Holly remained still, frowning as she looked Pyrus up and down. "Well, I guess that's all right then." To Hazel, she said, "I'll wait outside," then got up and walked out the door.

Pyrus rose from his seat and poured himself a cup of tea. He walked to a window and looked out as he sipped from the cup. "I understand you've not yet chosen a primary discipline. That you still only practice the discipline chosen in your childhood years. Weaving magic, if I recall correctly."

Hazel narrowed her eyes. "How would you know that? I wouldn't think a warlock would be privy to such information."

"I like to be well informed, and I have friends in the witches' Circle. I also hold the unpopular notion of wanting to do away with all this witch and warlock segregation. We are all practitioners of magic, are we not? It's unhelpful and unhealthy to work separately from one another."

"Hawthorn said you no longer attend the warlock Conclaves. I think I'm starting to understand why."

Pyrus smiled. "Exactly. I've too many bold ideas and spend too much time stirring the proverbial pot. Is it true though? You haven't chosen your primary discipline?"

Hazel closed her eyes and sighed. This was a conversation she was tired of having, and she never thought she'd be having it with a warlock. "Yes, it's true."

"May I ask why?"

Hazel shook her head and looked away. "They say you're supposed to know in your heart which discipline you belong to. But my heart is... torn."

"How so?"

She bit the inside of her cheek. This was none of his business, but she needed his help. "I always thought I'd dedicate myself to Weaving magic. But now with my father dealing in necromancy and... what he's done, Weaving no longer seems appropriate. None of the disciplines do."

"And so, like your father, you are also searching for elusive answers."

Hazel glared at him. "I am nothing like him."

"Willfully ignoring the truth will not help you. Are you a necromancer? No. Yet you would do well to acknowledge the similarities between you. It may help you find him."

"I know nothing about my father. How am I supposed to acknowledge any similarities?"

"By accepting the possibility that the two of you might be more alike than you'd like to admit. The truth of the matter is that no one knows where Ash has gone. If you can put yourself in his position, make decisions as he would have made them, then that may very well be your best hope in finding him. In the meantime, however, you need to choose your primary discipline, and you'd be well served to choose Wyr."

"I've considered it, but I find the notion... distasteful. All the illusions and nonsense." She fixed him in a level gaze. "It's a warlock's discipline."

Pyrus smiled. "It's true that many warlocks choose Wyr, and many witches often choose either Hearth or Weaving, with Wild being... well... the wild card of all four magics." He chuckled. "I need to tell that one to Cheswick later." He cleared his throat. "Wyr is, however, considered the most powerful of all the disciplines, boasting the widest range of spells. It is the most difficult to master, but it would undoubtedly be of the greatest use in helping you find your necromancer father. And as a Weaving witch, you are already well suited to the discipline."

"Weaving and Wyr are nothing alike."

Pyrus laughed. "Aren't they? Weaving magic almost exclusively deals with the manipulation of existing matter. Wyr, among other things, deals with the manipulation of conjured matter. Don't tell me you don't see a similarity. As a Wyr witch with a secondary in Weaving, you would be a force to be reckoned with. Together with your Wild and Hearth sister, the two of you would have a command over all four disciplines—over all four elements. That's quite a feat, don't you think? And this isn't even mentioning the fact that you've already begun using Wyr spells at a rudimentary level—without any training, I might add. And that, dear Hazel, almost never happens. It seems to me that your heart has already chosen Wyr, whatever you might tell yourself."

Hazel frowned at him. "What are you talking about?"

"I've heard about Hawthorn's party, the way you so expertly dispelled his glamour. No Weaving witch should be able to do that, Hazel. That is a Wyr spell."

She shook her head. "It was just a dispelling incantation. Nothing special."

"Oh, I quite agree. As far as Wyr spells go, it is quite base. I believe I learned it myself when I was around eight. What's remarkable is that you didn't realize you were doing it and that you did it without guidance. I suggest you find a way to move past your prejudices about the discipline. You were meant for Wyr, Hazel, the sooner you accept that, the better off you will be."

Hazel knotted her hands together as she studied him. "Why do you care? What difference does it make to you if I become a Wyr witch or not?"

Pyrus shrugged. "You come to me searching for information, yet you don't really know what you are asking. You don't know where your search will take you, what dangers you may face. I would hate if you came to harm because you weren't prepared for the information I gave you. Consider it my price."

"You haven't given me anything yet, and I don't know why you'd care what happens to me anyway."

"We are all in this together. What happens to one of us affects us all. When one of us starts tampering in necromancy, it affects us all. I'm an old man. The last thing I want to see in my final days is a horde of undead marching upon our Grove, or whatever it is Ash might have planned. Nor do I have an interest in joining the search for your father. I want you to succeed in this so I can remain here with my dogs in quiet solitude." He smiled. "Plus I think you'd enjoy being a Wyr witch. You have a strong mind, Hazel. None of the other disciplines would properly challenge you as Wyr would. And something tells me you're a woman that likes to be challenged."

Hazel worked her clenched hands. Then, raising her chin, said, "Very well, I'll do it. There are far too many Wyr warlocks anyway. Perhaps it's time we witches balanced them out."

Pyrus's smile deepened. "I couldn't agree more."

Tea with Tum

Holly hopped around Hazel as she left Pyrus's home.

"Well?" Holly said. "What did he say?"

"He gave me the name of someone we can talk to that might know where one goes to learn necromancy. I've also decided to become a Wyr witch."

Hawthorn scoffed. "A Wyr witch? Perhaps it would be better to stick to Weaving and leave Wyr to the men."

Hemlock put a hand over his face while both Hazel and Holly glowered at Hawthorn.

Holly pulled a tiny pinecone from her pocket. "Maybe you ought to say that one more time and leave the thumping on your noggin to the women."

"Don't bother, Holly," Hazel said. "Save your pinecones for a more worthy head."

Hawthorn straightened, looking offended. "What's wrong with my head? Is there something on it?" He put a hand to his forehead and lowered it again, blinking at his fingers. "Hemlock, is there something on my head?"

"Yes," Hemlock said. "You'd better go fix that."

Hawthorn gasped and ran to the coach, squinting and squirming as he tried to view his reflection in the windows.

Hemlock shook his head. "Idiot," he muttered. Then to Hazel, he said, "It's almost too easy."

Hazel couldn't help but smile. Hemlock smiled with her.

"Sooo," Holly said, sounding impatient. "Who are we supposed to go talk to? You never said."

"His name is Elder. Pyrus says he left the Conclave some years ago and might have changed his name. He suspects he lives in Sarnum now."

Hemlock frowned. "That's well to the south. What's he doing that far outside the Grove? And how does Pyrus know him?"

"He doesn't, but he's heard rumors. If they're true, he thinks Elder might be able to help us."

"And if they're not?"

"Then let's hope the worst that comes out this is a wasted trip."

They rode in the carriage back home in relative silence. Hawthorn, from time to time, would put a hand to his head, feel around, and then continue gazing out the window with a heavy sigh. They dropped Hazel and Holly off at their home, and the carriage rattled away again down the road.

"So," Holly said as they walked towards the cottage, "when do we leave?"

"I don't know. Not before the next Circle, and maybe not for a while after that. It depends."

"Depends on what...?" Holly began but trailed off as they walked through the door and found Tum and two other gnomes lurking inside. Tum was rifling through a dresser drawer while another gnome sifted through the ashes in the hearth. The third gnome held a bundle of spoons as he eyed his reflection in one of them. As soon as Hazel and Holly walked in, all the gnomes froze and glowered at them.

"What's going on here?" Hazel said as she glowered back.

"Nothing's going on, that's what," Tum said.

"That's what," echoed the gnome with sooty hands.

"It doesn't look like nothing to me. In fact, it looks like you're robbing me."

"Isn't any robbing here," Tum said. "Just taking what's owed."

"What?"

"We entered an agreement, me and the miss. Beer three times a week and a cut of the spoils. Well, there hasn't been any beer or spoils, so we're taking what's owed."

Hazel turned to Holly. "What's he talking about?"

Holly wrung her hands. "I might have forgotten to tell you I hired Tum."

Hazel closed her eyes and took a breath. Calm. She would remain calm. "Why?"

"Well... because..."

"Because I'm scrappy and resourceful, that's why," Tum said. "You'd do worse than having a scrappy cellar gnome."

Holly nodded. "Yeah, that."

Hazel tightened her jaw. "You forgot to mention *why* we need a cellar gnome at all. Scrappy or otherwise."

"Well," Holly said, still wringing her hands. "There's the rats."

The gnomes murmured among themselves and nodded.

"The rats? What...?" Hazel's temper flared. "You know what? I don't even care. We have more important things to consider right now. You figure out this problem with Tum's payment. And no, you may *not* pay him with our spoons." She walked up to the gnome with the utensils. He tried hiding them in his pockets, but she yanked them away from him, ignoring his squawking protests.

HOLLY WATCHED as Hazel marched up the narrow stairs to her room. A door slammed, and then all went silent.

"Well, someone's a grumpy frump," Tum said.

Holly put on the fiercest expression she could muster. "You shouldn't have done that—bring your friends here to take our stuff. You would've gotten paid if you just said something."

Tum shook his head. "Nope. Been in too many cellars where the owners conveniently 'forget' my payment. Then when I remind them, I'm booted out the door and the locks are changed. Now I take what's owed. You don't like it, then you'd best pay me."

"But... couldn't you just pick the new locks?"

"Don't change the subject."

"Well, all right." She scratched her head. "So what is it that you're owed? Some beer?"

"Yep, three bottles. Plus spoils."

"We don't have beer in the house. We have mead though. Will that do?"

"Nope, don't like mead. Too sweet. Needs to be beer."

Holly narrowed her eyes. "I don't know why you should get paid at all. You haven't been working for us for more than a day. How do I know you'll keep your end of the deal?"

Tum straightened and smoothed his shirt. "I'm a cellar gnome. We always keep our end. And cellar gnomes get paid in advance, see? Too many mishaps otherwise, and I don't abide mishaps."

"But... if you haven't done any work, then you're not really owed anything. Why not just leave instead of robbing us? Wouldn't that be more fair?"

"Don't change the subject. You gave me a job, and I'm owed pay up front. Always been that way." Tum put out his hands and waggled his fingers.

Holly pressed her lips together. Tum was a shrewd negotiator. "All right, fine." She thought a moment. "We haven't got any beer, like I said, but we'd probably be able to get some at the Green Man. I've even got some coin."

"Well, all right then," Tum said. "Let's go." He started for the door.

"Wait," Holly said.

Tum turned to look at her.

She waved towards the other gnomes. "Don't forget to call off your cronies."

The sooty gnome took on a wide-eyed and panicked look. He dove for the couch and tried to wedge himself under it.

"Go on, boys," Tum said. "Catch you later, right?"

"Yeah, all right," grumbled the spoonless gnome. He grabbed the ankles of the sooty gnome and pulled him away from the couch. The filthy gnome tried scrambling back towards his sanctuary when the other gnome shouted, "We're going!"

The sooty gnome calmed. Then, with a final glance at Holly, he threw a handful of ashes in the air, ran across the room, and hopped out an open window.

"That was weird," Holly said.

"Ben's a little touched," Tum said. "Good spoiler though." He nodded to the remaining gnome. "See you, Arn."

"Tum," Arn said as he strolled out the door.

With the gnomes gone, she and Tum left the cottage and headed for the Green Man.

"You're awful quiet," Tum said after they had walked for a while.

"Everything's changing. Hazel's going to become a Wyr witch, and then we're going to leave the Grove and head south, looking for some creepy warlock named Elder."

"And that's a problem?"

Holly shrugged. "I don't know. Part of me likes things the way they are. But then another part of me wants to help Hazel find our father. But if we do, then everything's likely to change."

Tum chuckled. "Everything changes regardless. It's just it usually happens too slow for most people to notice."

"Maybe," Holly said.

They followed the winding dirt road until they came to a thatched stone hut nearly overtaken by ivy. Holly rooted around in the vines until she found the door and pushed it open.

Inside, the tavern was surprisingly bright, given that the ivy blocked most of the sunlight that tried to filter through the leaded windows. Instead, most of the illumination came from scores of colorful lanterns that hung from the rafters and painted walls. Misshapen tables of thick, polished wood dotted the room, all surrounded by chairs made of bent branches.

A man stood behind a thick slab of wood that served as a counter, his face and arms tattooed with scrolling, intricate designs. His long brown hair was half-braided and half-tangled, the mess of which was pulled back in a monstrous tail.

"Haven't seen you here in a while, Holly," he said.

Holly smiled. "Been busy. It's good to see you though, Gael."

Gael nodded towards Tum. "Who's your friend?"

Holly's smile faded. "Not sure he's a friend yet. Friends don't rob one another."

"Wasn't robbing anyone," Tum said. "It was fair compensation."

Holly rolled her eyes. To Gael, she said, "Little monster needs beer."

Gael nodded. "We've got plenty of that."

Tum perked up. "Oh? What kind?"

"All kinds. All kinds of mead, too, and all kinds of wine. You want the stronger stuff, though, you go to the Burned Man for that."

"No, no," Tum said. "Beer's my only poison." He propped himself up on a stool at the counter. "Let's see," he said, sounding thoughtful. "Been a long time since I've had some apricot beer, though I doubt you have it."

"Got it," Gael said. "Anything else?"

"What? What about lavender beer?"

"Got that too."

Tum drummed his fingers on the counter. "Rose hip beer?"

Gael folded his arms. "Yep. You going to pick one?"

Tum stared at him. "Say, you need a cellar gnome?"

"Hey!" Holly said.

Gael shook his head. "No gnome is setting foot in my cellar."

Tum waved a hand. "I jest," he said to Holly. He eyed Gael a moment and said, "I'll have a cinnamon beer then."

Gael nodded, and Tum's mouth fell open. "What'll you have, sweetheart?" Gael said to Holly.

"Raspberry tea, please."

Gael nodded again and disappeared through a door behind the counter.

"Amazing," Tum muttered.

"We'll buy two for the road, and then we're even, right?"

"Of course," Tum said. "Well, except for the spoils."

"You get a cut of the spoils when there's spoils to be had. *That* was the agreement."

Tum screwed his mouth to the side. "That's debatable. However, since your payment in beer is of fine quality, I can make allowances."

Holly shook her head.

Gael returned with the drinks. Tum's was a tall glass of rich amber liquid with a bundle of smoldering cinnamon sticks resting across the foaming top. Holly's was as she expected—a round white cup topped with so much cream that she couldn't see the liquid beneath it. She took a sip, smiling as the sweet, tart taste of raspberries filled her mouth, followed by honey and bitter black tea.

Tum removed the bundle of cinnamon and, with both hands, grabbed hold of the glass and took a swig. He wiped away the foam from his face and let out a loud sigh. "Aye, that's the good stuff."

"You happy now?"

"Gimme two more bottles of that and I'll be happy indeed."

Holly nodded and sipped her tea.

Tum eyed her and waggled a finger. "It isn't right, you being so glum in the presence of such fine drink. We need to fix that."

"I suppose."

"Go on now, tell old Tum what's what."

Holly shrugged. "It's stupid."

"Isn't anything stupid that can put a smile on your face."

"It's not like that. It's just... well... I know Hazel's going to plan all sorts of things for our trip south. Not that she'll tell me any of it—she never does. But I want to help. I *can* help. I just... I don't know how or to tell her I can."

Silence fell between them.

"I told you," Holly said. "Stupid."

Tum clicked his tongue. "Stupid is letting that drink of yours go cold." He waved his hands. "Go on, drink up."

Holly took another sip as Tum took another gulp of his beer.

"As for Miss Hazel," Tum said, "well, we'll just have to think of something, now won't we?"

Odd Possibilities

Holly and Tum waited at the Green Man for night to fall. He drank three more beers, promising that the last was an advance on the following week's wages. When the day faded and darkness settled in, he hopped off his stool, tottered a bit, then righted himself and threw Holly a great big smile.

"Right," he said. "Off we go then." He shambled towards the door.

"Where are we going, exactly?" Holly asked as she followed.

He stopped and blinked at her. "Go?"

Holly folded her arms. "You're drunk, aren't you?"

Tum snorted and waved a hand, which caused him to totter again before he regained his balance. Then he looked at her with the utmost severity. "Perhaps."

Holly bent down towards him and whispered, "You're a cellar gnome, and you can't hold your beer!"

"Shhh!" Tum said as he flailed his hands. "Isn't anything of the sort. You tricked me with that fine beer of yours. Tricked old Tum into drinking an entire week's worth all in one go. You're a temptress, that's what."

Holly opened her mouth to reply but stopped. She put a hand to her hair and smiled. "Temptress? Really?"

Tum nodded, his expression solemn. "Oh yes. Perhaps even saucy, besides."

Holly giggled.

Tum blinked at her. "Now remind me. Where were we going?"

"I don't know. You said you knew someone who could help me convince Hazel to let me help her."

Tum blinked at her again. "That's a lot of helping."

"Well, yes, but it's what you said."

Tum scratched his chin. "Well, if I said that, then I must have meant Odd. He's real good at fixing and helping—all that stuff. We'll have to wait until night though. Odd sleeps during the day, and you don't want to wake him when he sleeps."

"It is night."

Tum smiled. "Well then! We best be off!"

He zigzagged down the darkened road and, before long, plunged into the brush of the surrounding woods. Tall ferns eclipsed his small form, and Holly was only able to follow by the cacophonous rustling and snapping of twigs that signaled his passage.

"Are you actually leading us somewhere?" Holly asked. "Or are you drunkenly wandering to nowhere at all?"

"Always have a purpose, I always say."

"What kind of answer is that?"

Tum poked a finger up through the ferns and into the air. "A most satisfactory one."

It wasn't satisfactory at all, but Tum did seem to be heading in a particular direction, so Holly let it lie.

The gibbous moon shone bright that night and bathed the woods in a silvery sheen. They came to a meadow within which a little cottage lay. Tum ran towards it. Holly followed.

As they neared the front door, Tum veered around a corner of the cottage and came to a pair of cellar doors. He hoisted one open and descended down a set of darkened stairs.

"Tum!" Holly hissed. She looked towards the cottage to see if anyone was coming, but the windows remained dark and the night still. And so, not knowing what else to do, she followed Tum into the darkness.

Holly had to descend sideways to keep herself from losing her footing on the steep and narrow stairs. She reached a hard-packed earthen floor.

On the wall to her right, a single candle flame wavered. She tried to split the flame for additional light, but nothing happened. She must be in a witch's home—her magic wouldn't work here.

She picked up the candle and waved it through the darkness as she made her way deeper into the cellar. The wavering, scratching sound of a violin met her ears, and she followed the music until she came to a door. She pushed it open and walked into a cozy room filled with light. Candles burned in sconces on the stone walls and in bottles on tables. A fire crackled within a plain stone hearth, sending wild shadows to cavort on the walls. A gnome-sized sofa faced the fire, and next to the sofa stood a table, upon which a little gramophone played the soothing strains of a violin concerto.

"Ah, there you are," Tum said. He wore a little red cap on his head and little curled slippers on his feet. On his body he wore a single suit of plush, soft material that reminded Holly of kittens and clouds.

"Did you change your clothes?"

Tum thrust a finger into the air. "When in the cellar, one's got to wear cellar clothes. For gnomes, that is. You"—he waved his hands at her—"will have to make do with what you have."

Another gnome wearing similar clothes emerged from a hatch in the ground, holding a pair of dark-tinted bottles. "I got cowberry beer and radish beer. Radish beer's got bit of a bite..." He trailed off when he saw Holly.

"Hello," Holly said.

The other gnome said nothing, his grip tightening on the bottles as he stared at her.

"Cowberry beer, you say?" Tum took one of the bottles from the gnome's hand. He squinted as he held it out for inspection.

Holly cleared her throat.

"What's that?" Tum said, snapping out of whatever reverie he had been caught in.

Holly nodded towards the other gnome, her eyebrows raised.

"Oh," Tum said and, waving a hand, added, "Miss Holly, that's Odd. Odd, Miss Holly."

Holly beamed at Odd. "Nice to meet you."

Odd grinned and shuffled his feet.

Tum broke off the wax sealing the mouth of the bottle and took a swig. "It's good. Maybe not as good as the cinnamon beer but good all the same." He scampered over to the sofa and sat down.

Holly said, "So... Tum. Are you going to explain why we're here?"

"Here?" Tum said as he peered at the bottle in the light of the fire.

"Yes, here," Holly said, growing annoyed. "Or have you forgotten again?"

"Of course not!" He waved a hand. "Odd'll help you."

Holly pressed her lips together. She took a step towards Tum but stopped when there was a tugging at her sleeve. She looked down, and Odd nodded towards a door at the other end of the room. Tum was enthralled with his beer bottle, so Holly let Odd lead her across the room.

They passed through the door and into a room filled with shelves laden with jars, vials, boxes, and a wide assortment of tiny little knick-knacks that Holly had never seen before. "What is this place?"

"My workshop," Odd said. He took a little white coat hanging from a peg and put it on. He took off his cap and hung it on the peg, then put on a pair of spectacles his fished out of his coat pocket. He scampered to a shelf, pulled down a box, then returned to Holly. Grinning, he lifted the lid and held out the box to her.

Holly leaned down and found a pair of violet flowers resting within. "How lovely," she said, but when she reached towards the flowers, the petals fluttered and stirred as if caught in a breeze. She yanked her hand back and giggled. "Is it magic?"

Odd smiled and shrugged. "Taste them."

Holly picked up one of the flowers. The petals were cold to the touch and slightly sticky. She popped it in her mouth, where the petals dissolved into a liquid. It tasted of grapes and fennel, with a hint of violets.

"Amazing," she said. "How did you do that?"

Odd smiled and shrugged again. "It's all in the method."

Holly didn't understand, but it didn't matter. "Has Tum explained my problem?"

Odd nodded.

"Well? What do you think?"

Odd blinked at her from behind his glasses. Then he snapped his fingers and wandered off.

Holly stood there, fidgeting with her hands. She eyed one of the shelves. There were little figurines made of what looked to be polished rocks but, when touched, felt soft like clay. There were flowers made of glass and glasses made of flowers. She lifted a lid of one of the little boxes but gasped and quickly snapped it shut when a pair of glowing eyes peered back out at her. There was even a little globe with a tiny house inside, and over the house loomed a grey cloud from which rain poured and lightning flashed. As she reached for it, the sky cleared and a rainbow streamed across the glass. Holly smiled and pulled her hand back, and the sky once again clouded and poured down more rain.

Odd returned, trundling a wheelbarrow that held a miniature potted clementine tree. He parked the wheelbarrow in front of Holly.

"What's that?" she said.

"Watch." He plucked a clementine from the tree and set it on a table. He tapped the fruit, and a stream of black ants filed from the tree and headed towards it. Odd rocked on his heels as he beamed at Holly.

"I don't understand," said Holly.

"Scouts," Odd said.

"Scouts for what?"

Odd's face fell. "Scouting?"

Holly shook her head. "It's very nice and amazing, but I don't think it will help."

Odd slumped. Then he straightened and snapped his fingers and again disappeared into the workshop. He returned after a moment, carrying a long, rectangular box. He held it out to her.

Holly took the box and, when she opened it, found a row of vials containing a clear liquid. "What's this?"

"Potions."

Holly peered at the bottles. She was familiar with potions, all Hearth witches were, but she didn't recognize these. "What kinds of potions?"

"The potential kind."

"What?"

"All potions have a purpose, yes? They are made to do one thing. These are for unlocking, but they unlock many things—possibilities, potential."

"I don't understand. How can a potion unlock... possibilities?"

Odd waved his hands. "Every day you decide things—what to wear, what to eat, where to go—these decidings direct your life. But the other choices, the ones you did not decide, still exist—you just don't experience them. These potions, sometimes they can help you experience those other decidings you did not make. And sometimes, by experiencing those other decidings, you can change the ones you *did* make."

Holly stared at him as her mouth hung open.

Odd scratched his backside.

"I've never heard of potions like this," Holly said. "How is that even possible?"

"Odd is cellar gnome to Miss Iris—most gifted Hearth witch to have ever lived. Well, possibly. But she spends all her days making potions, using equipment made by Odd. Together we make potions no one else can."

Holly looked down at the bottles. "I couldn't accept these. They sound much too dear for me to take." She tried handing the box to Odd, but he pushed it back towards her.

"Miss Iris makes many potions. Miss Holly can take these; no one will miss them."

She swallowed and nodded. "Thank you, Odd. I think these might be very helpful indeed."

Odd beamed up at her and then returned to the door where he donned his cap and removed his coat and glasses. "Now, time for beer."

Skyward Promises

Hazel and Holly walked along the darkening road as chirps of crickets and croaks of frogs pierced the warm twilit air. Hazel carried a lamp, but it would need to remain unlit for the time being.

"Are you nervous?" Holly asked.

"Why would I be nervous?" said Hazel.

"You're going to become a Wyr witch. That's kind of scary."

"It's just a formality. It's not like anything's going to change right away." She glanced at Holly. "And why is it scary?"

"No other witches practice Wyr except for Bellota, and she's scary."

Hazel tilted her head. "True."

"I suppose that means you'll have to learn from her."

"Maybe."

"You mean you won't?"

"I mean I want to see how far I get on my own."

"Oh."

They walked in silence a little longer. "Are you excited though?" Holly said.

"I think it's the right choice, if that's what you mean."

"But do you *want* to become a Wyr witch?"

"What I want doesn't matter."

"It matters to me."

Hazel sighed. "What do you want me to say, Holly? That I'm happy our father trapped our mother's soul? That I'm happy I get to spend my life trying to undo his treachery? Because I'm not, but it doesn't matter. I'm doing what needs to be done, and that's all there is to say about it."

"He already ruined Mother's life," Holly said in a near whisper. "You shouldn't let him ruin yours as well."

Hazel closed her eyes, letting her anger lessen. "He'll not ruin anything, not if I can help it. Now come on, or we'll be late."

They followed the road until it branched off into a winding path that led to a circular clearing bordered with towering oak trees. Their thick, gnarled boughs stretched overhead, mottling the dark cerulean sky with shadowed leaves.

A single torch burned at one end of the grove. Hazel walked over to it and used it to light her lantern. Then from the trees a line of witches emerged. They wore black dresses that matched both Hazel's and Holly's. Holly left Hazel's side and joined the other women.

A witch stepped forward. "Who approaches the Circle this night?"

Hazel sighed. "You know it's me, Aster."

Aster raised her chin. "The Circle does not recognize this response."

Hazel tightened her jaw. Aster always was a stickler for formalities. Taking a breath, she replied, "The Witch Hazel approaches the Circle."

The line of women moved around Hazel until they had formed a circle around her. Aster said, "The Circle accepts the Witch Hazel." She took a candle and lit it from Hazel's lamp. Then she used the flame to ignite another witch's candle and so on until each woman held a lit candle of her own.

Hazel gazed straight ahead, letting the flames around her fade into a haze of gentle light.

Aster stepped out of the circle and walked towards the torch. She lifted it from the ground and, with a spell, extinguished the flame. Then she thrust the torch back into the earth and transformed the smoking branch into a tall, forked staff. She turned back towards the circle.

"The Witch Hazel will step forward."

The women standing in front of Hazel moved aside, and Hazel stepped forward.

"Decree to the Moon and Sun, to the Trees and Sky, why you have come here this night."

"I come here to dedicate myself to the way of the Sky, if she will have me."

"Lady of the Sky accepts all who approach with humble hearts. How does the Witch Hazel approach?"

Hazel knelt on the ground in front of the staff. She held out her arms to either side, her palms facing upwards. "The Witch Hazel approaches with all due humility and respect for the Sky and for herself and for all her fellow witches." Hazel felt ridiculous for referring to herself in the third person. She wished the Circle would stop insisting on these rituals. They weren't necessary—not like this. Her choice of discipline was a personal one, and so any respect paid to the Lady of the Sky should also happen in private. Unfortunately, nobody else seemed to share her opinion.

Aster said, "Then rise, Hazel, Witch of the Wyr."

"Witch of the Wyr," said the other witches in unison, and Hazel got to her feet.

Holly squeaked and clapped but then stopped when no one else joined her.

The witches filed out of the grove. Hazel and Holly took up the rear of the procession.

"That went well," Holly whispered. "You did so much better than when I approached the Lord of the Trees. You didn't seem nervous at all."

"I wasn't nervous."

Holly blinked at her. "Really? I was so nervous I thought I might throw up. But then we had cake and it all went away." Holly pawed at Hazel's arm. "Do you think we'll have cake tonight?"

"Probably. It wouldn't be a proper dedication ceremony without cake, and Aster isn't one to deviate from propriety."

Holly sighed. Then, sounding wistful, she said, "I still remember the carrot cake from my ceremony. Do you remember?"

"How could I possibly forget? It's been three years since you dedicated yourself, and you *still* talk about that cake."

"I like carrot cake."

"You like all food."

"That's not true."

"All right, you like all food without meat."

Holly giggled. "Okay, that's true. Though there are worse things than liking something that keeps you alive."

Hazel snorted. "Is that how you rationalize it? Because the amounts you eat go well beyond the need for survival."

"You never know when a famine will come, and you can't let the food go to waste."

"And what about taking food from a poor old woman trying to eat her midday meal? Because there was no famine, and it certainly wasn't going to waste. So where does that incident fit in that perplexing mind of yours?"

"That was *one* time, and she was rude. People that rude shouldn't get delicious food to eat, especially not pie. They should get... lumpy porridge or something. *Cold* porridge. Served her right."

"I see."

The witches left the woods as they approached Aster's house. They formed into a line, and Hazel and Holly waited as each witch extinguished her candle at the threshold, left it in a box on a chair, then stepped inside.

By the time the sisters made it indoors, the room was cramped with all the women and the air stifling despite the hearth remaining cold.

Aster appeared from the crowd and thrust a silver spatula at Hazel as if it were a source of despair.

"You need to cut the cake," Aster said. "It's almost nine."

"Ah, yes, and the cutting of cake past the ninth hour is a dreaded ill omen." Hazel waggled her hands. "How could I forget?"

"Do not make light of such things. This is a dedication cake. You need to cut it by a certain hour, or it will lose its potency."

"Its potency? What potency is that, exactly? Will the Lady of the Sky strike us with lighting? Will we all get a bout of indigestion? I'm curious."

Aster narrowed her eyes. "Just cut the cake."

"Yes, ma'am," Hazel said and followed Aster through the crowd until they came to a table bearing a cake iced with a thick layer of whipped cream.

Aster wrung her hands as she watched Hazel. Hazel made a silent plea for rhubarb, then cut the cake, mildly disappointed when she found it was blueberry.

Aster exhaled a heavy sigh and said, "Let's eat!" She even smiled.

Hazel found a chair in a corner of the room and sat down as she ate.

She eyed the other witches, taking note of who attended and who didn't. Zinnia wasn't there, though that wasn't too surprising.

Holly bounced up to Hazel. "Blueberry!" She gave a purply grin. "Not as good as carrot cake but still yummy."

"I was hoping for rhubarb."

"Hearth witches sometimes get rhubarb. But usually lemon or orange. Sometimes raspberry."

"Aster needs to rethink her cake themes. There's no reason why a Hearth witch should get rhubarb and not a Wyr. It doesn't make any sense."

Holly shrugged and took another bite. "It makes sense to her. I just hope she doesn't go back to her fish cakes for Weaving witches. *That* was gross."

Hazel chuckled. "True."

Holly grew silent as she studied her plate. "So do you know when we're going to leave for Sarnum?"

"I'm not sure yet. Soon, hopefully."

"I can help, you know! You can't leave me behind! I've got potions and everything, so you have to take me along!"

"I was never going to leave you behind, Holly. You're a part of this and a grown woman besides—however you might not act like it. I can't protect you forever."

Holly blinked at her. "Oh."

"And what potions are you talking about?"

Holly poked at her cake and mumbled something incoherent.

"What's that?" Hazel said.

"Possibility potions."

"Which are...?"

"A gift from Odd."

"Of course, how silly of me." Hazel closed her eyes and shook her head. "Never mind, we can talk about it later. Apparently, cutting cakes and conversations with my sister are two things that shouldn't happen past nine."

Wyr Weariness

Hazel stood in the living room of their cottage as Holly held out a box of crystal vials containing a clear liquid.

"Possibility potions," Hazel said flatly.

"That's what Odd said they were."

Hazel reached out to touch one of the vials but pulled her hand back instead. "I don't understand. How are we supposed to use them?"

Holly shrugged. "He said that it will let us see decisions we never made. He said we might be able to change the decisions we *have* made."

Hazel frowned. "I don't understand how that's possible."

"Well, neither do I, but that's what he said."

"You're the Hearth witch. Potions are supposed to be your area of expertise."

"Hearth's only my secondary. I'm a Wild witch, really. You know that."

"You're right. I'm sorry." Hazel waved her hands at the box. "Well? What do we do with them?"

"I-I don't know. Drink them?"

Hazel wrinkled her nose and took a step back.

"What?"

"I don't trust them. Potions made by a gnome don't exactly instill confidence."

"Iris made them."

"Which were then tampered with by an alleged gnome named Odd."

"He's not alleged; he really does exist. And you should have seen his workshop. It was amazing. I bet these potions are amazing. They could help us."

"Or ruin everything."

"Well... maybe. But I doubt it."

"You doubt everything sensible."

"Not *everything*."

"My mistake." Hazel held up a hand. "Just... hold on to them for now. In case we get desperate or stupid enough to try them out."

Holly squeaked and jumped up and down. "I hope so!" Then she ran into her room.

Shaking her head, Hazel walked into the kitchen. On the table sat a thick, worn book nearly the size of a bread basket. She flipped open the cover, narrowing her eyes at the ridiculous and insulting title: *Waxing Wyr: Deception Made Simple for the Aspiring Witch*. Written by a warlock who called himself Nightshade. Pompous ass. It was the only book on Wyr magic the Circle had, and so it was all Hazel had to teach herself. But she couldn't even look at the book without getting angry. She'd have to go to Bellota for help, and that made her angrier.

She shut the book and poured herself a cup of tea. A knock came at the door. Hazel ignored it, hoping that whoever it was would go away. But the knocking continued.

Holly poked her head out of her room. "Are you going to get that?" she called.

"No, are you?"

Holly emitted a loud, exaggerated sigh and walked to the door. There was a murmured exchange of voices, then approaching footsteps. Hazel turned and found Hemlock standing in the kitchen doorway.

"Hemlock. What are you doing here?"

"We haven't spoken in a while. I wanted to see how you were."

"You mean you wanted to check on me. I assume you've heard about my Wyr dedication ceremony."

"I did, but that's not why I'm here."

"Is that so?"

He looked off to the side. "All right, perhaps it is. But I'm not here to check on you. I just wanted to see how you were doing. To see if... you might need any help."

"Of course, because a witch couldn't possibly learn Wyr magic on her own."

"You know that's not true."

"*I* know it's true. Do you?"

Hemlock held her gaze. "Wyr magic is a difficult discipline. Books on the subject are notoriously poor, filled with the blustered nonsense of self-important warlocks who are more in love with their own prose than they are with teaching anything of worth. Which means that if you don't want to subject yourself to the mind-numbing tedium of idiotic warlocks rambling about their own exaggerated qualities, you'll need to find a witch to teach you, and the only witch that can do that is Bellota." He rubbed the back of his neck. "I don't know the woman well, but she frightens me. I'd not inflict her on anyone."

"Not even Hawthorn?"

"Especially not Hawthorn. He'd probably enjoy it."

Hazel giggled before she could stop herself. Hemlock smiled.

She cleared her throat and straightened her back, trying to regain her composure.

Hemlock clasped his hands and took on a serious expression.

Hazel tightened her mouth, trying to find her previous anger, but it was gone. She let out a breath. "You're right, of course." She jabbed a hand towards the table. "That book is all but worthless. I can barely stand looking at it without wanting to pitch it in the fire."

"I know the feeling."

"I mean, really. *Nightshade?* Does he think that makes him sound mysterious? Intelligent? *Scary?* His real name's probably Bogwort or something."

"Or Pussywillow."

Hazel snorted and clasped a hand over her mouth. Then she laughed. Hemlock grinned.

She took a deep breath and wiped her eyes. "I don't know. If I cared enough about Wyr magic, I could probably suffer my way through that book. But I don't, not really. I'm just doing this to find my father, but I'm not sure it's enough."

"Let me help you, Hazel," Hemlock said softly.

She shook her head. "I don't want your help."

"I know, but maybe you need it. We all need help sometimes, whether we want it or not."

"And how do you propose to help? Warlocks aren't supposed to teach witches, you know."

"And witches aren't supposed to teach warlocks. Yes, I've read the pamphlets."

"Well then?"

He shrugged. "I thought you might like to take the opportunity to snub some of our society's more asinine rules."

Hazel grinned. "Well, I do love a good snubbing."

Hemlock grinned along with her. "I was hoping you would."

Aired Affections

Hazel trailed behind Hemlock as they climbed up the steep face of a rocky cliff. The stones were damp and coated with moss. Hazel grabbed on to a clump of the growth to pull herself up, but it tore free and she had to clutch on to a tree root to keep her balance.

Hemlock glanced down at her. "Are you all right?"

"I'm fine. Let's just keep moving before I fall and break my neck."

Somehow they managed to reach the top, and Hazel hoisted herself over the edge with about as much grace as a slug in a sink. Mud coated her dress, and a hole had been torn in a sleeve where she had snagged it on a branch. "Tell me again why we're here?"

Hemlock smiled and spread out his arms. "What better place to practice Wyr magic than atop a hill, where we can see the sky and feel the wind."

Hazel turned and looked over the vista. The Grove sprawled out before her, the treetops like a vast green blanket. "It's beautiful."

Hemlock rubbed his hands together. "I thought to start we'd talk about illusions."

Hazel took a breath and turned to face him. "All right."

"Now, how much do you know?"

She shrugged. "They're illusions. They make something appear different than what it is."

"That is one way to put it, yes, but there is more to illusionism than that."

"Such as?"

Hemlock put out a hand, and with a spell, a luminescent baby dragon materialized on his palm. It scampered up his arm and to his shoulder, then took flight to where it disappeared among the clouds. "Illusions can bring into being visions of what could be but still isn't. It is a sensory magic—it can elicit sensations of touch and scent, sight and sound, where there were before none of those things. It's very similar to conjuring. Yet conjuring doesn't require an observer to take effect, whereas illusions do. You could conjure the image of a cat that would exist in the world—even if there was no one there to observe it—for as long as the spell lasted. That dragon I created, however, only existed because you were here to see it, and it stopped existing as soon as it faded from view."

"What about you though?" Hazel asked. "You were here to observe the dragon. Isn't that enough?"

Hemlock shook his head. "Illusionary magic is about altering the perceptions of others. As I am the one creating the spell, it is not possible to alter my perception because I am already aware of every facet of the item I am creating. I am dictating how others will perceive it. It is, essentially, manifesting my will in a perceptible form, but others must be there to perceive it, or it will fail. Otherwise it is a conjuration and not an illusion, and conjuring is slightly different in terms of spellcraft and enunciation."

Hazel nodded. "I understand." Well, that wasn't entirely true, but she was sure she would once she had a moment to let all the information settle.

Hemlock eyed her a moment. "Why don't you give it a try?" He told her how to craft a spell and pronounce the words, and then he stood there, smiling and nodding and exuding an enthusiasm that Hazel didn't share.

"I wouldn't know what to create," she said.

"It could be anything. A scent, a sensation on the skin. It's best to start simple at first—like single sensations—and then work your way up to multisensory objects."

Hazel blinked and nodded again. She shouldn't hesitate. She needed to learn this, so there really was nothing for it than to give it a go. Her hands had turned clammy, and she rubbed them on her skirts. Then she spoke the words as she imagined the soft sensation of a warm, gentle breeze.

But nothing happened.

She rubbed her forehead. "I'm terrible at this."

"Everyone is terrible when starting out. You need to work your way up."

"Except I'm not anywhere. How can I work my way up from nowhere?"

He smiled. "It's hard, but it's possible."

She tried to feel encouraged, but it eluded her. "Have I made a mistake?"

"Your pronunciation wasn't exact. It needs to be exact for the desired effect to take hold."

"That's not what I meant."

Hemlock was quiet a moment. "No, you haven't."

"This should be simple. Trying to stop my necromancer father? *That* will be difficult. If I'm having trouble with this, then what hope do I have of stopping him?"

"This was never going to be simple, Hazel. Which is all the more reason why you need to do it. You get through this, and getting through to your father will be the simpler for it."

She tapped her fingers against her leg. She hoped he was right. She wanted to believe he was. He seemed to believe in her; she wanted to believe in him. "So the pronunciation needs to be exact?"

"Yes."

"Not even a little deviation?"

"That's the opposite of exact."

She took a deep breath. "All right, let's try it again."

Hazel returned home late that night, her dress even more muddied than before and the hem torn from a clumsy attempt at trying to navigate back down the cliff in the dark. She smiled. She couldn't help it. She was filthy, and her attempt at Wyr magic had been underwhelming. She should be angry, but somehow the anger never came.

She stepped inside the cottage, and Holly wandered out of her room as she rubbed her eyes. She was dressed for bed in her long white nightgown, her golden hair braided into pigtails. She squinted at Hazel as she clutched Robert—her well-worn teddy bear—close to her chest. "You're late."

"I was practicing."

Holly frowned. "You could've practiced here."

"I was with Hemlock. We were practicing on a cliff where the air is clearer."

Holly stared at her a moment, and then she grinned. "Oh, I see."

Now it was Hazel's turn to frown. "See what? And why are you grinning like that?"

"You like him."

"Who?"

"Hemlock."

"Don't be absurd."

"You do. Look at you. Your dress is ruined, you look terrible, and yet somehow you're not yelling at me."

Hazel folded her arms. "We can change that, you know."

Holly giggled. She grabbed hold of the skirt of her nightgown and swung it as she danced around Hazel.

"Stop that," Hazel said.

"You like him. You like him," Holly chanted.

"Go to bed."

"Are you going to get married?"

"You've lost your mind. Of course not."

"So you've talked about it?"

"What? No!"

"So you've *thought* about it?"

Hazel closed her eyes and took a deep breath. Leave it to Holly to ruin a perfectly fine evening. "I'm going to bed."

Holly trailed after her as she headed upstairs towards her bedroom loft. "You *have* thought about it!"

"I've done no such thing!"

"Do you think you'll move in with him? Not all warlocks and witches live separately, you know."

Hazel stopped and looked at her. "What? Like who?"

"Larch and Lily."

Hazel raised her eyebrows "Really? I had no idea." She screwed up her face. "Though I guess I shouldn't be surprised. Ridiculous name pairing, those two."

Holly grinned and clasped her hands together and leaned against Hazel. "Not like Hazel and Hemlock."

"Nope, that's pretty ridiculous as well, so it won't be happening." She opened the door to her room.

Holly remained on the stairs. "If you move in with him, can I come with you?"

Hazel made a disgusted sound, shouted, "No!" and slammed the door shut.

Holly's giggling faded as she made her way back downstairs.

Hazel leaned against the door as she let her annoyance fade. Then she smiled. Somehow she still wasn't angry, and the best part of all would be getting even with Holly.

Teatime Tribulation

Holly stared as Hazel set the table for tea. Hazel never set the table and definitely never with the china painted with the little yellow flowers that had been their mother's.

"What are you doing?" Holly said.

"Honestly, Holly, it's not complicated. We're having guests over. You're always saying how we should have guests over for tea."

"Yes, but we never do. You always say something like, 'Who decided that drinking tea needed to be a social event?' and then no one ever comes over. I have to invite myself to other people's tea." Holly poked at her hip. "I'm pretty sure Aster thinks I'm stalking her."

"Not without reason, I'm sure. And I don't see why you're complaining. If you've wanted this to happen for so long, you should be happy."

"I-I am. It's just weird is all."

"That's never stopped you before."

"It's never involved *you* before."

Hazel gave Holly a flat look and handed her a bundle of little lace doilies. "Here, place these on the table."

Holly's mouth hung open. "Doilies? You hate doilies!"

"We have company coming over, Holly. How I feel about doilies doesn't really matter, now does it?"

Holly stared at her sister. "Who are you?" she whispered.

Hazel rolled her eyes. "Don't be so dramatic. I can cancel the tea, you know, if you're finding it so upsetting."

"No!" Holly snatched the doilies from Hazel's hand. "I'll help." She placed the doilies under each cup and under the teapot. Hazel placed a jar of white and purple columbine flowers in the middle of the table.

Holly looked down at her clothes and realized she was wearing her ratty old house dress that she wore when cleaning. "I need to go change." She started towards her room when a knock came at the door. She froze.

"No time for that," Hazel said. "You look fine."

"I do not look fine! I look like I just crawled out from under a rock!"

"Could you get the door? I still need to put the scones on the table." Hazel returned to the great cast iron stove, grabbed a towel, and wrenched one of the heavy doors open.

There was another knock.

"Holly, please. I'm busy here."

Holly let out a heavy sigh. "Fine." She walked to the door and was about to open it when she remembered the handkerchief covering her head. She yanked it off, stuffed it in a pocket and, hastily smoothing her hair, opened the door.

Her heart lurched and then sank when she saw Hawthorn standing there along with Hemlock.

Hemlock smiled. "Holly, hello. Thank you for inviting us."

"Yes, thank you," Hawthorn said. He looked perfect standing there with his wavy chestnut hair and lavender brocade waistcoat and breeches. He even wore a matching cape that caught the light with dazzling effect.

"Is that a new outfit?" Holly asked.

Hawthorn beamed at her. "Why, yes it is. How astute of you."

Holly grinned as her cheeks grew hot. No one had ever called her astute before.

"I had it shipped from Sarnum." He rubbed a hand along the fabric on his chest. "You just can't get quality silk around here, you know?"

Holly snorted as she tried to laugh. "Oh, I know." She really didn't, but a little fib never hurt anyone.

"Are you going to make them stand out there all day, Holly?" Hazel said as she stood in the doorway to the kitchen.

"No," Holly said. The day they finally have guests over to tea and it turns out to be Hawthorn while she's wearing the worst dress she owned. She smoothed the garment as best she could and, stepping aside, said, "Come in."

Hawthorn swept his cape over a shoulder and strode into the cottage. "Ah, there we are."

Hemlock rolled his eyes and followed his brother in.

"One must always make an impressionable entrance," Hawthorn said. "Don't you agree?"

Holly nodded. "Oh yes, definitely. Yours was very nice."

Hawthorn smiled. "I thought so. The cape helps, you see." He unclasped it and, with a flourish, snapped it off his shoulders.

Holly squeaked and clapped. Then she reached out. "I can take that for you if you'd like."

"Yes, thank you."

Holly took the cape and managed to suppress a sigh as she ran her hands over the silk. It felt so smooth. She bet it even smelled like him. She resisted the urge to sniff it and scuttled away to her room where she draped the cape over her bed.

Another knock came at the door.

Holly stepped out of her room and frowned towards the entrance.

"More guests?" Hawthorn said, smiling. "How splendid." He turned to Hemlock. "See? I told you I wouldn't be overdressed."

"You're always overdressed," Hemlock said.

"So say the small-minded."

"You would know."

Another knock.

"Holly!" Hazel shouted from the kitchen.

"I know!" she yelled back. "Who else is coming?"

"You'll see."

Holly frowned some more. She didn't like surprises, not when they came from Hazel. Hazel always thought she was being so funny, but whatever it was usually turned out to be scary. Like that one time when Hazel had put nettles in Holly's night cream. Her face had gotten all puffy and itched for a week. She wondered if this surprise would also cause her to wrap her face in bandages like some kind of sickroom run-away.

She yanked the door open. "Rose! Uh... hello."

Rose smiled, showing perfect white teeth that rivaled Hawthorn's. "Hello, Holly."

Holly stared at her awhile. "You're here for tea?"

Rose laughed—a deep, throaty sound that made Holly feel frumpy and dull. "Of course. Why else would I be here?"

"Not for a nosebleed, I suppose," Holly muttered.

"Pardon?"

"Nothing." Holly forced a smile and stood aside. "Please, come in."

Rose swept into the room, pulling off the white gloves that covered her hands. She wore an emerald satin dress—completely unwrinkled—that matched her eyes and offset her perfectly curly auburn hair. Holly shrank away, smoothing the skirt of her rough-spun dress and wondering if she should put the kerchief back on her head.

"Rose," Hawthorn said as he walked over and took one of her hands. He kissed it. "Always a pleasure."

Rose inclined her head, her long porcelain neck arching like a swan's. "Hawthorn. As virile as ever, I see."

"You bring it out in me."

"I'm going to be sick," Hemlock said. He walked into the kitchen.

Holly also felt ill. Looking at Rose's perfectly ringleted hair and her perfect skin and her perfect dress. She was so... perfect that Holly wanted to pitch a potted plant at her. Even worse was that she looked good standing next to Hawthorn. The two suited each other, and that filled Holly with a panicked dread.

She marched up to them. "We should drink tea now!" Holly said much more loudly than she intended. She waved her hands at Rose. "Go on, scooch!"

Rose stared at her. "Did you just 'scooch' me?"

"I did, and I'll do it again. Best get moving if you know what's good for you."

Hawthorn extended an arm. "Shall we?"

Rose smiled as she placed a delicate hand on his sleeve. "Only if you promise not to ravish me on the way."

"I couldn't possibly make such a promise, my lady. Not when you show up wearing a perfectly rippable dress."

"You cad."

"Harlot."

Rose gave a throaty laugh, and the two sauntered into the kitchen.

Holly stood there staring after them. Her dress was much more rippable than Rose's—it was even torn in the armpit—but Hawthorn had barely even glanced at her. She marched into the kitchen and glared at Hazel. "You did this on purpose," she murmured.

Hazel smiled and thrust a crock of butter into Holly's hands. "I don't know what you mean. I would never torment you if I thought you liked Hawthorn. You don't like him, do you?"

Holly glared at her some more, then dropped the butter onto the table and slumped into a chair.

Hawthorn cut open a scone and spread some butter onto it. "You know, I've always thought a good butter resembles the creaminess of a woman's legs."

"My legs aren't creamy," Rose said. "They're firm like granite."

"Granite is grey," Holly said. "You would look like a corpse."

"I quite agree," Hawthorn said. "You have a complexion of porcelain, dear Rose. Or alabaster, or—"

"We get it," Holly said. "Rose is just like all the perfect stones in the world. Can we move on now?" She poked at her scone, no longer hungry. Just like Hazel to ruin their very first tea.

Hemlock said, "So, Holly, what have you been up to lately? Anything fun?"

"I never do anything fun. Hazel makes sure of it."

"Oh, please," Hazel said.

"Sounds like you've been wronged, Holly," Hawthorn said.

Holly nodded. "I have. Terribly."

Hazel scoffed. "The only time you've ever been wronged is when the postman misplaced your letter."

Holly narrowed her eyes. "And I bet you had something to do with that."

"Yes," Hazel said flatly. "I'm quite the devious mastermind. A true puppet master of all written correspondence."

"I knew it!"

Hazel shook her head and drank some tea.

Hemlock cleared his throat. "Surely things aren't as dire as you might think, Holly."

"You calling me stupid? You think I don't know when I've been wronged?"

"I quite agree," Hawthorn said. "Being wronged is a grievous offense, and we shouldn't make light of it." He turned to Holly. "You can borrow my dueling rapiers for when you demand satisfaction."

Holly blinked. "Satisfaction?" She wasn't sure what he meant, but she didn't want to ask and look stupid. Especially after she accused Hemlock of thinking she was.

Hazel leaned forward. "He means you can stab me with a thin little sword if it will make you feel better."

"What? That's terrible!"

"Well, yes," Hawthorn said, "but so is being insulted. I find it best to follow protocol in these kinds of situations."

Holly stared at her plate as she resumed poking her scone. "No, thank you," she murmured.

Hawthorn shrugged. "As you like."

"I'm confused," Rose said. "What happened that insulted Holly?"

"Yes, Holly," Hazel said. "What happened?"

Holly's face turned hot. Was Hazel taunting her? After everything she'd done? Holly stood up, bumping the table and sloshing tea onto the tablecloth. "You know what happened! You know I like Hawthorn! I didn't think you knew, but now I know you know because you have that smarmy look on your face when you think you're privy to some secret and you're feeling pretty special about yourself. You knew I liked him, so you invited Miss Perfection over here with her rippable dress while I look like the town idiot dressed in a potato sack. You always do this! You always take that tiny little thing that's mine that I love, and you find a way to ruin it!"

Everyone grew silent as they looked at her, and the realization of what she had just said crept in. Holly felt sick. Her lips trembled and her hands shook. Unable to look at Hawthorn, she turned and ran from the cottage.

She darted into the woods, letting branches tear at her dress. She hated her dress. She wanted to burn it. If it got torn enough, maybe she would. Tears streamed down her cheeks as she ran, but she didn't care. At least she hadn't cried in front of Hawthorn. After everything that had happened, at least she hadn't done that.

Holly came to a pond, and she stopped to lean against a tree. She could never go back there, not after what she'd said. She had said she liked him, in front of everyone. She might have even said she loved him; she couldn't remember—it all seemed so hazy now.

When she had been a girl, she had heard stories of solitary witches living out in the woods. Maybe she could become one. She'd hide from everyone. Squirrels never played tricks on her. Or mice or deer. It was safer out here, away from people.

"Holly?" Hazel said as she approached.

Holly scowled at her. "What? Have you come here to gloat? It wasn't enough seeing me humiliate myself? You need to come here and rub my face in it even more?" She turned around and stared at the pond, at the way the mottled light glinted on the surface.

"I'm sorry," Hazel said. "I... I didn't mean for that to happen."

"But you're glad that it did?"

"No, I'm not. I knew you liked Hawthorn, yes, so I thought I'd tease you a bit, kind of like how you were teasing me, remember?"

"It wasn't the same. What I did and what you did weren't even close to being the same thing."

"I realize that now, and I'm sorry."

"It doesn't matter. He probably thinks I'm a complete idiot or... crazy or something."

"Well... you are a *little* crazy."

Holly smiled, but then she caught herself and frowned.

They stood there awhile, letting the chirping birds and rustling trees be the only sound between them.

Then Hazel said, "You know Rose isn't the least bit interested in Hawthorn, right?"

Holly studied her. She couldn't tell if Hazel was being serious or not. "Really?"

Hazel nodded. "Really. Rumor has it that she and Linden have a thing going."

"Linden? But she's a witch."

Hazel smiled. "I know."

Holly's mouth fell open. "Oh. Then why was she flirting with Hawthorn?"

Hazel laughed. "Everyone knows Rose is a terrible flirt. Well, I thought *you* knew anyway. You usually know more about this kind of stuff than I do. It was part of the joke, and I thought..." She shook her head. "Never mind what I thought. I'm sorry."

Holly took a moment to consider. "Does Hawthorn know that she and Linden... you know...?"

Hazel shrugged. "I have no idea what knowledge that man holds in his head. That's for you to figure out, not me."

"I don't think he'll want to talk to me again."

"I wouldn't be so sure about that."

"Really?"

"Really."

"But how do you know?"

"Because you're my sister, and if having him in your life will make you happy, I will make sure he's there. Even if I have to drag him over kicking and screaming."

"Really?"

"Really."

Holly smiled and linked her arm in Hazel's and rested her head against her shoulder. "Thanks, Hazel."

Hazel rested her head against Holly's.

Then Holly said, "You know I don't *really* want you to drag him over, right?"

"We'll see."

"Hazel!"

"I'm kidding."

"You have a really terrible sense of humor, you know?"

"Well, we can't all be Miss Perfection."

Holly giggled. "No, certainly not."

Willowed Remorse

"Are we leaving soon?" Holly asked. She and Hazel sat at the kitchen table, sipping tea as a lantern cast fitful shadows along the darkened walls.

Hazel closed her eyes. "For the hundredth time, no. It's still too early."

"It's night outside. How is that too early?"

"I told you, we need to wait until past midnight."

"But why?"

"Because that's how this particular magic works, that's why."

"But why do we have to sit *here*, drinking tea? I'm bored. And tired."

"Because it's impossible waking you up early for anything once you fall asleep. And we're sitting here drinking tea because I *like* sitting here and drinking tea before I visit Mother. It gives me a chance to think."

"About what?"

"About how nice it is to have some quiet without my younger sister pestering me."

"If you'd let me sleep, I wouldn't pester you," Holly murmured.

"No, you'd just conveniently oversleep until it was too late to visit."

Holly turned quiet and stared into her cup.

"It's past time you saw her, Holly. I've been keeping you away from this mess for far too long."

Still staring at her cup, Holly nodded. "I know, and I want to. It's just... what if she's different?"

"She's dead, Holly." Hazel took care to keep her voice gentle. "Of course she's different."

"What if she doesn't remember me?"

"She talks about you every time I visit. She'll remember you."

Holly took a deep breath and drank some tea. "*Now* is it time?"

Hazel sighed. "Well, let's see. It's been about three minutes so... no."

The night passed excruciatingly slow. Between Holly's restless impatience and Hazel's own worries, every minute crawling by felt more like an hour. She almost cheered once the little clock on the mantle struck twelve. Holly had dozed off while resting her head against the table, so Hazel shook her awake and pulled her out the door.

Arm in arm they walked in silence as they made their way down the wooded path. Holly dragged her feet and made more noise than Hazel was comfortable with. Even so, she was glad Holly was there. It was nice not having to walk down the darkened road alone.

The brambles overtaking the cottage had thickened and become more lush since the last time Hazel had been there. She knew she should trim back some of the growth, but this was a garden she didn't know if she had the stomach to tend.

They slipped past the waterlogged door and into the cottage.

"Go start a fire in the hearth there," Hazel said. "I'll crumble the cake." She poured water into the basin, then pulled a cloth parcel from her pocket and unwrapped it. She broke off a piece of the rhubarb cake and popped it into her mouth. It was more tart than sweet—invigorating, really, which she welcomed at such a late hour. She crumbled the rest of the cake into the water.

Once the fire was lit, Holly came and stood next to her. "Now what?"

"Now we wait."

"For how long?"

"It depends."

"On what?"

"I don't know, Holly. It just does. Sometimes she'll appear quickly. Other times she won't. She's trapped by a product of dark magic. It's not exactly a specialty of mine."

Holly tightened her lips and narrowed her eyes. "How *did* you know how to find her here? She got sick and *died,* Hazel. She should be gone. How did you know she wasn't? How did you know about any of this?"

Hazel swallowed and looked away. "I don't know," she whispered.

"What do you mean, you don't know?"

Hazel shook her head, still unable to look at Holly. "I don't know. It was just a... a feeling I had that if I came here at a certain time and did a certain thing, that I'd see her again. I don't know how it works, and I don't know how I know, but I do." She forced herself to look at Holly. "What does that say about me that I knew those things?"

Holly's mouth worked soundlessly awhile. "I... I don't know. It doesn't have to mean anything, does it? You've always been the smart one. Maybe it's just you being smart, that's all."

"I have a natural inclination towards Wyr magic. That's what Pyrus told me. I've been practicing it at a rudimentary level without any training. That almost never happens."

"Because you're smart, that's why."

"What if it's the same with necromancy? Our father's a necromancer. What if I'm like him? What if I'm able to work this horrible, dark magic without any training at all?"

Holly looked away as she took a step back. She wrung her hands. "No. That's not true."

"Then why aren't you able to look me in the eyes?"

Holly swallowed but said nothing.

"Are you tormenting your sister again?" Willow said as she warmed her hands by the fire.

Hazel looked at her and then at Holly, who kept her gaze pinned to the floor.

Willow approached and reached out and touched Holly's hair.

Holly jerked away. Her eyes filled with tears as she looked at her mother, then she resumed staring at the floor.

Willow moved over to the bowl and leaned over it as she breathed in. She wrinkled her nose. "Rhubarb," she said, turning towards Hazel. "You know I don't like rhubarb."

"It was all we had, and you didn't want honey cake, so..." Hazel shrugged. "It's better than nothing."

Willow looked at Holly, but Holly wouldn't meet her gaze. She turned back towards Hazel. "So how have the two of you been? Any exciting news?"

Silence hung between them as Hazel tried to think of what to say. Holly didn't seem like she wanted to talk at all. So Hazel said, "We might know where Father has gone."

Willow clasped her hands and tightened her jaw, her expression still. "I see. And where would that be?"

"Sarnum."

Willow's expression remained cold. "I've heard that place is a sty. I don't envy you if you go there."

"You're not at all concerned with the news that we might know where Father is? You don't care?"

"You know my thoughts on the matter. Do we really need to have this argument again?"

Hazel looked away shook her head. "No. I suppose not."

Willow moved back to the fire and put her pale hands near the flames. "I want to know about the two of you. What have you been up to? Do you have any stories, Holly?"

Holly clenched her hands together, but she said nothing as she avoided her mother's gaze.

Crickets chirped, and in the distance, a frog croaked.

"I became a Wyr witch," Hazel said.

Willow smiled though it seemed weary. "Really? How nice."

"I need to go," Holly said and hurried out of the cottage.

Willow's smile faded as she stared at where Holly had gone.

"Give her time, Mother. This was her first visit here. It's difficult for her."

"It's difficult for all of us," Willow said.

Silence lingered between them. "I should go. Make sure Holly is all right."

Willow nodded.

Hazel took a deep breath. "I don't know when we'll be back. We're going to be leaving for Sarnum soon. So..."

"Have a nice trip."

"Is that really all you're going to say?"

Willow continued to stare at the waterlogged door. "Be sure to throw out the cake crumbs before the rats come in."

Hazel lifted her chin and set her jaw. Then she tossed the cake water out the window and walked out of the cottage.

The Tiresome Trail

Hazel and Holly waited in front of their cottage along with their luggage. Hazel stood near the road, her hands clenched as she watched for an approaching carriage. Holly sat on top of her steamer trunk, resting her chin on her hand with her elbow propped on her knee.

"Who's going to take care of the bees?" Holly said.

"Bees take care of themselves for the most part. But Aster said she'd check on them from time to time and harvest the honey when it's ready."

"She'll probably take it all for herself," Holly said sullenly.

"She's welcome to it. It's not like we'll be here to use any of it."

"But what about the garden?"

"We'll replant it when we return."

Holly fell silent.

"You said you wanted to come," Hazel said. "Why are you sulking?"

"I'm not sulking. It's just... we've never left home before. It makes me sad thinking about it all dark and empty."

Hazel looked at the cottage. "I know. Me too. But it's just a house, Holly. It's not what matters. We are. So as long as we stick together, we'll be fine. All right?"

Holly wiped at her eyes and nodded. She reached into her pocket and pulled out her mouse. "And Chester too. Don't forget about Chester."

Hazel had to make an effort to keep herself from cringing. "Chester too."

Holly smiled and ran her fingers over the mouse's furry back.

"Besides," Hazel said, "the house won't be completely empty. Tum will still be in the cellar, won't he?"

"Um, yeah," Holly said and put Chester on her shoulder.

A carriage rounded the bend in a cloud of dust. Hazel backed away from the road and waited until the carriage stopped in front of them. The driver—a stout man with a handlebar mustache—hopped down from the box and had started to load Hazel's luggage atop the carriage when one of the doors opened and Hemlock stepped outside.

He smiled. "You ladies ready for an adventure?"

Holly, still sitting on her trunk, poked at a rock with her foot.

"This isn't exactly a joy ride, Hemlock," Hazel said.

Hemlock cleared his throat. "Of course not. My apologies. Here, let me help with the luggage." He walked up to Holly, but she didn't move.

Hazel nudged her, and Holly looked up. "What? Oh, sorry," she mumbled and stood next to Hazel.

Once the luggage had been loaded and tied down, Hazel, Holly, and Hemlock climbed into the carriage. Hawthorn sat inside, and when Holly sat next to him, his back went rigid as he fixed his gaze out the window. Holly scooched away from him as far as possible and looked out her own window.

"Well, this is awkward," Hazel whispered to Hemlock.

Hemlock leaned close to her and whispered, "Hawthorn hasn't really been the same since that day we had tea at your house. I don't know what's gotten into him."

"This is going to be a long trip, isn't it?"

Hemlock shrugged and gave her a crooked smile.

Silence hung between them as the coach rattled down the road. Hawthorn stared out his window, and Holly did the same.

Desperate to coax some kind of conversation out of them, Hazel said, "Your glamour looks quite robust today, Hawthorn."

He said nothing as he continued to stare outside. Hemlock kicked him in the shin.

"Ow," he said, rubbing his leg. He pouted.

"You're brooding," Hemlock said, "and being rude. Hazel was talking to you."

"Oh," Hawthorn said. "I apologize. What were you saying?"

Hazel gave a tight smile. It was bad enough complimenting Hawthorn on his glamour once; she didn't really want to do it again. "I just said your glamour is well done."

Hawthorn smoothed his hair though his expression remained serious. He didn't seem to take pleasure in the gesture as he usually did. "Ah, yes. Thank you." He resumed staring out the window.

Hazel raised her eyebrows at Hemlock, but he just shrugged.

The journey was long and quiet. Hazel and Hemlock tried to make conversation, but with Holly and Hawthorn lost in their own worlds, it felt awkward. After a while, they gave up, and Hemlock spent the rest of the journey reading a book while Hazel stared at Chester as he nestled himself in Holly's hair. She shuddered.

The day waned, and as the sun began to set, they came to an old inn deep within a dark and wild part of the woods.

Everyone climbed out of the carriage. Holly walked to a patch of grass and set Chester down, and he scampered out of sight.

"Won't he get lost?" Hemlock said.

"No, he'll be fine."

"He's very resourceful," Hazel said.

Holly grinned.

"Ah," Hemlock said.

Hawthorn sniffed and pressed an embroidered kerchief to his nose. "What is this place?" He waved a hand towards the inn. "And what is that odor?"

"That odor is called nature," Hemlock said. "And this inn is where we'll stay the night. There's nothing else between the Grove and Sarnum."

"No, it's not nature. It smells like dust and..."—he sniffed again—"despair."

"That's not despair," Holly said, "it's horse dung and mildew. Despair is more spicy, like cloves and wet soot." She beamed at him.

Hawthorn's cheeks reddened. "Oh," he said and walked into the inn.

Holly's smile faded. She mumbled something incoherent and walked off to where Chester had gone.

Hemlock said, "Have I gone completely mad, or did my brother just *blush?*"

Hazel nodded. "And through his glamour too."

"I've never seen him so flustered. Could this really be from what Holly said at tea? Since when does a woman's admiration cause Hawthorn to become so unhinged?"

Hazel shrugged. "He's your brother. I hardly know the man."

"Should we do something?"

"Do something? Like what?"

"I don't know. It's just so awkward. I feel helpless."

Hazel grinned. "I'm sure they'll figure it out."

"I hope so." He straightened his jacket. "For all our sakes. It's painful watching them."

The driver climbed to the roof of the carriage, untied the luggage, and began throwing the trunks and bags down onto the ground. Hazel backed away from the rising dust just as Holly's trunk dropped in front of her.

There was a muffled grunt.

Hazel froze.

"What's wrong?" Hemlock said.

Hazel put up a hand. "Shhh." They both stood there, still as stone. Even the driver had stopped throwing the bags from the carriage.

"Did you hear that?" Hazel said.

"No," said Hemlock.

She opened the trunk, and there, tangled among Holly's dresses and petticoats, was Tum.

He hopped out. "*Finally.* Isn't too comfortable in there, even for a gnome."

Hazel put her hands on her hips. "Tum, what are you doing here?"

"Miss Holly said I could come along. Thought it for the best. Cellar gnomes aren't much good in empty houses, and beer has a tendency to dry up that way." He leaned into the trunk and started rummaging around.

"What are you doing? Stop that." Hazel nudged him with her foot, but Tum wouldn't move. She threw the lid closed, and he scrambled backwards to avoid getting struck by it.

"Hey!" he said. "You could've lopped my arms off!"

"That would have been a great tragedy."

"That's right. You remember that the next time you want old Tum to go spoiling. Can't exactly do that without any arms."

"You have feet."

Tum opened his mouth but then snapped it shut, his expression perplexed.

Hazel drew herself up. "Just stay out of my way and out of my things. You're Holly's responsibility. If you're going to steal anything, you steal from her. Otherwise, we're going to have a disagreement. Understand me?"

Tum waved a hand. "As you like. Though spoiling can't always be contained. It's a passion, see? And passion goes where it pleases, like the wind."

"Well, you keep your wind and passion away from me, and we'll be just fine." She thrust one of Holly's smaller bags at him. "Make yourself useful in the meanwhile."

Tum grabbed hold of it and grinned. "Tum's always useful." Then he scampered away with it into the inn.

Hazel shook her head. To Hemlock, she said, "I hope you didn't bring any valuables," and followed Tum inside.

Homeward Heart

Holly sat on a fallen tree trunk, twining together fern leaves into a wreath as Chester scampered in the brush. She'd like to make a matching wreath for him to wear, but her fingers weren't nimble enough for such tiny weave work. Maybe Odd had some tools she could use that would help her make such a thing. She'd have to remember to ask him when they returned. *If* they returned. Holly put down the leaves, staring at the darkening sky that seemed on the verge of swallowing her in its shadow.

"Holly?"

She turned and found Hemlock approaching.

"Are you all right?" he said.

Her throat clenched as she tried to answer, so she nodded instead.

He sat down next to her. "It's getting dark. Wouldn't you like to come inside?"

She shook her head. "I don't like it here. It's dark and depressing, and that's just outside. I don't want to see what it's like inside."

"It's actually not that bad. And that wreath you made is lovely, so it can't all be so depressing, can it?"

She shrugged. They sat in silence for a while, then she said, "Do you miss it?"

"What?"

"Home."

"Well, I..." He glanced at her out of the corner of his eye before letting out a breath. "No, not really."

Holly slumped. "Oh."

"I envy you, though, for missing it."

She frowned. "Why?"

"You have a place you have given your heart, a place where you belong. You have a *home*, Holly. I just have a place where I live with an annoying brother. There is a difference, and I envy yours."

"You could have a home if you wanted."

He gave a wan smile. "Maybe, though I wouldn't know how."

"Hazel would know."

Hemlock looked down at his hands.

Holly studied him awhile before saying, "Did she ever tell you what happened to our mother?"

He shook his head. "I know she passed away. I have gathered, given your father's tampering in necromancy, that maybe he had something to do with her death. Or... maybe with something that happened afterward."

"He trapped her soul in a geas. Hazel's been trying to figure out how to undo it."

Hemlock swallowed. "That is terrible. I'm sorry."

Holly looked off towards the trees and nodded. "I went to go see her—our mother—the other night. Right before we left. It was the first time I went since she died."

"How did it go?"

"Terribly. I couldn't even look at her, and then I left. Now we're here. I can't go back and tell her I'm sorry." She wiped at her eyes. "I might never get to tell her."

"I'm sure you will."

Holly stared at her hands resting on her lap. "If you have something you want to tell someone, you shouldn't wait."

"I beg your pardon?"

"Hazel. She likes you, and I think you might like her too."

Hemlock cleared his throat and adjusted his glasses. "Well, yes, but it's complicated."

"I know. Hazel always makes everything complicated. But you need to figure it out. She needs someone like you, though she'll never admit it."

He shook his head. "I'd like to believe that, but I'm not sure I do."

"Did you know that when I was six, our mother left us once?"

He blinked. "I... No, I didn't know that."

Holly nodded. "Just upped and left, didn't say where she was going or why or when she'd be back. Hazel was around twelve then, and she was furious. I remember her yelling and she threw something—a plate maybe, I don't remember what—and broke it. I cried. Hazel grew really quiet, and then she walked into the kitchen and grabbed a jar of honey. She took my hand and led me outside, and we walked to a pond nearby our cottage. We sat on a log together, kind of like this one, and ate the honey with our fingers until the sun set. Then we stayed out and watched the stars. It's one of my favorite memories, and I sometimes forget that it's only because our mother left that we did that at all."

Holly peered at Hemlock in the gloom. "Despite her rough edges, Hazel's always looked after me—after Mother too. It's who she is. I just hope that someday someone will come along who can look after *her*. I hope she can find someone to watch the stars with."

"I hope so too."

Holly nodded. "Well, all right then." She put her hand to the ground and waited until Chester scampered onto her palm. "Just don't wait too long."

She started to walk away when Hemlock said, "Hawthorn would be lucky to have you. If he doesn't see that, then he's a fool."

Holly smiled. "Thanks, Hemlock."

He rose and offered her his arm. "May I escort you back, Miss Holly?"

She giggled and linked her arm in his. "You may."

They strolled back towards the inn as the first stars of the evening sparked into the sky and crickets began to chirp.

"By the way," Hemlock said, "Tum has locked himself in your room. I thought you'd like to know."

Holly nodded. "I thought he might."

The inside of the inn was both creepy and cozy, if such a thing were possible. Racks of antlers hung on the walls, some of which served as sconces with tallow candles affixed to the branching, bony limbs. A massive chandelier wrought from yet more antlers hung from the ceiling of the common room, its candles dripping pale wax onto varnished walnut tables and the bare wooden floor. Black-painted walls sucked life and light from the room, only to give both back through warm, plush curtains and paintings of vibrant wildflowers and idyllic pastoral scenes. A single bookshelf boasted a modest library, and a fire crackling in the hearth helped chase away some of Holly's unease. Yet the room was empty, the popping of the fire the only sound. It made the place seem sterile. Dead.

"Where is everyone?" Holly said.

"The only people that travel between Sarnum and the Grove with any regularity are traders, and they usually sleep within their wagons so as not to be separated from their wares. Yet even they don't pass through as often as you'd think. The Grove has few traders of its own, and most traders from Sarnum find routes outside the Grove to be more worth their time."

"How do you know all this?"

Hemlock straightened his jacket, looking uncomfortable. "Let's just say Hawthorn's obsession with silk prices has kept me well informed of the local trade habits."

"It's quiet," Holly said as she surveyed the room.

"That's not so bad, is it?"

Holly pressed her lips together. "We'll see. If there are any of those antlers in my room, I'm tossing them out."

She walked to a counter and rang a little bell. After a moment, a thin man with a thinner mustache and ears nearly as big as his head walked out of a door and stood behind the counter. He beamed at her.

"We're going to need some beer," Holly said.

The man pointed at an open ledger on the counter.

Holly glanced at it and shook her head. "I don't understand. Did you hear what I said? We need beer." She raised her voice. "BEEER."

The man, still smiling, lifted a pen next to the ledger and handed it to her.

"I think he wants you to write it down," Hemlock said.

The man nodded and tapped the ledger one more time.

"What on earth for? He seems to have heard you. So why can't he hear me?"

"I don't know, but maybe just humor him?"

Holly sighed and wrote down: *Beer. Three. (Yes, three, and no they're not for me.)* She put down the pen and glowered at the man.

The innkeeper smiled and, with a flourish, ripped the paper from the binding and stuffed it in his mouth.

"Hey!" Holly said. "That's my order!"

He scampered back through the door and disappeared.

Holly stared at where he'd gone and then at Hemlock. "Is... is he coming back?"

Hemlock shrugged.

"What kind of place is this?" Holly said.

"The only place between Sarnum and the Grove, I'm afraid. It's just for one night."

A bell rang, and Holly froze. "Where did that come from?" They both kept still, and Holly held her breath as she waited. It rang again.

"There," Hemlock said and walked over to a wall. He slid open a door to a little hatch, revealing three mugs of beer on a shiny silver tray.

"Where did that come from?" Holly said.

"It's a dumbwaiter," Hemlock said. "We have one in our house though we rarely use it." He took the tray and handed it to her. Then he poked his head back into the hatch. "Intriguing design though. I wonder how they got a bell to ring..." He rapped on one of the inner walls and waited, but nothing happened.

Holly blinked at the foaming mugs. "Well, all right then. Which room is mine?"

"Oh, uh, room six."

Holly made her way upstairs and wandered down a hallway of doors, all painted black like the walls. She found the door with a brass "6" nailed to it and pounded on it with her foot, but there was no reply.

"I know you're in there, you little beast. I've got beer here, so unless you want me to drink all of it, you'd better open the door."

The door cracked open, and Tum poked his head out. "What kind of beer?"

"Does it matter?"

"It might. You should try lodging yourself in a cramped trunk full of dresses of middling quality for an entire day, and then see how *you* like drinking substandard beer as a restorative."

"This isn't supposed to be a restorative. It's supposed to be your weekly wages so you don't rob us all blind. And I told you before, you're not burrowing in with my good dress. I've only got the one, and I don't trust your grabby little fingers."

Tum's mouth fell open as he shrank back. "My fingers aren't *grabby!*" He stared at his hands as if unsure.

Holly walked in the room and set the tray down on a table. "Just drink your beer."

Frowning, Tum shuffled over to the tray and took a mug. He sipped some beer and glanced at her out of the corner of his eye but said nothing.

"Well? How is it?"

Tum shrugged. "Perfectly adequate. Utterly unremarkable."

"Good."

He sniffed. "After the glories of beer from the Green Man, 'adequate' is so much harder to bear."

"I'm sure you'll manage." She sat down on the floor, resting her back against the bed. Tum sat down next to her.

The room was brighter than the rest of the inn, with walls that had been papered with a butterfly pattern. It was actually kind of lovely. Especially the way the candlelight caught some of the wings, she could almost see the texture of them and... Holly narrowed her eyes as she tried to focus. Were they casting shadows?

She got up and examined a wall. To her horror, it was filled with scores of butterflies, all pinned to the plaster, their wings preserved in colorful splendor. She cried out and staggered back.

Tum poked his head up from his mug. "What's that?"

Head down, Holly bolted out the door and ran into Hawthorn in the hallway.

"I-I'm sorry," she said. Her vision blurred as her eyes filled with tears. Oh please, not now. Don't cry now. It's just butterflies. Who cares about butterflies? But that only upset her more, and she covered her face as a sob escaped her.

Hawthorn put a kerchief into her hands, and Holly cried into it. He stood there—she knew he did even though she dared not look at him. What he must think of her, running into him like that and then bawling for no reason like a crazy woman. She gulped down air and clenched her hands until she managed to calm.

Hawthorn shuffled his feet as he glanced around. He looked like he wanted to leave. "Are... you all right?" he asked.

Holly nodded, probably more vehemently than was proper. "Yes, sorry. I mean, thank you. It's just... my room. It took me by surprise." Her lips trembled, and she bit them to keep herself from crying again.

"What's wrong with it?"

Holly bit down harder and shook her head. After a while, she managed to say, "I can't stay here. This place, it's awful. I want to go home." Tears rolled down her cheeks again, and she hastily wiped them away.

Hawthorn cleared his throat and said, "You could take my room if you want. It's number eight, over there."

"What's in your room? Dead bears?"

"Lilies."

Holly sniffed and blinked at him. "Lilies?"

He nodded. "Lilies."

"But... where will you sleep?"

"In your room, I suppose. Or with Hemlock. Though whatever is in your room is probably less horrific than putting up with Hemlock's feet."

A giggle escaped Holly, and she nodded. "All right. Thank you." She remembered the kerchief and held it up. "I think I've ruined this."

Hawthorn waved a hand. "Not to worry. I buy them by the case." He gave a short bow. "Good night, Holly."

She smiled and clutched the kerchief to her chest. "Good night, Hawthorn."

He walked into her room and shut the door. Then, after a moment, it reopened and Tum came stumbling out, holding a mug of beer in each hand. He turned back towards the room just as the door slammed in his face.

"Hey!" he shouted. "I was in there, you know!"

"Come on," Holly said. "Hope you like flowers."

Haunted Heart

Hazel stood near the fire in the common room. The hour was late, and she suspected everyone else slept except for that creepy innkeeper, of course. Every now and then he would appear and fluff the pillows on the armchairs near the fire, grinning at her all the while and not saying a word. It was unsettling, and Hazel would glower at him, but the man seemed unconcerned with her displeasure.

She walked to the bookshelf and perused the odd selection. What kinds of books were these? *Pressed Wood Sprites that Impress; Seasonal Beverages for the Lunar Touched,* and her favorite, *From Melting Faces to Melting Cheese: How to Turn Your Culinary Mishaps into Appetizers that Dazzle.* Against her better judgment, she pulled that last title from the shelf. She cracked it open to a page with a wood etching of a cook brandishing a club at a cornered rat.

"Hazel?" Hemlock said.

She slammed the book shut and returned it to its place.

"What are you still doing up?" he said.

"I'm not tired. Though I could ask the same of you. You're not even dressed for bed."

Hemlock looked down at his dark jacket and slacks, still rumpled from the long journey. "Ah, yes. I thought I'd leave a note for our host, regarding breakfast." He held up a slip of paper. "It might make things easier."

Hazel suppressed a grimace as she recalled the image from the book and its unsettling title. "You might want to avoid ordering any meat. Or cheese."

"Oh? Why's that?"

"Let's just say I have my doubts about the quality of this establishment's food preparation."

Hemlock looked puzzled, but he didn't pursue it. Instead, he pulled out a pencil and, using the tea table as a desk, began striking out passages of whatever he had written.

She sat down next to him and stared into the fire.

Hemlock glanced at her as he made amendments to his list. "Something troubling you?"

"What do you think we'll find when we get there? To Sarnum."

"Hopefully we'll find Ash. That's the plan anyway."

"And since when does anything in life ever go according to plan?"

He tilted his head, scribbled something else, then set the pencil down. He turned towards her. "What do you think we'll find?"

She remained silent a while. Then, fixing her gaze on the fire, she said, "I'm afraid I'll find that my father and I aren't all that different."

"That's absurd."

"No, it's really not." She let out a breath and rose from the sofa. "I should go to bed."

Hemlock rose with her. "Wait." He took her hand. "You are not alone in this, Hazel. Whatever we find."

Hazel's heart quickened as she looked at his hand holding hers. She swallowed. "It's late, Hemlock."

He lingered a moment before letting go. "Of course."

Unable to look at him, Hazel turned and hurried upstairs. She passed painted black doors without really seeing them. Somehow she managed to find hers, jerk it open, and stumble inside.

She was such a fool. What had she been thinking, spending so much time with him? It had all seemed so harmless, so safe. But it wasn't. It never would be. She had been out of her mind in letting herself care for him. After everything that had happened. She'd been so worried about becoming like her father she had failed to notice that she was becoming like her mother.

Hazel had vowed never to make Willow's mistakes. It wasn't too late. Nothing had been done that she couldn't undo.

The night passed unbearably slow, measured only by the even, hollow beats of her heart. She lay in bed and, from time to time, would squeeze her eyes shut to try and sleep. But sleep wouldn't come, and so she had nothing to do but lie there and take in her surroundings.

As if insomnia weren't bad enough without being surrounded by tasteless decor. There were bear heads on the wall, a bear rug, a bear leg trash bin, and a paw with long, glossy black claws on the writing desk, though why it was there, Hazel certainly didn't know. She wanted to go downstairs and request a different room, but she didn't want to risk running into Hemlock, so she stayed instead.

By the time dawn started to peek through the heavy, fur-patterned curtains, Hazel was already dressed and packed. She ventured out into the hallway and knocked on Holly's door.

"Holly? Wake up. We're leaving early." She waited but was met with silence. She sighed. Waking Holly was always a near-impossible feat. Hazel opened the door, walked over to the bed, and shook the form burrowed under the covers.

"Honestly, Holly, just this once couldn't you wake up without my having to drag you out of bed?"

The covers pulled back, and Hawthorn blinked up at her, his glamour gone and his lined face puffy with sleep. He sat up, pulling the blankets up to his bare chest. "I am not *dragged* anywhere, madam. It is far too early and far too filthy a task."

Startled, Hazel jerked back. "Where's Holly?"

"How should I know? Do you see her here? I've not pinned her to the walls like so many butterflies, if that's what you're worried about."

Hazel hurried out of the room and into the hallway. "Holly! Where are you?" She returned to the room just in time to see Hawthorn's bare ass as he got out of bed. She reeled back and covered her eyes, unable to prevent herself from emitting a disgusted sound. "Are you *naked?*"

"Of course I'm naked. Only heathens sleep while clothed. It goes against nature, the very core of our existence."

Hazel took a deep breath and, still covering her eyes, said, "Where's Holly?"

"I told you, she's not here."

"Where is she?!"

"Great Grandfather's ashes, woman, you'll wake the dead. I gave her my room, as she didn't find this one to her liking. Why don't you go check there?"

Hazel staggered out and walked to Hawthorn's room. At least she thought it was his room. She'd find out soon enough. She pushed open the door, sparing only a fleeting hope that it wasn't Hemlock's room.

The walls were papered in a lily pattern the color of eggshells, vases of lilies adorned the end tables and desk, while a little pot of potpourri simmered over a hearth. As Hazel walked over to the bed, a passing twinge of envy gnawed at her that she hadn't been given this room. She gently pulled back the covers, saw Holly's golden hair, then ripped the blankets off her and dumped them on the floor.

"Get up," she said. "We're leaving."

Holly groaned and reached for the blankets, but her hands found only air and the bare mattress.

Hazel opened the drawers in the dresser and found men's clothes. She eyed Holly, and sure enough her sister was wearing a man's long shirt. "Are you wearing Hawthorn's clothes?"

Holly sat up, blinking and looking dazed. "What?"

"Why are you wearing Hawthorn's clothes?"

Holly blinked some more, then looked down at herself. She giggled. "Oh. Yeah. My clothes are still in Hawthorn's room. I mean my room, that's now Hawthorn's. And his clothes are here, so I borrowed a shirt." She snuggled down into it, burrowing her nose in the collar. "It still smells like him."

"Take it off and get dressed. We're leaving."

"It's not even light out."

"Dawn's broken; it's light enough. Get dressed. I'll not say it again." She marched out of the room and nearly collided with Hemlock.

Her cheeks turned hot, but she resisted the urge to look away.

"Is everything all right?" he asked. "I heard shouting." He wore a purple-and-black evening robe over what looked to be matching pyjamas.

The heat crept down her neck, so Hazel stiffened her back and, in an equally stiff voice, said, "Holly and I are leaving."

Hemlock raised his eyebrows. "So early? Has something happened?"

"No, I'd just prefer to get this unpleasantness over with."

He nodded. "All right. Hawthorn and I will get dressed at once, and then we'll be on our way."

"No, thank you, Hemlock. For everything. But I think it's best that we go alone. This is, after all, a family matter."

Hemlock's brow furrowed as he studied her. "Does this have something to do with last night?"

Holly poked her head out the door; she still wore Hawthorn's shirt. "What happened last night?"

"Nothing," Hazel said. "Go get dressed."

"Don't you think you're overreacting?" Hemlock said.

"This has nothing to do with last night," Hazel said.

Holly bounced out into the hallway with them. She clapped her hands. "Something happened? What happened? Did you kiss?"

"No," Hazel said. To Hemlock, she added, "You flatter yourself, but as I said, this is a family matter."

"Is someone kissing?" Hawthorn said as he walked towards them. He also wore a purple-and-black robe that matched Hemlock's.

"Hazel and Hemlock kissed!" Holly said as she bounded up to him.

"Nobody's kissed!" Hazel shouted.

"What are you afraid of, Hazel?" Hemlock said.

"I'm not afraid. I told you, it's—"

"A family matter. So you said, but I don't believe you."

"You can believe whatever you want. I don't care." She started to walk past him, but he grabbed her hand.

"I held your hand, Hazel. Like this. Nothing else. I didn't ask anything of you other than to remain near you. Why does that frighten you so much? Because up until last night, I think you've enjoyed my company just as much as I've enjoyed yours."

Holly clasped her hands and sighed.

Hazel went rigid. She wanted to pull away, but she dared not. She didn't want to prove him right or let him think she was afraid. So she looked him in the eyes and, hardening her heart, said, "Keeping your company was an obligation. The usefulness of that obligation has now come to an end, and I see no reason to keep up the pretense."

Hemlock flinched, then his face took on a stony calm and he let go of her hand. "I see. Well, I will certainly not keep you." He walked away.

Hazel swallowed as her stomach wrenched in a sickening way. It was better like this. It was always going to end badly between them—how could it not? Better to end it now and get it over with. Better to end it on her terms and not his.

Hawthorn followed his brother down the hall as Holly lingered behind with Hazel.

"Are you an idiot?" Holly hissed. "What's wrong with you?"

Hazel swallowed again. When she could, she said, "Get dressed. I'll wait for you downstairs."

❧

"Lover's spat, eh?" Tum said as Holly packed the dresses that he had strewn about her room.

"Hazel's an idiot," Holly said. "If Hawthorn ever held my hand or said anything like that to me, I... I don't know what I'd do. Probably die. But in a good way."

Tum nodded. "Death By Lover is the best way to go. It's how Uncle Shem went—had a big old smile on his face too."

"Well, I... I don't think I meant it like that."

Tum scampered over to the bed, picked up Hawthorn's shirt, and whistled. "Mighty fine shirt there. Is it silk?"

Holly marched up to him and snatched the shirt out of his hands. "That's not yours! I don't want you touching it or getting your... your beery, gnomey smell all over it. It'll be ruined then."

Tum sniffed his arm. "*Gnomey?* What's that smell like?"

"Like dirt and tobacco and... I don't know... strawberries that have been out in the sun. It's weird. You're underground all the time. Why do you smell like sunny fruit?"

Tum smiled and rocked on his heels. "All part of the charm. Sounds like a good smell to me. If you want, I can rub that shirt all over my bits. Give you the full experience."

Holly cringed and clutched the shirt to her chest. "What? No! You're not to touch it! It still smells like him. I know it won't last, but I want to enjoy it while it does."

"What do warlocks smell like?"

"Well, I don't know about other warlocks, but Hawthorn smells like chamomile soap and wig powder. Which is kind of weird since he doesn't wear a wig." She paused, her mouth hanging open. "Does he?"

Tum shrugged.

She shook her head. "It doesn't matter. It's what he smells like, and it's nice. So you don't touch it. Go manhandle one of my dresses if you have to."

Tum brightened. "Even the good one?"

"*Except* the good one."

He deflated. Even so, he helped her pack though his hands lingered on the fabric of her dresses a little longer than she was comfortable with. When they were done, Holly sighed.

"Well, I guess we're supposed to go then."

"Right. Meet you outside." He ran out of the room.

Holly remained. As much as she wanted to leave this place, she didn't want to leave like this—without Hawthorn and Hemlock. But she didn't know what else to do. She headed downstairs.

Hemlock was there, leaning against the innkeeper's counter. When he saw her, he straightened, gave her a half smile, then looked away.

When Holly stood next to him, he said, "I'm trying to make arrangements for the coach. The inn doesn't have their own, so you and Hazel will take ours to Sarnum, and then the driver will return here and pick up Hawthorn and me and take us home."

"You can't do that," Holly said.

Hemlock blinked. "I thought it the best solution, given the circumstances."

"No, you can't give up! You can't let Hazel go just like that."

He shook his head. "She let *me* go, Holly. I tried, but she has made her feelings very clear."

"But they aren't her feelings! She's just afraid. You even said so!"

"Perhaps. But I'm not going to force myself into her life if she doesn't want me there."

Holly wrung her hands. She felt like it was all falling apart even though she wasn't sure what "it" was. "Then stay for me!"

"What?"

She nodded and rubbed her eyes to keep them from filling with tears. "You and Hawthorn both. We wouldn't have gotten this far without your help. If you leave, we might get stuck again, and then it will just be a big mess. So stay and help *me*. Hazel can take care of herself."

"Holly, I—"

"Sarnum's a big place, isn't it? Hazel doesn't get to decide who goes there and who doesn't. And like you said, your coach is the only coach. You'd be doing *me* a favor by giving us a ride. Not Hazel. Who cares about Hazel, right?" She snorted as she tried to laugh.

Hemlock gave her a wan smile. "You are a dear girl. Though I'm guessing you don't want *me* to leave so much as you want my brother to stay."

Holly stared at her hands. "I want you both to stay," she murmured. "Besides, finding Father is just as much your business as ours, you being warlocks and all." She looked up at him. "Isn't that right?"

He smiled again. "Yes, I suppose it is."

She nodded. "So it's settled then? Nobody's going home? We're all going to Sarnum? Together?"

He shrugged. "It would seem so."

She grinned. "Good. So now there's no reason to skip breakfast."

Breakfast was silent and awkward. They all sat around a cramped circular table, eating waffles topped with blackberry jam and honey syrup.

"I don't understand," Hawthorn said. "Where is the bacon? I told you to order bacon."

Hemlock glanced at Hazel and said, "It was my understanding that the meat here was less than optimal."

Hawthorn sniffed and flipped his hair. "Hard to get bacon wrong," he murmured.

"The waffles are yummy though," Holly said. "Aren't they yummy?" She broke off a piece and dropped it in her pocket for Chester. The mouse grabbed it in his paws and nibbled on it.

Hawthorn wrinkled his nose. "Women eat breads for breakfast. Men need meat in their diet."

Holly screwed up her face at him. "That's just stupid."

Hazel snorted. Then she cleared her throat and put on a sober expression.

Holly kicked her under the table.

Hazel glared at her. "Stop being a child, Holly."

"*I'm* not the one being childish."

Silence settled among them again.

"What about sausage?" Hawthorn said.

Hemlock sighed. "Sausage is meat, brother, or didn't you know?"

He waved a hand. "It barely is. They could grind up just about anything in there, and you wouldn't be the wiser. It should be standard fare in places of ill repute."

"I was trying to avoid ill-reputed meat, but if that's what you want, then you go right ahead."

Hawthorn threw his napkin over his plate. "I will." He got up and wandered through the door that the innkeeper usually disappeared behind.

Holly removed his napkin and transferred the half-eaten waffle from his plate to hers. She topped it with extra jam and syrup, took a bite, and said, "It's nice of Hemlock and Hawthorn to give us a ride to Sarnum, isn't it, Hazel? Given their coach is the only one around. Bet you didn't think of that earlier."

Hazel glared at her. "No, I hadn't, and yes, it's very kind."

"Should we talk about what we're going to do when we get there?" Holly said. "How are we going to find Elder?"

"I know where he is," Hemlock said.

Holly's mouth hung open. "What? How?"

Hemlock cleared his throat and adjusted his glasses. "Well, it wasn't too hard, really. His name had been stricken from the Conclave records, though whether by himself or someone else, I couldn't say. So I asked around and found out where he once lived. I then went to the postman to see if Elder had left a forwarding address. He had, though the postman wouldn't tell me what it was until I gave him one of Hawthorn's scarves."

"His scarves *are* nice."

"Uh, yes. Anyway, I gave him the scarf, and he gave me the address of a Miss Abegail Thornton in the care of Ellison Browne's Culinary Institute for Women."

Holly scrunched up her nose. "That's weird. Did he change his name and become a woman?"

"Uh, no, I don't think so. I contacted the school and found out that

Miss Thornton was a resident instructor there who had resigned once she married. The headmaster was... reluctant to give me her forwarding address but relented after receiving a generous donation to the school." He reached into his pocket and pulled out a folded piece of paper and put it on the table. "That is, I hope, her and Elder's address. At any rate, it gives us a place to start."

Holly stared at him. "And you're saying all that was easy?"

He shrugged. "It was more time-consuming than anything."

"Well, all right. It's doubly good that you're coming along then." She gave Hazel a smug look. "Right, Hazel?"

Hazel tightened her jaw. "Of course."

HAZEL GLARED at Holly. She knew what Holly was up to. She was trying to throw her and Hemlock together. And it seemed to be working. Hemlock was going along with it as if nothing had happened. Hazel wasn't sure if she was upset or relieved that he had decided to stay. She admired him though. She doubted she could have behaved so well if he had said such cruel things to her. It made her feel even worse.

They finished eating in silence. Holly, wondering where Hawthorn had gone and if there were any more waffles to be had, got up and disappeared behind the door.

Hazel tensed, feeling awkward at being alone with Hemlock.

As if reading her thoughts, he said, "I don't want you to be uncomfortable."

"I'm fine."

"You clearly are not. You've hardly said a word, and you didn't snap at Hawthorn once. You're not yourself."

Hazel stared at her plate. Then, taking a deep breath, she said, "I'm sorry for what I said earlier. You were never an obligation, and I regret saying it. But I cannot give you what you want."

"I've only wanted to see you happy, Hazel. If your happiness does not lie with me, then I can accept that. But I still want to help you. That hasn't changed."

Hazel bit her lip. What was he up to? How could he just want to help her and want nothing in return? It made no sense.

Holly returned with a fresh stack of waffles while Hawthorn trailed after her munching on a handful of bacon. She set the plate on the table and, leaning towards Hazel and Hemlock, whispered, "You should see the cook. He's bald and massive, like a big wall with legs. I... I don't think he has eyes." She speared some waffles with a fork and dragged them to her plate. "Isn't that remarkable though? A blind cook?"

Hazel suppressed a groan. Who knew what went into the food? "Please hurry up so we can leave."

Holly nodded. "We can go right now. She flopped the waffles back onto the waffle plate before picking up the whole thing. Then she grabbed the honey syrup pitcher. "Ready."

"We can't take that with us."

"Sure we can."

"The dishes don't belong to us."

"And all the dead animals nailed to the walls don't belong to that creepy innkeeper. But he's done it anyway. It's what he gets."

Hemlock leaned over and whispered, "I can leave a little extra payment for the dishes."

"That's not really the point...," Hazel said, and then she closed her eyes and took a breath. It didn't matter. Holly would do what she wanted, no matter what Hazel said. "Fine, let's go."

Elder Night

Hazel glanced at the others in the carriage as it rattled down the dusty road. Somehow the mood inside seemed less heavy than it had the previous day. It was a wonder, given everything that had happened. But Hawthorn and Holly no longer seemed so uncomfortable around each other. And Hemlock seemed, well, like Hemlock. It was both comforting as well as puzzling. She didn't entirely trust him or his motives, and yet she was glad he was there.

Tum sat outside with the driver, and every now and then snippets of his voice would carry over the horses and carriage.

"Strawberries!" Tum shouted. "I smell like strawberries!"

"It's true," Holly said. "He does."

"Doubtful," Hawthorn said. "It's more likely you're associating his sweet, sickly, unwashed stench with that of fruit."

"You saying I don't know what a strawberry smells like?"

Hawthorn arched an eyebrow. "If you're insisting that little man smells like one then, yes, I am. It is an affront to all fruits and to those who eat them."

Holly opened her mouth but then snapped it shut. She slumped in her seat. "Well, that's probably true."

The journey to Sarnum stretched on. As the day faded, the forests of the Grove thinned until they, too, had gone with the light. The driver stopped to light the lanterns hanging on the sides of the carriage. Holly pressed her nose to the glass as she looked out the window.

"It's so dark out there," she whispered. "And empty. Why is it so empty?"

Hemlock squinted as he peered out the window. "I think it's a field. That pale patch there, I think that's grass."

"Creepy grass," Holly murmured.

"Indeed," Hawthorn said. "'Hair of the dead,' Father used to call it."

Holly shrank back into her seat. "What?"

Hemlock said, "Father drank too much."

"True," Hawthorn said, "but he did have a way with words."

Thankfully, the coach started moving again.

"Did your father come out this way often?" Hazel asked.

"On occasion," Hawthorn said.

"Why?"

He waved a hand, all murky and shadowed within the gloom of the carriage. "Why does anyone go anywhere?"

She shook her head and looked out the darkened window, but all she could see was the wavering light from a lamp as it swung to and fro.

The carriage slowed, men shouted, and there was a grinding of metal gears. They passed through a gate into an arched tunnel lined with torches, before coming to a city of brick houses and stone streets lit by flickering blue-and-green flames in tall iron lamps.

"Is this it?" Holly said. "Sarnum?"

"I certainly hope so," Hawthorn said. "Otherwise it's a wasted trip."

"Why is there a gate? Who are they trying to keep out? Or who are they trying to keep in?"

No one said anything.

"And why do those lamps have green flames?" she said.

"Alchemy," Hawthorn said. When everyone stared at him, he added, "Or so I've heard."

"How do you know so much about this town?" Hazel asked.

He shrugged. "Father spoke of it from time to time."

"He never spoke of it to me," Hemlock said.

"That concerns me how?"

Hemlock tightened his jaw and looked away.

Even though it was summer, the night held a chill, and the people on the streets wore long, dark coats with the collars pulled up against the wind. They walked hunched over, hurrying to get to wherever they were going, never looking up at the carriage as it passed or even each other.

The carriage turned onto a narrow street, then another, zigzagging through the darkness as the horses' hooves rang on the stones. Hazel clasped her hands in a tight grip, tensing even more as the carriage slowed and, with a final turn, stopped.

Everyone remained still. Outside came the sound of the driver's boots hitting the ground. Then the door next to Hazel and Holly opened. The driver smiled.

"I... I suppose we're supposed to get out now?" Holly said.

Hazel swallowed. She wished she didn't feel as unsettled as Holly sounded. She clenched her hands a little tighter and stepped from the carriage.

They had come to a great stone house flanked with sharply trimmed hedges. On either side of the great black door, a pair of wrought iron sconces displayed flickering blue flames behind pristine glass.

The others left the carriage and stood around her.

"This is it, isn't it?" Hazel said. "Elder's home."

"It should be," Hemlock said.

"It's awfully late," Holly said. "Shouldn't we wait until morning?"

"Probably," Hazel said. "But I don't want to stay in this city longer than we have to. Do you?"

Holly swallowed and shook her head.

Hazel took a breath and walked up to the door, grabbed hold of a heavy iron knocker in the shape of a lion, and gave it three solid raps. She tightened her hands as she waited, then harder still as the knob turned and the door swung open.

A round-faced little old man about as tall as Hazel's shoulder blinked up at her. "Yes?" He wore a red flannel robe over matching pyjamas and white bunny slippers on his feet.

Hazel said, "We are looking for someone named Elder."

The man smiled. "Well, you found him. What can I do for you?"

Hazel looked at the others, but everyone remained silent. Turning to Elder, she said, "Perhaps we could come in to talk?"

Elder chuckled. "Of course. How rude of me." He backed away and swung the door wide open. "Please, come in." As everyone filed inside, he tottered down a carpeted hallway lined with wildflower portraits. "Abby! We have company! Best put on the tea!" He returned to them and beamed. "Please, follow me."

He led them down the hallway into a wide and well-clothed room. That was really the best description of it. Tapestries hung from the walls, and carpets covered nearly the entire floor. Plush pillows padded the sofas, and knitted blankets were thrown over the backs of upholstered chairs.

Elder herded them to a pair of sofas by the hearth; when he turned around, he nearly collided with a little old woman wearing a red flannel nightgown and white bunny slippers of her own. She held a tray of sandwiches.

"Ah, there you are," Elder said. To Hazel and the others, he said, "This is my wife Abby. Abby, this is... Well, I don't know who they are, but I'm sure we'll find out."

"I'm Hazel. This is my sister Holly. That's Hemlock and his brother Hawthorn."

Hawthorn smiled and nodded. Holly studied the floor. Hemlock blinked a few times and murmured, "Pleasure."

"So many *H* names," Elder said. "Have you all banded together? Going to take on the *L* names by force? Or perhaps the *B*'s. The *B*'s can be so uppity, don't you think?"

Hazel stared at him. "I-I beg your pardon?"

He waved his hands. "Never mind."

Abby set her tray on a table. The sandwiches were made with fat rolls of floured, crusty bread. She beamed at them. "Tea will be out in a moment."

"Abby bakes the bread herself. Don't you, Abby?"

She giggled. "Oh, you," then poked her husband with a sturdy finger. He grabbed hold of her and tickled her ribs. Abby yelped and laughed, wrenched herself away, then slapped at his hands before running from the room.

Hazel stared down at her lap. Maybe they should have waited until morning.

Elder dragged over a chair and sat down. "So. What can I do for you fine folks?"

"I apologize for calling so late," Hazel said. "But our business is pressing and we didn't want to wait."

"Oh. Sounds serious." Elder grabbed a sandwich and took a bite. "Better eat up. Serious business needs serious food, I always say. And nothing's better for serious business than Abby's liver pâté and pickle sandwiches."

Hawthorn brightened. "Don't mind if I do."

Holly shrank back into the sofa.

"No, thank you," Hazel said. "The matter is my sister and I are looking for our father, a man named—"

Holly screamed, leaped from the sofa, and darted behind it.

Hazel started and turned around, and she also got up when she saw a toddler-sized creature—something between a monkey and a bear—with webbed bat-like wings and a long, scaly tail. It carried a teapot in its disturbingly human-like hands.

"Ah," Elder said. "You found Augustus."

"What... what is it?" Holly said.

"Friend. Manservant. Bearer of tea. He is so many things it defies description." Elder took the teapot and shouted, "Thank you!"

Augustus chittered.

Elder waved an arm at the thing. "I said thank you. Shoo, now. Shoo!"

Augustus squawked and half flew, half ran from the room.

Elder shook his head. "The lad's useful but a bit dense on the language front. We're working on it though."

"Hazel..." Holly whimpered.

Hazel swallowed as her stomach sank. "You're a necromancer."

Elder beamed. "Of course. Why wouldn't I be?"

Hemlock cleared his throat and adjusted his glasses. Hawthorn stopped chewing his sandwich as he glanced between Hazel and Elder.

Hazel clenched her hands. "Why wouldn't you be? Perhaps because it's an atrocity? An affront to everything that is good and natural in this world?"

Elder chuckled and shook his head. "You must be from the Grove. Yes, I should have seen it sooner." He waggled a finger. "It's been so long since I've been there I had nearly forgotten the closed-minded superstition that plagues the region. I see nothing has changed."

Hazel squeezed her eyes shut just as Hemlock got to his feet and put a hand on her shoulder.

"Hazel," he whispered. "Please breathe."

She clenched her jaw and took a deep breath. It didn't help. "Superstition?" Somehow she managed to keep her voice calm. At least calmer than she felt. "You are telling me my mother is trapped in a geas by superstition? That my father did nothing? That it's all in my head?!" Now she was yelling. She had tried, but some things were beyond her control. She pushed past Hemlock and glared down at Elder. "Where is he?" she growled.

"Who?" Elder said.

She grabbed him by the collar of his flannel pyjamas and gave him a shake. She wouldn't be toyed with, not by him. "Ash!"

Elder intoned a series of words, and the lamps in the room extinguished. The air chilled, and an icy pressure wound around Hazel's arms and towards her head. The chill sank into her skin, almost to her bones. She had felt that kind of cold before—at every new moon in a ramshackle cottage overtaken by briar and ivy. Hazel let go and staggered back.

Her breath turned shallow and rapid; her palms began to sweat. She needed to get out. Out of this house, out of this town. But the icy darkness continued to press on her, threatening to crush her until nothing remained.

"HAZEL?" HOLLY whispered, but there was no reply. When had it gotten so dark? She had been so shocked over that creepy tea-bearing bat thing, and then the next thing she knew the room had turned dark and cold.

She put out a hand and summoned a little ball of flame. It was always harder like that—calling the fire from nothing. But she didn't have a choice. She was just glad it worked even though the darkness that had been pushed back seemed like nothing at all. It was still so dark, and all Holly could see in the corners of her eyes were shadowed silhouettes that seemed to vanish as soon as she looked at them.

"Hazel," she said again, louder now as she found her nerve. Someone touched her arm, and she cried out and leaped back. She reached for a pinecone, then Hemlock stepped into her tiny circle of light and she relaxed.

"What's happened?" she whispered.

"Elder happened." His brow furrowed—he looked angry. Hemlock always seemed so collected; seeing him angry just concerned Holly even more.

"Where's Hazel?"

"I don't know." He patted his pockets and pulled out a silver watch. He threw it in the air, and the watch erupted into a ball of light, out of which sprung a small winged sprite. The fairy caught the glowing watch by its chain and flitted around the room with it. The darkness was pushed back a little more, illuminating tapestried walls that now looked foreign and sterile.

"Over here," Hemlock said, waving a hand towards the middle of the room.

The sprite flitted over to where he pointed. The darkness receded, and where Hazel had been standing was now only a vague, shadowed form, as if made from mist and midnight. A similar form sat on the nearby sofa, exactly where Hawthorn had been sitting.

Holly gasped and clapped a hand over her mouth. She extinguished her flame—it wasn't doing any good anyway—and walked up to the shadow that had been Hazel. She reached out to touch her, cringing at the way the air chilled the closer she got. But before she could, Hemlock grabbed her hand and pulled her away. Frowning, he shook his head, but Holly could see the fear lingering in his eyes.

Holly brought out a pinecone. She'd ignite the thing and throw it on one of those plush couches. That should get the chill out of the room. But then a narrow panel in a wall pulled back, showing a pair of suspicious eyes.

"What do you want?" Elder said, his voice muffled from the wall that stood between them.

"I want my sister!" Holly shouted. "You give her back, or I'll torch your house!"

"You try it and I'll set Augustus after you!"

Holly cringed as she suppressed a whimper. "You wouldn't..." That thing just wasn't natural.

"I would. You watch me!"

Holly wrung her hands as Hemlock walked up to the panel on the wall. He leaned down to meet the eyes that peered out at them.

"We know where you live, Elder," Hemlock said, his voice surprisingly calm. "I think the Conclave would be quite interested to learn of your... research down here in Sarnum. In fact, you've been out of the Grove so long everyone would be so thrilled to know of your whereabouts that I'm sure they'd all flock down here within days to see you."

Silence hung in the room.

"What do you want?" Elder said again.

"I'd like Hazel and my brother back, to start, and then I'd like us all to sit down and discuss matters quietly and civilly, as I'm sure we are all capable of doing."

"Your Hazel didn't seem capable of it to me."

"You took her by surprise. If you knew her, then you'd know why she was so upset."

"Well, I don't know her. I don't know any of you, and I don't think I care to."

"Very well," Hemlock said. "I'll return to the Grove and give the Conclave your regards." He turned to leave.

"Wait!" Elder squeaked.

Hemlock turned back around, but the eyes in the wall had gone. After a moment, a door opened and Elder shuffled in. He scowled at Hemlock and Holly. Then he raised his arms, and the darkness lifted. The shadows that clung to Hazel melted away, and the chill in the air dissipated. Hawthorn's shadows also faded, and he was once again sitting on a sofa with a half-eaten sandwich in his hand and a befuddled look on his unglamoured face.

"Hazel!" Holly said and ran up and hugged her.

ᄿ

HAZEL SHIVERED as the dreaded cold faded from her body, and then the next thing she knew, Holly was there, hugging her.

Feeling disoriented, Hazel put her arms around Holly as she looked around. Hemlock stood nearby. He let out a breath and gave her a crooked smile, then moved his gaze to the floor. Hawthorn blinked at the sandwich he held, as if mystified by its presence. When she saw Elder, the disorientation faded and she remembered what happened. She let go of Holly and took a step back. "What did you do?"

"Protected me and my family. Just when you think you're safe somewhere, a roving band of *H* names comes into your home and starts threatening you. How'd you like it if I came to your house, uninvited I might add, and throttled you, eh?"

Hazel looked down at her hands. He was a necromancer—an abomination—she shouldn't feel bad for what she had done. But she did. "I'm... sorry," she said in a tight voice. "You took me by surprise, and my experience with necromancy hasn't exactly been pleasant."

Elder grunted and nodded towards Hemlock. "That's pretty much what he said." He sighed and waved at a sofa. "Well, if you want to talk, let's talk and get this over with." He marched over to the tray of sandwiches, grabbed one, and took a big bite.

Hazel, Holly, and Hemlock all exchanged glances before sitting down. Hawthorn reacquainted himself with his sandwich and resumed eating it.

"So, you're looking for someone," Elder said.

Hazel nodded. "My father, Ash. He's also a necromancer."

"And you think I know him because of that? That we belong to some kind of club or something?"

"No," Hazel said, taking care to keep her voice calm. "We didn't know you were a necromancer at all. Someone told us you might know who teaches the... discipline, so that's why we're here."

Elder grunted again and took another bite of his sandwich. He fell quiet as he chewed, and Hazel clenched her hands together as she waited.

"Say I did know someone," he said. "What happens then?"

"We'd go and talk to him... or her... or... it?" Hazel cringed inwardly. She hoped it wasn't an "it." She couldn't believe she was even having this conversation.

Elder chuckled and waggled his sandwich at her. "Oh, no. I've seen the way you talk, and I'm not looking to inflict that on anyone. Some of us in this world still believe in decency. You stay here tonight and think about what you've done, and then tomorrow I'll think more about helping you."

Hazel opened her mouth to protest being called indecent by a necromancer when the rest of his words sank in. "What? We're not staying here."

Elder chuckled. "You're free to go if you'd like, but I'd not recommend it. You got here late. Clock's now past twelve." He pointed at a little silver clock on the mantelpiece. "Trust me, you don't want to be out there past twelve."

Hazel's stomach turned leaden. "Why not? What's out there?"

Elder gave her a wry grin. "Let's just say that I'm not the only necromancer in town. Far from it, and not everyone's companions are as pleasant as my Augustus."

Hazel swallowed as she struggled to keep her face calm.

"You'll have to double up," Elder said. "I've not got rooms for all of you. But I'm sure that's all right, isn't it?"

Feeling numb, it was all Hazel could do to nod.

He smiled, though his eyes lacked their previous warmth. "Excellent. Augustus will show you the way."

Holly whimpered before clapping a hand over her mouth. "Hazel..." she whispered.

But Hazel just shook her head. What could they do? She didn't think Elder was lying, though how could she be sure? Should she risk it? And if he was telling the truth...

"It's just for one night," she whispered.

Holly bit her lip and nodded, her blue eyes filling with tears.

Hazel felt wretched. What had she gotten them into?

The Long Dark

Hand in hand, Hazel and Holly followed Augustus as he led them up the stairs and down a dimly lit hallway. He stopped in front of a door and chittered at the sisters.

Holly flinched. "What does it want?"

"I think this might be our room."

Augustus's chittering turned to squawks as he hopped up and down.

"Or maybe it just wants our spleens," Holly said, covering her ears.

"We'd better go in." Hazel opened the door. Inside loomed the shadowed limbs of a four-poster bed, dimly illuminated by a stream of moonlight from a single sash window.

Augustus squawked again. Holly darted into the room, pulling Hazel after her, and slammed the door shut. Augustus's chittering continued a few moments before finally fading away.

Holly pawed at the door. "This thing got a lock?"

"Doubtful," Hazel said and went to a dresser near the door. "Help me move this thing over. It'll be better than a lock."

Hazel pushed as Holly pulled, and the dresser groaned when they slid it across the polished wood floor to barricade the door.

"Now what?" Holly said.

"I don't know." Hazel moved over to the window. Outside, an orb of pale blue light danced along the cobblestone street. Then the light skittered away, and in its wake followed a shambling shadow, dragging a heavy bag along the ground as it went. Hazel cringed and drew the curtains closed.

"What's out there?" Holly said.

"I don't know. I don't want to know." Hazel sat on the edge of the bed and buried her face in her hands.

Holly sat next to her and put a hand on her shoulder.

"Are you all right?"

Hazel took a deep breath. "I don't know. I think I've made a real mess of things."

"What do you mean?"

Hazel gave a wry laugh. "I mean this." She waved her hands towards the room. "I've been so intent on finding Father I never really stopped to look at where we were going."

"But we're getting closer. We've never been this close to finding him."

"*Are* we closer? I'm not so sure."

Holly remained quiet. Then she said, "What was it like when Elder... did what he did?"

Hazel shook her head. "I don't remember much. I just remember it being cold and dark and... empty."

"It was creepy. You looked all shadowy. Like you were gone but still there."

"How did you get him to undo it?"

"I didn't. Hemlock did. I threatened to burn down the house. That... didn't really work."

Hazel smirked. "It might have helped with the cold though."

"That's what *I* thought!"

They giggled.

Then Holly said, "You should have seen him though."

"Who?"

"Hemlock. He was so calm—he even conjured a fairy that brought in light. I... I couldn't have done what he did. It's good that he's here."

They fell back into silence.

"We should try to get some sleep," Hazel said.

They crawled under the covers and pulled the thick, downy blanket up to their chins as they lay side by side. From time to time, a shriek would resonate from outside. Each time it did, they flinched and Holly would grab on to Hazel's hand. They seemed to have stayed like that forever when there came a gentle knocking at the door.

Holly hid under the covers while Hazel took a deep breath and, struggling to keep her voice even, said, "Who is it?"

"Hemlock," came the quiet reply.

Holly exhaled and rolled out of bed. She tried to push the dresser out of the way, but it didn't move much. "Come help," she said.

Hazel hesitated. What did Hemlock want? But Holly threw her a sharp look, so Hazel got up, and they moved the dresser just enough for Holly to crack open the door and pull him inside. They moved the dresser back—Hemlock helped—and Holly ran back to the bed and dove under the covers.

Before Hazel could say anything, Hemlock said, "I wanted to make sure you two were all right. I wasn't expecting the barricade." He waved towards the dresser.

"More sturdy than a lock," Hazel said.

"Yes. Definitely."

The fell into silence for a while, so Hazel said, "We're fine, Hemlock. Thank you."

He nodded and started towards the door but then turned back around and said, "All right, that wasn't entirely true. The truth is I can't sleep, and I was hoping you two might want company. If... you know... you were also having trouble sleeping, that is."

"We are," Holly said. "We haven't slept at all."

"Mind if I stay a little while?"

Holly sat up on the bed. "We don't mind. Do we, Hazel?"

Hazel's mouth hung open a moment before she found any words. "N-no, I suppose not. But what about Hawthorn? Do you think he'll be all right alone?"

Hemlock shrugged. "He's already asleep. Which is another reason for my wanting to leave that room. He sleeps nude, you know."

Hazel cringed. "I know."

"What?" Holly said.

Hazel held up a hand. "Don't ask."

Holly frowned, looking puzzled. Then she brightened and bounced on the bed. "Ooh, we could play a game. Know any good games?"

"What games could we possibly play, Holly?" Hazel said. "Hide-and-seek? You go hide, and I'm sure Augustus will have a wonderful time finding you."

Holly both cringed and deflated. Then she perked up again. "What about stories?"

Hazel sighed.

"I know a story," Hemlock said.

"Really?" Holly said, sounding surprised. Then she grinned and patted the bed. "Sit down and tell it."

Hemlock glanced at Hazel, then walked over and sat on the edge of the bed. He adjusted his glasses and said, "Well, long ago there was a warlock who, afraid of growing old, decided to set out and find a fountain for eternal youth."

"How does someone find something like that?" Holly said.

"I-I don't know," Hemlock said.

"Does it exist? You can't just decide to find something that doesn't exist."

"I..."

Hazel said, "Do you want him to tell the story or not, Holly?"

Holly slumped. "Fine." To Hemlock, she said, "Continue."

He cleared his throat. "Anyway, so the warlock sets off into the woods to find this fountain, and along the way he comes across a witch's cottage. Smoke streams from the chimney"—he waggled his fingers in the air—"and smells of roasting meat and spiced wine."

"How does smoke smell of wine?" Holly said.

Hazel glared at her, and Holly shrank under the blankets. "Sorry," she murmured.

Hemlock took a breath. "So the warlock goes inside the cottage, and there he finds the most beautiful woman he has ever seen. Love-stricken, he gets down on one knee and professes his eternal devotion to this witch who has stolen his heart, forgetting all about the fountain of eternal youth. But the witch just watches him with a cool, hard gaze. Then, she grabs a knife, cuts out his heart, and eats it."

Silence filled the room.

Holly screwed up her face. "Is that it? That's terrible!"

Hemlock adjusted his glasses. "Well, I didn't say it was a good story."

Holly sat there, her mouth hanging open as she stared at him.

A giggle escaped Hazel, and she clapped a hand over her mouth. But it didn't help, and her giggles turned to laughter.

"What's so funny?" Holly said.

"It's terrible," Hazel said as she laughed. "Completely awful, horrible story." She bent over and put her hands on her knees, laughing so hard she could barely breathe.

Hemlock chuckled along with her.

"You've lost it," Holly said.

Hazel laughed a little more. "Probably. But that's likely for the best."

Hemlock smiled.

Holly screwed up her face again.

There was a knock at the door, and they all froze.

"Who is it?" Hemlock said.

"Hemlock?" came Hawthorn's voice. "What are you doing in there?"

Hemlock and Hazel moved the dresser, and Hawthorn stepped inside. Thankfully, he was clothed.

"Where did you go?" he said. "I woke up, and you were gone. I thought maybe Augustus got hold of you."

"I couldn't sleep," Hemlock said. "I didn't think you'd notice."

"Well, I did. This isn't exactly the most hospitable establishment, you know."

"It's not an establishment, Hawthorn. It's a necromancer's house."

"Exactly my point." He smoothed his rumpled clothes and looked around the room. "So what's going on in here?"

"Hemlock is telling us horrible stories," Holly said.

"Oh? I know some horrible stories." Hawthorn fiddled with his fingers and raised his eyebrows.

"Would you like to join us?" Hazel asked.

Hawthorn smiled. "I would love to, thank you." He sat on the bed near Holly's feet.

Holly grinned and snuggled down under the covers.

They passed most of the night swapping stories that ranged from mundane to completely awful, until Hawthorn and Holly both fell asleep sprawled across the bed.

Hazel sat on the floor with her back against the wall. Hemlock sat next to her. She looked towards the window and relaxed as the first light of dawn peeked in from behind the curtains.

Keeping her gaze on the window, she said, "Thank you, Hemlock."

"For what?"

Hazel shook her head and smiled. She looked at him and, in a quiet voice that was almost a whisper said, "Thank you."

Hemlock studied her a moment, then nodded and gave a small smile back. "You're welcome."

She looked back towards the window, closing her eyes and resting her head against the wall as the first bird chirped with the rising sun.

Elder Dawn

L ater that morning, Hazel and Holly ventured downstairs and found a slip of paper pinned to a wall with an arrow drawn on it that pointed down a hallway off the main room. They followed it and came to another sign that led them into a dining room, within which a monstrous wooden table took up most of the space as well as most of the light, despite the sunlight that streamed through the tall windows.

"What... what do we do?" Holly whispered.

Hazel shrugged. "Sit down, I suppose."

Holly took a deep breath and said, "Okay." She walked over to one of the high-backed chairs and screwed up her face. "Well, these chairs are ugly."

Numerous grotesques had been carved into the wood, snarling among bunches of grapes and thatches of fig leaves. The arms had been shaped into two long lions, their bared wooden teeth pricking Hazel's finger when she touched one. At least the seat of the chair was cushioned and relatively comfortable, all things considered.

Holly sat down next to her, her back as straight and nearly as rigid as the chair itself.

"Try to relax," Hazel said, hoping her words didn't sound as hollow to Holly as they did to her. She had to remind herself to breathe and to unknot the tension in her drawn-up shoulders.

"I'll relax when we're home," Holly said.

Hazel couldn't help but agree though she remained silent.

Augustus came in carrying a tray covered with a silver cloche. He stood on his tiptoes as he hoisted the tray up over his head towards the table. Holly kept her eyes shut, her hands clenching around the long bodies of the lions.

Hazel cringed as she watched Augustus teeter on his tiptoes before he finally managed to slide the tray onto the table. He chittered, then scampered out of the room.

"What's taking Hawthorn and Hemlock so long?" Holly said.

"Hawthorn said he needed to freshen up. Your guess is as good as mine how long that'll take." Hazel nodded towards the cloche on the table. "What do you think's under there? Should we look?"

"I don't know. What if it's pickled eyeballs?"

"I doubt it's eyeballs."

"You never know. Last night it was liver pâté sandwiches. That's almost as gross as eyeballs."

"Now you're just being dramatic." She elbowed Holly. "Go on, look."

"*You* look."

Elder walked into the room, and Holly tensed again as Hazel fixed her gaze ahead.

"Good morning," he said. "I hope you slept well." He pulled out a chair at the end of the table furthest away from the sisters and sat down.

Hazel hadn't slept at all, but somehow it seemed insulting to admit it, and she didn't want to cause any more trouble. "The room was lovely. Thank you."

Elder quirked his mouth to the side, but he said nothing. He reached for the cloche, and Holly sucked in a breath as his hand lingered on the handle before lifting it up, exposing a row of sliced brown bread. Holly exhaled.

Elder frowned. "Augustus!"

Augustus hopped through the door. Elder waved a hand at the tray. "Augustus, my lad, have you forgotten something?"

Augustus wrung his little hands and chittered.

"That's right," Elder said. "The relish plate. *Rel-ish.*"

Augustus squawked and ran from the room just as Abby walked in carrying a tray of six tall glasses filled with murky, dark beer. She set a glass each in front of Hazel and Holly, one to Elder and to herself. The last two she left in the empty places where Hemlock and Hawthorn would undoubtedly sit, should they ever come downstairs.

"Beer for breakfast?" Holly said.

"Of course," said Elder. "Nothing invigorates the constitution in the morning like Abby's bitter dark. Isn't that right, Abby?"

Abby giggled and waved a hand. "Oh stop."

Holly leaned towards Hazel and whispered, "Tum would love it here."

"Where is he anyway?" Hazel whispered back.

Holly opened her mouth to answer, but Elder interrupted her.

"No whispering over there. It's rude, you know. Honestly, did your parents never teach you any manners?"

Hazel tightened her jaw and fixed him in a level gaze. "No, as a matter of fact, they didn't." She and Elder stared at each other for a long while until, thankfully, Hemlock and Hawthorn walked in.

"Sorry we're late," Hemlock murmured. "It seems Hawthorn had a mishap with his clothes."

Hawthorn drew himself up, smoothing his red-and-black brocade jacket in the process. "Your... assistant... never fetched my luggage. And the driver was asleep in the garden shed." He fixed Elder in a pointed gaze. "The *garden shed.*"

Elder scoffed and waved a hand as he took a sip of his beer. "Not my fault the lot of you arrived unannounced and that your help doesn't know how to use a knocker. Maybe he wanted to sleep in the shed, you ever think of that?"

"*Want* to? Don't be absurd. He—"

"And Augustus doesn't fetch luggage," Elder continued, "so don't you go blaming him. You've got hands and legs of your own; it wouldn't hurt you to use them."

Hazel snorted and then composed herself by taking a swig of beer.

Hawthorn drew himself up even more, but before he could say anything, Hemlock said, "Perhaps it would be best if we sat down. We've kept everyone waiting long enough."

Hawthorn glowered at Elder, fidgeting with a button on his jacket before finally nodding. Hemlock sat across from Hazel; Hawthorn sat next to him, across from Holly.

Augustus returned with another covered tray, this one wider than the last. He scampered up to Elder and held it out.

"We have company, Augustus," Elder said. "Ladies first, you know that."

Augustus walked up to Holly and held out the tray.

Holly whimpered and squinted her eyes shut. "Hazel," she whispered.

Hazel swallowed. She didn't want anything to do with Augustus either, but it wouldn't do to show fear. Or be rude. Taking a breath, she held out a hand and said, "I'll go first."

Augustus wobbled over to her, struggling under the weight of the tray. She lifted the cloche, finding a selection of pickles in various bowls and jars. There were pickled onions and pickled beans, pickled beets and radishes, pickled herrings packed in a juniper-spiced brine, and a wedge of white cheese floated in oil among sprigs of rosemary and flowering thyme.

Hazel dished a little of everything onto Holly's plate—except for the herring—and did the same for herself. Augustus chittered and made his way around the table as everyone helped themselves to the proffered fare.

"Be sure to take some bread," Elder said as he took a slice for himself. "It's baked with the same beer as Abby's brewed, and is particularly good with the pickled herring and onions. Isn't that right, Augustus?"

Augustus chittered and hopped and nearly dropped the tray onto Hawthorn's lap before righting himself again.

Elder chuckled. "This is his favorite time of day. He loves the pickles, you see. The brine tickles his nose in a pleasing way."

Augustus made little chirping sounds that almost sounded like music. Once everyone had been served, he scampered back out the door.

"Do you always eat pickles for breakfast?" Holly asked.

Elder heaped herring, onions, and a couple of slices of beets onto a piece of bread. "Oh, yes. Like the beer, it's good for the constitution. The salt and brine are cleansing, you know. I haven't been sick in twenty years, and I owe that to the pickles."

Holly poked at the cheese with a fork and tasted a crumb. She seemed to relax a bit and grabbed a slice of bread.

"Perhaps we should discuss why we're here," Hazel said, "and then we can be on our way, which I'm sure you are awaiting with great anticipation."

Elder eyed her a moment as he chewed his breakfast before chasing it down with a swig of beer. "You want to find a teacher in necromancy."

"Yes."

"Why should I tell you anything? What assurances do I have that you won't go to this teacher's house, drag him into the street, and flog him?"

"I'm not in the habit of flogging people. Not to mention that, if necromancy is as common here as you say, then I doubt such a flogging would be tolerated by the townspeople. Wouldn't you agree?"

Elder narrowed his eyes and took a bite of his food. "I might."

He seemed unconvinced, so Hazel continued. "Look, I don't like you. I don't like necromancers. I think the lot of you are abominations that this world would be better off without. But I'm not here for you or any of your cretinous colleagues. I'm here for my father and no one else. The sooner I find him the sooner I can leave, and I think we can both agree that the sooner that happens, the happier the both of us will be."

Elder chewed his food a while longer and then chuckled. "You're a miserable woman, but I can't argue with the logic. Very well. I'll give you the address of a man named Baern. Talk to him and see where that leads you."

Hazel exhaled as she kept her gaze on her plate. "Thank you," she said, unable to look at him.

Elder grunted. "We shall see."

Sorrow, Bones, and Blood

They left Elder's house after they finished breakfast. Hazel clutched the slip of paper with Baern's address while Holly and Hawthorn clambered into the coach. Hazel was about to follow them but hesitated.

"Is everything all right?" Hemlock asked.

"I... I don't think I can face this man. Not yet. Not after Elder."

Hemlock studied her a moment, then stepped into the coach and murmured something to Hawthorn. Hazel closed her eyes, trying to gather her nerve to follow him in, but before she could, Hawthorn hopped out and walked around to talk to the driver.

Hemlock poked his head out the door. "Come on. We'll go somewhere else first."

"Where?"

"Hawthorn apparently knows of a place."

Hazel hesitated a little longer. Visiting a location known only to Hawthorn wasn't exactly compelling. Especially in this town. But then anything had to be better than visiting a necromancer. She stepped into the coach and sat next to Holly.

"Where's Tum?" Holly said. "We can't leave without him."

"I haven't seen him since last night," Hazel said.

"Well, we need to find him. We can't just leave."

"And we can't stay here either. We've already overstayed our welcome. Do you really want to go poking around and upset Elder even more? Not to mention his neighbors, who might be necromancers in their own right."

Holly shrank back into her seat. "No, but we can't leave him behind. What if something happened to him?"

Hazel rubbed her eyes. "I don't know, Holly. I'm doing my best to make sure something doesn't happen to *us*."

Holly wrung her hands and stared out the window. Hazel nodded at Hemlock. He rapped on the roof of the carriage, and the carriage started moving.

Everyone remained silent. Holly continued to wring her hands as she stared outside, and Hazel closed her eyes and tried to convince herself she was doing the right thing.

Sarnum was an improved sight during the day but not by much. Black slate roofs topped grey stone buildings that towered over cobblestone roads darkened by morning dew. The lamps that had flickered with blue-and-green flames now stood cold, the glass surrounding them crystalline and unsullied by smoke stains. Yet for all the cold stone, lush, green hedges lined almost every street and fenced nearly every house, which gave an unexpected warmth to the otherwise somber and sterile town.

The carriage eventually turned onto a tree-lined avenue of tall cotton-woods and came to a halt alongside an expanse of manicured grass. An occasional tree dotted the lawn, along with an overly large copper fountain that time had turned green. Further on, a pond glinted in the morning light as a collection of ducks glided across its smooth, placid surface.

"A park!" Holly said and jumped out of the carriage. Hawthorn climbed out after her.

Hazel raised her eyebrows at Hemlock, but he just smiled and shrugged and followed the others out.

As Hazel stepped onto the grass—soft and spongy in its thickness—a rustling came from the coach. She turned in time to see a rumpled gnome fling himself from the top of the carriage to the ground below.

"Tum!" Holly said, grinning. Then she grew serious and put her hands on her hips. "Where have you been? We thought we left you behind."

Tum drew himself up and smoothed his shirt. "Tum's never left behind."

"But where did you go?"

"Oh, you know, here and there. This place is an odd bucket o' gutted fish. They got shamblers here that come out at night. Shamblers! Don't they know shamblers will muss the lawn?" He peered at the well-manicured grass with narrowed eyes.

"Where did you sleep?" Hazel asked.

"I burrowed into one of your trunks, seeing as the luggage was left out. No reason to let a perfectly good bed of dresses go to waste." He thrust a finger into the air. "*Especially* when there's shamblers about."

Hazel wrinkled her nose and took a step back. "You were in my luggage?" She'd need to find a laundress to wash all her clothes. Either that or burn them.

"Aye. Figured it'd be a nice change from Miss Holly's trunk, but I was wrong." He sniffed and looked Hazel up and down. "A little finery wouldn't hurt, you know." Then he wandered off.

"I... I should keep an eye on him," Holly said as she watched him go. "Make sure we don't lose him again." Without waiting for an answer, she went after him.

"Father told me of that fountain," Hawthorn said, nodding towards the great copper sculpture. "He said that if you throw a copper penny into the water, then the two metals would bind together, making the fountain grow ever taller. Left behind would only be a memory of the coin, which you could then exchange for a wish."

"What would happen if you didn't exchange it?" Hazel said. "If you made no wish at all?"

Hawthorn shrugged. "I don't know; I never asked." He wandered over to it. Hemlock and Hazel followed.

The base of the fountain, though massive, wasn't all that impressive. It was of simple design, lacking any decorations or flourishes that Hazel would have expected for such a large structure. The single column that rose up in the center of the basin bore some wavelike embellishments, most of which were situated underneath the two smaller basins that the column supported. A thin trickle of water bubbled from the top of the fountain and drizzled downward, drip-dropping into a meager pool below. A few lilies floated on the surface of the water amid a film of algae that hid the glint of copper pennies.

"Well, that's disappointing," Hawthorn said.

"Do you have a penny?" Hazel asked.

Hawthorn arched an eyebrow at her as Hemlock rooted around in a pocket and pulled out a burnished copper coin. He handed it to her.

She tossed the penny into the fountain, breaking a hole in the algae and causing a lily to bob on its rippling wake. They all leaned forward as they stared at the water. Hazel realized she was holding her breath. She sucked in some air, hoping her foolishness didn't show.

Hawthorn harrumphed before he turned on his heel and headed towards a bench underneath a honeysuckle tree. Hazel and Hemlock remained by the fountain.

"Did you make a wish?" Hemlock asked.

"Why would I? It's all nonsense."

He smiled and shrugged. "You never know."

Hazel stared at the water, the layer of algae so thin it looked like paint. What would she wish for, if she believed one would be granted? Would she wish for the restoration of her mother's soul? It felt like an odd thing to spend a wish on, as her mother would likely depart from this world for good, never to be seen again. But it was what she had been working towards. It was the natural way of things; it was right even if the thought of it left a painful lump in Hazel's throat. Wishes were meant to be spent on something one desired, not obligations—however well intended. So what did Hazel want?

She stared at the water, swallowing as she realized she couldn't answer the question. No one ever asked her what she wanted—she never even asked herself. Her life seemed to have been a long string of duty and obligation, to be the will that kept the family together and safe. To be responsible and strong. To simply *be* there, no matter what. To be what her mother and father had never been.

Hazel had never wanted such a life, but it was the one she had taken upon herself to live. She had always thought it noble of her, but maybe she had just been afraid. Afraid to relinquish this illusion of control she clung so tightly to; afraid to be nothing more than a lonely leaf tumbling on an errant wind.

It all seemed so fragile, this flawed life of broken promises and tenuous illusions, of duty and heartache and lonely nights. It felt as if even a simple thought of a wistful wish would be enough to shatter it all, leaving her with nothing but cold and bitter regret. This life, such as it was, was all she had. Without it, she was nothing more than a hollow shell, a shadow left to shamble along darkened streets, dragging her sorrows behind her.

Unable to look at Hemlock, unable to answer him, Hazel returned to the carriage and sat inside. She folded her hands on her lap as she stared at the empty seats across from her, waiting for the others.

Waiting until this dull pain that had blossomed in her heart ceased to ache.

Hazel remained silent as the carriage once again rattled down the road. Her fear of meeting Baern had ebbed, replaced by a certain disquiet, a troublesome discomfort that disallowed any other feelings to take hold.

The carriage slowed and came to a halt in front of a modest home, one made from timber rather than the grey stone that seemed so popular in Sarnum. This home had no groomed hedges surrounding it. Instead, it bore only a few outcroppings of the same pale grass they had seen in the field surrounding the town.

Hazel smoothed her skirts as she took a deep breath. Then, squaring her shoulders, she left the carriage, marched up to the door, and gave the simple iron knocker three quick raps. She clasped her hands tightly together as everyone stood around her in silence. Then from the other side of the door came the shuffle of footsteps, and the door cracked open.

A single eye peered at them from the narrow opening. "Yes?" said a man's voice. "What do you want?"

"Are you Baern?" Hazel asked.

The eye narrowed. "Who wants to know?"

"My name is Hazel. This is my sister Holly and our associates Hemlock and Hawthorn. We've just come from Elder's house. He seems to think you know our father, Ash."

"And why would he think that?"

"You are a teacher in necromancy are you not? My father has taken up the discipline. Someone must have taught him. We're wondering if that someone is you."

Baern was quiet a long while as he looked her up and down. "I don't like visitors."

"I quite understand. I myself am not terribly fond of visiting the homes of necromancers. But it's important we find our father. If you could tell us where he is or, if you don't know, point us to someone who does, then we'll happily go on our way and leave you to your... business."

He remained silent, and then the door swung open. The man was thin and spindly, with greying tufts of hair that were unsettlingly similar to the pale grass outside. He wore an old suit, rumpled and patched, that seemed to have once held color but had since turned a wan greyish-brown. He turned and walked down the shadowed hallway and disappeared into a room.

Hazel, Holly, Hemlock, and Hawthorn remained huddled on Baern's doorstep.

"Perhaps we should go in," Hemlock said.

"Go in and get answers rather than stand out here like lackwits?" Hawthorn said. "Madness."

Hazel's rising annoyance at Hawthorn helped stifle her fear. So, taking Holly's hand in hers, she stepped inside.

It took a moment for her eyes to adjust to the gloom. The only light came from the open door. When Hawthorn closed it behind him, there wasn't even that. Then, from the walls, pale etchings of script came into focus.

The script scrolled across the walls and onto the floor and ceiling in a fluid, even hand. The writing was white, almost like chalk or paint, yet it gave off a faint, glittering light, as if Baern had ground up the stars and turned them into ink.

Gripping Holly's hand, Hazel made her way down the darkened hallway. She kept her gaze ahead, not wanting to look at the script too long, afraid of what she might find if she did. They came to a door that she believed was the one Baern had disappeared behind, and Hazel pushed it open and stepped across the threshold.

Inside, the room smelled dusty yet pungent with the odor of herbs and meat, ink and wet fur, and a host of other scents Hazel couldn't place. Strings of bones hung from the rafters, tied together in oddly arranged bundles. Baern sat at a table amid a mess of papers and a stuffed raven that looked out on the room with vacant glass eyes.

He motioned to an empty seat at the table. Holly tightened her grip on Hazel's hand. Hazel gave her a final squeeze, then let go and sat in the chair.

Baern blinked at her, then at the others. "Tell them to leave. What we discuss here is not meant for outside ears."

"Holly's my sister. She's not an outsider."

"Then she can take your place and you may leave. I will speak with only one of you."

Holly opened her mouth, but before she could say anything, Hazel said, "Wait outside. It will be all right."

Hawthorn shrugged and sauntered out the door.

Holly put her hands on her hips. "I want to stay."

Baern said, "Either one of you stays or all of you leave. Decide now, or leave me be."

"Wait outside," Hazel said. "It will only take a moment, I'm sure." She met Hemlock's disapproving gaze. "Please."

Hemlock glanced between Hazel and Baern. Then his frown collapsed, replaced by resignation. He put a hand on Holly's shoulder. "Come on. We'd better go find Hawthorn before he wanders off."

Holly pressed her lips into a fine line as she wrung her hands. Then she hurried out the door. Hemlock, casting a final worried glance at Hazel, followed her.

Baern got up and closed the door and returned to the table. Hazel swallowed. There was only a single window in the room, covered by heavy drapes that let in a sliver of light around the edges.

Baern turned up the oil lamp on the table next to the raven and shuffled through a pile of papers. He looked at her from under his brow and back at the papers again. After an excruciatingly long silence, he pushed the papers away, got up, and walked to one of the strings of bones hanging from the ceiling. He untied a bone before dragging his chair over to sit next to Hazel.

"Give me your hand," he said.

Hazel remained still, and he raised his eyebrows. He put out his hand, and Hazel, licking her lips and setting her jaw, put her hand in his.

He took her by the wrist, his skin cool and clammy. An untrimmed fingernail scraped against her skin as he traced a line along her palm. "When was the last time you saw Ash?"

"Why does that matter?"

"Everything matters."

Hazel took a breath. "When I was a girl. Around six or so."

"What was it like when he left?"

Hazel gritted her teeth at the thought of sharing intimate information with a man such as Baern. But she didn't know of any other way. She fixed her gaze past his shoulder, staring at a dried flower pinned to the wall. "It was quiet except for Mother's weeping. She locked herself in her room, and I was left to tend to Holly, who was little more than a baby."

"Did he break your mother's heart?" Baern asked as he continued to run a finger along her palm, almost like a caress.

Hazel suppressed the desire to cringe and looked him in the eyes. "I don't know. She never talked about it with me."

"Not even now, trapped as she is?"

Hazel narrowed her eyes and tried to pull away, but Baern tightened his grip, his fingernails digging into her skin.

"What would you know about that?" Hazel said.

"Ash took great pride in speaking of you. Hazel, his clever little daughter. Bound for greatness."

"He doesn't know a thing about me."

Baern inclined his head. "Perhaps." Still holding on to her hand, he used his other one to root around the papers on the table until he pulled out a short curved knife. Hazel tensed and got to her feet, struggling to pull away, but his fingers and nails only dug deeper into her skin.

"Let go of me," Hazel said, her voice barely above a whisper. "Now."

Baern fixed her in a level gaze and held up the knife in front of him, pinching the hilt near the blade between a pair of long fingers. "I am going to cut you, but do not cry out. Whatever you do, do not cry out."

Hazel tried to yank her arm free, but his grasp was firm. Breathless, she spoke a spell to knock over the lamp, but nothing happened.

Baern waved the knife towards the walls. "Your magic will not work here, not with these glyphs on the walls." He pulled her hand closer, and Hazel clenched it into a fist.

"Open your hand or I will cut your wrist, which is prone to profuse bleeding. I cannot guarantee the cut will be shallow. This knife is very sharp."

She kicked his leg and swiped at him with her other hand, but he leaned back out of her reach, and then she felt the cold, stinging edge of the blade against her arm.

"The hand or the wrist," Baern whispered. "You decide."

"You're a madman."

"You want to find your father. It's the only way I'm offering you."

Hazel's breathing grew heavy and ragged as her racing heart thundered in her chest. She glanced at the door as she sank back onto her chair. Biting her lip to keep it from trembling, she opened her hand.

"Remember," Baern said as he put the blade against her palm. "Not a sound. We are invoking spirits, and your screams will only call forth the unsavory ones. Do you understand?"

Hazel blinked several times and nodded.

A sharp pain lanced across her hand, followed by a warm rush of blood. Hazel bit harder on her lip, and an iron tang filled her mouth that matched the metallic smell in the air. Struggling to keep her breathing even, she again fixed her gaze on the flower on the wall. It looked like a cornflower, but she couldn't be sure in the dim light.

Baern pressed something hard against the wound on her hand, and she winced but kept silent. He intoned a spell, and the script on the walls grew a little brighter, just as the flickering light from the lamp grew a little darker.

Then he let go of her hand and rose from the chair. "We are done. You may leave now." He held out the small bone he had untied earlier, now stained red with her blood.

Hazel grabbed a handful of her skirts and used it to staunch the bleeding. She glared at Baern as she struggled to get her breathing under control. Anger settled over her, pushing all words out of her head, and all she could do was sit and fume.

He waggled the bone as he held it out to her.

"I don't want that disgusting thing, you sick piece of filth," she hissed.

"You will need it if you want to find your father. You two are bound by blood, and so by your blood will you find him."

"I'm not a necromancer. How am I supposed to use that to find him?"

A corner of Baern's thin lips twitched into a smile. "That will be for you to puzzle out. We shall see if you are as clever as Ash has made you out to be. Now leave. I am no longer feeling hospitable."

Hazel continued to glare at him, her mouth working soundlessly as she chewed on empty words that would not come. But she didn't want to be there anymore, so she grabbed the bloodstained bone and marched down the darkened hallway, wiping stinging tears from her eyes before she walked out the door and into blinding daylight.

Hallowed Hearts

Hazel bolted out the door, clutching a handful of her skirts in a throbbing, stinging fist. She kept her gaze ahead as she hurried through Baern's weather-worn yard, refusing to look at Holly or Hemlock, who now trailed behind her.

"What happened?" Holly said. "Are you bleeding? Why are you bleeding?"

Hemlock said, "Hazel, what happened?"

Hazel ignored them. She left Baern's yard and turned onto the stone-cobbled street, to the right, as there were no people or houses that way. They were at the edge of town, close to the wall surrounding Sarnum that cast a shadowy pall over the pale, wispy grass that grew wild in untended fields.

"What did he say?" Holly said as she trailed behind her. "Did he tell you where Father is?" When Hazel said nothing, Holly grabbed her arm.

Hazel rounded on her. "For once in your miserable life, Holly, shut your mouth and leave me alone!"

Holly's face went slack with shock, and in that moment Hazel hated herself. She turned around and kept walking. At least Holly and Hemlock didn't follow.

The air grew colder the closer to the wall Hazel got. The sun was out. It was supposed to be summer, but maybe that didn't mean anything in a place like this. Maybe the laws of nature meant nothing to the people of Sarnum, and so the laws themselves had abandoned them.

The grass rustled against Hazel's skirts, grasping at her like boneless fingers. A stunted pear tree stood nearby, it's gnarled, knobby branches laden with tiny hard fruit that likely would never ripen. Hazel sat down underneath it, into the tall grass that, she hoped, eclipsed her from view. She let go of her skirts, wincing as the fabric stuck to her wound before pulling away. Blinking, she stared at the cut, red and ugly that still trickled a thin stream of blood. She put her fingers to it and pressed, gritting her teeth at the pain, her stomach twisting in a nauseating way as the blood came faster.

Is that what her father had become? Living alone with writing scrawled on the walls, blood and spirits his only companions? Is it what he wanted *her* to be?

The grass rustled, and Hazel looked up, finding Hemlock walking towards her.

She looked away. "Leave me alone, Hemlock."

He stopped in front of her. "What happened in there, Hazel?"

"I don't want to talk about it."

"What happened to your hand?" His voice took an angry edge. "Did he hurt you?"

Hazel took a breath, struggling to keep her voice even. "I said I don't want to talk about it."

He crouched down in front of her and tried to take her hand. "Let me see."

Hazel clenched her hand shut, letting the pain fuel her anger. Then it was like the anger within her snapped, and suddenly she didn't care anymore. "You want to see?" She thrust her wounded palm near Hemlock's face. "Bastard cut me. Threatened to cut my wrist but I settled for the palm. I *let* him do it, Hemlock. Let him hurt me and draw blood so he could invoke his cursed spirits—all so he could give me this!" She threw the bloodstained bone at him. It struck him in the shoulder before falling into the grass.

Hazel laughed—a low, mirthless sound that sounded maddened even to her own incensed ears. "That's the best part of all. After everything we've done, after *letting* that monster put his filthy knife blade to my skin, I am then informed that I must somehow perform necromantic magic in order to find my good-for-nothing father. Only by becoming like him, will I find him. You have to appreciate the irony."

"Hazel—"

"Don't," she said, her voice low. "Don't tell me you want to help. Don't tell me I'm not alone. Don't sit there and pretend you don't want something from me when we both know that's not true!" She got to her feet. "You're all the same—men, warlocks—you all want the same thing: a woman for your pleasure and children for your legacy. Yet even when you have those things it's not enough, and you wander the world looking for something else, never once looking back at what you left behind. At who you've hurt in your wake."

Hemlock's brow knitted into a puzzled frown, and he shook his head. "What are you talking about? Who have I hurt? Who have I left behind? Not you. You're the one who's always leaving. You're the one that refuses to look back no matter who you hurt. And for what? So you can do all this yourself? So you don't have to feel vulnerable and ask for help? How's that working out for you, Hazel?"

Hazel raised her chin. "It's working just fine." A dismal lie that even she didn't believe, but what was the alternative? To say she needed him? The thought terrified her.

"Really? My mistake." He picked up the bloodied bone from the ground and handed it to her. "Good luck finding your father."

Hazel's stomach sank as she took the bone, the sight of the blood sickening her more than it had before. And as she watched Hemlock's back as he walked away, an old hurt bubbled to the surface—a helpless sorrow she had forgotten ever feeling when someone she loved walked out of her life and never returned. Before, she had remained silent. Before, she let it happen without so much as a protest. Not again. She wouldn't be silent again.

"You don't get to leave!" she shouted to Hemlock.

He turned around and spread out his arms. "You don't want me here, Hazel."

"That didn't stop you before, back at the inn. You came along anyway. Why?"

His arms went limp, and he stood there in the field, the grass brushing against his legs as it swayed in the breeze. Then he walked back to her. "Why?" he said, his voice low. "Why do any of us do anything? Why are you here searching for your father? Why are you trying to undo your mother's curse? Why have you looked after your sister for all these years, when no one asked you to do any of these things? Why do you do it, Hazel?"

Hazel frowned, swallowing. "They're my family."

"Family is just a word. You're doing it because you love them."

Her mouth worked soundlessly a long while, and she shook her head. "You don't love me."

Hemlock gave a wry laugh. "I'm afraid I do. I've loved you the moment you walked into my house and insulted my brother. From that moment, I knew you were a woman I wanted in my life. An intelligent, sensible woman capable of coherent conversation—one not taken by shiny baubles or fooled by the illusionary preening of warlocks who think too highly of themselves." He looked down at his hands. "I had hoped, in time, you would come to love me too. But even if you never did, I still wanted to help you. I wanted to see you happy, because if you were happy, then a part of me could be happy too. And maybe that part would have been enough."

The wind rustled the grass and the leaves of the pear tree above—a coarse, whispering reply that Hazel wished she had the voice to give, but her voice had gone.

Hemlock shook his head. "Foolish, I know."

Hazel swallowed. No, not foolish, but even those words failed her. And as if from a great distance, she watched as Hemlock once again turned to walk away. In that moment she saw, almost as plain as the skin on her hands, that this time he would not be back. That any words spoken by her next week, next month, next year, would be too late, the hurt inflicted by her dumbfounded silence too much to bear. And the idea of never seeing him again filled her with such an intense sorrow that her vision blurred as tears filled her eyes, and he faded entirely from view when she covered her face with her bloodstained hands.

Her mouth felt parched, her tongue swollen. Was this love? This uncomfortable, terrifying feeling as if she balanced on the edge of a knife? Would she slip and fall? Would he pull the knife out from under her, cutting her open? She didn't know, and Hazel didn't like not knowing. How could you protect yourself from danger—from heartbreak—if you couldn't see it coming? Her mother hadn't seen it coming, and look what happened to her.

She thought of Willow, alone in her tumbledown cottage, her once melodious voice taking on a more bitter edge with each passing year. Hazel had sworn she wouldn't let that be her fate, and yet in that moment when Hemlock turned his back on her, she could see it already was. She was a prisoner of her fear, destined to be alone because she refused to trust, to let someone in.

Hazel's body shook as she watched Hemlock move through the field. She felt heavy, paralyzed by the words she was so afraid to speak.

"Stay," she whispered, barely audible over the rustling leaves. She could say that to him; maybe he'd stay. Maybe it would be enough. She cleared her throat and, louder, said, "Stay."

Her voice must have carried, for Hemlock turned to look at her. "Why?"

Hazel swallowed and lifted her chin. "I don't want you to go."

Hemlock's features softened as he returned to her. "Why?" His voice was quiet; he sounded tired. "What's the point, Hazel?"

She narrowed her eyes. Was he trying to be cruel? Wasn't it enough that she wanted him to stay? "I can't love you, Hemlock. Because if I love you, then I don't know who I am anymore. What is my life if it's not mine alone?"

He took her hands in his, even the bloodied, cut one that he held with care. "You didn't answer the question."

Her eyes filled with tears again, and she looked away. "I'm afraid to love you, Hemlock," she whispered. "I'm afraid I won't recognize myself if I do. I'm afraid you'll crush my heart, and I won't have the strength to stand it."

"Hazel." He touched her cheek and gently turned her head to face him. "Why do you want me to stay?"

She closed her eyes. "Because I'm afraid that it's already too late, and if you leave, then you'll take my withered heart with you, and I don't know if I can bear that." She took a heavy, ragged breath. "I'm afraid of what my life will be if you're not there."

Hemlock put his arms around her, and Hazel, unable to hold back any longer, clutched on to him as she wept on his shoulder. Years of anger and resentment, tension and fear, it all seemed to pour out of her in a continuous stream of tears. Part of her felt like she shouldn't be there, crying like that—that she should pull herself together. But another part of her wanted it out; it felt good letting it out, just like it felt good standing in the warmth of Hemlock's body, feeling the weight of his arms as he held her close.

He said nothing as they stood there. He just let her weep and weep until, after an eternity, Hazel finally calmed and pulled away. She couldn't look at him, so she kept her gaze fixed to the ground. She wiped at her face and eyes, ignoring the throbbing pain in her hand. "What you must think of me," she said, no longer comfortable with the silence between them.

"I think you're beautiful," he said, handing her a kerchief.

She looked up at him, and he gave her a crooked smile that pulled a small smile from Hazel's own lips.

He pushed back strands of her hair that had become plastered to her fevered cheeks. He looked into her eyes as he held her face—just for a moment—and then he kissed her.

It wasn't an impassioned, desperate kiss; it wasn't tenuous or meek. It was steadfast, sturdy, almost matter-of-fact, as if this moment had never been in doubt. It was a kiss to endure life's turbulent throes; it was a kiss to comfort and ease the pain away. It was a kiss of love, pure and simple. And it... was perfect.

Finding Forgiveness

Hazel and Hemlock walked down the streets of Sarnum, heading towards an inn that Hawthorn had recommended. Apparently, after Hazel had run off to the field, Hemlock had sent the others away, and Hawthorn had said they would wait at the inn until she and Hemlock arrived.

Though as they turned down one road and then another, passing shops and doors and people disinclined to meet her gaze, Hazel wasn't sure she and Hemlock knew where they were going. Then again, she wasn't sure she cared.

They walked in silence, sidestepping oncoming people and the occasional dog. Even through all the bustle, Hazel had to keep reminding herself not to smile like a moonstruck idiot. Especially when Hemlock would take her arm and guide her away from stepping into a filth-laden gutter or—when she was looking up at him—from walking into a lamp-post. She suddenly felt so foolish around him, and yet somehow that foolishness was wonderful.

Not that he was faring much better. In the reflection of a window, she saw his gaze fall upon her just as he walked headlong into a man wearing a cape of a brilliant, shimmering material that would likely have made Hawthorn blanch with jealousy. Hemlock murmured an apology, but the man just huffed, swept his cape over a shoulder, and strode away.

Hazel bit her lip, but it wasn't enough to suppress a giggle. Hemlock smiled. He took her hand, and they continued on.

The chill morning waned into warm afternoon, finally taking on a semblance of summer. And though Hazel was reluctant to admit it, Sarnum really didn't seem so bad in the daylight. They passed jewelry shops displaying amulets that had been wrought into twining serpents with crystalline scales that sparkled in the light. Pastry shops boasted layered tortes and columns of cookies bundled together with bands of colorful ribbons. A tobacco shop sent an earthy, sweet scent wafting into the air, mingling with the smell of onion and meat, beer and char that came from elsewhere on the street. They even passed a dressmaker's shop that displayed an elaborate gown in the window; it had so many frills and flounces that Hazel could practically hear Holly squeal with delight.

The thought of her sister, and what Hazel had said to her, made her wince. She needed to make it right, though she wasn't sure how. By the time they finally found the inn—the Backwards Buck—Hazel was exhausted and filthy from the blood and dust that clung to her dress, and she could think of little beyond a bath and going to sleep despite the early hour.

They stepped inside, and Hazel hesitated at the threshold as she waited for her eyes to adjust. Her heart quickened, sweat stinging her cut palm as memories of Baern's dark home surfaced, and she clutched Hemlock's hand. But then she took in the flickering blue light from the sconces, and the dim interior of a common room came into view.

Tables littered the expansive room, populated by numerous patrons talking over mugs of beer or playing at cards. No one looked up as Hazel and Hemlock passed, even as she studied them while looking for Holly and Hawthorn.

They came to a counter, behind which stood a disinterested woman, her brown, greying hair pulled back into a single frizzy braid. When Hemlock enquired after Holly and Hawthorn, the woman raised her eyebrows, shrugged, and moved her gaze elsewhere. When they remained, the innkeeper sighed, murmured some room numbers as she waved a limp hand towards a set of stairs, then moved further down the counter.

Hazel and Hemlock headed upstairs and found one of the rooms the woman had mentioned—the other one further down the hall.

"Is this Holly's or Hawthorn's room?" Hazel asked.

"I don't know. The woman wasn't exactly forthcoming with information."

Hazel knocked on the door.

"Go away!" came Holly's reply.

"Well, I guess that answers that question," Hemlock said.

"I should talk to her alone," Hazel said.

Hemlock nodded. "I'll go find Hawthorn." He squared his shoulders and straightened his jacket. "This should be bracing, as always." Then he walked to the other door down the hall.

Hazel eased Holly's door open and slipped inside, not wanting to make too much noise. Holly lay on top of the bed, her back to Hazel.

Holly turned, scowled at her, then turned back around. "What do you want?"

"To say I'm sorry. I had no right to speak to you like that. I'm sorry, truly."

"You're always sorry, but you keep doing it anyway. I'm not a toy for you to kick around, Hazel."

Hazel sat on the edge of the bed behind Holly. "I know. I was scared and hurt and confused, and... I know that's not an excuse—I'm not trying to excuse it—but I don't deal with all that very well. Sometimes I need time to think, you know?"

"No, I don't know. Why don't you just say that? 'I need time to think.' It's not hard."

Hazel swallowed. "It shouldn't be, but it's hard for me."

Holly said nothing.

Hazel knotted her fingers together as she stared at her sister's back and her mess of golden hair spilling over the pillow. She opened her mouth but snapped it shut again. Then, gathering her courage, she said, "Hemlock and I kissed."

"No, you didn't."

Hazel blinked a few times. "Well, I suppose it's more accurate to say that *he* kissed *me*, but it happened."

Holly shook her head, an awkward motion as she lay against the bed. "You want me to think you did so I'll forget about what you said. But I won't forget. Not ever. Not this time."

"I don't want you forget, Holly. I hope you'll forgive me, but that's not the same thing. I'm not lying though. I..." She took a breath. "I think I might love him." Hazel stared at her hands as Holly sat up and studied her. Then before Hazel knew what was happening, Holly embraced her in a crushing hug.

Tears filled Hazel's eyes, and she smoothed Holly's hair as she hugged her sister back. They stayed there for a time until Holly pulled away. She grinned. "*Now* are you going to get married?"

A short laugh escaped Hazel as she wiped at her eyes. "I don't know. One step at a time, all right?"

Holly pursed her lips, but she nodded. "Let me see your hand."

Hazel let Holly take her hand, wincing as she poked at the wound.

Holly screwed up her face. "Why'd he cut you? He sick or something?"

"Probably, but he did it to make this." Hazel fished out the bloodied bone from her pocket and set in on the bed.

They stared at it as if the bone might scurry off the blanket and cavort about the room.

"W-what are you supposed to do with that?" Holly said.

"Find Father, apparently."

"But you're not a necromancer."

"Baern wasn't too concerned with that detail."

Holly stared at her, but Hazel kept her gaze fixed on the bone.

"What are you going to do?" Holly said.

"I don't know."

"Maybe if we returned to Elder..."

Hazel shook her head. "I think we've gotten all the help we're going to from Elder. And I'm not sure I'd want his help anyway even if he offered."

"But what choice do we have? You can't do necromantic magic, Hazel."

Hazel said nothing and continued to stare at the bone.

"Hazel?"

She looked up and met Holly's puzzled gaze, then forced a feeble smile. "I'm sure we'll think of something."

Holly frowned, but before she could say anything, Hazel swept the bone off the bed and returned it to her pocket. "I don't know about you, but I'm starving. Let's go get something to eat." Hazel hurried out of the room, leaving her silent sister behind.

HOLLY GLOWERED at Hazel's back as she followed her sister down the hall. This was all wrong. This wasn't how it was supposed to be. They were supposed to find their father, yes, but not with necromancy. Hazel couldn't possibly be considering it, could she? Holly wanted to believe that, but there had been a look in Hazel's eyes. A look of... resignation. Holly almost wished that the look meant Hazel was giving up, that they'd soon return home, and everything would go back to normal.

Except it wouldn't be normal—it hadn't been normal for a very long time, only Holly had been too preoccupied to see it. It seemed so frivolous now, all her fussing over dances and making the perfect dress. What did dresses matter when the person you loved most in the world was probably in trouble?

Holly had been so happy letting Hazel shoulder the burdens of their life while Holly did nothing. She had told herself that's how Hazel wanted it, but now Holly wished she had done more. If she had, maybe they'd have found another way—maybe Hazel wouldn't now be walking with a bloody bone in her pocket as she pondered unthinkable thoughts.

Hazel hurried downstairs, but Holly lingered on the landing. Hemlock and Hawthorn sat at a table in the common room. Hemlock waved Hazel over, and she joined them. When Hazel looked back at her, Holly followed and sat between Hazel and Hawthorn.

Hemlock and Hawthorn were eating pies stained with thick, dark gravy that had bubbled over the crust. A serving girl came and gave Holly and Hazel pies of their own. Holly poked at hers. She wasn't hungry. It probably had meat in it anyway.

Holly studied Hazel as she and Hemlock talked. Her sister looked different. There was color in her cheeks, a brightness in her eyes. It should have made Holly happy seeing her like that, but she only felt sad. She couldn't let Hazel ruin everything now, not after her sister finally found happiness. And how could Hazel's life not be ruined when necromancy was involved?

Holly murmured a half-sincere apology as she got up from the table and headed upstairs. Returning to her room, she went to the trunk housing her good dress and unlocked it with a key she kept around her neck. She rifled around the layers of taffeta and mismatched beads. Why had she brought the monstrous thing; did she expect to go dancing? Underneath the fabric, she found a narrow wooden box.

She pulled out the box and opened it, her heart thumping a little harder as she peered at the clear liquid in the crystal vials that Odd had given her. Before, Holly had been so eager to try the mysterious potions, but now she wasn't so sure. Now she was desperate; she didn't know what to do. It was hard to be enthusiastic, feeling like that.

Holly put the box in a dresser drawer, ready for when she might need it, though she didn't know when that would be. Hopefully never, though she doubted it.

Dark Decisions, Dark Deeds

Hazel lay awake in bed as Holly slept next to her. The inn was fully booked and hadn't had any extra rooms for Hazel or Hemlock, so they had to share with their siblings. Hazel stared at the shadowed silhouette of the bone as it rested on the end table near her head. The room was dark, but the bone looked darker still, soaking up shadows as if any light refused to touch it.

Hazel couldn't rest with that thing so close to her. She had told Holly they'd think of something and had suffered a pang of guilt for the lie, but she didn't know what else to do. It was the only way. Holly would never understand. She didn't *want* Holly to understand. Hazel wanted her sister to retain her naive optimism. Something the darkness couldn't touch.

Holding her breath, she slipped out of bed and dressed carefully and quietly so as not to wake Holly. She probably didn't need to be so careful—Holly would sleep through crashing pots and pans and howling dogs. But Hazel didn't want to risk it. Not tonight.

Once dressed, Hazel took the cold, hard bone from the table and slipped out the door.

A single oil lamp burned on a narrow table in the hallway, illuminating the way to Hemlock's door. She gently knocked upon it, and after a minute or so, the door opened.

Hemlock blinked at her. "Hazel," he said, sounding surprised. He glanced behind him before stepping out into the hallway with her and closed the door. "You know Hawthorn's in there, right?"

"I don't want to come in. I need you to come with me."

Hemlock grinned and stepped closer to her. "Oh? Where?"

She fished the bone from her pocket and held it out.

His face fell, and he sucked in a breath. "What are you doing, Hazel?"

"Finding my father."

"Now? Tonight? Do you even know what you're doing?"

Hazel shook her head. "I have no idea. But I'm never going to know. Now's a good a time as any."

"And what does Holly think of this?"

"I don't want her involved."

"She's already involved. It's her father too. She has a right to know."

"I know, but not with this. Not until it's done and over. I don't know what's going to happen. I don't even know what's out there after dark. It's why I need you to come with me. You'll be able to deal with what's out there a lot better than her—better than both of us." She took a breath. "I'm asking for your help, Hemlock."

Hemlock rubbed his forehead and nodded. "All right. Just... let me get dressed."

Hazel paced around the dim hallway until Hemlock returned, smoothing the jacket of his rumpled black suit.

She managed a feeble smile. "I'm afraid we both have the look of getting dressed in the dark."

Hemlock grinned, straightening his shoulders. "People might get the wrong idea."

"Let's hope that's the worst thing that happens tonight."

They walked down the hallway towards the stairs.

"I wouldn't mind, you know," he said, "if they got the wrong idea. Or... even the right idea..."

"Focus, Hemlock."

"Right."

She glanced at him out of the corner of her eye and bit her lip to keep herself from grinning like the fool she was. She also needed to focus.

The common room was empty, save for a man sleeping at a table, his face buried in his arms. Hazel lingered by the door. Then, taking a deep breath, she opened it, picked a direction, and started walking.

"Do you know where to go?" Hemlock asked as he followed her.

She shook her head. "No, I... I figure we'll just walk and see what happens."

Hemlock said nothing.

They came across a tiny orb of blue light weaving in and out between the black bars of an iron fence. From the shadows came a rough, scraping sound of something heavy being dragged along the road. Hemlock took her arm and pulled her away. Yet a tension tugged at Hazel's mind, drawing her attention to a darkened alley on the other side of the road, opposite of where Hemlock was headed.

The dragging sound became louder. Not wanting to waste time, Hazel took Hemlock's hand and, before he could speak, ran with him across the street and into the shadows of the alley. Whatever was out on the street didn't follow them.

They walked past low shuttered windows. When Hazel passed an uncovered window, she glanced inside before hurrying on. Then her breath caught, and she stepped back to it. Beyond the window the room stood dark, yet she still managed to make out the shadowed silhouettes of bookshelves lining the walls. A private library, nothing special. She should move on, but instead Hazel lingered there, her breath fogging the cold glass.

"What is it?" Hemlock said.

Hazel didn't answer. She didn't know what to say—how to explain the tension tugging at her mind. Maybe she was just afraid to say the words, because then it would be real.

A low arched door stood next to the window. Hazel walked to it and pulled on the handle, and the door creaked open.

"What are you doing?"

"I need to go in there."

"Why?"

"I don't know." She ducked inside and walked down a pair of stone steps that took her into a darkened hallway. Hemlock closed the door behind them.

"Who lives here?" he whispered. "Do you know?"

"No idea." She listened for any sound—footsteps, hushed voices, or the even, feathered breath that came from sleeping bodies. But there was nothing. No clock ticking, no crackling of embers as they cooled in the night. Not even a scratching from rats in the walls—a sound which Hazel never thought she'd miss, but she missed it now. It was too quiet.

She ran her hand along the wall as she walked down the hallway. Dust clung to her hand and floated into the air. Hazel sneezed.

Both she and Hemlock froze, but everything remained eerily silent.

Hemlock pulled a handkerchief from his pocket and handed it to her. "I think the house might be empty."

Hazel nodded, took the handkerchief, and wiped her nose. "I hope so. How anyone could live in all this dust is beyond me." But she remained tense. The amount of dust suggested that no one had lived there in some time, yet the house was furnished. Shadowed portraits hung on the walls; dusty carpets padded her steps. When Hemlock pulled out his pocket watch and conjured from it a fairy that, along with the watch, emitted a brilliant white-gold light, Hazel could finally see the true state of the house.

Dust-laden cobwebs hung in the corners, fluttering in a draft that Hazel couldn't feel. Faded paper had peeled from the wall in places. Further down the hall stood a narrow table with a porcelain vase containing an arrangement of dried red roses that almost looked black. Webs stretched between the drooping heads of the flowers, and when Hazel touched one, the petals fell apart and fluttered to the floor in a papery cascade.

The fairy continued to flit down the hallway, and the shadows shrank away as it approached. They followed it and opened a door to a bedroom—the covers on the bed lay flat and undisturbed, their color indistinguishable underneath the dust. A photograph portrait of a woman rested on the night table in a silver frame. Her face was blurred, as if she had refused to sit still. Hazel made her way back down the hall to the door she believed led to the library. When Hemlock and his fairy came close enough to illuminate the cracked and peeling paint on the door, she nudged it open and stepped inside.

The smell of dust was thicker here, moldering in its stench. Hazel put the kerchief over her nose to keep from sneezing again. She stared at the stacks of books and wondered what to do.

Hemlock followed her in, and the fairy carrying his glowing pocket watch flitted to the shelves. The light seared across Hazel's vision, and she closed her eyes, leaving a ghostly winged afterimage imprinted on her mind.

"Extinguish the light," she whispered.

"What?"

"The light, put it out." She took a breath. "Please."

Hemlock remained silent a moment. Then he released the fairy and returned his watch to his pocket.

Hazel opened her eyes. Moonlight filtered through the window, and she could make out some of the muted colors of the leather-bound tomes. Dark green and maroon. Midnight blue, black, and chocolate brown. Some of the titles were visible on the spines, even underneath the dust that coated everything like powdered breath. *Whispering Wights and Intelligent Sprites: How to Imbue Cognizance into Your Summoned Spirits. The Misunderstood Virtues of Blindweed and Direction for its Proper Application. Silenced after Sunset: 50 Counterspells for the Mischievous Familiar.* Necromancer books. Hazel wished she could feel surprised. She pulled a book from the shelf and cracked it open, wrinkling her nose as a waft of musty air hit her, smelling like stagnant water and decomposing leaves. She held her breath and brought her face closer to the pages, trying to make out what was written. But the text was faded, and the paper was blotted with a rash of mold like liver spots on old, withered skin. She pulled out another book and opened it, but the pages were the same. Then another but it, too, was illegible.

Hazel stood there, her arms limp at her sides.

"Hazel," Hemlock said, his near-whispering voice carrying through the silence with surprising clarity. "Perhaps we should leave."

"There's something here. I know there is."

"Yes," Hemlock said. "That's what worries me."

She made herself look at him. "I can't turn back. Not until this is done. I think you know that."

An expression passed over his face that Hazel couldn't quite read. He looked sad but also strangely defiant, his shoulders squared and back straight as he met her gaze.

Hazel reached into her pocket and pulled out the bloodied bone. She held Hemlock's gaze a moment longer. Then, looking away, she tossed it into the air.

The bone clattered onto the wooden floor, clearing a path through the dust before it rolled to a stop at the clawed foot of a dense cherrywood bookshelf. Hazel bent down to pick up the bone and as she did, felt a draft of cool air coming from behind the shelf.

"There's something here," she murmured. She tried to push the shelf aside, but it was too heavy. "Help me move it."

Hemlock walked to the other side of the bookshelf, and on a count of three, they edged the monstrous thing away from the wall as it groaned and screeched across the floor. In the wall where the shelf had stood was the outline of a door. There was no handle or knob, only a hole in the wood where a knob should have been. Hazel hooked her finger into it and pulled, and in a cloud of dust and a squeaking of rusty hinges, it opened, revealing a dark passage beyond.

Silence lingered as she and Hemlock peered into the blackness.

"Well, that doesn't look foreboding at all," he said.

Hazel smiled, but it was fleeting and faded as a cold fear settled over her.

Hemlock looked at her. "Do you want to go first or should I?"

She closed her eyes, thankful beyond words that he was there. "I'll go first, but we need some light. Maybe something less brilliant than the fairy though?"

Hemlock shook his head. "This is a warlock's house. I'll need an object of mine for the magic, and the fairy is the only thing I can conjure from the watch. You're under no such restrictions though, unless a witch lived here as well." He looked around. "Which I doubt." Then he smiled. "Have you been practicing your Wyr pronunciation?"

"In the Grove, yes, but not since we came here."

"Try the moth spell I showed you."

She spoke the words Hemlock had taught her, feeling both elated and relieved when a little white moth glowing like moonlight unfolded into being. It flitted into the passage and illuminated a narrow set of stairs that headed downwards.

Hazel took a deep breath to steady her nerves, then started her descent. The stairs creaked under her weight. She kept a hand to the wall, trying not to dwell on what made the rough stones slick underneath her fingers.

She looked back at Hemlock. He was frowning, but when he saw her looking at him, he gave her a crooked smile. Hazel tried to smile back, but the effort felt beyond her, and she probably looked more pained than pleased. She continued on.

At the bottom, Hazel's boots scuffed against irregularly shaped flagstones that paved the floor. The moth's light was feeble down here, and Hazel resisted the urge to ask Hemlock to summon his fairy. She didn't know why, exactly. The extra light would be welcome. But at the same time, it also felt... wrong.

The wound on her hand throbbed in time with the beating of her heart. The cold air fed into her nerves a strange kind of energy. She felt excited. And beyond that, a faint and terrible understanding.

Thoughts and images came to her mind, unbidden and unknown, but there was truth beyond them. Like when she had known that on each new moon at the tumbledown cottage near her home, if she made a fire and crumbled cake in a water-filled basin, she'd see her mother again. Hazel had that same kind of feeling now. She knew what to do to push back the darkness beyond the little moth Hemlock had taught her to summon, only she wished that she didn't. Especially now with Hemlock there. She didn't want him to know that about her.

Hazel reached into her pocket and wrapped her fingers around the bone that now felt warm against her cool, clammy skin. She worked a spell—similar to a Weaving spell of Transformation but with altered pronunciation and harder consonants. Into that spell she wove another one similar to a Wyr conjuration but also with the altered pronunciation and a longer drawing of the vowels. When she finished, blue points of light flared in the darkness. They wove around each other until each light found a sconce on the wall, then erupted into flickering flames as they attached themselves to tapered candles, and the darkness receded.

A long rectangular table stood before Hazel. On the table was a plain silver goblet, a mortar and pestle, and a wooden box about the size of a thick book onto which intricate designs had been carved. There was also a bottle of wine, a thin, narrow knife, an unadorned ceramic bowl, and a clean white cloth that had been folded into a neat little square. It occurred to Hazel that there was no dust down here—the cloth looked freshly laundered and pressed, and the dark glass of the bottle gleamed in the flickering blue light as if it had been polished.

Everything looked deliberately placed, each item carefully arranged. And the absence of dust could only be the work of magic. Someone wanted to keep this place just so. But why? Did they plan on returning? Or had they known she would be there—that *someone* would be there—and if they had, then what did that mean?

She stepped closer to the table, studying the items. There was a pattern among them—a symmetry in their arrangement, an evenness of the spaces between them. It was as if they fit into her mind like pieces of a puzzle, and Hazel knew what to do.

She took the bone from her pocket and put it into the bowl-shaped mortar. Hemlock came to stand next to her, but Hazel kept her gaze on her work. Her nerves had calmed, and the excitement she had felt now became an enthusiastic curiosity as her mind buzzed with a potential solution she was eager to prove right.

Picking up the heavy stone pestle, she ground the bone into dust. She then tipped the powder into the goblet, using her fingers to scrape the mortar clean. Moving on to the wine bottle, Hazel picked up the knife and hesitated. The knife had to be there to open the bottle—there was no other use for it, if she was right. Puzzled as to why a corkscrew hadn't been left behind, she handed the bottle and knife to Hemlock, murmuring instructions for him to open it.

He gaped at her, knife and bottle in hand, but Hazel returned her attention to the table. She opened the wooden box, finding stalks of dried herbs and plants bundled together with pieces of twine. There was lavender and mugwort, marigold, jasmine, anise, and vervain. There was ash bark, yarrow, and a few withered, deadly nightshade berries dangling from a stalk along with dried leaves. Hazel sifted through them, running each plant's properties through her mind, searching for the way each one fit into her puzzle. Not all of them did. There were more here than what she needed.

She took some mugwort and jasmine and broke off some of the fragile, flowering fronds of the anise and crumbled them between her fingers into the goblet along with the bone dust. Her hands hesitated over the ash bark. She wanted to reach for it, grind it up in the mortar like she had the bone. But it didn't quite fit. Not as well as the yarrow. So Hazel took some of the dried flowers from that instead, ground them with her fingers, and added it to the goblet.

She turned to Hemlock. He had gotten the cork out of the bottle, his expression a mixture of puzzlement, fear, and concern.

"What are you doing, Hazel?" he said as she took the bottle from him.

"Finding my father."

"How, exactly?"

Hazel didn't answer. There was no time to explain, not if she wanted to hold on to this idea long enough to see if it worked. She poured some wine into the goblet and stirred it with the handle of the knife. Then she sucked in a breath—she had almost forgotten an ingredient. Hazel returned to the box and plucked a nightshade berry from its stalk and ground it into a jammy paste with the mortar and pestle. She mixed it with some wine, then poured the slurry into the goblet. She gave it another stir, then brought the goblet to her nose and sniffed. It smelled like wine, mostly, but more earthy, with hints of jasmine and anise coming through. Not all that unpleasant, really.

"Nightshade is poisonous," Hemlock said. "Please don't tell me you're thinking about drinking that."

She turned to look at him again, the haze clearing from her mind now that she had done what she wanted to do, and a twinge of shame gnawed at her. Yet she couldn't turn back. Hazel still hadn't gotten her answer, and she wouldn't be able to rest until she had.

Hazel brought the goblet to her lips and tipped it back.

The liquid was thick and sludgy, tasting like chalk, ash, and iron. She downed it quickly, not wanting to dwell on the taste or let the sediment settle to the bottom. She almost laughed. *Sediment.* As if the sandy consistency was a natural occurrence in the wine and not ground-up bone that had been slathered with her blood. The thought almost made her retch, but instead she coughed and managed to keep it down. The chalky taste faded, replaced by sweet, floral notes from the wine and jasmine before giving way to the aromatic sharpness of the anise, and then to bitterness that she could only assume came from the nightshade.

Hazel's heart quickened, and sweat beaded across her brow. She put a shaking hand to her head, not wanting to think about how foolish she had been or what a terrible mistake she had undoubtedly just made. This was the only way. It had to be.

Hemlock stood in front of her and grabbed hold of her shoulders as he studied her face. His knees were bent, bringing his eyes level with hers, and she realized his eyes were hazel. Green flecked with brown—colors of the earth. The color of her name. Why hadn't she noticed that before? He must not have noticed the similarity either, or he wouldn't have been frowning like that. She giggled, wanting to tell him, but her laugh came out sounding gurgled and foreign. She sobered, acutely aware of her racing heart and of the shadows that had gathered around her vision.

Her legs buckled, and Hazel collapsed onto the floor. The shadows grew, turning white and wispy as they took over her sight. They gathered around Hemlock, pulling at his skin and eclipsing his face, but the stillness in his body indicated he didn't notice. Hazel closed her eyes as they throbbed with a dull and distant pain that made the world shiver. When she opened them, Hemlock had gone, and all that remained were the pale, wispy shadows, as if all life had been leeched from the world, leaving behind only a smoking, pallid husk.

Her breath echoed through her chest and ears as if she had been hollowed out like a harvest-time gourd. Alone, alone, dead and alone. The thought echoed in her mind along with her breath, and she grabbed hold of her head and bent over in an effort to quiet them.

Silence. No, a heartbeat, fluttering and florid. Like a butterfly trapped in a jar, wings singed by searing sun. When had she become like sand, dissolved by wind and whisked away by the rapids of a rushing river? She looked for an anchor, letting the pale wispiness of the world wash over her like shimmering sunlit water.

She calmed, and the room came back into focus. Hemlock was there, kneeling in front of her on the ground. But it wasn't really him—it was only a pale shadow, an outline of a mirage that shimmered and pulsed like a heart with a beat of its own. Hazel reached out to him, but her hand passed through where his face should be. Her movement displaced the shadows, only to congeal back into place once she withdrew.

The rest of the room looked much like Hemlock—bleached and bland, a shimmering, tenuous echo of what had once been there. Hazel got to her feet, and the room shifted, moving along with her, though for some reason Hemlock's shadow remained fixed in place.

She walked to the table, but the stone floor became like sifting sand, pushing her back even as she struggled to move forward. Yet still she managed, coming to a pale and wan table that seemed to disassemble itself and then reform every time Hazel blinked.

The table looked much the same as far as Hazel could recall through the haze of her mind. There were the clean white bowl and neatly folded cloth, the herb box, wine bottle, and mortar and pestle. There was the goblet with its dregs of wine and silt of bone dust drying along the silver edges of the cup. The bone dust gleamed like crystalline snow.

Hazel looked up and out beyond the room, beyond the shifting hollow mist, and looked for the same sparkling gleam out in the world. And there, beyond the shivering, shadowed stones that served as a wall, a glimmering that matched the cup winked in the distance.

She held her breath, wondering if it were true or if she had only imagined it. How could she be sure of anything here, a world that refused to solidify into color and bone, stone and blood?

Hazel passed through the table, sending it to ripple in her wake as if she walked through water. She made her way to what served as a wall, and then she walked through that as well. The city of Sarnum rippled into shape before her, as if a mist had dissipated in the morning sun. It was neither night nor day; everything was equally wan and devoid of color. She fixed her gaze on the glimmering point of light winking through the haze like a candle in a distant window. But where was it? She had no bearings. There was no sun to tell her east from west, no stars to tell her where the north lay. It was all just haze and fog, shimmering heat and rippling water for air. She tried to focus through it all, the same way she had when the room had coalesced from the mist. Again she let it wash over her until in the distance... Was that a hill? There was something on it—a house or maybe a mill. Hazel narrowed her eyes, trying to see, but then her stomach cramped, and she grabbed her abdomen as she doubled over.

"Hazel?"

The voice boomed in her mind, making her wince even as bile rose in her throat. She swallowed and inhaled a deep breath, relaxing with momentary relief before she doubled over with another sickening cramp. This time she retched, the mist cleared, and she was back on the floor in the cellar of the abandoned house.

The solidity and vivid color of her surroundings were jarring. Hazel could only blink before she doubled over again, vomiting onto the floor.

Hemlock grabbed the ceramic bowl off the table and set it on the floor in front her. Hazel emptied her stomach into it—purple-brown sludge peppered with bits of desiccated leaves. She closed her eyes, not wanting to look, fearful of getting sick all over again.

A minute or so passed, then Hazel spit acid from her mouth and pushed the bowl away.

Hemlock handed her a cloth—the neatly folded linen square from the table. Hazel managed a feeble smile. She had been right about the puzzle of items—though it was difficult feeling particularly pleased while her nose and throat stung.

"Are you all right?" Hemlock said.

Hazel wiped at her mouth with the cloth. "Yes."

Hemlock, crouching on his haunches, moved his legs out from under him and sat on the floor. He let out a heavy breath and ran his hands over his face. "What was that, Hazel? What were you thinking?"

"I was thinking I was trying to find my father."

"By performing necromantic magic? Do you understand what you've done?"

Hazel stiffened her back. "I'm not a fool, Hemlock. I know what I've done."

He stared at her, his brow furrowed. "Then how can you sit there and pretend that it's all right?"

Hazel tightened her jaw. "I'm not pretending anything. I did what I needed to do!"

"Do you hear yourself? Do you even recognize yourself? Because from where I'm sitting, I'm not sure I recognize you at all. Maybe you're right—maybe you are just like your father. Maybe I'm the fool for not listening."

Hazel swallowed and looked away, feeling as if he had wrenched a knife in her gut—wishing his words hadn't held so much truth.

He sighed. "I'm sorry. That was unworthy of me."

"No, you're completely right." She made herself look at him. "I am undoubtedly just like him. How else can you explain what I've done? I know how to work necromancy, Hemlock. I wish I didn't, but I do. I doubt it's a coincidence."

They fell into silence.

"What do we do now?" Hemlock said.

"I... saw a light after I drank the potion. I think that might be where he is."

He frowned. "A light? What kind of light?"

She squinted her eyes. "It's hard to explain. But the bone I ground up, after I drank the potion, it's like it glowed. I saw the same light off in the distance. I think it might be him."

Hemlock stared at her, and Hazel forced herself to hold his gaze. Then he asked, "How far was it?"

"I don't know. The world looked different. I couldn't say how far. I don't even know *where* it was. A building, perhaps a mill, up on a hill."

He nodded. "Well, then. I suppose that means we'll have to find the hill."

"You don't have to come along."

"What?"

"I know you're not comfortable with this. *I'm* not comfortable with it. But I need to see this through. You don't." She took a breath. "I wouldn't blame you if you wanted to leave."

Hemlock shook his head and took her hand. "There's no turning back now, Hazel. For either of us."

He helped Hazel to her feet, and they left the house and returned to the inn.

But when they got there, they found their shared rooms empty and their siblings gone.

In the Midst of Midnight

"Where could they have gone?" Hazel said. She had to remind herself to breathe. Nothing had happened. There was no need to worry.

Hemlock shook his head. "I don't know. Hawthorn is more familiar with this town than I am. If he and Holly are together, they could be anywhere."

"That's not reassuring."

He smiled. "I'm sure they're fine."

"We need to go look for them."

"They're probably out looking for *us*. It might be best to wait here. They could come back at any moment."

Hazel stared at the empty bed, still rumpled from where Holly had lain. "You can wait here then. I'll go out." She turned and headed down the hallway.

Hemlock hurried after her. "You don't know what's out there, Hazel. You shouldn't go out alone."

"I'm going. Whether or not I'll be alone is up to you, isn't it?" She hurried to the stairs and was about halfway down when she heard Hemlock's footfalls following behind her.

Neither one said anything as they crossed the common room before stepping outside into the dark night.

∾

"It's dark," Holly said, her breath pluming in the sterile blue-green light of a lamppost. "And cold. Why is it so cold here? It's supposed to be summer."

"It's cold and dark because we're out in the middle of the night," Hawthorn said. "Perhaps you should have thought about that before you dragged us out here."

"Old Uncle Orn always liked to go walking at night," Tum said as he kept up alongside them. "Usually without pants. He wasn't too fond of the cold either."

Hawthorn wrinkled his nose. To Holly, he said, "Did you have to bring the gnome?"

"We're not leaving anyone behind. If Hazel and Hemlock hadn't run off without us, then we wouldn't be in this situation at all."

"Speaking of which, how are we supposed to find them exactly? Or is blindly wandering the streets the extent of your grand scheme?"

"I don't know," Holly said. "Hazel's got a gross bloody bone and a mind to do necromancy. Where would someone go for that?"

"For necromancy or bloodied bones?"

"Both."

Hawthorn thought a moment. "A butcher shop or a graveyard?"

"Really?"

He shrugged. "Plenty of bones and blood at butcher shops. And graveyards seem like the natural lurking ground for those inclined towards necromancy."

Holly wrung her hands. "Is there a graveyard here?"

"Of course. A rather extensive one, from what I've heard."

She took a deep breath. "All right. Let's go there then."

∾

"Do you have any idea where she would go?" Hemlock said as he walked next to Hazel. He kept his voice low, eyeing a shadowed form further up the street.

Hazel stopped walking. When she felt certain the shadow wasn't coming towards them, she sighed and said, "I don't know. They could be wandering blindly. Holly wasn't ever one for planning."

"Does she know about the bone?"

A shiver crawled up Hazel's neck. "Yes."

"So she knows then, what you had intended to do?"

Hazel shook her head. "I never told her my plan. I didn't even *have* a plan. I told her not to worry about it. But..."

"She knows. So where would she think you'd gone to do necromancy?"

"I'm such an idiot. I shouldn't have ever shown it to her."

"She had a right to know. You can't protect her forever, Hazel."

Hazel bit her lip. "I know. But this... I would happily let her charge into whatever danger she likes if she didn't have to be involved in necromancy."

Hemlock put a hand on her shoulder, and Hazel looked up at him.

"So, you're Holly," he said. "You wake up in the night and find your wonderfully willful and enchantingly clever older sister gone to do necromancy. You march down the hallway, drag a pretentious old warlock out of bed—under the threat of ruining his finest silk vest—and head out to find said sister. Where would you go?"

Hazel suppressed a giggle. "How do you know it happened like that?"

"I honestly can't see it happening any other way."

The giggle escaped her, and she clapped a hand over her mouth. She glanced at the shadowed figure ahead, but it seemed transfixed with one of the shop windows. "I don't know," Hazel whispered. "She couldn't know about the house. *I* didn't know about it, and I don't think Holly has the same... inclination as me."

"So not knowing anything about necromancy, where would you go to find it?"

Hazel rubbed her forehead. "Wherever there's death, I suppose." She looked at Hemlock. "A graveyard. Where do we find one?"

He shook his head. "I have no idea. And there isn't exactly anyone around whom we can ask for directions."

Hazel fixed her gaze on the shadowed form down the street. "I bet that thing knows."

"We don't even know if it's capable of thought."

"There's only one way to find out." She started towards it.

"Hazel!" Hemlock hissed.

But Hazel kept on. Her quickening steps pulled the thing's attention, and the shadows around it shifted as it turned towards her.

Hazel faltered a step, but she clenched her hands and continued on. The shadow lumbered towards her. It moved into the light of a lamppost, but the shadows remained, clinging around its form like black-stained gauze. Beneath the shadows, Hazel caught glimpses of pale, lacerated skin, the cuts looking red and angry.

It lunged towards her, and Hazel darted out of the way. Before it could turn around, Hazel flicked her hand and spoke a single word. "Secant."

The shadows clinging to the thing's skin gathered and pulled away. They formed into the shape of a man, leaving exposed the scarred husk of a body that slumped its shoulders and lowered its head.

Hazel stood in front of it. It had yellow, watery eyes that watched her as she moved. Its shadow stood off to the side. It would walk away a short distance, shiver as if strained, then move back to stand next to its fleshy counterpart.

This thing had once been a man. Hazel could see that now it no longer had shadows to clothe it. But now it was nothing more than a collection of flesh, cut and scarred, made to ambulate through town for reasons Hazel couldn't figure. It stared at her with its yellowy eyes, looking on the verge of weeping pus-filled tears, and Hazel felt sorry for it.

Hemlock stood next to her. His brow was furrowed and his hands clenched, his gaze shifting between Hazel and the flesh golem.

Hazel met the golem's gaze. "The graveyard. Can you take us there?"

The golem remained still, but its shadow nodded. It headed down the street while its scarred collection of flesh lumbered behind it.

Holly, Hawthorn, and Tum zigzagged their way through town. Darkened forms shambled along the shadowed streets, following flickering lights that flitted around like springtime swallows. Each time a shambler crossed their path, the group had to alter their course. So their progress—and the night—dragged on. It felt like dawn should be approaching, but the sky remained dark and devoid of stars save for a scattering of the brightest ones that managed to wink through the alchemical haze of light emanating from the lampposts lining the streets.

"Are we almost there?" Holly whispered as they crouched behind a collection of leafy, thorny shrubs. A shambler a stone's throw ahead of them made wet, rasping sounds as it breathed through its mouth. Holly cringed and resisted the urge to clench her eyes shut. She needed to know if the thing decided to come towards them.

When it finally moved away, Hawthorn whispered, "It shouldn't be much further." He rose and started walking.

Holly reached into the shrubs and poked at Tum. "Come on, we're going."

Tum stuck his head out through the leaves. "Isn't right, being out with the shamblers. If you and Miss Hazel had any sense, we'd all be drinking beer in the cellar."

Holly didn't much care for beer, but she had to admit it sounded more appealing than being on these creepy darkened streets.

They followed Hawthorn and soon came to a tall stone wall adorned with snarling gargoyles perched along the top. They followed the wall until they came to a massive wrought iron gate, over which arched the words *In Morte Divinitas.*

"What does that mean?" Holly said.

"In death there is divinity."

She screwed up her face. "What kind of saying is that?"

Hawthorn shrugged. "I make no claims over the quality of such slogans. But that is what it says."

Holly narrowed her eyes at him. "You know an awful lot about this town, with all its creepy streets and creepy sayings in weird creepy words. More than you ought to from stories alone."

He pushed the gate open—it didn't so much as squeak—and gave her a flat look. "Well, we're here. Shall we go in? Or have you reconsidered?"

Holly pressed her lips together. "We'd better go in and look around." She passed through the gate, followed by Tum. Hawthorn quietly closed the gate after them.

They walked along a stone path that snaked over grassy hills, past shadowed tombstones and mausoleums with lanterns of flickering blue flames hanging near thick, iron-studded wooden doors. Statues dotted the hills and lined the walkway, like sentinels watching their passing with lifeless eyes. One statue was of a woman in a full dress looking off towards the horizon, another of a baby lying in an intricately carved crib guarded by a sleek dog. Winged and snarling grotesques crouched in thatches of wild grass, then a pensive man, perusing a book.

"Are these all people who died here?" Holly asked while eyeing the statues.

"Probably," Hawthorn said. "Except for the grotesques, of course. I imagine those are more for protection than remembrance."

"Protection from what?"

He shrugged. "Whatever these people might fear after death."

They came to an empty, open grave. A shovel rested against the lichen-encrusted tombstone.

"Or maybe they fear whatever they dig up," Holly said.

Tum tottered over to the grave and hopped down into it.

"Tum!" Holly hissed, trying to keep her voice low. "Get out of there!" She couldn't even see him down in the shadows of the hole.

"It'll be all right," came Tum's voice from the darkness. "Closest thing I'll find to a cellar here, and a cellar is where old Tum belongs."

"You're supposed to help us find Hazel."

"I'll keep an eye out. Stand guard, see? Makes more sense to have eyes in many places than all in one place."

"Well, I... I suppose. Will you be all right here alone? What if whoever dug this grave comes back? Or a shambler?"

"No shambler'll see me down here in the dark. And anyone else, well, old Tum will give him what-for, that's what." He flung some dirt up into the air.

Holly backed away from the flying soil. She didn't want to leave him, but she didn't want to stay there either. A bent shadow stood silhouetted against a distant lamp near one of the mausoleums—much too near for Holly's comfort.

"Well, you come find us if there's any trouble, okay?"

"Right!" Tum shouted as he flung more dirt.

Holly hurried on. She glanced behind her, but the shadowy thing didn't look to be following. Hawthorn strolled at her side, seemingly at ease, which did nothing to settle Holly's nerves. It didn't feel right, him being so calm.

They passed under towering great oaks that cast mottled, moonlit shadows along the path. Eventually they came to a great stone building that looked like a mausoleum only much bigger. Massive wooden double doors adorned with intricate iron scrollwork formed an entryway, flanked by a pair of smooth stone columns around which twines of ivy grew.

"The path ends here," Holly said. "I... I guess we should go in then."

Hawthorn grabbed hold of a great iron ring attached to a door and pulled. The door creaked and groaned on its massive hinges, and Holly cringed. She glanced around the graveyard and at the shadows, hoping beyond all reason that they weren't overheard. She hurried inside, feeling strangely grateful when Hawthorn pulled the great door shut.

Silence settled around them as they stood in a vast chamber with a high ceiling that disappeared into darkness. In the center of the chamber stood an alabaster statue of a woman shrouded in a long veil. A circle of lit candles surrounded her on the floor, washing her in a warm, gentle light. Her hands were outstretched, and in one she held some dried flowers, in the other a few sprigs of wheat. The veil, despite being carved from stone, looked sheer, showing the outline of her closed eyes, her shapely nose, and delicate mouth.

"She's beautiful," Holly whispered. How could something so beautiful exist in a place like this?

"Mother of the Lost," Hawthorn said. "She is said to guide wayward souls to rest and offers protection to those buried without proper rites. She is often revered by the lonely—those without any family to speak of, who have no one to care for and, in turn, have no one to care for them."

"How sad."

"I suppose. Not everyone is blessed with a loving family. Such people normally have no one to turn to. At least they can turn to her."

Holly studied him as he looked up at the statue. "How do you know so much about this place, Hawthorn?"

He said nothing for a while. Then, still looking at the statue, he said, "I lied earlier. I've been here before. Several times."

"Why would you lie about that?"

"Father used to bring me here, to Sarnum, though to this graveyard as well. He thought it an important part of my worldly education to learn of this place. Of the customs here, both good and bad."

"But why lie about it?"

"Father always favored me, in his way. I was the eldest, heir to the estate. He... never showed much interest in Hemlock, and Hemlock envied our relationship." He shook his head. "Perhaps I shouldn't have lied, but I feared Hemlock wouldn't understand."

Holly stared at him. "You're looking out for him. You care about his feelings."

Hawthorn frowned and glanced at her out of the corner of his eye. "You needn't sound so surprised. I am his brother. Of course I care."

She smiled. "It's nice of you."

He turned towards her, and before she knew what she was doing—before Hawthorn knew what she was doing—Holly kissed him.

"I-I...," Hawthorn stammered, his cheeks turning red.

"Sorry!" Holly said as her own face turned hot. "I don't know what I was thinking."

"N-no, it's fine. Really. You just took me by surprise is all."

"Really?"

"Y-yes. Of course."

Holly nodded, trying to feel reassured, but it eluded her. She never felt so mortified in her entire life. Well, except for that time at tea she had made an utter fool of herself in front of Hawthorn.

So it was almost a relief when the great double doors swung open.

HAZEL AND Hemlock walked into the vast mausoleum to find Holly and Hawthorn standing before a statue, both looking flustered and uncomfortable. Holly wouldn't meet Hazel's eyes.

"Is everything all right here?" Hazel asked. "I've been worried sick about you, Holly."

Holly, looking away, nodded. "Sorry. I..." She trailed off without finishing the thought.

Hawthorn, meanwhile, took a great interest in studying the statue. Hazel gave Hemlock a questioning look, but he just shrugged.

She turned back to Holly. "Never mind about it. Let's get back to the inn. It's not safe being out here like this."

As if on cue, the creature Hazel had subdued shambled inside. Its severed shadow shivered and lost cohesion and wrapped itself once again around the scarred flesh of the golem's body like a shroud.

"What is that?" Holly said, sounding panicked. She took a step back.

Hazel spoke the word that had earlier brought the golem under her control. Nothing happened.

A rhythmical sound erupted from the fleshy husk, slow and guttural, almost like a laugh. Then the sound altered, taking on a cadence like language, but it wasn't any language Hazel knew.

From within the shadows of the mausoleum came a screeching of grating metal. A whispering stirred the air, causing an icy breeze to snake across Hazel's skin. The candle flames surrounding the statue flickered in agitation. Some went out.

Holly grabbed a candle and whispered a spell. The candle flames around the statue grew brighter, revealing numerous glinting eyes peering out from the darkness.

Hazel searched her mind for that dark part of herself that told her things she didn't want to know, but it remained quiet. Her mind went blank, and all she could do was stand and watch as Hemlock and Hawthorn stepped forward to conjure shimmering, prismatic creatures with long crystalline limbs and wings of spun glass. The conjurations soaked up the feeble candlelight and cast it back out to the shadows, banishing the darkness and exposing the creatures that lurked within it.

They were horrible. Grey twisted things with gaping wet mouths and black, shiny eyes like chips of polished coal. Lines of ribs protruded through dusky, desiccated skin stretched taut across their bodies like old book bindings. And the smell—growing stronger as they shuffled forward—was sharp and acrid like rotting teeth and stomach bile. They squinted their glossy black eyes while peering up at the prismatic creatures but otherwise advanced unhindered.

Hawthorn backed away. "Perhaps we should leave."

Holly started for the door but stopped when she found it blocked by the flesh golem.

Hazel cringed. What had she been thinking? Dabbling in forbidden magic she didn't understand, putting them all in danger, and justifying it by saying it needed to be done. Hemlock was right—she didn't recognize herself. Here she was not only practicing but *depending* on necromancy, and when it failed her, she turned helpless? That wasn't who she was.

That wasn't who she wanted to be. She was a Weaving witch, been one most of her life. How could she forget that?

The shadowed golem shuffled towards Holly, and she cried out and staggered back. She pulled flames from the candles and threw the fire at the creature. But the shadows surrounding it extinguished the flames.

One prismatic creature swooped at the golem and poked at its eyes. From its own shadows, the golem summoned an imp with blackened wings like curling smoke. The imp leaped at the shimmering form, dug its claws into it, and both creatures disappeared.

Enough. Hazel worked a spell of Transformation, and the statue of the veiled woman groaned as the stone turned pliable and began to move. She stepped over the candles, knocking some over with the solid veil that trailed behind her, and moved towards the horde of grey, husk-like creatures that balked at her approach.

Turning aggressive, the prismatic summons darted at the husks, poking at them and harrying them before flying away. Those that weren't harassed seemed transfixed by the massive statue that moved towards them. The statue dropped the bundle of dried flowers she had been holding and extended her hand, and several of the creatures scurried away.

"We can't leave with that thing guarding the door," Hemlock said, nodding towards the golem.

A brown field owl flew into the chamber and circled over Holly's head before flying around the room, swooping down with clawed talons at the grey creatures and the golem's shadowed head only to fly away again before any of them could react.

Hazel conjured for the statue a gleaming silver sword with beveled edges. The statue leveled her sword at the golem and advanced on it. The golem, seeing the threat, split its shadows into two darkened figures shaped like men. Hawthorn created an illusion of himself—smart jacket and all—wielding a long silver sword that it used to swipe at one of the shadows and sent it leaping back.

The grey creatures began to scurry forward. Hemlock summoned a dragon the size of a horse with white, pristine scales that shimmered with color depending how the light hit it. The dragon opened its maw and exhaled a crystalline breath. Most of the grey creatures scurried out of the way, but the breath caught one and its murky skin paled like frost on a windowpane before it shattered into dust.

Dumbfounded, the creatures stared at the remains of their fallen companion. But then their shiny black eyes hardened, the gaping holes of their mouths widened, and in collective body they hissed, filling the chamber with their acrid stench that made Hazel gag. The husks swarmed at the dragon, stepping over the ones that got caught in the dragon's breath and collapsed on the floor in frozen, ashen heaps.

Hazel made the statue quicken its step. It lifted the sword and brought the blade down on the golem's shoulder and severed its arm. The shadows battling Hawthorn's double retreated and shrouded themselves around the golem's fleshy husk once more.

But before the golem could open its wretched mouth and speak more of its foul words, Hazel infused the sword with gleaming light, and the statue ran the sword through the golem's head. The shadows dissipated, and the golem thudded to the ground and remained motionless.

With the dragon overpowered, the grey creatures scrambled towards them. Hazel and the others ran out the door—the owl flying after them—and slammed it shut. Hazel made the lock catch and fuse together.

Tum strolled over, covered head to toe in black dirt. "Hey, Miss Holly. Told you I'd find Miss Hazel. Easy." He made a futile effort to brush some of the dirt off his hands, then pointed at the mausoleum. "What's in there? Any good spoiling?"

"No," Holly said as she took him by the arm and marched towards the cemetery gate. "Everything's already been spoiled."

Archived Amity

Nobody spoke as they walked back to the inn. When they reached the Backwards Buck, Holly threw the door open and ran upstairs. Hazel and the others followed her. Except for Tum. He grumbled something about beer and returned to the inn's cellar.

Hazel walked down the lamplit hallway and to the room she shared with Holly. Hemlock and Hawthorn followed close behind her, right up to her door. She raised her eyebrows at them, but Hawthorn just waved impatiently at her, so she opened the door and they all stepped inside.

Holly sat on the bed, burying her face in her arms while hugging her knees. Hazel sat down next to her as Hawthorn sat in the chair by the desk, leaving Hemlock to sit on Hazel's luggage.

Hazel stared at her hands, waiting for the accusations to be flung at her, but they never came.

"It was my fault," she said, no longer wanting to wait for the inevitable discussion. "Everything that happened tonight..." She took a deep breath. "My fault."

"I'm sorry," Hawthorn said. "Do you mean to tell me you summoned those ghastly things and set them upon us?"

"No, but I brought that golem to the mausoleum and then lost control of him. I shouldn't have done that. None of this would have happened if I hadn't done that."

Holly peered at her. "What's happening to you, Hazel?"

Hazel shook her head, blinking away stinging tears. "I don't know," she whispered.

"Is it all really because of Father?"

"I don't know. I can't keep blaming him, certainly not for the poor judgment I've shown tonight. I'm not even sure why I'm here anymore."

"To save Mother."

"At what cost?"

Holly fell silent a long while. "Where did you go tonight?"

Hazel told her about everything—the potion she made and then drank and the otherworldly vision that it caused.

"But potion-making is a Hearth skill," Holly said. "What business has necromancy in making potions?"

"I don't know. I really can't explain any of it."

Holly pressed her lips into a fine line. "And so you think that's where he is? That Father is at this house on a hill or whatever it was you saw?"

"I honestly can't say for sure, but... I think so."

Holly glowered at Hemlock. "And you let her do this?"

Hemlock met her gaze with a steady one of his own. "Would you rather she do such things alone, without anyone there to look out for her?"

"Don't talk about me as if I'm not here," Hazel snapped. "My mind is my own, Holly. You know that. You have a problem with what I did, you talk to *me* about it, not Hemlock."

Holly shifted her glower to Hazel. "And what if it had been me? What if you found out I snuck out in the night to do necromancy? What would you do? How do you expect *me* to react?"

Hazel took a breath. "I'm sorry for putting you in this position. I never wanted that. It's... why I left without telling you."

Holly opened her mouth, and Hazel interrupted her by adding, "Which I know I shouldn't have done."

Holly snapped her mouth shut and frowned some more as she glanced between Hazel and Hemlock, then let out a heavy breath and closed her eyes. "Well, now what?"

"I suppose we try to find the hill I saw, though I really don't know where to start. It looked like it might be outside of town, but I can't be sure."

"Do you know, Hawthorn?" Holly asked.

Hawthorn, cleaning his fingernails, stopped when he noticed everyone looking at him. "What's that?"

"The house and hill Hazel saw from drinking the potion. Do you know where it is?"

He waved a hand. "There are a lot of houses and hills around here. I don't know how I'm supposed to figure out which one from a second-hand account of a hallucinatory dream."

Holly glowered at him and firmly said, "Try."

Hawthorn sighed and squinted up at the ceiling.

Holly narrowed her eyes and looked the ceiling too. "What're you looking at?"

"I'm *thinking*."

"The ceiling help you with that?"

Hawthorn ignored her. To Hazel, he said, "Were there trees on the hill? Landmarks?"

"I don't know. Maybe?"

He gave her a flat look.

"I don't remember. There might have been a tree or two. But that's all, I think. It was the building that caught my attention."

"That may be a house or a mill, according to your account."

"Yes."

Frowning, Hawthorn rubbed his chin. Then he brightened and began smoothing out his clothes.

"Well?" Hazel said.

"I have no idea."

"Helpful."

"It's quite out of my hands. I am not a man of miracles, as shocking as that realization may be."

"Yes," Hemlock said. "We're all dumbstruck by the news."

"So that's it then?" Holly said. "We just give up? After everything?"

"Nobody's giving up," Hazel said. To Hawthorn she asked, "So who would know something like this? There's bound to be some elderly person who's been around as long as dust that would know every facet and detail about this town."

"You could always try the city archives," he said.

"The archives?"

"Yes, archives. You know, old papers, books, people. They'll probably have something there that can help."

Hazel narrowed her eyes. "Why didn't you say that in the first place?"

Hawthorn shrugged and resumed cleaning his nails. "You didn't ask."

They spent what remained of the night in Hazel and Holly's cramped little room. Hawthorn wedged himself between the sisters on the bed and promptly fell asleep. Holly followed shortly after. Hazel, finding herself in closer proximity to Hawthorn than she ever would have liked, relocated to the floor. Hemlock sat next to her, and so she spent the night resting her head against his shoulder as she drifted in and out of fitful slumber.

The next day, it was nearly afternoon when they left the inn, got in the carriage, and headed towards the archives.

The sky was overcast and drizzled a fine mist of rain. The carriage wound along the streets, coming at length to a great stone building surrounded by an almost equally great stone wall.

"This is it," Hawthorn said as he hopped out of the carriage.

The others followed. Hazel craned her neck as she stared at the building. The thing was monstrous, made with massive blocks of stone occasionally interrupted by a window. It looked more like a fortress than a public building of information.

"Well, that looks formidable," Hazel said.

"Knowledge is power," Hawthorn said. "It must be protected from uppity rabble-rousers looking to drag us all into an age of ignorance."

"What must be protected? The knowledge or the power?"

He shrugged. "There cannot be one without the other."

"We do just fine in the Grove without an archive."

He arched an eyebrow at her. "Yes, but we have our libraries, some of which are restricted depending on the magic one practices. It is the same idea."

Hazel frowned. She didn't like it when Hawthorn was right.

They crossed an expansive stone courtyard before coming to stairs that led to a wooden pair of great double doors. Pulling one of the heavy doors open, they walked into a darkened entry hall. A feeble stream of light filtered through a window high up on the wall, illuminating a patch of the woven, basket-like design of the parquet floor. Most of the light came from lamps that hung on the walls. The lampshades were made of frosted glass. They pulsed with a gentle red-orange light, waxing and waning like slow, steady breath. It made the room feel alive. It made Hazel uncomfortable.

Hawthorn led them into a vast room filled with desks and tables, each one illuminated with what looked like an oil lamp exuding the same unsettling living light as those in the entry hall. A row of shelves took up one part of the room, bearing massive tomes that looked nearly identical. A man perused the shelves while a few others sat scattered among the tables, leafing through papers and books.

Nearby, a man sat perched on a stool at a podium, peering over half-moon spectacles that rested upon his hawk-like nose. A lamp on the podium illuminated his face irregularly, shifting from shadows to light to shadows again as the warm light pulsed and faded.

Hawthorn strode up to him. "We need access to the city planning documents."

The man shifted his gaze between them before finally picking up a pen and poising it over a ledger. "Name?"

"Warlocks Hawthorn and Hemlock, and witches Hazel and Holly. From the Grove, but we're currently staying at the Backwards Buck."

The man scribbled the information down. "Follow me." He hopped off the stool and headed across the room to a door near the shelves. He led them down a narrow hallway, then into a smaller room with only a couple of tables and more shelves along the walls. He pulled a monstrous book from one of the shelves and set it on the table with a resounding *thud.*

"This is the directory," he said. "It will list the different documents and where you can find them on the shelves." He narrowed his eyes as he looked Hazel and Holly up and down. "And no silliness. I've documented your use here, so if anything is amiss when you leave, we'll know. You *don't* want to have a run-in with one of our collectors." He turned on a heel and strode out of the room.

"Charming man," Hazel muttered.

"Why'd he think we're the silly ones?" Holly said. "Is there something on my face?" She prodded her cheeks.

"I think he's used to seeing withered old men here most of the time," Hawthorn said. "Young ladies undoubtedly ruffle his limited world view."

"Maybe we should come here more often then," Holly said.

"Or not," Hazel said.

Hemlock riffled through the directory. He ran a finger along the lines as he scanned the pages.

"Well?" Hazel said. "Any mills or houses built on hills?"

Hemlock shook his head. "I don't know. These listings aren't terribly clear. They're arranged by year, then by district, then owner, *then* by types of buildings constructed. Land specifics aren't mentioned here, so I expect we'll have to consult the individual planning documents to see whether or not a structure was built on a hill. Since we don't know what district we are looking for or when it was built, I don't know how we'll find it without pulling each document for a house or mill listed in this directory."

"That'll take ages," Hazel said.

"Exactly."

Hazel rubbed her eyes. There had to be a better way. "What about buildings outside of town?"

"Outside?"

"I'm not certain that what I saw was inside of town. Perhaps it would be easier to search outside as I'm certain there will be fewer buildings to account for."

Hemlock blinked at her a few times and then down at the ledger. He flipped towards the end of the book and scanned the pages. "I think this directory only lists buildings inside of town."

Holly sighed and flopped onto a chair. Hawthorn began perusing the shelves. Hazel went to the shelf that had housed the directory and examined the other books and ledgers. Most were labeled with enigmatic numbers and letters, probably in accordance to whatever was listed in the directory. She walked as she scanned the spines of books and labels of bundled-up papers for something that stood out. It wasn't until she reached the corner of the room that, down on the bottom shelf next to the wall, was an old vellum-bound book. It looked much older than any of the other tomes in the room. When she pulled it from the shelf, numerous emblems in wax and tin dangled on strips of leather protruding from the bottom of the book.

She took it to a table and opened it. The pages were handwritten in fading ink, the style overly elaborate and difficult to read. A reddish-brown wax emblem was affixed to the bottom of the first page with a leather tab.

Holly, who had been playing with Chester, leaned towards Hazel as she eyed the book. "What's it say?"

Hazel squinted and brought her nose closer to the page. "'Wicke and warren byway af...'" She tilted her head. "'...Randal's rue betwixt baine and barrough...'"

"What gibberish is that?" Holly asked.

"The Old Tongue," Hawthorn said. "An earlier dialect of our current language."

"It doesn't make any sense."

"Language, like all things, changes over time."

"'...Shall evermoore be hearthshippe, hearthwoorne, and hearthhallowed te ye fyne familyshippe af Austenwalde fromme this daye the Twelfthe af Desending Windren in the Twain-Hundredth and Eighty-Eighth Sycle.'" Hazel fell silent as she stared at the page. "I think it's a land deed. And almost seven hundred years old by the looks of it."

"Fascinating," Hawthorn said, "but I don't see how it helps us."

Hazel carefully turned the pages, looking for something that might be helpful, though she honestly didn't know what. Combing through a seven-hundred-year-old deed book was probably fruitless at best, but she couldn't bring herself to stop. The feel of the leathery, yellowed pages, the enigmatic, scrawling handwriting. It was like a piece of time sliced from the world and pressed into a book, existing only in this place of dust and forgotten documents.

She came to a page that had a twig attached to it instead of an emblem. The first part of the document had been faded from time, but the rest of it was fairly legible. "'...do here and bye avowe to relinquish the Northrend lands in to perpetuity, and that the Southron shall ne'er interfere, neither in governshippe, knowledgeshippe, nor in kinshippe, and that the Northrend lands of Forest and Grove shall here and by after be in accordance, and ne'er interfere with Southron governshippe, knowledgeshippe, nor kinshippe of the Flatlands, or the new and budding townshippe of Sarnum...'" Hazel trailed off as she continued to study the page. "It looks like some kind of concord between Sarnum and the surrounding lands and... the Grove." She looked up at Hemlock. "Have you ever heard of this?"

He shook his head. "No."

"Have you, Hawthorn?"

Hawthorn fidgeted with the cuff of his sleeve and shuffled his feet. "I may have heard something about it."

"Care to elaborate?"

Hemlock folded his arms. "Yes, brother. Please do elaborate."

Hawthorn glowered at them, then exhaled and looked resigned. "Very well, but not here. We skipped breakfast, and one shouldn't tell long, complicated stories on empty stomachs."

Soup and Secrets

They traveled across town to a cramped little district where the buildings were built too closely together, all bending with the weight of years pressing upon them. Hawthorn hopped out of the carriage, and the others followed him into a rickety-looking establishment that had a sagging roof and wooden walls blackened by pitch that gave off a slightly burned and pungent smell.

Inside, the burned smell was replaced with pleasing aromas of cooked meat, onions, and herbs. The walls were spared the pitch treatment from the outside, and the naked wooden walls were adorned only with pots of herbs and trailing vines that supplied a rather homely feel.

The room had a few tables scattered about, all of them filled with patrons holding on to steaming mugs or slurping soup from chipped clay bowls. Behind a counter stood a little old woman who was barely tall enough to peer over the top of it. Great copper kettles surrounded her, all containing simmering soup that fogged the windows behind her with their steam.

She squinted at them from behind a pair of thick glasses as they approached. Then her face split into a luminous smile. "Hawthorn, my boy! What brings you here?"

"Hello, Ada."

Ada came around the counter and put out her hands, and Hawthorn took hold of them.

"Little Hawthorn," she said, blinking up at him several times. "Unchanged from the last time I saw you. You still fooling around with those silly glamours?"

Hawthorn grinned. "You know me. I always like to look my best."

Ada tsked. "You always were a handsome boy. Probably more handsome now as a man. You shouldn't hide that." She blinked as she took in the others. "You must be Hemlock. You've the look of your father, make no mistake."

Hemlock shifted his feet. "You and Hawthorn know each other?"

"Oh, aye. Little whelp's been coming here with Lupinus for years." She turned back to Hawthorn and squinted at him. "When was the last time you were here? It's been a while."

"Before Father died."

Ada spit on the floor then smeared it with her foot. "Sad business, that. But the inevitable end for us all, I suppose. But enough of my rambling. I'm guessing you came here to eat and not reminisce with an old woman."

Hawthorn flashed her a bright smile. "You were always too clever for your own good."

Ada scoffed and slapped his arm. "And you were always too charming for your own good. That charm get you in trouble yet?"

Hawthorn grinned. "Not yet."

"Then you're luckier than a hog in a midden heap. I'll take you to the back." She turned and headed through a door that led them down a narrow hallway before herding them into a cramped but cozy room with a single round table. An oversized window nearly took up an entire wall, washing the snug room with light and turning it pleasantly warm.

They situated themselves around the table, and after a few minutes, Ada returned, carrying a great round tray filled with various bowls and mugs. She set them out on the table.

"I've brought you a bit of everything. You all look like you could use a good warm lunch. If you need anything else, I'll be out front, so you just let me know." She turned and left.

Holly was the first to grab a bowl. She sniffed it, then passed it to

Hazel before grabbing another. She passed on two more before finding one of the mugs to her satisfaction. She sipped from it as she glanced at the others.

Everyone remained silent. Hemlock ignored the soup Holly had set in front of him as he glowered at Hawthorn.

"Care to tell me what's going on, brother?" Hemlock said. "You've been here before. Why lie about that? Why wouldn't you tell me?"

Hawthorn sighed. "To avoid this very conversation. Father brought me here from time to time when I was younger. I never asked him to, but he did. So there it is."

"He was trying to spare your feelings," Holly said.

Hemlock glowered at her. "You knew? Does everyone know except me? Have you all had a good laugh playing me for a fool?"

"No, I—"

"Not everything is about you, Hemlock," Hawthorn said. "You've always been so sensitive about Father and me. Can you blame me for wanting to avoid all this nonsense?"

"Nonsense?" Hemlock said. "Is it nonsense to want to be included? To feel like I belong in a family? Because I never have, Hawthorn. I expected this sort of thing from Father, but it's worse that you're still doing it even though he's long been in the ground. You truly are his heir, in every conceivable way." He got up and left.

Silence fell around the table. Hawthorn stretched his neck and straightened the cuffs of his shirt. He fixed his gaze on Hazel. "Shall we get on with it then?"

Hazel thrust a finger at him. "You wait there." She got up and walked out to the main room, but Hemlock wasn't there. She went outside and found him sitting on a squat barrel underneath the drooping eave of a particularly ramshackle building further down the way. His head was lowered as he rested his weight against his knees, so he didn't see her as she approached.

"Are you all right?" she asked.

He looked up at her and then away again. He stared out towards the street a long while before saying, "Somehow it always manages to take me off guard how much of an ass Hawthorn can be. You'd think I'd be used to it by now."

"Does it matter so much that he lied about coming here?"

Hemlock shook his head. "It's not that. It's everything. It's lifelong years of being overlooked and of having to brace the brunt of Hawthorn's smug indifference. And I'm... tired. I don't know why I've continued to care. I've tried not to, but..."

"Everyone wants to feel like they matter."

Hemlock said nothing.

Hazel leaned against the building. The wooden slats were damp, and a chill began to seep through her clothes, but she remained anyway. "Mother always favored Holly. She tried to pretend like she didn't, but I could tell. Her face never lit up when she looked at me like it did with Holly. Even now, after her death..." She shook her head. "Some things never change."

"Your sister adores you though."

"I can only wonder why. I haven't always been a good sister to her. I've tried, but... well, sometimes it's hard to do the right thing, to say the right thing, especially when you don't know what the right thing is."

Hemlock screwed up his face as he looked at her. "Are you *defending* Hawthorn?"

Hazel scoffed. "I wouldn't go that far. But he is your brother. I'd be willing to wager that somewhere beyond that puffed-up exterior of his he cares about you. He probably just doesn't know any other way."

"You *are* defending him!"

Hazel winced. "Good grief, I am." She took a breath. "I'm not saying you don't have a right to be upset—you have every right. Had I been in your place, I doubt I'd have handled things nearly as well. But he is your brother. Your mother and father are both gone. He's all you have left."

"I thought I had you."

"I can never fill that part in your heart that belongs to your brother. Just as you can never fill that part of mine that belongs to Holly. You owe it to yourself to find a way to mend this rift."

"You don't think I've tried?"

"Try harder."

He shook his head. "No. I'm done trying. I'm just... I'm done."

Hazel tightened her jaw. These brothers, pigheaded the both of them. She marched back inside the soup shop and to the back room, grabbed Hawthorn by the sleeve of his brocade jacket, and hauled him out of the chair.

"Unhand me, you shrew," Hawthorn said. "You'll rumple the fabric or stain it with those sweaty paws of yours."

Hazel ignored him, tightening her grip on him as she dragged him outside.

Hemlock got up as they approached and glowered at Hazel. "I've nothing to say to him."

"That will be a refreshing change," Hawthorn said. "I've no need for a wife with your nagging at me all the while." He smoothed out his jacket once Hazel let go of him.

"Enough of this," Hazel said. "You two can't stand each other, is that it? Well, let's have it out then. Let's air out every grievance you have with each other."

To Hazel, Hemlock said, "I know what you're trying to do, but it won't work. Not with him. He's got his head so far up his ass that's it's a wonder he can walk."

"Ah, yes," Hawthorn said, "the ass quips. Your standard fallback of insults. One would think you'd find more material after all these years."

"Why? Your sorry ass proves to be most ample in that regard."

"My ass is many things, but ample is not one of them."

"You see?" Hemlock said to Hazel. "There's no talking to him. Everything's a joke. Everything is cheapened and made superficial. I'm sick of it, and I'm done." He turned to leave, but Hazel got in his way.

"Why have you come here, Hawthorn?" she said, looking at him past Hemlock. "Why do you care whether or not Holly and I find our father?"

Hemlock tried pushing past her, but she put a hand on his chest and gave him a sharp look that took some of the fire out of his eyes. He stiffened his back and stared past her, but he remained still.

"I didn't have much choice," Hawthorn said. "You've dragged me into this whole business of finding your father."

Hazel narrowed her eyes. "Don't give me that. You've helped us, and you didn't have to. Why?"

"Of course I had to. Can you imagine the mess you all would have made without me?"

Hemlock rounded on him. "Of course, without you we're all just a group of bumbling idiots. Nothing and no one has any worth until you decree that it has. How foolish of us for not realizing that."

Hawthorn fixed him in a cool gaze. "Indeed."

Hemlock's face twisted, and again he turned to leave, but Hazel grabbed him by the arm.

"Hazel, let go."

"Why do you care whether or not we make a mess of things?" Hazel said to Hawthorn as she tightened her grip on Hemlock's sleeve with everything she had. "What does it matter? Is it because of Holly? Do you want to be near her?"

Hawthorn's smug look dissolved into a dumbfounded stare. "I... What? N-no, not exactly."

"Then why?"

Hemlock pried her hand away, so she latched onto Hawthorn instead, grabbing him by the collar of his jacket and giving him a shake. "Answer me!"

"I wanted to be included!" Hawthorn shouted as he wrenched himself out of her grasp. "Mercy alive, woman, you can be a loud little thing."

Hemlock, who had been walking away, now turned back. "Oh no. You don't get to feel left out. Not about this. You don't get to make *everything* about you!"

Hawthorn glared at him. "You think you're the only one who's felt left out in life? You think you're the only one who's ever been lonely? You've always been so jealous of me and Father, but you didn't miss a whole lot. Do you think he was affectionate? That we shared some bond? The man barely spoke to me and only when it suited him. Even on our trips here together he kept me at arm's length. Combine that with a younger brother who despises you, and what did you expect me to do? Grovel at your feet so I can take more of your scorn? Have you look down on me with that air of superiority you're so fond of? You've always thought you're better than me. Smarter. You're an arrogant jackass, just like Father."

Hemlock's face blanched, as if he had taken a blow to the stomach. "I... I never despised you."

"Yet you've held no love for me either. You're not the only one who's felt excluded from family, Hemlock."

The two brothers stared at each other, and Hazel remained frozen as she held her breath.

Holly wandered out of the soup shop and walked towards them. "Why're you all out here? Are we leaving?"

No one said anything for a long while as Hemlock and Hawthorn continued to stare each other down. Then Hawthorn turned towards Holly and brightened. "I hope you haven't eaten all the soup. I'm starving." And then he walked back into the shop.

Holly glanced between Hazel and Hemlock, shrugged, and followed Hawthorn inside.

Hemlock, without looking at her, said, "What just happened?"

"I have no idea. But maybe we should follow them inside."

Hemlock continued to stare outwards before he slowly shifted his gaze to her. "What?"

She smiled and took his hand. "Come on." She led him back inside and to the little room. Ada threw them a quizzical look as they passed, but said nothing.

Hawthorn took a great interest in his bowl of soup when they entered. Holly sipped from her mug as she glanced between them. Hemlock stood there, staring at the table yet not seeming to actually see it. Hazel nudged him, and he started and sat down in a chair.

Holly raised her eyebrows at Hazel, but Hazel shook her head. Hemlock proceeded to stir his soup with a spoon, staring at the food as if divining its contents.

Hazel's soup was a thick chowder, both warm and filling. "So, Hawthorn," she said as she ate. "What was it you were going to tell us about the Grove? Some history with Sarnum?"

Hawthorn looked up at her, then glanced at Hemlock, but his brother kept his gaze on his soup. Hawthorn cleared his throat. "Yes. Well. Long ago—"

"How long?" said Holly.

"Um, about seven hundred years."

"Then you should say that."

"Holly...," Hazel said.

"What?"

Hawthorn raised a hand. "Seven hundred years ago, there was no Grove, and there was no Sarnum. There wasn't much of anything really, just small townships and communities, each paying homage to their own patron god or goddess."

"What kinds of gods and goddesses?" Holly asked.

"The same ones we pay homage to today. The Ladies of the Sky and

Sea, and the Lords of the Trees and Sun. Yet there was another that we in the Grove have long since forgotten: the Shapeless One, the Nameless Father, the Barren Mother, Keeper of the Stars, and Siphoner of Souls."

"A lord of necromancy?" Hazel said.

"Some say a lord, others say a lady. Some say that it's neither, a being that's transcended beyond the limitations of gender. But it's not necromancy that it guides, it's ether, the element of the Otherworld, that intangible substance that permeates us all and cannot be measured. That is the element that guides necromancy, just as air guides Wyr, and fire guides Hearth. And the Shapeless One is the deity of that element."

Hemlock came out of his stupor and stared at Hawthorn. "You've studied necromancy?"

"I've studied the theory of it but never the practice. Father forbade it, but he said it wouldn't do to be willfully obtuse. Necromancy exists in the world, and the best way to fight it is to understand it."

"Why didn't you ever tell me?"

"Would you have wanted to know? Would it have helped your estimation of me to know that I studied such things?"

Hemlock said nothing and looked back down at his soup.

"What does this have to do with the Grove and Sarnum?" Hazel asked.

"I'm sure I don't have to tell you that necromancy is a grim discipline. It focuses on manipulation of spirits and the dead, of the darkness that seeps into the cracks of the world. Yet for all its grimness, it's highly complex. It's similar to Wyr magic in that regard. And, as with the Wyr discipline, there are many who thought—that continue to think— that the discipline's complexity makes it superior. This was further compounded by the nature of the discipline's element. Ether: the fifth element. Quite literally *quintessential*. This brought about the mindset among necromancers that there are only two types of people in the world: those who practice necromancy, and those who are too inept to do so.

"As you can imagine, all this was not met well with non-necromancers. Regardless of the deity one pays homage to, respect still needs to be afforded to all. Equally. But necromancers continued to disparage and disregard the other deities of the other elements. An unmendable rift formed among the people until the only recourse was to split from the necromancers. Those who followed the ways of earth and air, water and fire, headed north and settled in what is now the Grove. The necromancers remained behind and built their walled city so that they could practice their dark arts in quiet seclusion.

"It was decided long ago in the Grove to forbid necromancy in all forms, fearful of repeating past events. Father always thought it foolish. That only through ignorance will the errors of the past be repeated, but he never spoke out about it. He simply taught me in secret instead."

"I can see why he and Pyrus were friends," Hazel said.

"Indeed. Though I never knew Pyrus's thoughts on the matter. He left the Conclave before I joined. But it does make sense."

"But how does this help us?" Holly said. "What does it mean that Hazel can work necromancy on her own?"

"It's difficult to say. There are avid followers that might say she's been chosen by the Shapeless One."

"What?" Holly said. "That can't be true."

Hawthorn shrugged. "I doubt it is. I've never been fond of such literal representations of the Divines at any rate. But there are some who believe it."

"But I had also worked Wyr magic before I learned about it," Hazel said. "Does that mean I've been chosen by the Lady of the Sky as well?"

"I have no explanation for your magical aptitude. But if I were to wager a guess, I'd say you're better at intuiting the nuances that each discipline has. There are similarities between them. Perhaps you are just better at making the leaps between the gaps than most people are."

Holly beamed at him. "You think she's good at magic. What happened to 'Wyr magic is for the menfolk' nonsense?"

Hawthorn shifted in his chair. "It was a position I had not been challenged on until your sister. Prior to that, I believe I was quite accurate in my assessment."

"You were wrong, you can admit it."

"I..."

"Go on"—Holly poked him—"admit it."

Hawthorn took a breath and fixed his gaze on the ceiling. "I suppose I was wrong," he mumbled.

Holly grinned like she had just snagged a pie from a windowsill. "There now. That wasn't so hard."

Hawthorn kept his gaze upwards as he shook his head.

"What happened to the scattered communities and townships?" Hazel asked. "Do they still exist?"

"I believe some do, yes. Though I've never been to any town outside the Grove other than Sarnum."

"Can we go to one?"

"I don't see why not. I'll ask Ada. She might know where the closest township lies."

Harvest Home

The following day, Hazel, Holly, Hemlock, and Hawthorn were back on the road in the carriage. Tum sat with the driver. He had made quite a fuss in leaving the comforts of the cellar of the Backwards Buck. But for all his howling, he didn't want to be left behind.

Ada had directed them to the nearest township she knew of, though she had warned them to be on guard. No one she knew ever traveled to the few scattered towns outside of Sarnum, and she didn't know what to expect. She had heard rumors, even though she refused to repeat what she had heard. She just warned them to be wary, and that was it.

They had left at dawn, and now midday approached, yet the carriage still rattled down the dusty road as the sun glinted at them from behind fluffy white clouds. The fields of pale, wispy grass had cleared, replaced by patches of farmland, orchards, and untamed hills of wild sweetgrass and great gnarled oaks. Some of the green leaves were beginning to turn, signaling the approach of autumn. It gave Hazel a twinge of sadness. She missed her garden and her bees. She wished she were home, harvesting and canning and preserving, but instead she was here. She needed to get this ugly business with her father sorted. Then she could go back.

They stopped alongside the road to stretch their legs and eat a simple meal of bread and marmalade. Grasshoppers and cicadas chirped and buzzed from the surrounding fields, and the light alternated from sunny to shadowed as dark, towering clouds threatening rain and thunder passed momentarily across the sun.

"How much further is it?" Holly asked.

"Ada said it was a long day's journey," Hawthorn said. "So I imagine we have a few hours yet to go."

"But what if there's nothing there? Then we'll just have to come back this way all over again."

Hazel said, "Do you have any other ideas?"

"Well, no."

"So it won't hurt visiting this town and seeing what it offers."

Holly frowned and pursed her lips, but she said nothing.

Hemlock remained silent. Ever since his argument with Hawthorn, he had seemed distracted. He hadn't bothered with reading as he usually did while riding in the carriage. Instead, he had just stared out the window, letting the scenery drift by without any discernible reaction. Hazel wished she could cheer him up, but she didn't know how, so she just left him alone.

The sky darkened again as foreboding clouds shrouded the sun. In the distance, a faint boom of thunder rolled in from beyond the hills. Holly put away the marmalade, and they clambered back in the carriage just as cold, heavy raindrops started to fall.

The downpour that followed chased them into the night. Rain dripped in through cracks along the doors and windows, and they all sat cramped together as they tried to avoid the moisture. The rain disallowed any lanterns to be lit, so they continued on at a crawling pace. By the time they reached something resembling a town, it was well into the night. Hazel was exhausted, cold, and, despite her best efforts, damp from the rain that had seeped through the carriage. At least she had been inside rather than out; she didn't want to imagine how Tum and the driver must feel.

She climbed out of the carriage and landed in ankle-deep mud. The town looked tiny, with only a couple of buildings that Hazel could make out in the gloom. She squelched her way through the mud to a house and knocked on the door. When no reply came, she tested the knob instead.

The door was unlocked, so she carefully eased it open and poked her head inside. But there was only darkness and a distant *tock-tocking* of a grandfather clock. The air smelled sweet and fragrant, like a summertime field.

"Hello?" Hazel said quietly. She couldn't bring herself to raise her voice any higher—it was the middle of the night. This was all beginning to feel like a great big mistake. What if this was a necromancer's house? She shouldn't be walking in uninvited and unannounced.

"What's happening?" Holly whispered.

"No one's home," Hazel said. "Or they're all asleep. I don't know what to do."

"We go inside, that's what." Tum said, his drenched clothes plastered to his little frame. He pushed his way past them and toddled into the darkened room, leaving a trail of water behind him.

"Yes, please," Holly said and followed him in, shadowed by Hawthorn.

"I guess we're going in," Hazel said.

"It looks like it," Hemlock said.

She tried to study him through the gloom, but it was too dark. "Are you all right?"

"I'm fine," he said and followed the others.

He didn't sound fine, but Hazel said nothing as she walked inside, gently closing the door behind her.

"Someone got a lamp or something?" Tum said, his voice carrying cringingly loud in the quiet night.

"For the love of the Lady," Hazel whispered, "keep your voice down."

A little flame bloomed in Holly's cupped hands, illuminating her face in a flickering orange-yellow glow that pushed back some of the darkness.

The room looked unremarkably ordinary. A long, shadowed form of a sofa stood before even darker shadows of an open hearth. A narrow table stood behind the sofa, upon which sat an unlit lamp. Everything else remained in shadows. Holly walked over to the lamp and lit it with her flame, and the darkness receded a little more.

Sheaves of wheat and straw littered one corner of the room. Rows of shelves lined the walls—nearly from floor to ceiling—upon which little shadowed figures sat. Hazel picked up the lamp from the table and walked over to a shelf. The shadowed figures were dolls made out of woven wheat and clothed in rough-spun dresses. Most were faceless, but some had been given expressions fashioned out of black beads for eyes and strips of red string for mouths.

Tum grabbed a doll then scampered down a darkened hallway.

"Tum!" Hazel hissed, but he had already gone.

Wooden floorboards creaked overhead, and Hazel froze. She thought about extinguishing the lamp but decided against it. If they were going to be discovered, better that they get discovered in the light rather than skulking in darkness.

From the hallway where Tum had disappeared came a wavering glow of candlelight. It dimly illuminated a set of stairs, and then a pair of slippered feet appeared with bony ankles peeking out from underneath a long nightshirt.

"Hello?" Hazel called, thinking it best to make their presence known. "The door was unlocked, so we let ourselves in."

A thin, birdlike man in his elder years descended the stairs and blinked at her from underneath an oversized nightcap that slouched over his wrinkled brow. "*We?* Are there more of you?"

Hazel waved the others into the hallway, and they all filed in. Hawthorn gave a slight bow, Hemlock a slight nod. Holly seemed transfixed with the man's knobby ankles.

"Goodness me," the man said, pushing back his cap and raising his candle as he blinked at them some more.

"I apologize for our intrusion," Hazel said, "but the weather turned dreadful, and we didn't know where else to go."

The man nodded. "Yes, of course. You had to come in. I heard the thunder booming out there and I thought to myself, 'Francis, you take your two coppers and chuck 'em out the window, 'cause you're not going to get any luckier than this.'"

Hazel glanced at the others, but they all looked as perplexed as she felt. "Um, yes. Exactly."

Francis beamed at her. "So what brings you out here? And in such a mysterious manner?"

"I'm afraid the mysterious manner was unintended, as the weather delayed us. But we've come for... Well, it's a long and complicated story. But the short version is we're looking for someone."

"And you think this someone came here?" He shook his head. "No one comes here. Why, I don't think we've had a visitor in our town since... well... the crop blight some twenty years ago. Sad business, that. But nothing a good tarring and feathering won't fix." He beamed at her again. "Am I right?"

Holly pulled her gaze from his ankles and stared at him in horror. "You tarred and feathered someone?"

Francis chuckled. "Goodness me, no. That was Emmond, our mayor." He put a hand to his chest. "*I* was merely in charge of collecting the feathers. Had to raid Martha's chicken coop for all it was worth, but we got a nice feast at the end of it, so all in all, a good day."

The grandfather clock *ticked* and *tocked* in the silence as everyone stared at him.

"You folks hungry?" Francis said.

Holly screwed up her face. "That depends. You got any creepy servants lurking around here?"

"Creepy servants? Lurking? Goodness me, I hope not. I've not paid any servants wages, so if they're lurking, I'd rather not find out what they're planning." He turned and headed further down the hallway, leaving Hazel and the others to trail after him.

He led them to a kitchen where an extinguished lamp sat on a table. He lit it with his candle, turned up the wick, then took it with him as he rummaged through the cupboards.

Strands of wheat littered the table and floor. From the ceiling hung a legion of dolls among bundles of herbs, braids of garlic, and nets of cured ham.

"You sure have a lot of dolls," Holly said as she stared at the ceiling.

"Of course I do. I'm a doll maker."

"Do you manage to sell any dolls out here?" Hazel asked. "Wouldn't you be more successful selling them in Sarnum?"

Francis pulled a stack of plates from a cupboard. "Selling? Goodness me, these dolls aren't for selling. They're for protection."

"Protection? From what?"

"Oh, the usual. Pox and blight. Stillborn babies and calves. You know how it is."

"You need protection from all that?" Holly asked.

"The town does, yes. Had to step up production after that blight twenty years ago, but we haven't had one since, so it must be working." He set the plates on the table along with a loaf of bread. He then grabbed a long knife and, climbing atop a chair, teetered on his tiptoes as he cut down a cured ham among a thatch of dolls and bundles of dried sage.

"What utter nonsense," Hawthorn said as he poked at a doll hanging over his head. "Wheat dolls don't do anything other than produce mold and invite in moths and vermin."

Francis dropped the ham onto the table with a resounding *thud* that made the plates clatter. "What did you say?" His knuckles gripping the knife whitened.

The air turned tense, and everyone shifted their gazes to Hawthorn. He opened his mouth, but instead, Hemlock said, "I think what my brother means to say is that we're not familiar with such forms of protection. It is undoubtedly most effective, and I'm sure we could learn much from our most gracious host." He turned to Hawthorn. "Isn't that right, Hawthorn?"

Hawthorn glanced between Hemlock and Francis and then inclined his head. "Of course that's what I meant. Apologies if I was unclear."

Francis beamed and hopped off the chair with a sprightliness that was unexpected for his advanced years. He waggled his knife at Hawthorn. "I knew I liked the look of you folks. Coming in with the turn of the weather like that, good omens, I say. Good omens. But you can never be too careful nowadays."

"I'm not disagreeing with you," Holly said, "but how is us coming in with the weather a good omen? The weather's horrible. Seems like it'd be a bad omen to me."

Francis pointed the knife at her before using it to cut away the netting encasing the ham. "I can see why you'd think that, and I know some folks that'd agree with you. But not me. Oh sure, foul weather can be frightful and unpleasant, but ultimately it's a good thing. The water nourishes the ground and keeps the crops thriving. And I don't care what that old crank Robert says, if your barn gets struck by lightning and catches fire and burns down, then I say it's 'cause you did something awful and had it coming. I don't got anything to fear from lightning, let me tell you."

"That's good," Hawthorn said as he sat down at the table, "because with all this straw and wheat in here, the house would likely go up faster than a harlot's skirt."

Francis cackled as he sliced the ham. "Don't I know it!" He put slices of ham and bread onto a plate and set it out for the others, along with a pot of mustard that he fetched from a cupboard.

"Do you have anything else?" Holly asked. "Something without meat?"

Francis looked crestfallen as he blinked at her.

Holly shifted in her seat, but then Francis brightened and hurried to a door on the other end of the room and disappeared behind it.

Hawthorn helped himself to the food. Hazel and Hemlock did the same. Holly nibbled on a piece of bread.

After a while, Francis returned with a jar of pickled eggs. He set the jar on the table and, leaning towards Holly, said, "I think I found one of those unsavory servants you mentioned. A short little man was lurking in the cellar while changing into a pair of pyjamas. He ran me out, clearly displeased over his lack of wages. I... I'm not sure what to do."

Hazel had to bite her lip to keep herself from snickering. But Holly just looked at Francis with the utmost severity and said, "Beer. Give him lots of beer."

Early Ambitions and Ablutions

Francis was a kind and generous host even if he did seem a little soft in the head. They ate sandwiches of ham and mustard (eggs and mustard for Holly) until they were all full and nearly falling asleep at the table.

"I've only got a single spare room," Francis said, "so you need to decide amongst yourselves who gets it. The rest of you can stay in the barn."

To Hazel, Hemlock said, "You and Holly take the bed. Hawthorn and I will sleep in the barn."

"Absolutely not," said Hawthorn. "I refuse to sleep out in the cold and filth with unwashed animals."

Hemlock stared at him. "You can't be serious."

"Do not test me, Hemlock. I've put up with much, but I can only be pushed so far. I don't care who I share that bed with, but I *will* be sleeping in it."

"It's fine," Hazel said. "Holly and I will sleep in the barn. Right, Holly?"

Holly clapped her hands. "I've always wanted to sleep outside with the horses!"

"See? It's fine."

Hemlock rubbed his eyes and nodded. "I'll join you out in the barn, if you don't mind. I'll send in the driver, and he can bunk up with Hawthorn." He turned to his brother. "If that's all right with you?"

Hawthorn drew himself up. "Why wouldn't it be? I'm nothing if not reasonable. Have him bring in the luggage while he's at it."

Francis showed him to his room upstairs while the others made their way outside to the barn. They had a lamp this time, so they were able to avoid the swathes of mud that the rain had caused. The downpour had lessened to an even pattering of drops that thrummed against the wooden planks of the barn. Despite the storm, the interior was surprisingly dry in most places. Holly walked around to pet the horses before making a little bed of hay for Chester. Then she gathered a great big pile of hay for herself and lay down in it. By the time Hemlock had finished helping the driver carry in Hawthorn's luggage, she had already fallen asleep.

"That didn't take her long, did it?" Hemlock said as he sat down next to Hazel in a pile of hay.

"She's a champion sleeper," Hazel said.

"I wish I could sleep so soundly."

"You and me both."

They fell into silence.

"Do you want to talk about it?" Hazel said.

Hemlock shook his head. "I don't know what to think anymore. Hawthorn can be a real bastard sometimes. But now... I don't know. Maybe I'm just as bad as him."

"You're not as bad as him."

"And yet I'm still as much to blame for our strained relationship. I... I never realized that before. I feel awful."

"So fix it."

"How?"

"By doing better. By *trying* to do better. I don't know if it's enough. All I know is that I've put my foot in it more times than I can count when it comes to Holly and me. But I always try to own up to it when I'm wrong, and I try to do better. It all seems terribly inadequate, but it's all I have. It's all I know how to do. I need to believe that it's enough. I hope it is."

"I hope so too," he whispered.

She took his hand, and he peered at her through the gloom. Then he kissed her, gently, and they lay down in the hay together, finding comfort and warmth in each other's embrace.

Hazel awoke to a cock crowing in the silver-lighted gloaming. She groaned and rolled over, covering her ears with fistfuls of hay, but it didn't help dampen the racket. Unable to fall back asleep, she sat up, picking strands of hay out of her hair as she blinked at her surroundings.

Thin streams of blue-grey light filtered through the wooden slats of the barn. The air smelled sweet and, despite the animals they shared their lodgings with, surprisingly fresh. She nudged Hemlock and woke him up.

Hemlock blinked at her, then groaned and rolled over. "No."

"What do you mean, 'no'? It's morning."

"It's *dawn*. That's not at all the same thing."

"Well, it is today. I can't sleep."

"Lie down, and then you'll sleep."

"Come on. You're as bad as Holly."

"She's clearly the wiser sister."

"Oh, don't even." She took his arm and tried pulling him up, but instead, he grabbed her and pulled her down on top of him.

He grinned. "That's better."

Hazel tried to look annoyed, but the smile stretching across her face betrayed her. "You're really pleased with yourself, aren't you?"

"Quite."

Hazel let the moment stretch on, enjoying the quiet closeness with Hemlock, wanting to linger there with him just a little while longer. "We should get up," she whispered.

Hemlock smiled and continued to look into her eyes in such a way that made the heat creep up her neck and her heart quicken. Then he nodded and let go, and they both got to their feet.

Holly remained oblivious and continued to sleep like a felled tree.

"Let her sleep longer," Hemlock said. "We can wake her after we look around."

Hazel nodded, and they made their way out of the barn.

Yesterday's storm had passed, leaving a clear morning to shine upon a freshly washed world. Hazel could see now they weren't in a town at all. It was just a house and a barn, surrounded by tree-dotted fields.

"Is this it?" she said. "I thought this was supposed to be a town."

"It was difficult to see last night in the storm. We might have taken a wrong turn somewhere. I'm sure Francis can point us in the right direction."

"He seems like an odd one, doesn't he?"

"Well, we don't exactly keep normal company ourselves."

Hazel chuckled. "True."

The cock continued to crow behind the barn, so Hazel and Hemlock headed in the opposite direction, past the house to a quaint field surrounded by a wooden fence with a ramshackle shed in one corner.

"What do you think's in there?" Hazel asked as she nodded towards the shed.

"Farming supplies? Outhouse?"

"Let's go look." She started towards it.

"If it's an outhouse, I really don't think we'll want to look," Hemlock said as he trailed after her.

"We'd smell it, if that was the case. And I don't smell anything." She reached the shed and nudged the door open. The shed was windowless and dark inside—not much bigger than a closet—and the air was thick with dust and smelled of rusted metal. An assortment of tools hung on the walls. A table took up most of the space and bore a crate covered with a filthy cloth. A few flies buzzed around it. Hazel reached out to take a peek.

"You looking for something?"

Hazel started and jerked her hand back, spinning around to find Francis standing a stone's throw away. He was dressed in stained overalls and a fraying straw cap. His overalls were too short, and his bony ankles peeked out over his well-worn, plain leather shoes.

"No, just looking around. We didn't think anyone was up yet."

"I'm always up with Rufus. Didn't you hear him?"

"Rufus?"

"The rooster."

Hazel suppressed a grimace. "Yes, I did."

Francis studied her a moment, then nodded. "Breakfast'll be on in a minute. You can go inside and wash up if you've a mind."

Hazel smiled, hoping it didn't look forced. "Thank you. I think we will." She and Hemlock headed towards the house.

"What was under the cloth?" Hemlock whispered.

"I don't know, but I'm pretty sure it wasn't farming tools."

He eyed her. "It was just a covered crate. I'm sure it wasn't anything remarkable. Certainly nothing we need to worry about."

Hazel pursed her lips, but she nodded. "You're probably right."

They walked into the house and found Hawthorn milling about in the front room, perusing the shelves of dolls. "There's water on in the kitchen for you to wash up."

Hemlock lingered a moment, fidgeting with his hands. He opened his mouth but then snapped it shut again and headed towards the kitchen. Hazel trailed after him.

He busied himself with transferring some of the heated water on the stove to a pitcher, all while avoiding Hazel's gaze. "I don't know if I can do it," he said eventually. "Apologize to Hawthorn."

"You don't need to explain yourself to me, Hemlock."

He stared out the kitchen window as he held on to the steaming pitcher. "I know. I just... I don't want you to think less of me."

She took the pitcher from him, and he turned to blink at her. "The man is insufferable at the best of times," she said. "So, trust me, my esteem of you is in no threat of diminishing in that regard. Just make sure that whatever you decide to do—or not do—it isn't something you'll later regret."

Hemlock nodded.

"I'd better go wake up Holly." She held up the pitcher and smiled. "Thanks for the water."

He smiled with her. "My pleasure."

She walked out to the barn and to where Holly still lay sleeping in the monstrous pile of hay. Hazel nudged her with a foot. "It's time to get up."

Holly groaned and mumbled something incoherent, then fell back asleep.

Hazel pursed her lips. Then she grinned. She tipped the pitcher over Holly—just a little—and dribbled some water onto her face.

Holly twitched and swiped at her cheek but remained sleeping.

Hazel increased the dribble to a steady stream, and Holly bolted upright as she sputtered and coughed.

"Good morning," Hazel said, smirking.

Holly wiped her face with a sleeve. "You poured water on me?"

"Quite effective, don't you think? I might do it again in the future.

Gone will be the days of struggling to get you out of bed. I don't know why I didn't think of it sooner."

Holly glowered at her. "You really need a hobby."

Hazel grinned. "Don't be sore. We need to wash up anyway, and be thankful that this water was warm."

Holly opened her mouth but then seemed to think better of it and snapped it shut again. They both used the water to wash up—which was little more than them splashing it on their faces and drying them on their skirts. Hazel would have liked to wash up properly—with soap and everything—but not here in a drafty barn with Francis potentially skulking about.

"You and Hemlock have fun last night?" Holly asked, grinning. Her voice had taken an overly sweet, taunting tone.

"Wouldn't you like to know?" Hazel said drily. "But you were asleep, so I guess you won't."

"Was it amazing?" Holly said as she leaned into Hazel. "Was it *magical?*"

Hazel moved away from her. "Honestly, Holly, who needs a hobby now? Go pester Hawthorn if you're in need of romantic frivolity."

Holly sobered, and Hazel frowned in confusion. "What's wrong?"

"I... I kissed Hawthorn."

"What? When?"

"Back in Sarnum. In the graveyard."

"Is that what happened? I knew something was weird when Hemlock and I walked in."

"It *was* weird, that's the thing. I... I don't think he enjoyed it. I don't think *I* enjoyed it. I don't know why I did it."

"Maybe because you've been pining for Hawthorn since the day you met him?"

"I haven't been *pining.*"

Hazel raised an eyebrow.

"All right, I'll admit I might have been rather keen in my fondness for him..."

"Mildly obsessed is more like it."

"But I'm not pining," Holly continued, ignoring Hazel's interruption. "You're making it sound like I'll wither away and die if he doesn't notice me."

"You mean you won't?"

"No!"

"Just asking."

"Besides, I'm pretty sure he has noticed me now. I think I made sure of that in the graveyard."

"You do have a knack for getting noticed."

"It's just... I'm not sure it's his attention that I want anymore. I'm not sure if it feels right." She peered at Hazel with dewy eyes. "What does that say about me?"

"Good grief, Holly, it doesn't say anything other than you perhaps having a dreadful sense of timing."

"But if I don't love him, then who? What if I never find someone to love? What if I'm not capable of it?"

Hazel took hold of Holly's shoulders in a firm grip. "Now you listen to me. You're the most infuriatingly loving girl I know. You take the most wretched of us into your heart, even the ones who don't deserve it. Including me. Including Hawthorn even if you might not love him the way that you hoped. It's going to take an exceedingly rare soul to be worthy of your love, Holly, so don't you be sad about this. You just keep being you, and if it's right, it will happen."

"But what if it's never right? What if it never happens?"

"So what if it doesn't? You'll never be alone, I promise you that. Not as long as I draw breath."

"But you have Hemlock now."

"And you have the both of us. For as long as you can stand us."

Holly wiped at her eyes. "Promise?"

Hazel nodded and swallowed. "Promise."

Holly took a deep breath and gave a shaky smile. "All right then."

Hazel squeezed her shoulders. "Feeling better?"

Holly nodded. "I think so."

"Good, because there's a shed I need you to go investigate while Francis is eating breakfast."

Witnessing Trouble

Holly could only stutter incoherent half protests as Hazel herded her out the barn door and prodded her towards the house.

"All right," Hazel said in a low voice once they reached the steps of Francis's home. "You wait here while I go inside. If I'm not back in five minutes, you come inside too. Otherwise, I'll come back out and let you know it's safe to go investigate the shed."

"Why? What's going on?"

"There's no time to explain. But we need to make sure Francis doesn't catch us poking around. He already caught me once this morning, so I can't do it."

"But *why* are we poking around?"

"Because I don't trust him, that's why. I want to know what we're in for here, and I feel like he's hiding something."

Holly frowned and pursed her lips.

"Oh, don't give me that look," Hazel said. "You've talked me into more ridiculous schemes. Remember Zinnia? You owe me this one."

Holly let out a heavy sigh. "Fine. I'll wait here."

"Remember, if I'm not out in five minutes, you come inside."

"And do what, exactly?"

"Nothing, just come in. Don't make a bigger issue out of this than it needs to be."

"Right, *I'm* the one making a big issue out of things."

Hazel ignored her and disappeared into the house.

Holly lingered by the steps, poking at her skirts and kicking at rocks. How long was five minutes anyway? She didn't have a watch. Was she supposed to be counting? Because she hadn't been counting. So was she supposed to start counting now, or was it too late? Would she need Chester with her? She thought about running back to the barn to fetch him when Tum appeared from around the house. When he saw her, he smiled.

"Pretty good digs we've got here, eh? Not much in the way of beer, but that Francis fellow piled up a bunch of those dolls around the cellar door. He must want me to have them. Not too shabby a payment."

"He's probably hoping they'll ward you away. The dolls are supposed to be for protection." Holly screwed up her face. "And what do you mean, 'payment'? You're *our* cellar gnome, not his."

Tum thrust a finger into the air. "Never refuse a payment, I always say. Even ones not owed." He looked her up and down. "Besides, your payments have been a little lacking."

"We've been busy traveling! You've nabbed more than enough beer and goods on this trip, and you only got those because we brought you along, so you can't complain."

"We'll see about that."

Holly rolled her eyes.

Tum squinted up at her. "Why're you standing out here?"

"I'm waiting for Hazel. She wants me to go poking around some shed, but she told me to wait here first."

"A shed, you say? I seen a shed. I'll go look."

"No, wait!" Holly said, but Tum had already run off around the house and disappeared.

Well, now what? Should she go after Tum? Should she wait for Hazel? Had it been five minutes yet? She imagined Hazel sitting inside silently fuming at Holly for botching up what should have been a simple plan. It must have been at *least* five minutes, right? Holly was fairly certain she was supposed to go in now.

She eased open the door and stepped inside. Voices carried from the kitchen, but the main room was empty except for all the shelves of creepy dolls. She hastened across the room and passed through the threshold into the hallway and nearly collided with Hazel.

A fork clattered to the floor from the plate Hazel held in her hands. On the plate were more pickled eggs along with a wedge of lumpy bread that looked like solidified porridge.

Hazel's expression tightened, but before she could open her mouth, Francis appeared in the hallway behind her and beamed.

"Ah, Holly," he said. "Feeling better, I hope?"

"What?" Holly said.

"You said you weren't feeling well," Hazel said, giving Holly a weird look. "So I was going to bring you breakfast out in the barn. But you seem to be feeling better now. Right?"

Holly's mouth hung open as her mind reeled at what she was supposed to do, how she should act. What should she say? She'd never been any good at thinking on her feet, not like Hazel.

"Of course she's feeling better," Hawthorn said as he walked out of the kitchen and took Holly's arm. "Why else would she be here? Though with you crowding her as you are, I wouldn't be surprised if she needed more air. I'll take that." He took the plate from Hazel and, holding on to Holly's elbow, led her back outside.

"What just happened?" Holly said once they left the house.

Hawthorn kept on walking until they reached the barn, then he handed her the plate of food. "I just salvaged whatever plot you and your sister have been scheming."

"We haven't been *scheming*."

He folded his arms and cocked an eyebrow.

"It was Hazel's idea! I was just going along with it."

"What is she up to?"

Holly told him of Hazel's plan to get her to the shed unnoticed.

"How ridiculously complicated," he said. "Why don't you just walk over there and look inside?"

"I don't know! She told me to wait, and then I lost track of time. And then Tum... who *knows* what Tum is doing!" Holly shook the plate of food at him.

Hawthorn backed away from the plate as an egg wobbled over the edge and fell to the ground. "It's fine. We'll go look together. All right?"

Holly took a deep breath and nodded. She poked at the lumpy bread as they walked past the house. "What is this stuff anyway?"

"I have no idea. I don't think I want to know. You can thank me later for saving you from that as well." He took the bread from her plate and pitched it into a nearby field enclosed in a wooden fence. Next to the fence in a corner was a little shed.

"That must be it," Holly said, squinting. "It doesn't look special."

"What did you expect?"

"I don't know, something more grand, for all the fuss Hazel's making about it."

As they approached, Tum slipped out of the shed and then froze when he saw them.

"Well?" Holly said. "What's in there?"

Tum rubbed his hands on his shirt. "Isn't anything in there. Not anything that concerns you anyway."

"And it concerns *you*?"

Tum drew himself up. "I'm a cellar gnome; most everything concerns me."

"I should hope not," Hawthorn said. "I'd rather rats take an interest in my affairs than a grubby gnome."

Tum looked offended. "I'm not *grubby*! *Rats* are grubby."

"What's in there, Tum?" Holly said.

"Told you. Nothing."

She reached for the collar of his shirt, but he darted out of the way, straight into Hawthorn who grabbed him and hoisted him off his feet.

Tum howled in protest and flailed his arms and legs as Hawthorn swung him away from the door for Holly to open. A pile of Francis's dolls were heaped upon a table, with some scattered on the bare earthen floor.

Hawthorn dropped Tum on the ground outside the shed and wiped his hands on a handkerchief.

"Those are mine!" Tum cried. "Don't you touch 'em!"

"What are you doing with all these dolls?" Holly said.

"They're mine! He gave them to me!"

"You mean you *took* them." She scrunched up her face. "How'd you get them out here so fast? You didn't even know about this shed until just a little while ago."

But Tum just darted past her and Hawthorn into the shed, grabbed a couple of dolls, and ran away.

Holly shook her head. Other than the dolls, she couldn't see what was so special. There was a table and some tools hanging from the walls. And there was a crate covered with a grimy cloth. She pulled it aside and gasped and jumped back, stumbling into Hawthorn.

"What is it?" he said.

"I... I'm not sure what it is. But it's looking at me."

Holly ventured another peek into the box, and just like before, a disembodied face peered back at her. Yet as she looked closer, she could see that there were only holes instead of eyes and that the skin was really molded wax.

"It's a mask," she said. "A creepy, horrible mask. Why is it out here?"

"I certainly don't know, but now you have something to tell Hazel."

"I guess we'd better get back."

They returned to the house and rejoined the others. Holly still had her plate with the eggs, and Francis, seeing her missing bread, supplied her with a new slice while beaming at her and complimenting her appetite.

"Well?" Hazel whispered as Holly sat down next to her.

When Holly told her, Hazel just gaped at her. But she couldn't ask any more questions, because Francis took to talking instead.

"So you mentioned last night you were looking for someone. This person got a name?"

"His name is Ash," Hazel said. "He's mine and Holly's father. And we're not sure if he came through here or not. We've only come here on some far-fetched theory."

Francis perked up. "Oh? Those are the best ones. What's your theory?"

Hazel glanced at the others and then, folding her hands on the table, said, "Our father, unfortunately, has involved himself with some rather unsavory magical practices." She studied Francis as she spoke, but Francis just smiled and nodded as he spooned some beans onto a plate. He handed the plate to Hemlock.

Hemlock sniffed the plate and, with a look that said he was throwing caution out the window, started eating.

"I'm speaking of necromancy," Hazel said.

Francis waved his spoon at her. "Not sure I follow what's so unsavory about that."

Holly sucked in a breath as Hazel clenched her jaw and stared at Francis the same way she usually looked at Holly when she was trying really hard not to yell at her (but usually did anyway).

"It's an atrocious practice," Hazel said, her voice tight. "It is manipulation of the dead for one's own personal gain. How can you not see the unsavoriness of that?"

"Death is a part of life. I don't see how manipulation of dead things is any different than manipulation of living things. You a worker of magic? You ever manipulate living things?"

"Well, yes, but—"

"But there you go. We're all in the same boat. All magic is finding different ways of steering that boat. But we're all going to the same place, regardless of how we get there."

Hazel's mouth worked soundlessly, but words seemed to have abandoned her.

"How do you know so much about magic?" Holly said. "You a warlock?"

Francis chuckled. "Warlock? Goodness me, no. I'm a simple doll maker. But as a doll maker, I understand that there are forces in the world beyond us and that sometimes we can talk these forces into working *for* us."

Hazel narrowed her eyes. "Is that what the mask is for? Out in the shed?"

"Hazel!" Holly hissed.

Francis paled. "You saw the Witness?"

"No, she didn't— Ow!" Holly said when Hazel dug her nails into her hand.

"I saw everything," Hazel said, raising her chin.

"Oh, no, no, no," Francis said. "This changes things. This changes everything!" He got up from the table, flapped his arms uselessly for a while, then ran from the room.

"Well, that can't be good," Hawthorn said. "Pass the beans, Hemlock."

Hemlock stared blankly at him and then at Hazel as he pushed the pot of beans over to his brother. "What just happened?"

"Hazel got us in trouble!" Holly said.

"We don't know that!" Hazel snapped. Then she straightened her back and folded her hands on the table. "Let's just see what happens before we jump to any conclusions."

Hawthorn pointed a spoonful of beans at her. "I think you'd better hope old Martha is clean out of chickens."

Meeting the Mayor

"He's not *really* going to tar and feather you, is he, Hazel?" Holly asked.

"Perhaps we should think about leaving," Hawthorn said, "before we find out."

"Would someone please tell me what's going on?" Hemlock said. "Why am I the only one not in on this?"

Holly told him of the morning's events while Hawthorn continued to glower at Hazel.

"What I don't understand," Hawthorn said, "is why you must purposefully aggravate the man. Why have Holly sneak out to the shed only to tell him you were out there? What was the point?"

"I don't know!" Hazel said. "He was just so... so *smug* talking about how 'natural' necromancy is that I couldn't help myself. This certainly wasn't how I thought the morning would go."

"You do have a gift for the unexpected," Hawthorn said. "So well done with that."

Hazel glared at him.

"What's done is done," Hemlock said. "We need to figure out what to do next."

"I think we should leave," Holly said. "We're leaving, right?"

"I should think so," Hawthorn said.

Hazel said, "We're not leaving."

"Has anyone ever told you that you have the most dreadful sense of humor?" Hawthorn asked.

Hazel narrowed her eyes. "Yes, as a matter of fact. But we're still not leaving."

Hawthorn put up his hands and then, shaking his head, returned his interest to the pot of beans.

"Hazel," Holly said, "be reasonable."

"No, I will not be reasonable, because this is an unreasonable situation. Where else can we go? To say that coming here was a long shot in finding Father is being overly optimistic. But right now it's all we have, and I am *not* giving up!" Hazel's voice had risen, and she cleared her throat as she tried to regain her composure.

"Leaving's not an option," Hemlock said. "So we need to focus our attention on how we're going to keep Hazel—and quite potentially all of us—from getting tarred and feathered."

Everyone grew silent.

"Anyone?" Hemlock said.

Hawthorn sighed and rubbed his forehead. "I really need new friends," he muttered.

Francis returned to the kitchen, his wrinkled face flustered. He flapped his hands at Hazel. "Time to go. I got the wagon ready, so we better be off. The rest of you... ah..." He flapped his hands some more. "We'll figure it out later. But you and me," he said to Hazel, "we're going into town."

Hazel got up from her chair. "I'm doing no such thing."

Hemlock got up with her. "She's not going anywhere."

Holly and Hawthorn remained sitting, staring up at everyone.

"I must insist," Francis said. "You saw the Witness. Isn't anyone supposed to see the Witness unprepared."

"I don't even know what this Witness *is*."

Francis thrust a finger at her. "Exactly! Come quietly, or I'll have to get the rope and branding irons from Norris. And you don't want to be on the poking end of Norris's branding irons. The man hasn't had any cattle for years, so he's itching something fierce for some skin to burn."

Hazel drew herself up, even as she struggled to keep the horror from showing on her face. "If you think I'm going to make it easy for you to inflict whatever twisted form of punishment you have planned for me, then you're sorely mistaken."

"Punishment? Goodness me, I don't decide any punishments. I just need to get you to Emmond. He's the one that does all the deciding. I'd prefer if you came quietly, but I'll fetch Norris and his irons if that'll help motivate you."

"And what is it you think Emmond will decide to do? Can I expect to be tarred and feathered?"

Francis blinked at her a few times. "Well, I suppose that depends on whether or not he decides to run you out of town. At times like this, it's always better to come in nice and quiet. The more trouble you make... Well... we don't like trouble."

Hazel looked at Hemlock, but he just shrugged. She turned to Francis and raised her chin. "Very well. I will accompany you to meet this Emmond."

"I'm coming with you," Hemlock said.

"Me too!" Holly said.

"I'll wait here then," Hawthorn said.

Holly kicked him under the table.

"You wanted to be included," Hemlock said. "Well, this is being included."

Hawthorn glanced at them all, then pushed his plate of beans away. "Very well. We'll all go."

Holly squeaked and clapped her hands.

Hazel said, "We're not going on a picnic, Holly."

"I know, but that doesn't mean we can't have fun."

They all filed out of the kitchen and followed Francis outside to a wagon that he had hitched to a couple of horses. Hemlock and Hawthorn's driver stood nearby, brushing his own horses while he watched, rather forlornly, as everyone crawled up into the back of Francis's wagon. Except for Hawthorn. He seemed to reconsider his display of solidarity when he saw the filthy wagon bed. But when Francis crawled in the driver's seat and flicked the reins, he hopped up and joined the others just as the wagon started to roll away. He tried brushing a clean patch next to

Holly, but the wagon jolted, and losing his balance, he groped at Holly to keep himself from falling face-first onto the grimy wood.

"Hey!" Holly shouted as she pushed him away. "Hands off, mister... *handsy*!"

"Honestly, Hawthorn," Hemlock said, smirking. "You could at least bring her flowers first."

"That's funny," Hawthorn said. "I don't recall you ever bringing Hazel flowers."

Hemlock's cheeks reddened.

"All right," Hazel said. "We're changing the subject. Right now."

To Holly, Hawthorn said, "Apologies, madam, for my unsolicited forwardness. It was not my intention."

Holly looked him up and down and said, "Well, all right then. Just sit down before you grab something else."

Hawthorn sat next to her, and the group fell into silence as they watched the countryside ramble by. Wooden fences and rough stone walls divided farm fields, orchards, and untended, overgrown meadows. They passed an apple orchard where people harvested the fruit from atop long wooden ladders and stowed the apples in canvas sacks slung across their shoulders. Hazel wished she was out there with them rather than sitting in a rickety wagon rolling towards some unknown fate.

The wagon turned up a narrow dirt road flanked on either side by a low stone wall that bordered wild, grassy fields. Their pace slowed as the road led them up a long, steady hill. They rounded a bend, and further up the hill, the wide and flat slats of a windmill came into view.

Hazel held her breath. This was purely coincidental. It couldn't possibly be the mill she had been searching for, especially since she'd never been certain it was a mill she'd seen in the first place. But there it was, a mill at the top of a hill, just like she thought she had seen after drinking the necromantic potion.

She looked at the others and found everyone watching her. Holly looked stunned and frightened, Hawthorn critical, and Hemlock concerned.

"I'm sure it's just a coincidence," she said. But everyone kept staring at her, apparently unconvinced.

"Do you think Father's here?" Holly asked, her eyes growing wider.

Hazel shook her head. "No, absolutely not. Why would he be?" But the more Hazel thought about it, the more uncertain she became. She wasn't ready to face her father. What would she say to him? What would she do? Her stomach twisted with nerves, so she gave another resolute shake of her head. "Just, no."

Next to the mill was a tiny cottage, smaller than Hazel and Holly's cottage back in the Grove. They stopped in front of it, and Francis hopped down and opened the back of the wagon. Once everyone had clambered out, he stuffed one of his dolls into Hazel's skirt pocket, winked at her, then headed inside.

Hazel stiffly followed him, willing herself to leave the doll alone and not wrench it out of her pocket and throw it away. Or worse, at the back of Francis's balding head. Hemlock, perhaps noticing her struggle, took one of her clenched hands and gingerly held it. She managed a feeble smile just as they stepped over the threshold and into the cottage.

Dried bundles of herbs and flowers hung from the rafters, filling the air with a pleasant aroma. A black potbelly stove stood at one end of the room, near a sofa with cushions embroidered with flowers and leaves that rested on a woven carpet depicting a forest scene. At the other end of the room stood a polished wooden table, decorated with a beveled glass bowl filled with apples and surrounded with high-backed chairs padded with embroidered cushions that matched the sofa. The room was a lovely, cozy space in which Hazel would have liked to spend her time. She didn't know how to feel about that, given the circumstances.

A door along one wall opened, and in walked a stout man who looked more square than round. He had greying black hair, a beard to match, and a thick oxen-like neck. He walked up to Francis as he peered at the others.

"What's this?" he said as he clapped Francis on the back with a meaty hand. "Visitors?"

Francis nodded. "Came in with the storm. Normally that'd be a good thing, you know? But these have gotten into some mischief." He blinked at Hazel a few times before turning back to Emmond and in a low voice, said, "She saw the Witness."

Emmond's broad, smiling face darkened. "Well now, that's serious."

"It's just a mask," Hazel said. "I don't see what all the fuss is about."

"Just you then? No one else?"

"I—" Holly began.

"Just me," Hazel said. "No one else."

"But, Hazel..."

"It's fine, Holly. You don't need to worry."

Holly frowned and pressed her lips into a thin line, but she remained silent.

Emmond nodded. "Come with me then."

Hemlock said, "I saw the mask too."

"Hemlock!"

"So I need to be included in this."

"He's lying," Hazel said. "He didn't see anything."

Hemlock shrugged. "My word against hers, and she's just trying to look out for me. I'd not take any chances though, if I were you."

Emmond nodded again. "All right, the both of you, with me." He peered at the others. "Anyone else?"

Holly's mouth hung open as she stared between Hazel and Hawthorn.

Hawthorn glowered at Hemlock a long while, but Hemlock just gazed back at him. Hazel thought she saw Hemlock give a slight nod towards Holly, but she couldn't be sure. Then Hawthorn let out a long breath as his expression calmed. He turned to Emmond and said, "No, it was just them. We didn't see anything."

"You two wait here then." To Francis, Emmond said, "You bring Norris's irons?"

"No, they came quietly enough. I didn't think they'd be needed."

"Well, there's a poker near the stove there. You start a fire if you want and get the poker nice and hot."

Francis beamed. "Yes, sir!"

And with that, Emmond led Hazel and Hemlock through the door from which he had come and into a tincture room. Shelves of bottles and little pots lined the walls except for where a great wooden cabinet stood. A desk took up most of the space on the floor and left little room for the round table that had been tucked into a corner with a couple of chairs. Emmond indicated to them to sit, so Hazel and Hemlock did.

Emmond leaned against the cabinet and ran a hand over his face. "So you saw the mask. What is it you're expecting to happen right now?"

Hazel and Hemlock glanced at each other. Hazel said, "Honestly, I don't know. I suspect your man Francis would enjoy a good branding. Either that or we'll be tarred and feathered."

Emmond chuckled. "I knew I never should've tarred and feathered that man all those years ago. But I had recently been made mayor and, well, wanted to make good with the townsfolk. Francis talks about that incident far too much. He's a good man but a little touched, you know?"

Hazel was inclined to agree, but she feared it might be a trick. "So what do you have planned?"

"I'm not sure yet. I'm hoping we can figure something out together."

Hazel narrowed her eyes. "I don't understand."

"Truth be told," Emmond said, "I hate that mask with its lumpy wax skin and vacant eyes. It's creepy. But Francis, see, he's a bit old-fashioned. That mask represents an old way of thinking, back when it was used in rituals to pray for healthy crops and children. I've been encouraging Francis to focus on his dolls, hoping he'd forget about that stupid mask. But instead, he's latched onto both." He shook his head.

"Why do you go along with him then? What was all that nonsense about the hot poker just now?"

Emmond scratched the back of his head and winced. "Yeah, sorry about that. But see, Francis isn't the only one who thinks that way. There's plenty of folks around here who are of a similar mind, and Francis is well respected. It won't do to make light of their beliefs. Not if I want to live here and definitely not if I want to be mayor. So we got to play along."

"Even if it means getting branded with a hot poker?"

Emmond scoffed and waved a hand. "Francis is mostly harmless. He won't do anything unless provoked."

"*Mostly* harmless? Is that supposed to make me feel better?"

"Let's get down to business," he continued. "We need to come up with a punishment for you two, and it's better if you help decide. We can please everyone that way."

"You're as touched as Francis if you think I'm going to be pleased with devising my own punishment for a ridiculous and made-up offense."

"All offenses are made-up. And for Francis and the like, it's as real as daybreak. So you play along, or I'll come up with one all my own. We both know Francis has been itching for another tarring and feathering. I think he'd be real happy to see another one."

Hemlock leaned towards Hazel and quietly said, "Maybe we should just come up with something so we can move on and focus on why we came here."

Hazel shifted in her seat. "I suppose I could apologize."

Emmond chuckled and shook his head. "Apologizing's just good manners. It's not a punishment. I'm not sure you grasp the severity of this. Do you know that in the old days, they'd put out a man's eyes for looking upon the Witness uninitiated?"

"You can't be serious," Hemlock said.

Emmond put up his hands. "Now I'm not suggesting we do that. I just want you two to understand how fortunate you are to be sitting there having this conversation with me right now. The alternative could've very easily been a lot more grim."

"So what *are* you suggesting?" Hazel asked.

Emmond scrutinized them under heavy brows as he rubbed his chin. Hazel struggled not to roll her eyes.

"Thing is," Emmond said, "the folk love a good show. Especially Francis. That's really all they're looking for, I reckon. So I figure that's what we need to give them."

Hazel frowned as she studied him. "What kind of show?"

"The base kind, unfortunately. You know, with whips and chains and all that. It's utter rubbish. But the folk, see, they love it, and it's been some time since we've had anything of the sort. Don't get too many visitors passing through these days."

"I can't imagine why," Hazel muttered.

"It'll all be for show though," Emmond continued. "I'll rattle some chains, and you'll scream for a bit, the folks'll be appeased, and then we can have a good laugh about it later." He smiled. "What do you say?"

Both Hazel and Hemlock stared at the man.

Seeing their lacking enthusiasm, Emmond said, "I'm open to other ideas if you've got any."

Hemlock leaned over to her and whispered, "We can still make a run for it if you want."

She shook her head. To Emmond, she said, "And it'll all be staged? You won't actually flog us or anything?"

He shrugged. "I can't guarantee you won't get a welt or two. I'm handy with a whip, but sometimes it gets away from me, you know? But a little welt never hurt anyone, I always figure."

"Are you serious? Of course welts hurt! That's why they're welts."

"I don't know where you're from, but out here, we take our lumps and welts with a measure of pride. Sounds like you could do with a few."

Hemlock rubbed his eyes. Dumbfounded, Hazel could only stare at Emmond. Seemed like Francis wasn't the only one touched in the head.

"If we do this," she said, "then I want something from you in return."

Emmond's eyebrows shot up. "Something other than you walking out of here whole and hale for looking on the Witness when you shouldn't have? You've got gumption, my friend."

"I'm looking for my father. If we agree to this, then I want your word you will do all you can to help us find him. If not, I'm walking out of here and telling Francis you're a fraud and taking my chances out there with him."

A slow smile stretched across Emmond's face. "You've got a bit of fire in you, don't you? I like that. All right, I'll help you with what I can. Just don't be upset if it turns out to be less than you'd like."

Disastrous Discipline

"Have you gone mad?" Holly shouted as she and Hazel stood alone in the main room of the cottage. "You're going to let him *flog* you?!"

Hazel flinched. Holly wasn't usually one to shout. "*Pretend.* He's going to pretend to flog us."

Holly folded her arms. "Right. And I'm going to sprout wings and fly around the sun. You can't possibly believe him!"

"He has no reason to lie. If he was going to flog us, he'd just do it without the pretense. So, yes, I do believe him. And he's promised to help us find Father. We need this, Holly."

"No, we don't. We've gotten this far on our own, haven't we?"

"Yes, and the path we've been following has been getting exceedingly narrower. Where do we go from here, Holly? Can you tell me that?"

"You don't even know if he *can* help us. You could be doing all this for nothing."

"And what would you suggest we do instead? I don't see you providing any ideas."

Holly looked away. "We still have the potions," she murmured.

"What?"

"The potions Odd gave me. We should drink them. They might help us."

Hazel had completely forgotten about the potions. "What good will they do?"

"I don't know. Maybe more good than whatever potion it was that *you* drank."

"I—" Hazel began but was interrupted when Hemlock and Hawthorn walked in.

"They're here," Hemlock said as he approached Hazel. "We need to go."

Francis hurried into the room, brightening when his gaze fell on Hazel and Hemlock. "Ah, there you are. The wagon's ready to take you to the town square. We best get moving; folk don't like to be kept waiting, eh?"

Hazel wanted to say something to Holly. Something to reassure her and let her know everything would be fine. But the words seemed to die on Hazel's tongue, and Francis's impatient prodding only jumbled her thoughts. Before she knew what was happening, Hemlock was gently leading her out the door and into the back of Francis's wagon that had been strewn with fresh straw. Strings of dolls had been nailed to the outside of the wagon, and the two horses each wore a wreath of the things around their necks.

"Why so many dolls?" Hazel asked. "Surely you don't mean to protect us?"

Francis looked offended. "I always offer protection to the condemned. It's only polite. Best sit down so you don't get jostled from the wagon and break your neck." He skipped up to the driver's seat, flicked the reins, and the wagon started moving.

Holly and Hawthorn walked out of the cottage. Holly took a few steps forward, as if to follow them. But then she clenched her hands and remained still, watching until the wagon rounded a bend and fell out of sight.

Hazel put a hand over her eyes. Maybe Holly was right. Maybe she was being foolish and this whole show would be nothing but a terrible mistake.

"She'll be fine," Hemlock said. When Hazel looked up at him, he added, "So will we."

Hazel wanted to believe him, but a sickening weight had settled in her gut, keeping her from feeling anything but a heavy dread.

The ride to the town square was long and quiet. The sun gleamed in the clear blue sky, shining upon a renewed world after the storm. They passed fields of rye and wheat with long, golden stalks that rippled in the wind. They even passed a field of sunflowers. The great yellow flowers had withered and browned, and their blackened faces drooped towards the earth rather than the sun. Amid the fields and orchards was an occasional house. Sometimes a person would be standing out front, shouting something incoherent as the wagon rolled by. Probably curses, given the circumstances.

After they passed a few of these houses, people started to follow them. Some carried bulging burlap sacks as they hurried after the plodding wagon. Others carried long walking sticks as they briskly kept pace. Then on the road behind them, a rickety wagon came into view, and the people who'd been falling behind scrambled up into it.

But one man with a sturdy walking stick kept pace with Hazel and Hemlock's wagon. He drew close to them and asked, "So did you see it?"

"What?" Hazel said.

"The Witness. Did you really see it? Or was it all just stories?"

"Why else would we be here if we didn't see it?"

The man shrugged. "I'd always heard a man'd get smited to ash if he ever looked upon the Witness unprepared. You're not smited, so I'm wonderin' which story is false."

"Use your imagination."

"See, now, I've been tryin' for that. But my 'magination can't fathom much when it comes to the Witness, you get me?"

"I'm sure I don't."

"So... did you see it or not?"

Hazel fixed him in a level gaze. "What would you say if we didn't see it? That this whole display was a ridiculous sham? What would you say to that?"

The man blinked at her a few times, then scratched the back of his head. "Well, now... I'm not sure what I'd say to that."

"Best news I've heard all day."

The man stopped walking and stared at them as the wagon pulled away, and he soon fell out of sight.

"Do you think that was a good idea?" Hemlock said. "What you told him?"

"I don't know. I just wanted him to leave us alone. So I guess that worked, at least."

By the time they reached the town, two wagons filled with ogling passengers trailed behind them, along with a pack of people on foot that had managed to keep up the entire way.

The town consisted of a handful of buildings nestled between a pair of sloping, grass-covered hills. Signs in front of a few of the buildings identified them as a notary, a dry-goods store, and a barber. The rest were signless so probably just houses. In the middle of it all, a wooden platform had been erected and decorated with colorful ribbons, braids of woven wheat, and more of Francis's dolls.

"You have a hand in that?" Hazel asked, nodding towards the platform when Francis came around to help them out of the wagon.

He beamed at her. "You've got a good eye. Benjamin did the woodwork—I'm useless with a hammer, see?—but the dolls will look out for you in your time of need."

"You seem awfully concerned for our welfare, considering what we've done."

"I don't wish you ill, if that's what you mean. I figure it was plain stupidity and ignorance what made you search out the Witness like that, rather than any sort of malice."

"How reassuring."

"But we got rules," Francis continued, "and you broke 'em. So you get a good learning here, and then we can all have a good laugh and a picnic and then go home."

At first Hazel thought his reference to a picnic was just his addled wit, but then she noticed people sitting on blankets out in the grass while fishing goods from baskets and parcels. One of the wagons that had been following them slowed to a halt in the town, and people clutching bulging burlap sacks hopped off, ran to the grass, and set up little picnics of their own.

"Looks like we're the day's entertainment," Hemlock muttered.

"I guess we should be glad they're not throwing anything at us," Hazel said.

Francis looked affronted. "Wasteful to throw perfectly good food away, either for menfolk or the pigs. Now you two get up on the platform there and wait for Emmond."

"You mean he's not here yet?"

"He likes to make an entrance."

Wonderful, Hazel thought, but remained silent. Francis was eyeing her, so instead, she said, "Let's get this over with," and she and Hemlock walked to the platform and ascended the set of wooden stairs.

Hazel fiddled with her skirts, feeling awkward at standing there on display. More and more townspeople began to take notice of them. Some left their blankets and food on the grass to come get a closer look.

Emmond arrived riding a mule. The animal had been adorned with a wreath of wheat and wildflowers crowned around its long, twitching ears. Some of the townsfolk cheered, and he smiled and waved as if he were in a mummer's parade.

"Good grief," Hazel muttered.

"He knows how to charm a crowd, at least," Hemlock said. "Let's hope that works in our favor."

Emmond hopped off the mule, and the animal wandered off to graze in the grass. He was dressed in a finely tailored brown vest and linen shirt with the gold chain of a pocket watch glinting in the sunlight. He joined Hazel and Hemlock on the platform and raised his arms.

"Friends!" he shouted as more of the crowd came forward. "We gather here on this fine day not for companionship, nay, but to right a grim wrong. This man and woman"—he pointed at Hazel and Hemlock—"I fear have committed a grievous crime. You may have heard rumors. You may have suspicions. Let me say it now: this man and woman have looked upon the Witness."

Murmurs and gasps rustled through the crowd. Hazel had to focus to keep her expression neutral and to not roll her eyes or do anything else inflammatory.

Emmond nodded. "Yes, it is so. No one in the past hundred years has looked upon the aspect of the Witness unprepared, and it pains me greatly to relay this most unfortunate news."

"Put out their eyes!" a man shouted from the crowd. There were a few nods and murmurs of assent.

Emmond nodded again. "We could do that, yes."

"What?" Hazel began, but Hemlock put a hand on her shoulder, and she bit the inside of her cheek and forced herself to remain silent.

Emmond cast her a quick glance before turning back towards the crowd with his ready-made smile. "But are we not more civilized than that? Are we not more illuminated and restrained?"

The crowd members glanced at one another with questioning looks. Someone coughed.

"Are we not more *merciful*?" Emmond added.

"Yes?" a woman said.

"Exactly, goodwife Beatrice!" Emmond exclaimed, and Beatrice donned a smug smile as she looked around the crowd.

"We are indeed more merciful," Emmond went on. "The putting out of eyes is well beneath us, and I put it to you good folks to find a better form punishment for these two wayward, yet repentant, souls."

"Throw them in a pit!"

"Tar and feather 'em and run 'em out of town!"

"Cover their heads with sacks of bees!"

This last suggestion came from a squat man in the middle of the crowd, and judging by the aghast looks of his neighbors and his reddening cheeks, he had gone too far. He shuffled his feet and wrung his hands and, in a meek voice, suggested, "Flog them?"

Emmond smiled and pointed at him. "You always had a nose for justice, Ernie, along with the oddly dramatic." This elicited a few chuckles among the crowd, and Ernie's blushing cheeks reddened even more.

"Yes, good folk, I put forth that these two make amends with a proper, honest flogging."

"Except it's not honest," came a man's voice. The crowd parted, and Hazel's heart sank when she saw it was the same man that had been pestering her on the way over. "The whole thing's a sham." He pointed at Hazel. "She told me herself!"

Emmond put on his smile and forced out a stiff chuckle. "What nonsense. Have you been spending your nights in the cider cellar again, Tobin?" He grinned around at the crowd, but only one or two managed to chuckle feebly along with him, the rest were scrutinizing Tobin, Hazel, Hemlock, and Emmond with dark gazes.

"Did she not really see the Witness?" one lady asked.

"Are you making fools of us, Emmond?" a tall, burly man asked, his ham-like hands balled into fists. "You know I don't like being made a fool."

Emmond's syrupy smile faded, and he put up his hands. "Nobody's making a fool out of anyone, Dennet. I swear to you, they confessed to me they saw the Witness. Why would they lie about that, knowing it would bring repercussions?"

"But they haven't been smited into ash!" Tobin said. "They must be lying!"

The murmurs surrounding the man grew louder, and beads of sweat began to collect on Emmond's brow. He put up his hands again. "Friends, please!" But then someone lobbed an apple from the crowd that *thunked* against Emmond's head.

The crowd grew eerily silent for the span of a breath. Then chaos erupted. People started shoving each other. Those who came near Dennet soon found themselves facedown on the ground. Ernie scuttled away and hid behind a tree. For a moment it looked as if everyone had forgotten Hazel and Hemlock. Then Tobin cried out and started towards them and, in doing so, drew the attention of the others. Hazel and Hemlock backed away. Emmond hesitated, glancing between Hazel and Dennet, who was now advancing on him. He gave a quick bow, then hurried to his mule grazing in the grass and made a hasty retreat.

Hazel went for the stairs, but Beatrice grabbed hold of her sleeve.

"What do we do with them?" Beatrice shouted to the others.

"Cover their heads with sacks of bees!" Ernie shrilled from behind his tree.

"You're a freaky little git, Ernie," Dennet said.

"Get out of my way." Hazel yanked her arm out of Beatrice's grip and tried to push past her. But Beatrice grabbed hold of her again, and as Hazel struggled to free herself, Dennet came up behind her and put a thick, heavy hand on her shoulder.

Hazel froze and peered up at him.

Dennet smiled a broad, gap-toothed grin.

Hemlock cast a spell, and in the middle of the crowd, a towering man shimmered into being. He was head and shoulders taller than the tallest man there and wore a long black cloak that covered the narrow frame of his body. The face that peered out of the hood was sallow and lumpy with a fixed, vacant expression and empty blackened holes for eyes.

"It's the Witness," someone said. A woman gasped and fainted. Ernie bolted from behind the tree and ran down the road until he was out of sight. Everyone that remained froze in place and stared at the Witness in wide-eyed wonder.

The Witness raised a hand and pointed a long, pale finger at Beatrice.

"She's been marked!" Tobin shouted. Half the remaining onlookers charged at Beatrice, the other half followed Ernie's lead and made for the hills. But Dennet remained unfazed. He tightened his grip on Hazel's shoulder, and so Hazel summoned a sharp gust of air and hit him square in the gut with it.

He staggered back, arms flailing as he struggled to keep his balance.

Hemlock grabbed Hazel's hand, and they ran.

Chester's Field Day

Holly sat on the steps of Emmond's front porch, resting her chin on her palm with her elbow propped on her knee while Hawthorn paced back and forth behind her. Of all the stupid ideas Hazel had ever come up with, this one had to be the worst. If Holly had tried such a thing, her sister would have thrown a fit fierce enough to make her go cross-eyed. But when it was Hazel's idea, Holly was supposed to go along with it and pretend everything was fine. It wasn't, and she was getting tired of the game.

"How long is this thing supposed to take?" she said. "They've been gone forever."

"They've been gone for an hour," Hawthorn said.

Holly turned and squinted up at him. "Don't tell me you're taking her side."

"Were we taking sides? I wasn't aware. In that case, I'll take *my* side and leave this place to find an establishment that will serve me a decent glass of wine absent of any local... flavor."

"You can stop the act. I know you're worried about Hemlock just as much as I am about Hazel or else you wouldn't be pacing like that. What

I'm wondering is why we're just sitting here doing nothing while they're getting flogged."

Hawthorn stopped pacing and looked down the bridge of his nose at her. "*Pretend* flogged."

"Say that to me one more time and I'll pretend flog *you*."

"What would you have us do? We have no means of transportation, having left our own carriage and driver at Francis's house—a brilliant move in and of itself, by the way. Are you suggesting we take to foot and march down the road searching for them? We don't know how far the town is from here or how long it will take for us to get there. So, if we're lucky, it might only take us some hours, and when we get there, we'll be exhausted and filthy and all the excitement will have long since been over. Marvelous idea."

"You got a better idea then?"

"Other than waiting here as we all agreed to do? No."

"Well, that's just great."

Hawthorn started pacing again, and Holly resumed waiting on the stairs when a man riding a donkey came trotting up the hill.

Holly got to her feet. "Is that Emmond?"

Hawthorn turned just as Emmond hopped from the moving animal and ran towards the cottage.

"Hey!" Holly said as Emmond bolted past her. She followed him inside. "Where's Hazel and Hemlock?"

Emmond ignored her and walked into a snug room cluttered with a potion cabinet and desk. He rifled through one of the drawers.

Holly marched up to him and slammed the drawer shut, causing Emmond to stagger back to keep his fingers from getting smashed.

"I'm talking to you!" she said.

Emmond jabbed a finger at her. "Your sister's crazy, you know that? Has absolutely no sense of self-preservation, that one."

"What happened?"

He threw his arms up into the air. "She blew the whole thing, that's what! Why on earth would she tell Tobin of all people that the flogging was a sham? She soft in the head or something?"

"Who's Tobin? What are you talking about?"

Emmond closed his eyes and took a breath. "Look, I like you. Honest, I do. You come here looking for your father, completely clueless about the kind of town you've stumbled upon. I get it. Really. But you people got to meet me halfway, see? Your sister getting a peek at the Witness was like her poking a hornet's nest. Now her telling Tobin that the whole punishment thing was a fake, well, she's done and taken that hornet's nest, thwacked it against a wall a few times, and then thrown the ruined remains at me. The townsfolk aren't pleased. They aren't pleased a mite. So if I were you, I'd be scootin' on out the door before they come here looking for justice." He returned to the desk, rummaged around in the back of one of the drawers, and pulled out a little black wallet. He held it up and nodded at Holly before he hustled back out the door, hopped onto his donkey, and disappeared among the grass and trees.

Hawthorn stood beside her as she stared at the road where Emmond had gone. "Why am I not surprised that your sister's impetuousness has gotten her in trouble yet again?"

Holly glared at him, but before she could say anything, Hawthorn started down the road.

"Are you coming?" he said as he turned to look at her. "Or are you going to wait here for the angry mob to arrive?"

Holly grabbed her skirts and ran after him. "What happened to 'we agreed to sit and wait'?"

"I never agreed to get mauled."

They hurried down the road in the direction Francis had taken Hazel and Hemlock only an hour or so before. They had no idea how far the town was, and the expectation of an angry mob to come charging down the road at any moment made Holly tense.

"Maybe we should get off the road," she said. "Keep to the grass and trees." She glanced at the surrounding farm fields and fallow meadows that, at best, boasted only a handful of trees. "Well, when there are trees."

"Do you know how much this jacket cost me?" Hawthorn said as he smoothed the lapels of his coat. The jacket was longer than usual—reaching down to his knees—with gathered material in the back and wide cuffs and dyed a purple so deep it looked black until the sun hit it. "You can't get material like this in the Grove. I had it shipped from Sarnum, and the stars only know where *they* got it, given the price I paid for it. So, no, I will not go traipsing through mud and overgrown weeds to avoid a few toothless rustics and whatever pitiful display of pitchfork waving they have planned as a means of entertaining themselves."

As if on cue, a group of people appeared on the road ahead of them, headed their way.

"Well, that's just wonderful," Holly said. "If you want to stay here and debate the quality of fabrics with them, then be my guest. But I'm guessing they won't be nearly as impressed with your coat as you are. Getting a little mud on your sleeve will be a lot better than whatever they have planned. Me? I'm not staying." She headed into a field, but Hawthorn just stood there, stiff-backed and scowling at the distant group that now grew closer. Holly didn't care. She wouldn't stop. If he wanted to be stupid and stubborn, well, that was his problem. She was leaving.

Holly stopped, closed her eyes, and sighed. She headed back to Hawthorn. "What's wrong with you?" she shouted at him. "You can't possibly think protecting a stupid coat is worth getting throttled?"

Hawthorn took off his jacket, folded it, and gently laid it on a thick patch of grass. He wore a white linen shirt under a vest made of the same material as his coat. He started to roll up his sleeves. "Look at them"—he nodded towards the approaching group—"frothing-mouthed lackwits out for retribution for catching a glimpse of a hideous, filthy mask. I mean, honestly. Ant colonies have a higher sense of purpose than these back-water, inbred dullards. So, no, I will *not* run. Not from them. We should have done this from the beginning instead of going along with the ridiculous fictional floggings our wayward siblings so strongly advocated."

He wove a spell, and the air in front of him glimmered like sunlight reflecting off a pond. The shimmering glare coalesced into form, taking the shape of a hulking man wearing polished silver armor and holding a sword that looked like it was made of glass and sunlight.

Holly squinted as her eyes watered. She had to turn away as the brightness emanating from Hawthorn's conjuration was too much to bear. If they were going to face the townsfolk, then she'd better find a way to help. She reached into her pocket and pulled out Chester.

"I know you're hungry," she whispered to him, "but there's no time for food just yet. I need you to find us some help with the people coming. I don't think they're too happy with us, so we might need a *lot* of help." She put Chester on the ground, and with a squeak he scurried away into the grass and disappeared.

The crowd approached, close enough now to catch snippets of their voices. Some were pointing at Hawthorn and Holly, others were taking measure of the hulking, shimmering sword-bearing man blocking their way on the road.

"Turn around," Hawthorn called out as the crowd stopped in front of his conjuration. They were staring up at the shimmering man, some with gaping mouths, others shading their eyes. Most were eyeing his glass-like sword with open apprehension.

"I'm sure there is nothing of interest to you here," Hawthorn continued. "So you can just scurry back to whatever hole you crawled out of." When the crowd remained, Hawthorn waggled his fingers at them. "Go on. Shoo, shoo."

A man in the crowd stepped forward and thrust a finger at Hawthorn. "You and your friends come to this town sullying our good traditions. You're the ones that need to get."

"Traditions? You mean the mask? You need better traditions, my friend. Horrendous thing. It's not fit for the fire. It would've been a mercy to you all if I'd thrown it on the midden heap."

Others in the crowd gasped as the man growled and took a step towards Hawthorn, but the armored conjuration touched his sword to the man's chest and the man backed away.

Hawthorn smirked. "As I said. You'd better run along now."

The group conferred among themselves. Then the man, balling his fists, said, "We're not going anywhere."

"Very well."

The armored hulk swung his sword at the crowd, but everyone scattered and ran into the field, surrounding them.

"Hawthorn...," Holly said as she tried to keep track of everyone. "What now?"

Hawthorn altered his spell, and the armored conjuration split into three smaller and less formidable identical aspects. They chased the townsfolk into the grass, but there were close to a dozen people—if not more—so they were well outnumbered.

Holly crept closer to Hawthorn as she watched one of the townsfolk dodge a sword jab before grabbing hold of the armored man's arm. The light emanating from the conjuration faded as they struggled, and when others joined in, the spell failed and the conjuration vanished.

Hawthorn sucked in a breath as the townsfolk, seeing their victory, swarmed upon the remaining two.

"*Now* we should leave," Holly said.

"Never," Hawthorn said and brought up a crystalline wall as thin as paper that surrounded them both. It went up just as one of the townsfolk bolted towards them. He ran into the wall and bounced off it with a bloodied lip and dazed expression.

"That's nice," Holly said. "But now we're stuck here. I don't think you really thought it through."

"I don't see you assisting in our current situation beyond suggesting we run and hide like a pair of willowy ladies."

"*Willowy ladies?*"

Hawthorn fixed his attention beyond her. When Holly turned to look, she saw Chester scamper out of the grass. She crouched down to pick him up, but her hand ran into Hawthorn's wall.

"Let down the wall," she said. "We can't leave him out there."

"Oh no," Hawthorn said. "No, no, no."

"Oh yes. You can't just..." Holly trailed off as Chester scampered away, and behind him, a swarm of rodents poured out of the grass and onto the road. There were mice and voles, rats and weasels, and blind little moles. There were squirrels, chipmunks, and wild jackrabbits with their long legs and longer ears.

"Lady preserve us." Hawthorn gasped as he brought out a handkerchief from his pocket and used it to cover his mouth and nose.

Holly grinned. "Good boy, Chester!" she shouted, hoping he could hear her through the wall. The rodents moved in packs, looking like living earth that shifted and heaved upon the field.

At first none of the townsfolk seemed to notice them. But when weasels started twining around people's legs, mice crawling up underneath pants and skirts, rabbits kicking at anyone who came near, and all the other rodents nibbling at whatever they could find—panic erupted. People swatted at their legs and chests as rodents crawled up them. One man ran into Hawthorn's translucent wall, his arms flailing as two squirrels clung to the back of his shirt. A woman tripped over her skirts and fell down on the road in a cloud of dust. The rodents swarmed over her, eclipsing her form under a writhing mass of furry little bodies.

One man ran away. When another tried to help the fallen woman, the rodents swarmed over him as well, and the rest of the group of townsfolk lost their nerve and ran down the road in the direction they came.

Hawthorn continued to press the kerchief to his mouth, his eyes wide and filled with horror.

Holly folded her arms grinned at him. "What were you saying about me not contributing?"

He closed his eyes and took a deep breath. "Wild witches," he said and turned to look at her. "Crazy like a pack of sodden badgers."

Holly's grin widened. "And don't you forget it."

Through the Keyhole

Just as Hawthorn let down his crystalline wall and retrieved his jacket, a carriage came rattling down the road behind them. The carriage slowed as it approached, and Tum glowered down at them from his perch next to the driver.

"You think you can just ditch old Tum? Placate him with dolls and leave him in the cellar? Not nearly enough beer to ditch me in a place like that. So if you want to keep on my good side, you'd best think again the next time you're of a mind to be playing your tricks."

"We weren't trying to trick you, Tum," Holly said. "We meant to come back. We—"

Tum put up a hand. "Tricksters' tongues wag only lies. Old Uncle Tid told me that one. You calling my uncle a liar?"

"I... what?"

"Get in the carriage and let us be done with it. I've still words to share with Miss Hazel, so let's go find her before my mood changes."

Hawthorn opened the carriage door. A rotten draft of air wafted out, and inside on the floor lay a heap of Francis's wheat dolls. A few tumbled out and landed in the dirt.

Holly clapped a hand over her nose and mouth. "Ugh, what's that smell? And where are we supposed to sit?"

"You should have thought of that before you crossed me." He thrust a finger in the air. "Never cross a cellar gnome. Not if you want to live to tell about it."

Hawthorn, covering his nose with a handkerchief, said, "The only thing threatening our lives is the stench emanating from my once pristine coach. Did something *die* in there?"

Tum sniffed. "I may or may not have broken a jar of those pickled eggs in the coach. Not that it should matter. In my day, we were lucky if a jar of eggs broke on our heads, and then if we were *really* lucky, we got to eat the glass afterwards."

"That makes *no* sense," Holly said.

Tum waved his hands. "You coming or not? Time's wasting, it is."

They clambered inside. Hawthorn shoved most of the dolls out onto the road, ignoring Tum's shrieking protests. Then the carriage started moving, and both Holly and Hawthorn unlatched the catches on the windows and stuck their heads out into the cool, clean air.

HAZEL AND Hemlock hurried along the road. They had managed to escape the town undetected with the help of a few well-timed spells that had diverted unwanted attention. Well, from the people that had remained behind anyway. Hazel kept a sharp eye out for the mob that had left in case they came back.

So when she saw a pack of people on the road ahead, she grabbed Hemlock's arm before he had a chance to react, and they both darted into a field and flattened themselves in the tall grass. They remained there even after the shuffling footsteps and murmuring of voices had faded in the distance.

"Well, that was—" Hemlock began, but Hazel clamped a hand over his mouth as she strained to listen.

"I think a carriage is coming." She removed her hand, and they both peeked over the grass in time to witness their carriage rattle along the road while Holly and Hawthorn both hung halfway out of the windows.

"Do they think they're on a joyride?" Hazel said and got to her feet to run after them.

"Would that surprise you?" Hemlock said as he followed her.

"Hazel!" Holly shouted. "Tum, stop the carriage!"

"Tum stops for no one!" he shouted back.

The carriage careened down the road, leaving Hazel and Hemlock behind. There were some unintelligible shouts, then the carriage stopped. Then somehow it managed an awkward turn on the narrow road and headed back.

Holly hopped out of the carriage before it stopped and ran over and hugged Hazel. Then she pulled away, put her hands on her hips, and gave her a severe look. "What were you thinking with that stupid plan of yours? Did you have a plan for when it didn't work out? Because it *didn't* work out, did it?"

"It didn't work out because I don't know when to keep my mouth shut," Hazel said.

Hawthorn had also left the carriage and stood next to Holly. "Shocking. Perhaps you should stop putting yourself—and all of us—in situations where keeping your mouth shut is imperative."

Hazel scowled at him, but before she could say anything, Holly grabbed her arm and pulled her towards the carriage. "We'd better get out of here before the townspeople come back. They got a good scare with the voles and weasels, but I doubt it'll last long."

"What?"

"I'll explain later. *Come on.*"

"We need to go back to Emmond's house," Hazel said as she freed her arm from Holly.

"Um, no?" Holly said. "We need to leave. Right now."

"Listen to your sister," Hawthorn said. "At least one of you has sense."

"Hazel," Hemlock said as he shot Hawthorn a sharp look. "I don't think going back would be a good idea."

"It's a terrible idea!" Hazel said, throwing up her hands. "But we still need to do it. There's something there connected to Father. I know there is."

"Ah, yes," Hawthorn said. "Your 'vision' from a necromantic potion. It's not enough for you to dabble in the dark arts, now you feel compelled to drag us all into the mire with you?"

Holly elbowed him. To Hazel, she said, "You don't know it's the same place."

"I know it's the only place we've come across that resembles what I saw. We have to go back."

When no one said anything, Hazel lifted her chin. "Fine, I'll go back myself." She started down the road, but Hemlock stopped her.

"Nobody's going off alone. We'll go with you." He looked at the others. "Right?"

Holly wrung her hands, but she nodded. "Right."

Hawthorn remained distinctly silent. Holly swatted him on the shoulder, and he sighed and said, "Right."

They all headed towards the carriage. Hazel covered her nose. "Ugh. What's that smell?"

"Your charming gnome had his way with the carriage," Hawthorn said.

"It's not too bad if you stick your head out the window," Holly said.

"I'm not sticking my head—" Hazel began, but then her throat clenched shut when Hawthorn opened the carriage door and the smell of vinegar and sulphur hit her like a wall. "Show me how."

What a sight they must have been, Hazel thought as she leaned nearly halfway out the window. Four adults hanging out of a moving carriage like drunken revelers.

Hemlock smiled at her as the carriage rattled along. "It's rather refreshing, don't you think?"

"Oh yes," Hazel said. "Very refreshing what with all the gnats and flies bouncing off my face." She grimaced. "I think I swallowed one."

Hemlock laughed and closed his eyes as he lifted his face towards the sun.

Thankfully, the trip back was blessedly short. For once, Hazel didn't wait for the carriage to stop and hopped out as soon as it had sufficiently slowed. Holly yelped and clapped, then did the same.

Hazel looked around. None of the townsfolk were in sight, though they'd probably show up soon enough. She hurried up the steps and, holding her breath, eased the door open and poked her head inside. The room stood quiet and dark, save for the diffused streams of sunlight filtering through the linen curtains.

"Hello?" Hazel called, but no answer came. She stepped inside and headed to the cramped tincture room where Emmond had proposed his ridiculous plan.

She opened one of the desk drawers and rifled around through sheaves of paper. She glanced at a few of them, which looked to be nothing more than bills and invoices and inventory lists for nearby farms. She opened another drawer and found an array of steel-tipped pens and sealed pots of ink. Another drawer held a bundle of Francis's dolls, and Hazel slammed the drawer shut a bit harder than she intended. The desk held nothing of interest that she could find, so she turned her attention to the cabinet.

Inside she found an array of ointment pots and jars and little bottles similar to the ones on the shelves lining the walls. None were labeled though. How was anyone supposed to find anything if nothing was labeled? She picked up a narrow, cylindrical jar about as big around as her thumb and twice as tall. She pulled out the cork stopper and sniffed the contents and nearly dropped the thing when her eyes stung and watered and she staggered back in a fit of coughing.

"Careful," Hemlock said as he stood at the door's threshold.

Holly poked her head in. "What're you sniffing at?"

Hazel wiped her eyes. "I don't know. You're the Hearth witch, maybe you'd do a better job going through all this stuff."

"Maybe, if I knew what I was looking for."

"Yes, well, unfortunately we don't have that luxury."

"Then what's the point?"

"The point is to find something that stands out that will hopefully give us a hint to where Father has gone."

"You do hear yourself, right? You do realize how nonsensical that sounds?"

Hazel snorted. "You're the queen of nonsense. This should be your area of expertise."

But Holly was not amused. "There's nothing here!"

Everyone turned quiet. Hemlock, flanked by the sisters, tried to press himself into the door's threshold as he studied his feet. Hawthorn stood out in the main room, shaking his head as he otherwise pretended not to notice their argument.

Hazel tightened her jaw as she stared at Holly. Holly's cheeks had turned a deep red, but she stood her ground and glowered back at Hazel.

The silence broke when Tum tottered inside the house. "Hate to break up the party, but we got a band o' those townsfolk coming up the way, so we might want to skedaddle, if you catch my meaning."

"We need to go, Hazel," Holly said.

"Excellent idea," Hawthorn said and followed Tum out the door.

"We can come back later," Hemlock said. "After they leave."

"You mean after they ransack the place?" Hazel said. "I don't think so."

"Hazel, please," Holly said.

"You can leave if you want. I'm staying here."

Holly planted her hands on her hips, but before she could say anything, Hemlock took her by the arm and led her out.

"SHE'S LOST it," Holly said as Hemlock gently led her across the main room. "Her mind's finally snapped, and she's gone the wrong way round the bend."

They reached the door, and Hemlock opened it and led them outside.

"I mean, you agree with me, right?" Holly said. "We shouldn't be staying here."

Hemlock stopped as they reached the bottom of the steps at the base of the porch. "It doesn't matter what I think. Hazel's dug in, and she's not going to change her mind. Arguing about it isn't going to help us at this point. Not when we've got an angry mob headed our way. We need to decide what we're going to do about *that.*"

Holly threw up her hands. "I don't know! I don't know what to do that will scare them away again. I don't think they'll be chased off twice by weasels and moles." She scratched her head. "I could try to bring a pack of wolves over, but that's trickier. A *lot* trickier."

"So," Hawthorn said as he came over to stand next to them. "We have a choice of either getting mauled by an angry mob or by a pack of wild wolves. Brilliant."

"I pick the wolves," Holly said.

"Nobody's getting mauled," Hemlock said. To Hawthorn, he added, "Have you ever done a keyhole illusion?"

Hawthorn arched an eyebrow. "A couple of times. Why? Have *you?*"

Hemlock shook his head. "I've read about them, but no, never tried one."

"What's a keyhole illusion?" Holly said.

Hawthorn held up a hand at her. To Hemlock, he said, "You're not suggesting we try one, are you?"

Hemlock remained silent a moment as he met Hawthorn's gaze. "You have any other ideas?"

Hawthorn chuckled and rubbed his hands together. "Well, this should be interesting. Do you have an illusion in mind?"

Hemlock nodded. "I created an illusion of the Witness earlier, and it worked for a little while. But it was too simple, too crude, and they saw through it. If we can work a keyhole illusion of the Witness, well, if that doesn't send them running for the hills, nothing will."

Holly waved a hand between the two brothers. "Hello? Will someone please tell me what we're talking about?"

Hemlock took a breath and turned towards her. "A keyhole illusion is basically a cross between a conjuration and an illusion and requires two practitioners in Wyr magic to pull off."

"Only the tricky part," Hawthorn added, "is that whoever does the conjuring bit risks breaking his own mind."

"What?" Holly said. "How?"

Hemlock rubbed the back of his neck and said, "The summoner, in this case... conjures the entity within him, rather than externally."

"He *becomes* the conjuration, essentially," Hawthorn said.

Holly's mouth hung open. "I don't understand. Is it a spirit? This sounds like necromancy."

"Don't be absurd," Hawthorn said. "No souls are involved—it's not at all the same."

"The discerning difference between a conjuration and an illusion," Hemlock said, "is that others must be present to observe the illusion for it to work."

"But since others can't see what is inside oneself," Hawthorn added, "it must be a conjuration in this particular instance."

"But what will it do?" Holly asked. "Why can't you do the conjuration outside yourself?"

Hawthorn said, "Despite the complexities in summoning them, conjurations are simple creations. You can create a conjuration of a giant or a fierce beast, but they will not necessarily act as you wish. They have no souls, no wills of their own. They are not *alive*, and just like an illusion, they can sometimes be seen for what they are."

Hemlock said, "But if you summon a conjuration within you, well, it's like it changes you. You... become what you summon. At least mentally. Externally, you'll look the same."

"Which is where the second person comes into play to apply all the necessary outwards illusions."

"Oh, I see," Holly said. "So you basically give the thing *your* soul. Tell me again how it's not like necromancy?"

Hawthorn gave her a flat look. "I'm not *giving* it anything. *Lending* perhaps is as far as I would go. And you would be surprised how thin a line separates many of the disciplines from one another. But this is strictly a Wyr spell, I assure you."

"Though it *is* forbidden," Hemlock said.

Hawthorn chuckled. "Ah, yes. The Conclave wasn't at all pleased at the rising number of drooling warlocks cooking their brains from attempting keyhole illusions."

"But why the conjuration at all?" Holly said. "Why not just act the part?"

Hawthorn shrugged. "I suppose one always could take that approach, but you will never get the same kind of *authenticity* by acting. For all intents and purposes, we will be bringing the Witness into the world in a way that acting could never replicate."

"It's why it's called a keyhole illusion," Hemlock said. "Because they say it's like looking through a keyhole into another world."

"Or like bringing another world *through* a keyhole," Hawthorn said. "It depends who you ask."

From further down the road, the murmuring of voices and the scuffling of footsteps grew louder.

"I'll do the conjuration," Hemlock said. "You do the illusion."

"Absolutely not," said Hawthorn. "You've never done this before. I'll do the conjuration."

"It's my idea; it's my risk to take."

"And all of us are at risk if it's not done properly. We have one shot at this, and we don't have time to argue."

Hemlock glowered at Hawthorn, but before he could say anything else,

Hawthorn started his spell. He spoke a series of unfamiliar words, and the familiar glint in his eyes faded and was replaced by something wholly foreign. A chill bore into the base of Holly's neck, and she took a step back.

"WHO DARE STANDS BEFORE ME UNPREPARED?" Hawthorn's voice boomed as he spoke. There was a sliver of his usual voice present, but the rest sounded like someone else. Hemlock worked his illusion, and right before Holly's eyes, Hawthorn transformed.

He grew taller in stature, his purple-black coat replaced with a long, black tattered cloak. His beautiful features were eclipsed with a horrid waxen mask, similar to the one Holly had seen earlier. She clapped a hand over her mouth to stifle a gasp. She hadn't really thought it possible, but Hawthorn was gone. This *was* the Witness.

"YOU WILL ANSWER ME," the Witness said as he took a step towards her. "OR BEAR MY WRATH."

"I..." Holly began.

Hemlock, standing behind the Witness, waved towards the road.

Holly nodded and took a deep breath. "*They* stand before you unprepared!" She thrust an accusatory finger at the throng of people just as they topped the hill.

The Witness rounded on them, and as he did, the entire group froze. For one hopeful moment it looked like they might run away. But then a man stepped forward.

"It's all a trick!" he said. "This isn't the Witness!"

That solidified the courage in the rest of the group, and they charged forward.

The Witness lifted his arms, and the entire group ran into an invisible wall with a series of grunts and cries of pain. Several of them staggered back and fell down with bloodied noses.

The Witness bent down next to a man on the ground cradling his jaw and grabbed the back of his head. The man seemed to shrink within himself as the Witness brought his face close to his. He stared into the Witness's eyes, and then he began to scream.

"It's him! It's the Witness!"

Panic broke out among the crowd. Most were trying to cover their eyes as they scrambled to their feet, resulting in a clumsy dash as the townsfolk collided into one another as they ran for all they were worth back down the road.

Holly let out a breath, then the Witness turned on her.

"YOU," he said. "YOU MUST ATONE."

She staggered back. The illusion fell from the Witness, and he looked like Hawthorn again, but he still came towards her with a gleam in his eyes that Holly didn't recognize.

"Hemlock?" she said as she backed up against the porch.

Hemlock worked another spell, and the foreign gleam in Hawthorn's eyes faded, replaced by one of befuddlement. Then he fell over.

Holly ran over to him. She fell to her knees and scrabbled at his coat and patted his cheek.

"Hawthorn? Wake up. Please wake up." She looked up at Hemlock and felt a pang of panic at his distressed expression.

"How do we wake him up?" she said.

Hemlock shook his head as his mouth hung open. "I... I don't know."

"What do you mean, you don't know? Do something!"

"I—"

Hawthorn groaned and put a hand to his head.

Holly helped him sit up. "Are you all right?"

He stared at her and mumbled something incoherent.

"He's cooked his brain!" Holly said.

Hemlock said, "Just... give him a minute." He squatted down and put a hand on Hawthorn's shoulder. Looking into his eyes, Hemlock said, "You've ruined your best jacket, brother."

Hawthorn's expression remained vacant as his jaw slackened.

Hemlock tightened his grip on Hawthorn's shoulder. "Not to worry though. I'm sure Holly can sew you a new one out of the curtains."

Hawthorn continued to stare at his brother for several heartbeats when his brow twitched into a frown. "Curtains?" he murmured, his voice raspy and strained. "On me?" He let out a sharp wheeze that might have been a laugh. "Only if you put it on my cold, turgid corpse."

Hemlock smiled and gave his brother's shoulder another squeeze. "He's fine."

Holly wrapped her arms around Hawthorn and hugged him tight. Then she shoved him. "You stupid idiot! What were you thinking, doing a spell like that?"

Hawthorn grinned. "I was magnificent, wasn't I?"

"No, you were creepy. Don't do it again."

"Creepy because I was magnificent. You've never seen anything like it before, have you?"

"No, and I don't want to. So promise you won't do it again."

"I'll do no such thing."

Holly grabbed one of his ears and twisted it.

"Ow!" he cried. "Let go, you torturous harpy."

"Promise!"

"Fine, I promise. Now unhand me."

Holly pursed her lips and let go. "Well, all right then."

Hemlock hid a smile behind his hand.

Hawthorn smoothed his hair and attempted to brush his jacket clean, but he gave up and sighed.

"Come on," Hemlock said as he clasped Hawthorn by the forearm. "Let's find you some clean clothes."

Milled Messages

Hazel walked out of the tincture room with the latest drawerful of bottles as Hemlock and Hawthorn walked in. Hawthorn was filthy, and he dragged his feet as Hemlock helped him towards the sofa, his head hanging as if it were too much to bear.

"What happened?" she said. "I heard commotion out there. I've been trying to pack up everything I can find so we can leave."

"Resplendent victory happened," Hawthorn said in a sudden display of renewed vigor. "Victory!" He stumbled over his feet and fell onto the sofa.

"Is he drunk?"

Hemlock chuckled and shook his head. "He just cooked his brain a little, but he'll be fine." At Hazel's perplexed look, he added, "I'll explain it all later, but the townspeople have gone and I don't think they'll be coming back. So we should have some time."

Hazel let out a long breath as she set down the drawer of tinctures on the floor near the door along with three others. "I can't say I'm not thankful for that. I have no idea what I'm looking for here. My only plan was to grab everything not nailed down to take with us and sort out later. I could really use the extra time."

Hemlock smiled. "Well, you have it." He nodded towards Hawthorn.

"I'm going to find him some new clothes. I'll be right back." He walked out the door as Holly walked in. She started for Hazel, but then noticed Hawthorn curling up on the sofa, and headed towards him instead.

She pushed Hawthorn's legs aside, sat next to him, and prodded at his arm. "I don't think you should lie down, in case you fall asleep. You probably shouldn't fall asleep so soon after cooking your brain."

Hazel asked, "Why does everyone keep saying he's cooked his brain?"

"Well, he didn't *actually* cook it, but it's not like he didn't give it a good go."

Hemlock came back with a bundle of folded clothes. He took them over to Hawthorn and roused him out of his half-asleep stupor.

"What took you so long?" Hawthorn murmured.

"Sorry, but I'm unable to summon your cherished vestments with a snap of my fingers."

"Do work on that."

Hemlock let out a sharp breath that almost passed for a laugh. "Sure."

Hawthorn got to his feet and swayed as he began to unbutton his coat. Hemlock reached out to steady him. Holly just stood there, looking on.

Hazel said, "Holly, I could use some help searching the mill outside."

Several moments passed before Holly started and turned to look at her. "What?"

"Come help me outside. Hemlock can help Hawthorn get dressed without you looking on like a creepy window lurker."

"I wasn't *lurking*," Holly said as she headed towards the door, casting one quick glance back at Hawthorn as he peeled off his dirty jacket.

"No, but you have the creepy part covered well enough."

Holly opened her mouth again, but Hazel said, "Oh, just come on."

Once they were outside, Hazel said, "I thought you said you weren't interested in Hawthorn anymore."

"I'm not, but," Holly lowered her voice to a whisper, "he's still very pretty."

Hazel shook her head and opened the door to the mill. Inside, the few narrow windows were shuttered and the room stood dark. A little flame blossomed in Holly's cupped hands.

Her wavering light showed a cramped, circular interior dominated by a pair of great millstones, one stacked atop the other. A thick wooden shaft that turned the bottom stone—when the mill was in use—disappeared into the low timber ceiling that served as the floor of the second level, accessed by a narrow set of stairs along one part of the wall. The air smelled stale and dusty but also tinted with a pleasant nutty aroma.

"Well," Holly said, "what are we looking for?"

"I don't know. Let's just see what we can find."

Holly ran a finger along the hopper that fed grain into the stones. "Why would Father come here?"

"I don't know, Holly. The reasons why Father has done anything in his life are well beyond me."

The two sisters poked around the ground floor of the mill, but all they found was dust and remnants of old flour and a scattering of tools hanging from pegs. They took the stairs to the second floor but didn't find anything there either.

"There's nothing here, Hazel," Holly said as they ascended to the third and final floor. The space in which they had to stand was narrow and cramped as the low ceiling arced to a point a few feet above their heads. They had to keep near the wall, as the shaft that came through the floor was capped at calf height by a wooden gear almost the size of their kitchen table at home. It connected perpendicularly to an even greater gear pinioned by a shaft that led to the windmill sails outside. Holly peeked through the little window that accommodated the shaft connecting to the sails.

"It's starting to get dark outside," she said. "Are we going to spend the night here? Because, you know, I'd rather not."

Hazel said nothing as she looked around the cramped chamber. There were no tools or cupboards or anything else that looked out of place. There wasn't even so much as a scuff on the floor to indicate their father had ever come here. Hazel let out a long breath as she peered out the tiny window alongside Holly. What was she supposed to do now?

The sun sank towards the horizon, turning the sky golden and sending shadows from the trees to stretch across the wild, untended grass. As the fading light slanted across the windmill sails, a small, boxlike object cast its own shadow.

Hazel narrowed her eyes as she tried to get a better look. "What is that out there?"

"What's out where?" Holly said as she craned her neck and brought her head closer to Hazel's. "I don't see anything."

"There's something on one of the sails."

"Where?"

"On the uppermost one to the right." Hazel pointed. "There, near the edge."

Holly wrinkled her nose as she squinted out the window. "I don't see it."

"Never mind about that. How do we get that sail down within reach?"

"Um, I don't know. Get it to turn. With some wind. We need wind."

A slight breeze stirred outside. Hazel worked a spell that intensified it, but the sails remained still. "They didn't even budge."

"Try it again."

Hazel did but with the same result. She turned around to eye the machinery in the mill. "Is there a brake that's keeping the sails from turning?"

She and Holly poked around the gears and shafts.

"Here's a lever," Holly said, and before Hazel could reply, she pulled on it. There was a clanging sound, and a wooden band rose from the great gear that joined the smaller one just above the floor. Outside, the sails lazily rotated about an arm's length before they stopped again.

"Closer," Holly said.

"But not close enough." Hazel summoned more wind, but the breeze was still too gentle.

"You need to step it up a bit."

"I thought I was," Hazel said. "Obviously, the nuances of conjuring wind intensity is a skill I've yet to master."

"Go get Hemlock," Holly said. "Maybe he can help."

"Help with what?" Hemlock said as he walked up the narrow set of stairs into the tiny loft.

"Hazel needs help conjuring up some wind."

Heat crept into Hazel's cheeks, and she folded her arms. It was silly, feeling so defensive about such a trivial matter, but she couldn't help it. "I can conjure the wind just fine. I just need more of it."

"There's a little box or something on one of the sails," Holly said. "I can see it now, right *there*." She pointed.

Hemlock adjusted his glasses and nodded. "All right. Sounds simple enough. Go outside and get ready to grab whatever's on that sail as it goes by."

"If they get going too fast," Holly said, "here's the brake." She patted the iron lever.

"Good to know."

Hazel and Holly made their way outside and positioned themselves inside the sails' arc. The sails themselves were massive—the bottommost ones brushed the tips of the knee-high grass.

The wind kicked up, and after a few moments, the sails eased into motion. The joints creaked and groaned. After a few seconds, the one with the box swung low to the ground. The sail wasn't moving particularly fast, but even so, it swung by and out of reach before Hazel had a chance to grab the box.

"It's moving too fast," she shouted up to Hemlock.

"Right!"

She waited for the sail to come around again. Holly hunkered down as she readied herself. The wind calmed, but the sails kept on at the same speed. When the sail with the box made its way back down, a groaning sound resounded from within the mill, and the sails shuddered before slowing to a stop.

The box on the sail was about as wide as a ring box but twice as long. It looked to be built into the wood of the sail itself and didn't want to come off.

"I can burn it off," Holly said.

"Not when we don't know what's inside it," Hazel said.

Hemlock joined them, but he remained silent as Hazel poked around the box.

There was no way in, not that she could tell. The sails were massive slats of wood, and the little box looked to be a natural part of that.

"Maybe it's not supposed to come off," Holly said. "Maybe it belongs there."

Maybe she was right. Hazel's stomach sank. She had been so certain that she would find something here.

The sun dipped below the horizon, lighting the sky on fire in brilliant shades of orange and red.

"We should go," Holly whispered.

"Where? We've nowhere to go."

Holly said nothing. She put a hand on Hazel's shoulder, but Hazel couldn't bring herself to meet her sister's eyes. Then Holly turned and headed back inside the house.

Hemlock stood next to her but remained silent. The fire in the sky faded, cooling to a deep, pristine blue. A few stars winked into existence, studding the fabric of the young night like luminous pearls.

On the box, a faint, silvery script began to glow.

"What is that?" Hemlock said.

Hazel leaned in to get a closer look. "I don't know. It looks like a symbol of some sort. A circle that's been intersected with a cross and crowned with a tiny star." She leaned back. "Have you ever seen anything like it before?"

"No, never."

What could it mean? Did it mean anything? Maybe it was like the Witness mask—a relic from a bygone age that only held superstitious significance for those who cared to remember it. Was it a mark of protection? Or maybe a spell to bring bountiful harvests?

Her attention fixated on the cross that divided the circle into four parts. Four was a significant number in magic. There were the four elements of fire, water, air, and earth. There were four Divinities—the Ladies of the Sky and Sea, Lords of the Trees and Sun. Yet if Hawthorn was to be believed, there was also a fifth element, a fifth divinity. Was that what the little star meant? Outside the realm of nature yet still belonging. A Lord of Ether. A Lady of Night and Stars. A siphoner of souls.

A chill crawled up Hazel's neck. This couldn't be a coincidence—finding a potential necromantic symbol in a place similar to what she had seen in her vision. Again, she tried to remove the box, but it remained immovable. Growing frustrated, she cast a Weaving spell that altered the sail behind the box. The wood cracked as it softened, but the box itself began to darken as if it had taken to rot. The glowing symbol began to fade. Fearful she might destroy it—and whatever it might contain—Hazel canceled her spell, and the symbol regained its muted glow.

Necromancy. Leave it to a rotten art to rot perfectly sound wood. She tried her spell again, only this time she altered it, souring the wood herself, twisting it into something ugly, something dark. She focused her spell directly onto the box. The circular symbol glowed brighter, and the box fell to the grassy ground.

Hazel picked up the box and opened it. Inside was a lock of golden hair, tied together with a stiff white ribbon. Underneath it lay a slip of paper. Hazel took the paper and unfolded it, but it was too dark outside to read.

Hemlock summoned a glowing moth that fluttered around her hands, illuminating in its soft light the following message:

It is time.

"Time for what?" Hemlock asked.

Hazel stared at the paper as a cold veil of realization settled over her. "It's time to meet."

"Who?"

"My father," she whispered.

"How do you know?"

Hazel said nothing. She took the lock of hair and dropped the empty box on the ground. The hair was like spun flax. Just like Holly's hair. Just like their mother's. With shaking hands, she untied the ribbon and pulled it free. On one side of the stiff fabric was a scrawling of writing in charcoal ink:

In the Star Shrine anchored beyond the Sea, a love tempered in death will bring you back to me.

Hazel felt light-headed, as if all her blood had pooled in her feet.

A love tempered in death...

Memories of Willow's sickness came back to her. The way her mother had weakened until she faded away. The empty silence that followed. The itching that had nagged in Hazel's mind and taken her to the tumbledown cottage on that first new moon.

...will bring you back to me.

Her father had trapped her mother's soul, and now Hazel was holding a lock of her mother's hair that had been bound in a ribbon that spoke of the deed. Was it part of the spell? Was this somehow part of the key of undoing her mother's geas? Or was it an act of pride that made her father pen these words in ink? For the first time in her life, Hazel wished she was a necromancer. So that she could understand. So she could undo what had been done.

Hazel's hands trembled so much she nearly dropped the ribbon and hair. Gently Hemlock took the ribbon from her, and she put the lock of hair in her pocket.

He read the writing. Then, sparing a single glance at her, he turned and hurried back into the house. Hazel followed.

Hawthorn sat upright on the sofa, sipping a clear liquid from a glass vial and wincing at the taste. Holly sat next to him.

"It's disgusting," he said.

"It's willow bark extract," Holly said. "It'll help with your headache."

He sipped more of the liquid when Hemlock walked up to him and handed him the ribbon. Hawthorn read it, then shook his head and looked up at him. "What is this?"

"You've been to Sarnum before," Hemlock said. "You know the place. What is this sea he's talking about?"

"Who's talking about what?" Holly asked.

"Father," Hazel said. "About Mother."

Holly's mouth fell open, and Hawthorn tightened his jaw. He read the ribbon again and then took a deep breath. "The only sea I know about around here is the Sea of Severed Stars."

"I didn't know there was a sea nearby," Holly said.

"It is not a sea of water."

Holly shrank back a little. "Then what is it?"

"There is a prevalent notion in necromantic circles of a connection between stars and souls. Both are objects over which the Shapeless One reigns. Some even believe stars and souls to be one and the same and will use the words interchangeably. Which would make this sea..."

"A sea of severed souls," Hazel said.

Hawthorn nodded.

"Is that even possible?" Holly asked.

He shook his head. "I have no idea. I certainly hope not. I hope it's just a colorful name for a murky pond in someone's back garden that has been overly embellished throughout the years. But if I were to wager a guess in what 'sea' that note was referencing, then that would be it."

"Where is it?" Hazel said.

"I don't know."

"How can you not know?"

Hawthorn gave her a sharp look. "This is a closely guarded secret that only practitioners in necromancy are meant to know. The *only* reason I know anything about it is because some necromancers' tongues are too easily loosened when plied with enough wine. But even they would not reveal the location, not for any price or promise. If you want to find out where it is, you'll have to become a necromancer."

Everyone fell silent.

"How would I do that?" Hazel asked in a near whisper.

Everyone stared at her.

After an unbearably long moment of silence, Hawthorn said, "Necromancers have their own version of our Circle and Conclave called the Shrine. Perhaps if you appealed to them, they'd take you in."

"This is madness," Holly said. "You can't become a necromancer, Hazel!"

"What happens if they do take me in?" Hazel said. "What will they do? What will they... want me to do?"

Hawthorn shook his head. "I have no idea."

Holly said, "Hemlock, talk some sense into her!"

"We'll find another way, Hazel," Hemlock said.

"Like what?" Hazel said. "Tell me of this other plan you've devised that will lead us to my father. I'd love to hear it."

When Hemlock said nothing, Holly said, "The potions!"

"What?" Hazel said.

"The potions Odd made, remember?"

Hazel rubbed her forehead. "How will those help us?"

"I don't know. That's why we drink them and find out. It's got to be better than becoming a necromancer."

After a while, Hazel nodded. "Fine, but not here. We should return to Sarnum first. I don't want to be here when the townspeople finally regain their nerve and come back."

They took the tinctures and potions and carried them out to the carriage. The doors stood wide open, and Tum and the driver fanned the air with swathes of clothing.

"Is that my dress?" Hazel said.

"Dunno, maybe," Tum said. "But that's not the pressing issue here."

"Here we go."

"The issue is that I haven't gotten paid in... well... a while. I'm out of a jar o' eggs, a pile o' dolls, and there isn't any beer to be found anywhere. What have you got to say about that?"

"Absolutely nothing. We have bigger problems than your sobriety. So you can either help us load up these potions or find your own way back to Sarnum."

Tum stopped fanning and eyed her. "Potions, you say? What kinds of potions?"

Hazel thrust the drawer of tinctures at him. "Look for yourself."

Tum grinned and tottered away with his newfound loot.

The egg smell clinging to the carriage had faded to tolerable levels, and once the driver had lit and hung the lanterns, they were on their way. The waxing moon shone brightly above, washing the grassy hills in shifting shades of grey.

The night stretched on. Holly and Hawthorn slept slumped against each other. Hemlock dozed with his forehead resting against the window. But Hazel remained awake, watching as the whitewashed world rolled by and faded into darkness.

Cats and Contemplation

They made it back to Sarnum in the afternoon of the following day. Everyone had slept fitfully on the carriage, and they were all exhausted. They didn't return to the Backwards Buck though. Hawthorn directed them to a different inn—one that, he claimed, had far better hospitality.

The inn didn't look like much from the outside—a narrow timber building wedged between two of grey stone, like a spindly child trapped on a sofa between her two great aunts. A brass placard near the walnut door displayed the inn's name of Sensi's Contemplation.

"That's a weird name," Holly said.

"Are you sure this is an inn?" Hazel said.

Hawthorn drew himself up. "Of course. Although..."

"What?"

He shook his head. "Nothing. Just... apologies in advance." Without further explanation, he stepped inside and the others followed.

A pleasing aroma of rosewater and mint hung in the air, but all pleasantries ended there. A garish floral print papered the walls that clashed disorientingly with the mosaic-patterned carpets. The curtains were made of heavy chiffon, in lavender, and dozens of paintings of cats and kittens hung on the walls. There were kittens in baskets and hatboxes of yarn, another of a cat curled up next to a blazing fire. One portrait of a white-and-orange-patched cat was painted so intricately that Hazel felt like its brilliant green eyes followed her.

The main room was snug, with only a handful of round tables near the door. On the far end of the room, the hardwood floor rose a step, which led to a firelit hearth and a sofa where three elderly women sat knitting. A grey-striped cat lay on one of the sofa's arms.

Holly's mouth hung open as she took in their surroundings. Hemlock stared at the wallpaper with a dubious expression, as if expecting the flowers to hop off the walls and advance on them. Hazel didn't know what to make of it, so all she said was, "Oh my."

Hawthorn sighed. "The decor is atrocious. But they have the softest beds in town and the fluffiest biscuits topped with the most delectable cream." He nodded towards the trio of women. "I'm fairly certain those women were knitting on that sofa the last time I was here several years ago. I think they might be a permanent fixture."

"It's no wonder," Holly said as she gazed around the room. "This place is amazing!"

A stout, jovial innkeeper greeted them and escorted them upstairs, which was surprisingly vast compared to the overly snug common room downstairs. They were each given their own room, and once Hazel stood in hers, she stared in horror at a mural painted on the wall behind the bed depicting a collection of flowers with cat faces for blossoms.

Holly walked in and wrinkled her nose. "That's actually pretty creepy."

"Lucky me," Hazel said. "What's in your room?"

"A pirate ship with a crew of cats. It's the best painting in the house, as far as I can tell. So I'm not swapping."

"I'll contain my disappointment."

Hemlock walked in and froze when he saw the mural. "That's... impressive."

"What's in your room?" Holly asked.

"A line of cats wearing mismatched boots."

She giggled. "That sounds funny. Mine's still better though."

"Where's Hawthorn?" Hazel said.

"He's already fallen asleep. He's right about the beds; they are comfortable."

"What painting is in his room?" Holly asked.

"A pair of cats dueling in full plate armor."

Holly gasped. "Really?" She started for the door.

"Let the man rest, Holly," Hazel said.

Holly's shoulders sagged. "Fine."

"Should I be concerned about the cat infatuation here?" Hazel said.

"Only if you're allergic," Hemlock said, grinning. Then he sobered and cleared his throat. "Sorry."

"So, the potions," Holly said. "Should we drink them now?"

"Can it wait?" Hazel said. "I'm hungry and tired—not exactly the best condition when experimenting with suspicious gnome-enhanced potions."

Holly nodded. "All right then. We'll do it in the morning." She turned and left.

"Want to go downstairs and get something to eat?" Hemlock said. "I'm rather curious about those biscuits Hawthorn was going on about."

Hazel nodded.

They went down to the common room. The three women were still on the sofa, their needles click-clacking as they unapologetically eyed Hazel and Hemlock.

"What do you think they're knitting?" Hemlock whispered.

"Probably a cat."

They sat at a table and waited in silence as a willowy young waitress brought them a plate of biscuits topped with cream and jam. Hemlock took a big bite of one, then nodded as he chewed.

"Hawthorn wasn't kidding about the biscuits. They're incredible."

Hazel gave him a tight smile and took a bite of her own, but she couldn't find it within herself to share his pleasure.

"What's the matter?"

She stared at her plate a long while. "Would it be so bad if I became a necromancer? It's not like it'd mean anything. Just words I'd say to find Father. But if it would lead me to him, wouldn't that be worth something?"

Hemlock tightened his jaw and set down his biscuit. "Except it wouldn't be just words, Hazel. Words have meaning. Power. You know that. What you don't know is what they would require of you. These people manipulate human souls. How do you know they won't require yours?"

Hazel said nothing as she stared at the table. Hemlock took her hand. "We will find a way. Don't worry."

She forced a smile and nodded. "All right."

They finished their meal and retired to bed early—Hazel to her room and Hemlock to his. She lay in bed as she stared at the ceiling. Despite the fatigue that stung her eyes and ached in her bones, Hazel still couldn't sleep. Her mind wouldn't quieten, and an unaccountable fear settled deeper and deeper into her heart. What if becoming a necromancer was her only chance to find her father? What if it was the only way? The others would never let her go. Holly would likely tie her to a chair and haul her back to the Grove. And Hemlock... Hazel wouldn't be able to look him in the eyes again, and somehow that frightened her far more than necromancy ever could.

Hazel squeezed her eyes shut, telling herself to sleep, telling herself to believe Hemlock that they would find another way. But her unspoken words held no power for her. This *was* the only way. The sooner she accepted that, the sooner it would all be over.

A painful lump caught in her throat. She swallowed it down, along with her rising regret. She walked to the little desk in a corner of her room and scribbled a note by the gentle moonlight filtering through the window. Then she got up and walked into the night.

Enshrined

H olly.

Holly sipped her tea. She sat at their little kitchen table at home, seated across a squirrel twice her size.

"It's all rubbish, you know," she said. "Gathering acorns for winter is one of the world's greatest hoaxes. Everyone knows that summer is eternal and that winter is just a clouding of the mind."

The squirrel chittered and nodded, then buttered a piece of bread.

"Holly!"

Holly jolted awake. Hemlock stood over her as a little glowing moth illuminated his haggard face.

"Hazel's gone," he said.

"What?" Holly sat up and rubbed her eyes. "Gone where?"

He dropped a note on the bed and went over to the closet. "You need to get dressed."

Holly blinked several times as she tried to clear the haze of sleep from her eyes. She squinted at the paper, illuminated just enough by Hemlock's fluttering moth.

Hemlock,

I'm sorry, but there is no other way. I need to do this, though I don't expect you to understand. Please look after Holly for me and make sure she gets home safe. Tell her I'll find a way to make Father undo what he's done. Tell her—just tell her that.

Hazel

Holly flipped over the letter, but there was nothing else. "Where did you get this?"

Hemlock pulled out a dress from the closet and threw it onto her bed. "The night man slipped it under my door. I couldn't sleep, so I noticed when it came in. After I read it, I went to her room, but she'd already gone."

"But she said—"

"Get dressed, Holly," Hemlock said, his voice quiet and strained. "We need to go get her before it's too late."

∽

THE STREET was quiet and abandoned, for which Hazel was grateful. The night man on duty at Sensi's Contemplation had told her where she could find the Shrine and even had helped her find a late-night carriage to drive her there. He had promised to deliver her letter after she'd gone. She had made him repeat the promise until she had believed him.

Now she stood on the Shrine's wide doorstep, the stone immaculately clean and freshly scrubbed.

She gripped her mother's lock of hair as she stared at the black wooden door carved with an elaborate motif of stars and bones. The building itself was a massive stone affair, as clean as the doorstep upon which she stood, though there was nothing but darkness beyond the tall windows.

Curtains. They were dark because of curtains. Or because everyone was asleep. Surely there would be light somewhere inside. She was being silly, fretting over trivialities that didn't exist other than in her mind. She tightened her grip on her mother's hair. Just one more minute to gather her nerve. To tell herself she wasn't making the biggest mistake of her life.

Just one more minute.

∾

HEMLOCK WALKED into Hawthorn's room without knocking. Holly trailed after him, quietly closing the door behind her, though her care was unnecessary.

"Get up," Hemlock said as he went to Hawthorn's closet.

Hawthorn groaned. "I have never slept so poorly in my entire life than I have in the company of you three."

"You mean us *two*," Hemlock said. "Hazel's gone."

"Shocking." Hawthorn sat up and ran a hand over his face. "Has it ever occurred to you to simply let her go? The woman's more trouble than she's worth."

Hemlock's expression tightened, and he stared at his brother with a coldness that Holly had never seen in him before.

Hawthorn sobered and cleared his throat. "I... Where did she go?"

"To the Shrine," Holly said. "She's actually going to do it. She's going to become a necromancer." Holly couldn't believe it. She spoke the words, yet they still felt hollow to her. How could Hazel possibly do such a thing?

Hemlock said, "Which is why you need to get up and take us there."

Hawthorn nodded. "I... Of course." He got up and took the shirt and pants that Hemlock held out to him. He opened his mouth, like he wanted to say something, but instead he just nodded and started to get dressed.

Holly walked out and waited in the hall, only then realizing that Hawthorn had been naked and she didn't even care. She didn't care about anything other than finding her sister.

∾

WITH A final, deep breath, Hazel squared her shoulders and pulled on a thick, braided cord by the Shrine door. She clenched and unclenched her jaw, twisted the lock of hair around her finger until it hurt.

The door opened, and a man shrouded in a black robe peered out at her. "Yes?"

Hazel froze. She should leave. She should just turn on her heel and head back to the inn, let Hemlock's hands warm her own, let his assurances warm her heart. Instead, she said, "I'm here to become a necromancer."

The man stared at her a long moment. Then he chuckled a low laugh. He started to close the door, but Hazel put out her hand and stopped him.

"We don't take in trash from the streets," he said. "To be a necromancer is to be chosen. And you... you are not a chosen one."

Hazel gritted her teeth. "If I'm trash, then you're a pus-filled boil. How dare you? If I wasn't chosen, then how could I know of your Sea of Severed Souls? How could I work necromancy without learning a single thing about it? I'd wager I'm more of a chosen one than you, so you go back in there and find me someone with real authority."

The man smirked at her. "Of course. Wait here." He had nearly gotten the door closed when Hazel thrust her foot in the threshold.

"I'm not an idiot." She fished out the ribbon from her pocket and handed it to him. "If I wasn't supposed to be here, then why do I have that? Why would it tell me to come here? That is what it's telling me, right?"

The man summoned an orb of silvery light and read the ribbon. He regarded her a long moment from under his brow, then he swung open the door. "Follow me."

Hazel wiped her sweating palms on her skirt and hoped that, one day, Hemlock and Holly would forgive her.

HOLLY, HEMLOCK, and Hawthorn sat silently in the carriage as it hurtled down the street. Hemlock stared out the window, biting his nails as his legs mindlessly bounced up and down. Hawthorn stared at his hands. When the carriage slowed, Hemlock jumped out and ran to the Shrine and pulled on a braided cord that hung by the door. Holly and Hawthorn followed close behind.

Hemlock tapped his hands on his legs as he waited. The door opened, and they were met by a man wearing a black robe.

"A young woman came here tonight," Hemlock said. "Her name's Hazel. We need to see her."

"We are not a boarding house," the man said. "We do not take visitors. We do not betray those who pass beyond our walls."

"But she came here, right?" Holly asked.

"I couldn't say."

Hemlock grabbed the man by the collar of his robe, yanked him away from the door, and sent him stumbling out into the street. Hemlock tried to walk into the Shrine, but it was as if he had walked into an invisible wall. He staggered back.

The necromancer laughed. "As if you were the first who ever tried to trespass on our Shrine. As if we weren't prepared for such inevitabilities."

From within the Shrine, three more black-robed necromancers came to the door. From the shadows on the streets, dark forms shambled into the light. They watched Hemlock and the others with weeping yellow eyes. Hemlock took a step back.

"That's right," the necromancer said. "You'd better leave, and you'd better leave now."

Holly whispered to Hemlock, "We need to find another way in."

Hemlock clenched his jaw, but he nodded. They returned to the carriage and drove away.

❧

Hazel waited in a dark, well-appointed, windowless chamber. She sat on a plush, deep blue velvet sofa, eyeing the blue-and-green flames that flickered behind glass sconces on the stone walls. The lights illuminated tapestries woven into scenes of star-studded night skies, which gave the room a feeling of openness that Hazel had not expected. It was strangely comfortable, and that made her uneasy.

The door opened, and a man wearing a black robe embroidered along the sleeves and hem with glimmering silver thread walked in. "So. I'm told you want to become a necromancer."

Hazel stood and regarded him. His features were shrouded within his robe's hood, so she couldn't get a measure of him. She clasped her hands and straightened her back. "That's right."

"Why?"

She blinked a few times. "I'm sorry?"

The man chuckled and lowered the hood of his robe. He was younger than she'd expected—perhaps a little older than herself—with wavy brown hair and kind eyes. "What's your name?"

"Hazel."

"Like the tree? You must be from the Grove."

"Does that matter?"

"Not really. But it does make me question your motives. Necromancy is forbidden in the Grove, disdained by its people. It makes me wonder why you are here, saying you want to become one."

Hazel's mind whirled. She didn't know what to say to him. She didn't want to become a necromancer—she just wanted to find her father. Should she tell him that? He seemed kind; maybe he would help her. But then again, maybe he wouldn't. Maybe he'd throw her out and she'd have squandered her one chance in finding Ash. "I've told you my name, what's yours?"

"Verrin."

"Have you ever been to the Grove, Verrin?"

"I have not."

"It's a beautiful place, lush with trees and flowers. Life flourishes there, and I've always thought it well that necromancy was forbidden."

He raised his eyebrows.

"But we're a peculiar people," Hazel continued. "We're set in our ways with customs that don't always make sense. Men and women largely live separately, for example. Even if married, they don't necessarily share their lives together."

Verrin folded his hands. "Fascinating."

Hazel gave him a level look. "What I'm trying to say is that I haven't always agreed with how life is lived in the Grove. Perhaps change... could be good for us."

He narrowed his eyes. "Are you saying you want to take necromancy to the Grove?"

"No... I... nothing that drastic."

"Because you still haven't told me why you want to become a necromancer."

Hazel sat down on the sofa and buried her face in her hands. She let out a long, heavy breath and looked up at him. "I'm searching for my father, Ash. The trail has led me here. And so I want to become a necromancer to find him."

"Now that," Verrin said, "is much more interesting. What trail, exactly, led you here?"

Hazel told him about the bloodied bone, the potion, and the vision she'd had, and of the little box with the lock of hair bound with a ribbon bearing a scrawled message.

Verrin smiled. "One moment, please." He gave a short bow then left the room.

Hazel took a deep breath, trying to calm her racing, fluttering heart. Was he finding men to throw her out? Was he preparing whatever ritual she'd need to do to become a necromancer?

He returned a few minutes later. "Please, follow me." He headed back out the door, and Hazel hurried after him.

They walked down a long corridor illuminated with cool, sapphire light.

"Where are we going?" Hazel said. "What's going on?"

"Don't you know? It's why you came here."

Hazel swallowed. "Is it a ritual of some sort? What will I have to do?"

Verrin chuckled. "Ritual? No. I thought you wanted to see your father."

Hazel stopped walking, and Verrin turned to look at her.

"You know where he is?"

"Yes."

"And you're just going to take me to him?"

Verrin frowned, looking puzzled. "Would you prefer we did something else?"

Hazel's mouth fell open. "No, I... I just thought I'd need to become a necromancer for any information about him."

"We do not accept initiates into the Shrine who come here out of desperation. But your aptitude is real and your presence expected. Perhaps you will join our ranks after you meet with Ash." He turned and kept on walking.

Hazel hurried to keep alongside him. "What do you mean, my presence was expected?"

He smiled at her. "You might want to keep some of your questions for your father."

They came to a door. Verrin opened it and gestured for her to step inside. Hazel studied him a moment longer, then crossed the threshold into a vast room much colder than the rest of the Shrine. A lit pair of sconces flanked the door, illuminating a black-lacquered coach embossed with ornate silver scrollwork that surrounded a skeleton dancing amid a curtain of stars. Two robed initiates—Hazel assumed they were initiates given they lacked the silver needlework adorning Verrin's robes—were busy hitching two black horses to the coach. A man dressed in a black coat, breeches, and top hat sat in the driver's seat. Behind the coach, all else remained shrouded in shadows.

"Your ride," Verrin said, extending a hand towards the coach, "to the Sea of Severed Stars."

HOLLY HAD to sit on her hands to keep herself from wringing them. "I don't think he's going to be happy to see us," she said. "Elder, I mean."

"His happiness does not concern me," Hemlock said.

"Well, no, I don't mean that." She scratched her nose. "Just that he's creepy and he might try his creepy necromancy on us again."

Hemlock said nothing as he stared out the window.

Holly sighed, then clenched her hands and put them on her lap. "Well, he's welcome to try. Right, Hawthorn?"

Hawthorn cocked an eyebrow and gave her a look that suggested he was questioning her sanity.

She elbowed him, and he rolled his eyes and said, "Yes, quite right."

She smiled, but Hemlock never looked away from the window.

The carriage slowed as they pulled in front of Elder's house. A pang of sorrow stabbed at Holly. The last time they'd been there, Hazel had been with them. She'd been the one to knock on the door and lead the way.

Hemlock hopped out, strode to the door, and rapped with the knocker in several quick successions.

Minutes passed, but no answer came. Hemlock knocked again.

The door opened a crack, and Elder's round face peered out at them. "You again? Are you people incapable of calling at a decent hour?"

"We need to get into the Shrine," Hemlock said. "And we need your help to do that."

Elder fell into a raucous laugh. "Oh, that's a good one." He turned towards the hallway and shouted, "Augustus! Augustus my lad, did you hear that? They need to get into the Shrine!" Elder let go of the door, and it swung open wider as he rested his hands on his knees, laughing.

"It's really not that funny," Holly said.

Elder straightened, chuckled some more, then wiped tears from his eyes. "Oh, my dear. Yes, it is. It's quite hilarious. Not only your audacity in coming here, asking for my help, but in also thinking that I would actually help you. And with a matter that would be considered sacred among some."

"But not to you," Hemlock said. "It's not sacred to you."

Elder's mirth faded. "Highly irrelevant either way. Even if we were good friends, which we're not, I still wouldn't take you into the Shrine. The Shrine is for necromancers, and you're not necromancers."

"Hazel's gone there to become one," Hemlock said.

Elder snorted. "The one that got so riled up over necromancy? There's hypocrisy for you."

"We need to stop her."

Elder eyed Hemlock for a while. "I'll admit, I'm not too excited over the prospect of having her in the club, so to speak, but that decision isn't mine to make. Isn't yours either."

"But if I get to her in time, I might be able to talk her out of it."

Elder shook his head. "If you're here and she's there, then it's probably already too late."

"What do you want?" Hawthorn said.

Everyone turned to look at him.

"I beg your pardon?" Elder said.

Hawthorn folded his arms. "You're a warlock of the Grove that came here to practice necromancy. I imagine quiet and solitude are important to you."

"Oh no," Elder said, wagging a finger. "That threat isn't going to work on me twice. If dealing with the Conclave is what I have to do to be rid of you folks, I'm beginning to think it will be worth it."

"It's not a threat, it's an offer. Sarnum's all well and good, especially for those inclined towards necromancy, but don't you miss the quiet of the forest? Don't you miss the way the air changes as the sun sets and the ground cools? Don't you miss the whispered hush of the wind rustling the trees? You might have solitude here in Sarnum, but you don't have quiet. I—we—can give you that."

"I can't go back to the Grove," Elder said. "That bridge is burned and buried."

Hemlock said, "But maybe we can bring the Grove to you."

Elder narrowed his eyes. "How?"

"An atrium!" Holly squeaked. "A garden inside your house, all quiet and cozy."

Hemlock nodded. "I was thinking more of a garden extension, but yes, an atrium would work."

"With an area for a library within it," Hawthorn added.

"I have a library," Elder said.

"But not a library in a miniature forest, I bet," Holly said. "Wouldn't it be amazing, to be at home reading but to also be sitting under a tree with the sun shining down on you."

Hawthorn nodded. "A glass roof is a must."

"*And*," Holly said, "since the garden would be protected, you could grow all kinds of things you normally can't around here. Like orchids and orange trees." She sighed, turning wistful. "I wish I had an orange tree."

Elder pursed his lips as his brow furrowed. "I'll admit, an orange tree would be an enviable item, but—"

"Imagine what Abby could do with all those oranges," Hawthorn said.

"Orange juice for breakfast," Holly said.

"Remarkable for the constitution."

"And orange tarts!"

"Orange cordial."

"Orange *beer!*" Holly giggled. "Tum would love that one."

"Orange blossom tea," Hawthorn added. "That's an expensive import around here. And you could have your very own supply."

"Ooh, and orange cake!"

"Yes, yes," Elder said. "It would all be quite wonderful, I'm sure. But I don't see how any of this is feasible."

"We would build it for you, of course," Hemlock said.

"That would cost a small fortune."

"I don't have a fortune, but I do have some money set aside from my father's inheritance. It's all yours if you help us."

"As is mine," Hawthorn said. "I believe our combined inheritance suffices as a small fortune."

Hemlock turned to stare at him. "Hawthorn, I..."

"And I can grow the garden," Holly said. "I'm a Wild witch. I can make just about anything grow with the right materials. You'll have the most beautiful garden and without having to do anything at all."

Elder studied them for a long and critical moment. "All right. Come in and we can discuss it."

Holly squeaked and hopped up and down.

"*But,*" he added, "I make no promises."

"I never trust anyone who does," Hawthorn said.

The Sea of Severed Stars

Hazel walked towards the coach. The silver scrollwork and stars caught the flickering blue lights on the walls, making them look as if they had been wrought from water.

Verrin came up behind her. "I'm afraid there is one condition for this arrangement."

Hazel turned and Verrin held up a black strip of cloth. "You will need to be blindfolded."

Hazel's heart quickened as her apprehension intensified. "And if I refuse?"

"Then you are free to leave by way of the front door. That you have been granted access to the Sea of Severed Stars without first being initiated is a great honor—one that has been extended to you solely upon your father's reputation and good standing with us. But our goodwill can only go so far. You will go blindfolded, or you will not go at all."

Hazel swallowed and nodded. She had come so far; she couldn't go back. She turned around, and Verrin put the blindfold over her eyes and tied it snugly behind her head.

With his help, Hazel climbed into the carriage and sat down on a soft, pillowy seat. The carriage smelled like anise seed and juniper berries. Verrin sat down next to her, and the carriage started moving.

∿

"THE PROBLEM with your plan," Elder said as they sat in his living room eating freshly made sandwiches, "is that you overestimate my influence within the Shrine. I could get you in but little else beyond that. As soon as they realized your intentions—which would be rapidly, I assure you—then you would be thrown out and I along with you. Orange trees are lovely but not if the cost is permanently losing my position in the Shrine, nominal though that position may be."

"Could you get us in without them knowing it was you?" Holly asked. This time Abby had made a selection of different sandwiches, and Holly grabbed one filled with honey and soft cheese.

Elder took a bite of his own sandwich—spiced salami with marinated olives and fresh herbs and greens. "Possibly. But to what end? What are you going to do once in?"

"Find Hazel," Hemlock said, "and convince her to leave."

"And if it's already too late?" Elder said. "What if she's already made her vows? What if she's not even there? She didn't tell you she was going there, did she? You've just been working on that assumption. What if she came up with a completely different plan than what you've expected? So what I want to know is what do I do about the aftermath of this plan that might end up being a complete waste of time."

"She's trying to get to the Sea of Severed Stars," Holly said.

Hawthorn covered his face with a hand. Elder choked on his sandwich. He set the food on a plate and took a big swig from his glass of sour cherry cider. "You shouldn't even know about that."

"Then you should tell your fellow necromancers to stop drinking wine," Hawthorn said. "They get entirely too chatty."

"And if she's not at the Shrine," Holly said, "then she'd be at this sea."

"Would it be possible for a new initiate to gain access to the sea?" Hemlock asked.

Elder scoffed. "*Possible?* Yes. Probable? No." He waved his hands at them. "I mean, you shouldn't even *know* about it, yet you do, so at this point I'd say anything's possible."

"We need a two-layered plan," Hemlock said. "One that accounts for us finding Hazel at the Shrine and one that..." He cleared his throat. "One that doesn't. If she's not there—and she's not at the inn—I think we should assume she's found a way to get to the sea. And so we need to come up with a backup plan to get us there."

Elder shook his head. "Getting you into the Shrine is one thing, getting you to the Sea of Severed Stars is quite another. I cannot help you."

"We'll make sure they'll never know it was you," Holly said. "We *promise.*"

Elder chuckled, but it sounded forced and nervous. "You don't understand. I'm not at all concerned with the other necromancers finding out. Not when compared with the *real* threat."

When everyone stared at him, he continued. "The Shapeless One. She will know I led you there. There aren't any secrets in the world that she does not know. And I don't think she will take kindly to my leading a band of trespassers onto her sacred grounds."

"What utter rubbish," Hawthorn said. "So now you're suddenly pious when a few moments ago you were a skeptic?"

"I don't take chances where it concerns the Siphoner of Souls and neither should you. I think you should leave now."

"But you said you'd help," Holly said.

"I promised nothing." Elder's voice had taken a hard edge, but there was a tremor underneath the gruff that matched a slight tremor in his hands. "I'm sorry, but you are on your own."

Hemlock ran his hands over his face as they left Elder's home. "This can't be happening."

Nobody said anything for a long while. In the distance, the sky began to lighten with the coming of dawn.

"I... might have an idea," Holly said. "But you might not like it."

Hemlock shrugged. "At this point, I'll try anything."

"Well... I have these potions..."

❧

THE CARRIAGE didn't jostle nearly as much as Hemlock and Hawthorn's carriage. The thought of them brought a painful lump to Hazel's throat. She coughed. "How far is it?"

"That would be telling," Verrin said. He sat close to Hazel, closer than she was comfortable with. Not that she was comfortable with much of anything in this situation. The carriage seats were soft and cozy. All comfort ended there.

"You'd be surprised how much one's perception of time is altered when one cannot see," Verrin continued. "I'm sure you understand."

Hazel had absolutely no perception of time. Despite her frayed nerves, the gentle swaying of the carriage and the clattering of the horses' hooves had lulled her into a slumber. She had no idea how long she had slept. Day had broken—given the cracks of light that seeped through the edges of her blindfold—but she couldn't say whether it was morning or afternoon.

"You seem young," Hazel said after a long bout of silence. She didn't want to drift off to sleep again; talking helped keep her awake. "How long have you been a necromancer?"

"I was eight when I first started to learn, much like yourself, I assume. Don't Grove warlocks and witches join their first school of magic around then?"

"Yes, we get to choose our first discipline at that age. What made you choose necromancy? Or did you have a choice?"

"Oh yes, I had a choice. Not all magic practitioners in Sarnum are necromancers."

"Only most?"

He chuckled. "A fair amount, yes. The truth is we excel in necromancy. Those who are interested in the other disciplines are better off pursuing them in the Grove rather than in Sarnum."

"Except we don't take in outsiders."

"You sure about that? You're selective, yes, but it's not unheard of for people to go there, make their case—ardently so, perhaps—and be accepted. It usually involves a name change to adhere to your quaint naming convention of trees and flowers. But I know of two people who have done just that."

Hazel frowned. "Who?"

"That would also be telling. But surely you can't be surprised by that. You know of people who have left the Grove for Sarnum, why wouldn't it be possible for people to do the opposite?"

Except it did surprise her, as obvious as it all now seemed. She had honestly never heard of people coming to the Grove who were not born there—she had never even considered it. Then again, she'd never been one for local gossip. She wondered if Holly had known.

The carriage rattled on. Hazel dozed in fitful bouts of shallow slumber. The light creeping in around her blindfold faded until everything was once again as dark as the sable fabric that covered her eyes.

∽

Holly, Hemlock, and Hawthorn stood in Holly's room at Sensi's Contemplation. She held out the box of potions that Odd had given her in what now seemed like ages ago.

"What will they do?" Hemlock asked.

"I don't know," Holly said. "Odd said they will show us the decisions we haven't made and that they might help us change the decisions we *have* made."

"Wonderful," Hawthorn said. "Except the only decision that needs to be changed is Hazel's, and she's not here."

"I *told* you that you might not like it."

"Let's bicker about it later," Hemlock said. "We need to try something." He took a vial and, turning to Hawthorn asked, "You have any better ideas?"

Hawthorn tightened his jaw and shook his head.

Hemlock uncorked the vial and downed the clear liquid in one big swallow. He gave the empty vial back to Holly and sat down on the edge of her bed.

Holly studied him a moment, but nothing seemed to be happening. She turned to Hawthorn. "You next?"

He shook his head. "If we're going to be experimenting with suspicious, gnomic concoctions, I think one of us should abstain and keep a sober eye on things. You go ahead."

Holly nodded. She took a vial and drank its contents, then sat next to Hemlock.

She waited.

Nothing happened.

Holly frowned. She got to her feet, intent on finding Tum to yell at him about the untrustworthy nature of gnomes, when the walls rippled like raindrops on water. She lost her balance, and Hawthorn caught her before she fell to the ground.

"You have to hand it to us," Hawthorn said as he helped Holly back onto the bed. His voice sounded oddly distant, as if he were at the bottom of a deep chasm and not right next to Holly's ear.

"Things are never dull around here."

~

THE CARRIAGE was still moving when Verrin reached behind Hazel's head and untied the blindfold.

She blinked, but the interior of the carriage was too dark to see anything other than Verrin's shadowed silhouette. "What's happening? Are we there?"

He reached over her and pushed aside the curtain covering her window, and Hazel gasped.

Night had returned to blot the sky in an inky blackness. Stars filled the void, and along the shadowed ground hundreds of soft, flickering blue lights stretching to the horizon echoed the ones in the sky.

"There is nothing like it," Verrin said quietly. "Witnessing the sea for the first time. I envy you."

Hazel opened her mouth to reply, but her throat clenched shut. The beauty of the softly glowing lights gnawed at her heart, exposing a raw longing she hadn't known existed. "Are those souls?"

"Depends who you ask. Some fervently believe so and that these are sacred grounds to the Keeper of Stars. Others will argue it is merely a natural, though unique, phenomenon."

"What do you believe?"

He was quiet a moment. "I believe not everything needs to be explained."

They fell back into silence. She had so many questions, but she couldn't bring herself to ask them. Not here. Here, surrounded by starlit sapphires, speaking seemed like a perverse intrusion. She folded her hands and leaned back in her seat, letting the cool lights pass across her gaze until it was as if she floated among them, weightless and unseen.

Odder Possibilities

Ripples warbled across the walls of Holly's room. It was as if the sea on the wall bearing the pirate ship of cats had spread itself beyond the confines of its painted surface. Concentric lines extended and then contracted across every visible surface, again and again, hypnotic yet strangely anchoring.

She leaned back on her bed, nuzzling down in the covers as she tried to get more comfortable, when the rippling walls stilled for a fragile moment before they shattered.

She was back in the Grove, lying in a patch of grass outside the cottage.

"Holly!" came her mother's voice from inside the house.

Holly's breath caught in her chest. She sat up, and the world rippled again. In the corner of her vision, a little girl ran by. No, not running. She was blurred, as if constantly in motion even though her pace to the cottage was measured and even.

Holly followed her inside, and her throat constricted when she saw her mother alive and well and as beautiful as Holly remembered her.

Willow folded her hands as she looked down at the little girl. "We will be going to the Circle soon. Have you decided on your discipline?"

"Hearth," whispered Holly. She remembered this moment, when she had picked her first magic discipline upon her first visit to the witches' Circle.

But the little girl said, "Weaving."

Holly frowned. She had been so excited in the weeks prior to her first visit to the Circle that she hadn't been able to decide on her first discipline. Hazel had become a Weaving witch, and for a while Holly had thought she'd do the same. But when her mother had asked her, she had blurted out, "Hearth," surprising herself though perhaps not her mother.

Willow's eyebrows arched upwards at the little girl's response, but she simply nodded and said, "Very well. Be ready to leave within the hour."

The walls rippled like a rock thrown in a pond, then they gave way and Holly stood in a grove of trees. Another version of herself stood nearby, blurry like the little girl had been but clear enough to see that she was a few years younger than Holly was now. This other Holly held hands with a freckle-faced young man, and Holly gasped.

She walked up to him for a closer look. He didn't react to her in any way; his attention remained fixed on the other Holly, who shifted between solidity and impermanence like crystalizing clouds.

She recognized the boy—a warlock named Oak who practiced Weaving and Wild magic. He wasn't conventionally handsome—not like Hawthorn—but he had a strong nose and kind eyes, and when he smiled, his face would flush, which made his freckles stand out in a curiously endearing way. Holly had never noticed that about him before. She only knew him as a quiet and somewhat awkward young man. She'd never spoken to him—had never seen a reason to.

"What am I going to do?" Other Holly said as tears streamed down her cheeks. "What am I going to do without Mother?"

Oak put his arms around her, and Other Holly rested her head against his shoulder.

"You're going to let me take care of you. We'll marry. Everything will be fine."

Other Holly nodded and held on to him. Then her blurriness intensified, and she split into three different people. Each form wavered as if about to dissolve, only to coalesce together again like flesh-bound smoke.

Each form walked in a different direction. Oak faded into nothingness, and Holly felt a stab of panic on which form she should follow. Each figure looked the same, and none seemed to be headed anywhere specific. So Holly picked the closest one and followed.

The sky clouded over, the air in front of her rippled, and Willow's decrepit cottage came into view. Holly cried out and stumbled back. She didn't want to be there, not now. But her blurry reflection kept on walking until she rounded a corner and came upon Hazel, who sat on a pile of collapsed stones that had been overtaken by vines.

The other Holly solidified again, so much so that she looked just as real as Holly herself. "Don't blame yourself," she said. "You did everything you could."

"It wasn't enough," Hazel said. "It's never enough."

"You've done more than anyone would dare ask." Holly's counterpart smiled. "I heard you were invited to the warlock brothers' Mid-Ascension party. Hemlock and Hawthorn. Did you go?"

Hazel scoffed. "Why on earth would I ever go? I'm only thankful you weren't around to drag me to the nonsensical affair. I heard everyone had to wear masks. Can you imagine?"

"I bet it was magical."

"I bet it was headache inducing." She eyed Other Holly. "Don't tell me you're bored with married life already?"

Other Holly beamed. "Of course not. But that doesn't mean I'm still not fond of a good party."

"Well, *I'm* fond of a quiet evening alone. And on that thought..." Hazel rose. "I should get home."

"You should come by for dinner sometime. You're little Willow's only aunt."

Hazel gave a tight smile that didn't quite reach her eyes. "I will. Soon." Then she left.

Other Holly's form wavered again. The sky continued to cloud over until there was only darkness. Holly's own breath rattled in her ears, thunderous like a roiling storm. Wisps of breath plumed from her lips, the only thing visible in the blackness that surrounded her. The breath clung to her, then spread out into the shadows, turning the darkness into light and the light into a snow-wrought world.

Holly stood at the cottage she shared with Hazel in the waking world. But the windows stood dark, the chimney cold despite the freezing air. Holly walked up the steps and through the door, and the air inside was just as frigid as the air without.

Sheets were draped over the furniture; a layer of dust coated the floor. Holly walked into the kitchen, but the table stood empty, the oven cold and unused for some time, judging by the dust that coated it along with everything else.

She headed upstairs to Hazel's room, but Hazel wasn't there. Instead, a woman sat on the edge of Hazel's sheet-covered bed. At first Holly thought it was her mother, but this woman was a little too old. Then familiarity crashed into understanding: this was the other Holly—some future version of herself that she had yet to live through.

Someone came through the door downstairs.

"Mama?" called another woman's voice.

Footsteps came up the stairs, and a young woman walked through the door. She looked to be around the same age as Holly was now—the real Holly watching these events unfold—new to womanhood and all its complications. She also looked strikingly similar to Holly. She had the same golden hair and round, rosy cheeks, though this girl had freckles dotting her fair complexion that Holly lacked.

And Holly knew, without hearing her name, that this girl was Willow—her daughter in another life she had never lived. A daughter she had named after her mother. And as she looked upon this girl that looked so much like herself and yet so different, Holly's chest tightened in a way she couldn't explain.

"Mama," Willow said. She knelt down next to Other Holly as she sat on the bed. "You need to stop coming here."

"I dreamed about her last night," Other Holly said. "I dreamed that we were young again and that we still lived here. Everything was like it used to be, when we would stay up all night to watch the summer sun rise or drink spiced tea by the winter-side hearth. I thought... I thought maybe she had returned."

"She left, Mama. She's not coming back."

"You don't know that."

"I know she turned to necromancy," Willow said, her voice tinged with harshness. "I know you think she had her reasons, and maybe she did. But whatever those were, she can't come back. She just can't, Mama."

Hazel turned to necromancy? Even here in this otherworld where everything was different? It was as if a heavy burden settled over her. It all felt so pointless—no matter what they did, Hazel would become a necromancer and then nothing would ever be the same.

Why had Holly come here? What was the point? To witness a could-be life that ended in ruins for Hazel and, in some ways, for Holly as well? She wanted to leave, to go back to where things were real instead of wallowing in fruitless possibilities.

As soon as the thought entered her mind, the world around her began to dissolve. The walls gave way to snowy forest, and the snow, in turn, gave way to nebulous mist. It was all about to shiver away into eternal nothingness when a thought entered Holly's mind: What was she supposed to change?

Odd had said she'd see the decisions she did not make and maybe even be able to change the ones she did make. Well, that's what she needed. She needed to change something, but what?

The mist solidified once again and took on the form of a great wood-paneled hallway. Portrait frames hung on the walls in between candlelit sconces. But instead of paintings, within the frames were fragments of her life.

In one, she and Hazel sat on a log next to a pond while eating honey with their fingers as the sun set. In another, Holly was making the dress she had worn to Hawthorn and Hemlock's party. She walked on, cringing as she watched herself act like a complete fool in front of Hawthorn and everyone that day Rose came to tea. And there, further on, she did it again as she kissed Hawthorn in the graveyard. Part of her wanted to stop and change those events. They made her cringe just to think about them; how nice it would be if they had never happened.

But that's not why she was here; they weren't what mattered. Holly kept on walking until the candles lighting the hallway dimmed and fell into shadow. She turned and looked at one of the smaller frames—one showing how she went to sleep that night when Hazel had left.

What if Holly had never slept that night? What if she had taken the tinctures they'd taken from Emmond's home and fashioned a potion that would make Hazel sleep instead? More than that, what if Holly had gone to the Shrine? Hazel always took it upon herself to do everything. But what if Holly had gone there, convinced them she was destined for necromancy instead of Hazel?

The last of the candlelight guttered and died, and Holly was plunged back into darkness.

Whispers rasped within her mind, like bees in a hive hibernating for winter. She tried to listen but couldn't make out any words. Then, further on, a light appeared—soft and blue like twilit water.

She came to a heavy black door that led into a darkened room where, on the far end, she could make out the silhouette of a man. As she walked towards him, he turned to look at her.

Holly froze. His eyes met hers, registering surprise. But he couldn't possibly be as surprised as she was. How could he see her? None of the others had. More than that, though, there was something about him that looked distinctly familiar.

He looked a lot like Hazel.

"Holly," he said.

Holly bolted upright on the bed and cradled her head in her hands. That man... could he have been her father? Holly had never known him; he had left just as she had been learning to walk—or so she'd been told. She'd never mourned his absence. Why would she? He was someone she'd never met and never loved. Why would she mourn someone she didn't know?

But now, seeing a man that so clearly resembled Hazel, Holly, for the first time in her life, felt as if her heart had cracked with an emptiness she'd never known was there.

Hawthorn handed her a tall glass of water. She gulped it down, only then realizing just how thirsty she was.

"Easy," Hawthorn said. "Slow down."

She ignored him, drinking down the water like a man drowning. She was so thirsty. Then her stomach constricted, and she bent over and threw it all up onto the floor.

"I did the same thing," Hemlock said. He sat in a chair in a corner of the room, his face waxy and pallid.

Holly blinked at him and then at Hawthorn, the events from the potion floating in her memory like a distant, disturbing dream.

"What happened?" she said. "Did it work?"

Hawthorn shrugged. "How should I know?"

"Did I change it? Did it work?"

"Did *what* work?"

"Hazel, is she here?"

"No."

Holly's arms went limp. Nothing had changed. It had all been an illusion.

But it hadn't felt like an illusion. Even now, as the memories clung to her in a dreamlike haze, it still felt real. She looked at Hemlock. "What did you see?"

He frowned and shook his head. "Lots of things. It was all kind of jumbled. Mother was there, and Father, and Hawthorn of course. But a lot of the time I was alone. I switched to Hearth magic at one point." He stared off into the distance. "I'm pretty sure a gnome had taken up residence in my cellar..."

"But what about Hazel?"

He shook his head again. "I never saw her. It was like she didn't exist in that world."

"She must have existed."

"She may have, but our paths never crossed." He ran a hand over his face. "I didn't much care for that world, truth be told."

"With a gnome in your cellar," Hawthorn said, "who could blame you?" He wiped his hands together as if dusting them off. "Well, it sounds to me like this whole affair was a magnificent waste of time. But that's Hearth magic for you—withered, anemic witches and warlocks tinkering with worthless potions. Ludicrous. I don't know why the Conclave still sanctions it. Let me know when either one of you comes up with a plan that will actually produce results." He left the room.

"I hate to say it," Hemlock said, "but I think he's right."

"Hearth magic is perfectly respectable!" Holly said.

"That's not what I meant."

Holly flopped backwards onto the bed and stared up at the ceiling. She wanted to tell him he was wrong, it *had* worked somehow. Only Holly couldn't see how it had, so she didn't say anything at all.

A Love Tempered in Death

Hazel gazed out the window as the carriage continued through the field of starlight. What was she supposed to make of this? Those couldn't possibly be souls out there. Souls were incorporeal—an indescribable element that could not take shape in this world as blue lights or anything else. And yet how could she be sure? It was becoming increasingly apparent that there was more in the world that she didn't understand than she did. Maybe necromancers understood more than she would have liked to admit.

In the distance, a great shadowed silhouette of a mountain loomed on the horizon, blotting out the stars as if someone had stolen them from that part of the sky. It towered ever taller the closer they got, and eventually Hazel could see man-made elements upon its natural surface.

Tall, rough-hewn pillars supported crags of irregularly shaped stone, between which tiny windows had been carved. Some emitted soft light, others remained dark. Lanterns of flickering blue-green flames illuminated narrow stairways that crisscrossed up the mountain face before disappearing into shadows. At the top of the mountain, a crown of silhouetted trees stretched towards the starlit sky.

The carriage stopped at the base of the mountain, and Verrin hopped out. Hazel, taking a deep breath to steady her nerves, followed him to a narrow set of stairs.

He summoned a ghostly apparition—childlike in size—that was nothing more than a shifting haze of flowing ribbons, like silk swatches caught underwater. It emitted a pale white light that illuminated the path for them as it moved up the stairs.

The stairway was only wide enough for one person, so Hazel trailed after Verrin in silence. The stairs themselves were perilously narrow and slick with moisture, so Hazel dared not take her gaze off them. Ferns and other small, leafy shrubs grew out of cracks in the stone, thriving in small rivulets of water that dripped and dribbled along the rough rock.

They came to a cramped landing before the stairs switched back in their ascent of the mountain. Next to the landing stood a polished black door, its glossy surface reflecting the light of the apparition.

Verrin released his spell, and the apparition dissipated like morning mist. He opened the door. They walked into a snug stone chamber illuminated by sconces of the same blue-green light that had illuminated the stairs outside and the streets of Sarnum. The cold air bit into Hazel's skin. It smelled of minerals and dirt, like rocks pulled up from a riverbed. At the other end of the chamber stood another black door. It lacked the swirling grain of regular wood, and when Hazel put her fingers to it, felt strangely sticky.

"Nightwood," Verrin said. "It grows only atop this mountain, and it secretes a resin that is repellant to water. Useful, given the surroundings." He opened the door and walked past her into another room.

Crags of rough rock jutted from the walls, casting irregularly shaped shadows from the flickering sconces. The middle of the floor gave way to a pool of water, fed from a narrow stream that trickled from a wall and collected into a basin encrusted with crystalline formations. Rivulets of water overflowing from the pool snaked across the uneven floor before draining into cracks in the stone.

"Remarkable, isn't it?" Verrin said.

It was remarkable, but Hazel didn't want to admit that to him. It didn't seem right that such beauty could exist in a place like this, where necromancers congregated and worked their dark arts. Instead, she said, "Why are we here?"

He gestured to another black door on the other end of the room. This one led back outdoors, onto a narrow pathway bordered by cliffs of sheer stone on either side. Sheets of water glided down the cliff faces, polished smooth by what she could only assume were centuries of water passing over it. They crossed the narrow walkway and came to another door that led them into a cramped chamber illuminated by moonlight. A set of stairs led out of the chamber and disappeared into the darkness of the mountain. As Hazel started up them, the mountain above blocked out the moonlight and everything went black.

Her breath quickened, and she was about to summon the little glowing moth that Hemlock had taught her, but Verrin was quicker in summoning his ghostly apparition.

Hazel stood aside for him, but he indicated for her to go first. So she did.

She ran a hand along the wall as she ascended the stairs, partly to keep her balance but also to let its solidity reassure her. Where were they going? What would happen to her when they got there? How would she find her way out again if this all turned out to be a dreadful mistake?

Ahead, the apparition crested the stairs and rounded a corner. The stairwell darkened, but Hazel was close enough that a portion of its light still reached her. She rounded the corner after it and gasped.

The room before her was vast and open. To the right, the room retreated deeper into the mountain, the walls smooth and polished. At the far end, a vast hearth had been carved out of the wall, within which a lively fire burned. Black bookshelves and tables carved out of nightwood furnished the room, along with a comfortable-looking sofa and chairs and carpets that padded the cold stone floor. But what pulled Hazel's attention was the left side of the room that opened up to the clear night sky. Great granite columns held up the stone ceiling, and beyond those a balcony overgrown with ferns, ivy, potted plants and herbs stretched into the star-encrusted night.

Verrin came and stood behind her.

"Beautiful, isn't it?" said a man who was *not* Verrin.

Startled, Hazel whirled around and staggered back.

There, smiling at her as if nothing were wrong, stood her father, Ash.

He put out his arms as if to embrace her, but she moved back.

All words escaped her. It had been so long. She hadn't seen him since the day he left, close to sixteen years ago. He had changed very little from what she could remember, yet a spell was not at work here. His face bore lines she didn't recall, his brown hair now liberally dusted with grey. But he looked healthy. Vibrant. Somehow that made her angry. Her mother had died, and here he was, vigorous and full of life.

Ash put down his arms. "It's been a long time, hasn't it?"

Long time, indeed. Too long to stand there and chat as if more than a decade didn't stand between them. Hazel clenched her hands and reminded herself why she was there. "What did you do to Mother?"

A flicker of emotion passed over his features that she couldn't quite read. Was it remorse? Anger? Or was it something else entirely? But a heartbeat later the look faded and he smiled. "You've come a long way. Let us first talk as father and daughter before venturing to less pleasant topics."

Hazel narrowed her eyes. "Father and daughter? We haven't been father and daughter for sixteen years! I am not here to sit with you and hold polite conversation. I am here because you trapped Mother's soul in a geas. I am here to make you undo it!"

He smiled at her again, but this time it was a knowing kind of smile that made Hazel's anger deepen. "You always were such an extraordinary girl. I saw it in you as soon as you began to speak your first words. I'm glad to see nothing has changed."

Hazel's voice turned cold. "You know *nothing* about me."

"I know a great deal more than you think."

Hazel had opened her mouth to protest when Verrin walked up behind Ash, holding an empty silver tray.

"I've set some tea and refreshments out on the table. Will there be anything else?"

"No, Verrin," Ash said. "Thank you."

Verrin nodded and left.

"A considerate young man," Ash said as he turned back towards Hazel. "And gifted too. I've always liked to think that if I'd had a son, he would have been much like Verrin."

"Sorry to be such a disappointment."

Ash gave her a saddened smile and shook his head. "Oh, you misunderstand me, Hazel. You were never a disappointment. And now with you standing here..." He shook his head again as his eyes glittered with unshed tears. "I have never been so proud to call you my daughter as I am tonight."

Hazel frowned, uncertain how to react.

"Shall we have some tea? The view is beautiful, but at this time of year it becomes too cold to stay out here for too long." He swept an arm towards the inner portion of the room. "Please."

Hazel tensed but remained still. She did not want to go inside and drink tea, even though the wind was harsh and cold and she was more than a little hungry. She did not want to let herself get comfortable. She did not want to let this man think, even for a moment, that she had forgiven him. So instead, she stood there, giving him a look cold enough to match the wind.

Ash gave her a wan, tired smile. "Well I, for one, am quite hungry. You are welcome to join me, should you so choose." He walked into the room and to the table.

Hazel remained on the balcony, clenching her jaw at the ridiculousness of it all. She felt like a child, pouting because she wasn't getting her way. What was she supposed to do now? Stand out here and freeze? Leave? That, of course, wasn't an option. So, straightening her back, she walked inside and joined her father at the table.

He passed her a cup of tea, and Hazel said nothing as she took it. She assembled herself a sandwich from the platter of bread, cold meat, and cheeses. She was hungry; she wouldn't apologize for that. Them eating a meal together didn't mean anything.

"How have you been?" Ash said. "And Holly?"

Hazel chewed a mouthful of food a long while. "I told you, I'm not here to chat. How I've been is none of your concern."

"Do you blame me for caring about your welfare?"

"You don't care about me. You never have."

"That is absolutely not true."

"Then why did you leave? Why did you never show any interest in my life? You never came to check on us after Mother died—not once. You didn't even send a letter! Instead, you trapped her soul and left Holly and me to fend for ourselves. You don't do that to people you care about!"

Ash's expression tightened. "You don't understand the situation."

"Oh, I understand perfectly. You left your family behind to pursue necromancy. Then when the opportunity presented itself, you trapped Mother's soul in a geas, for whatever twisted ends I'm sure I don't know. I *am* wondering, though, did you kill her? Or was her illness just a convenient coincidence?"

"I loved your mother," he whispered.

"You ruined her!"

Ash slammed his hand on the table. "I saved her!" He took a deep breath as he regained his composure. "You've spun quite an elaborate fiction. Is that what your mother told you?"

"Mother refuses to even utter your name. And I can't say I blame her."

He looked down at the table and nodded. "I see. So, then you know that our *arrangement,* as she liked to call it, was her idea and not mine? You know that I wanted us all to live together like a family, and she refused? You know of the other men she consorted with, despite our vows of marriage? She told you all this, yes?"

Hazel's heart hammered in her chest. "You're lying. When you left, Mother was inconsolable."

"Yes, because she no longer was getting her way. I loved Willow, more than you could ever know. And in the beginning, I think she might have even loved me back. But as time went on, it became clear to me that she never wanted a husband so much as she wanted someone to father her children. And once she got her two daughters, her need for me rapidly dwindled. She grew restless and increasingly difficult. She sought out other men, but I forgave her that. I of all people know what it's like to be searching for something, for a sense of completeness. But I wanted more. I no longer wanted to be just one of her many diversions, to be a... *convenient* element in her life. I confronted her about it, and when it became clear that our aims in life were no longer compatible, then yes, I left.

"But what she did not tell you—and I knew she would *never* tell you— was how badly I wanted to take you with me. We fought about it. Bitterly. Cruel words were exchanged that hurt us both deeply. But in the end your mother prevailed, and I left you and your sister in peace, as she wanted it."

"I don't believe you," Hazel said. "If you had truly wanted to take Holly and me, you would've contacted us somehow. Especially after she died."

Ash shook his head. "I didn't want to take both of you. Just you, Hazel.

Holly was always your mother's daughter. But you... you were always mine. And I did contact you. You know I did."

A chill crept down Hazel's spine. "What are you talking about? You never contacted me."

"I suppose not in the traditional sense of written letters or messages, but I most certainly did contact you. How else could you have found your way here? Did you think it was coincidence? Luck?"

"I..."

"You were always *my* daughter, Hazel. Always."

A Reluctant Ally

Holly leaned against the wall in her room as she stared out the window. The sky had begun to lighten with dawn, but she hadn't been able to sleep. That had never happened to her before, being unable to sleep. This was all an ugly mess. Hazel leaving to become a necromancer and now them unable to figure out where she'd gone. Hazel was always the one who fixed things, just not lately. Lately it was almost like she'd become another person.

Except maybe that wasn't true. Maybe this was who Hazel truly was, only Holly could never see it before. Even in the weird potion dream, Hazel had turned to necromancy even though they had never come to Sarnum or done any of the things that followed. As long as their mother's soul remain trapped, Hazel wouldn't ever stop. She *couldn't* stop—Holly could see that now. And maybe... maybe Holly wasn't ever meant to stop her. Maybe she was just supposed to help her through it. Maybe that was the decision the potion meant for her to change.

Holly rubbed her eyes. When had life gotten so complicated? She didn't like it—not one bit. It was time she took life by the scruff and rattled it some before it got too big for its breeches.

She marched to the door and yanked it open, nearly crying out when she saw Hemlock there. His hand was poised as if he had been about to knock on the door.

"What are you doing here?" Holly said once her heart felt like it was no longer going to run out of her chest.

"I haven't been able to sleep, thinking all night, but I keep coming to the same conclusion." He took a breath. "I need to become a necromancer. I need to go after her."

"You're not doing any such thing."

"If that's what it takes to get me in the Shrine to find out where she's gone, then I'll do it. She shouldn't be alone in all this."

"I know, and she won't be. That's why we need to go back to Elder."

"Elder? He already said he won't help us."

"Yeah, well, we'll see about that."

"He's got beer, you say?" Tum said as he, Holly, Hawthorn, and Hemlock stood outside Elder's home. Dawn had broken, and a thin mist lingered along the damp ground.

Holly nodded. "*Lots* of it. Bitter dark. Abby brews it herself. I reckon they'll have a full cellar of the stuff."

Tum rubbed his hands. "Full cellar's good. What else?"

"Well, the house is big. And nice. There's got to be all kinds of spoils in there."

"It's been far too long since old Tum's gone spoiling, I'll tell you that."

"Well, now's your chance. You've got to spoil it for everything you're worth."

Tum drew himself up, looking offended. "I always do."

Hawthorn said, "Don't forget about Augustus."

Holly cringed.

"Who's that?" Tum said.

"Elder's creepy little butler," Holly said. "He's not even human... or gnomish or anything."

"He'll probably try to bite you," Hawthorn said.

"Well, he's welcome to try," Tum said. "He might just find out old Tum bites back."

Hemlock asked, "How are we supposed to get Tum inside?"

Tum drew himself up again. "Please. I'm a cellar gnome." He thrust a finger in the air. "There's never been a cellar Tum couldn't get into."

"Unless it's chained shut with a big fat lock," Holly said.

Tum shuffled his feet. "Well, yes, but these Sarnum folks aren't familiar with cellar gnomes—few of us live in these parts. If he's chained his
cellar shut, I'll eat my pyjamas."

"Perhaps I should chain it shut," Hawthorn said, "because I'd like to
see that."

Tum opened his mouth, but Holly interrupted him and said, "We
need to get moving. Elder's going to be up any moment now—if he's not
already. We need to get inside."

They walked around the house as they searched for a cellar door. But
when they ended up back where they had started without finding one,
Holly grew concerned.

"Maybe he doesn't have a cellar." It honestly hadn't occurred to her
that Elder wouldn't have a cellar. Her whole plan hinged on it.

"Nonsense," Tum said. "If he's got as much beer as you say he does,
then he's got a cellar, mark my words."

They walked around the house again, only this time Tum poked
around the bushes and hedges.

"Here we go!" he shouted as he rummaged behind a prickly goose-
berry shrub. "There's a window here."

Holly peered through the bush and spied a narrow window on the
wall of the house right above the ground. "It's tiny."

"Big enough for a gnome." Tum pushed on the window, then tried to
pull on it, but the window didn't budge. "Blasted thing's locked."

Holly turned to Hemlock and Hawthorn. "Either one of you know
Weaving magic?"

"Don't be absurd," Hawthorn said and snorted. The man actually
snorted. "Weaving magic." He smirked and shook his head.

"Sorry, Holly," Hemlock said. "We're both strictly Wyr warlocks."

Glass shattered and Holly flinched.

"Got it!" Tum said as he cleared away the broken shards of the window. "Not anything a good rock couldn't fix."

Holly remained speechless for a couple of heartbeats before she regained her senses. Which was good, because Tum was squirming through
the window and, before she knew it, had disappeared inside.

She bent down towards the window. "You all right, Tum?"

"Tum's always all right," he replied from within the darkness.

"Well, good then. You get to work." She turned towards Hemlock and Hawthorn and grinned. "This is going to be fun."

She and the two warlocks walked to the front door, where she grabbed the knocker and gave it several quick raps. Holly clasped her hands together and tried to put on a solemn expression, but she couldn't do it. A wide grin had spread across her face that she couldn't dispel. She felt confident, and that confidence filled her with an unexpected glee.

Elder opened the door in his red flannel pyjamas and bunny slippers. "Sweet biscuits and jam. Not you again."

"You know," Holly said, "I don't think there was any way this was never going to happen. I never used to believe in destiny, but now I'm not so sure."

Elder's brows knitted into a puzzled frown. "What are you talking about?"

From within the house, Abby screamed, accompanied by Augustus's squawking. There was a metallic clanging and a loud, hollow thud.

"Abby?" Elder said as he turned around. "Abby!" He ran down the hallway, his red robe billowing behind him. Holly and the brothers followed him in.

They passed the living room and headed towards the kitchen. Except for Hemlock—he and Holly exchanged quick glances before he hurried upstairs. Elder hadn't seemed to notice.

In the kitchen, they found Tum and Augustus playing tug-of-war with a shiny silver tray while Abby ran around the room until she found a rolling pin. She swung it at Tum.

"Hey!" He let go and tumbled out of the way, and Abby clipped one of Augustus's wings instead. The blow sent him into a fit of squawks and hopping.

"I'm outta here," Tum said, and he darted back into the cellar and slammed the door shut.

Elder rounded on Holly. "What was that thing? Did you bring it here?"

Holly smirked at him. "At least he's not some weird monkey-bat thing."

"Why is it in the cellar? What does it want?" He rattled the cellar door, but it wouldn't budge.

"All your beer's in there," Holly said. "And he's got it. You're from the Grove. I'm sure you've heard of cellar gnomes."

Hawthorn said, "They're really nothing more than a vermin infestation, if you ask me. Except that these particular vermin will drink all your beer and steal your silver, so, in fact, they're actually worse."

"What will happen to your constitution?" Holly said. "You won't be able to have your beer for breakfast."

"Or the pickles."

"Oh yes, Tum loves his pickles. That is, when he's not vandalizing carriages with them."

"You don't have a carriage, do you?" Hawthorn said. "The wretched gnome ruined mine with pickled eggs. I don't think it'll ever recover. I'm going to have to burn it."

"Let's just hope he doesn't get into your linen closet," Holly added. "With his grabby little hands, who knows what he'll ruin. One day you'll pick up a pair of your knickers, only to find out they smell like beer and old cheese."

Hawthorn shuddered. "I would have to move. Honestly."

Holly nodded. "Oh, absolutely. Once a cellar gnome gets dug in, there's no getting rid of him."

"Not until the beer runs out at least."

"Which"—Holly smirked at Elder—"I'm sure won't happen here for quite some time."

Abby crouched on the floor, tending to Augustus's wing. The creature made a pitiful whining sound. Then Abby straightened and leveled her rolling pin at Elder. "I want that thing out of my house, Elder." She shook the rolling pin at him as her round face purpled. "Out!"

Holly flinched. Abby had always been so pleasant and jovial. This side of the woman was a little bit scary.

"I'm taking Augustus to see the doctor," Abby continued. "If that thing isn't gone by the time we get back, then you'd better find yourself a new home, a new wife, and so help me, a new hide." She took Augustus's little hand and marched out of the room while the imp hopped frantically alongside her.

Elder stared at where she had gone, his arms limp and mouth hanging open. He looked like a man who had just woken up in the middle of the forest, missing his shoes along with any recollection of how he had gotten there.

"So," Holly said. "We need to get into the Shrine. You help us do that and we'll leave, take the gnome with us, and you'll never see us again."

Elder ran a hand over his face. He looked exhausted. "I told you, I can't help you get to the Sea of Severed Stars. If I did, I'd likely suffer worse than a ruined marriage." His face crumpled a little, but then he sniffed and composed himself.

Holly began to feel bad for inflicting Tum on Elder like that. But they were desperate—she needed to push on. "I know. We're not asking you to take us to the sea. We just need to get into the Shrine here in Sarnum. That's all. If we're lucky, Hazel will still be there."

"And if she's not?"

Holly shrugged. "It's doubtful she managed to get to the sea. We'll look someplace else."

Elder snorted. "Right, and I'm a plucked chicken ready for roasting."

Holly stared at him, unable to keep herself from imagining Elder sitting naked in a giant pot as Augustus basted his fleshy limbs.

Hawthorn nudged her, and she started back to attention.

"Look," she said, "you help us get in there, and we'll take Tum away. We'll even get you that orange tree we promised. What we do or don't do later won't involve you at all. After we get in the Shrine, we'll part ways, and you'll never hear from us again. That's all you know."

From beyond the cellar door came a crashing sound. Then a moment later, the sharp smell of vinegar permeated the air.

Elder closed his eyes and sighed. "Fine. I'll get you in."

Summoning Visions

Hazel got up from the table and backed away. Ash got up with her.
"You're lying," she said. "You didn't contact me." But the words
felt hollow. Deep down, she knew her father spoke the truth, and that
frightened her more than she wanted to admit.

Ash's expression softened. "You know that I'm not."

Hazel closed her eyes. The windmill where she had found the enigmatic message with a lock of Willow's hair. The abandoned house with
the pristine alchemical table in the cellar. The first time she had summoned her mother's aspect in that abandoned cottage back in the Grove.
She clenched her eyes shut tighter for one more treasured moment, then
opened them and looked at Ash. "You planted those things for me to find.
At the windmill, at that house."

Her father smiled. "Yes."

Hazel fought down her rising anger at his pleased expression. "Including Mother. Did you..." She swallowed. "Please tell me you didn't
trap her soul in a geas for me."

"I didn't do it for you," he said quietly.

Hazel studied him, looking for any sign of falseness, but he gave none.
"Then why did you do it?"

Ash averted his gaze. "It is not always an easy thing to understand one's own mind and heart. To confess the truth, I cannot say for certain why I did it."

"That's not good enough. There has to be more than that."

He scowled at her. "Of course there is more. A great deal more. So much so that one is hard-pressed to make any sense out of the emotional racket going on in one's mind. I left your mother. I was through with her, and yet..." He shook his head. "Can we ever truly leave behind those we love? Can we live the entirety of our lives without them, either in presence or in thought?"

"You tell me. You've had more experience than me in that regard."

Ash gave her a cool look. "Yes, to my great regret. But you know the answer already. That you stand here now is all the answer either one of us needs."

Hazel and her father shared a tense, silent moment as they regarded each other.

"How did you do it then?" Hazel asked. "If you can't tell me why, then tell me how."

Ash frowned, looking mildly puzzled. "I'm afraid the practical application of such spells is much too advanced for you to understand right now. You are gifted, Hazel, but some things remain beyond your understanding."

Hazel clenched her hands. "I don't care about the spell! How did you know she was sick? How did you even have the opportunity to do what you did?"

Ash regarded her silently for a moment. Then he said, "Come with me," and walked to a door hidden behind a tapestry depicting a forest scene populated with woodland animals dining under a twilit, summer sky.

Hazel followed him into a dark hallway illuminated by a single flickering blue light at the far end. There they turned left and walked a few steps further to another door that Ash pushed open. It led to a chamber that looked to be a combination of a workroom and library. There were benches and desks littered with jars and vials, piles of papers, and an occasional bowl or ewer or other receptacle for holding water. Tall bookshelves lined the walls to the left and right, but straight ahead the wall remained bare.

Ash walked to the wall and to a table that bore a single tallow candle, a mirror, a wide shallow bowl, and a tall silver ewer. He turned to Hazel. "You are familiar with such implements, I am sure. They are quite similar to the magic you performed to summon the aspect of your departed mother."

Hazel flinched despite her efforts to remain calm and collected. He hadn't told her anything she hadn't already known—she had realized herself that each time she had called upon her mother at each new moon that she had performed necromantic magic even if she didn't understand how she had managed to do it. But it still shocked her to hear him say it out loud, like she had crossed a bridge that had now collapsed into an endless chasm behind her.

Hazel cleared her throat, struggling to collect her thoughts. "I'm not familiar with the mirror or candle," she finally managed to say and almost immediately regretted it. Was she really going to discuss necromancy with her father?

Ash nodded. "The flame from the candle serves as a beacon that leads a soul through the Void with its light and warmth. The water poured from an ewer to a bowl serves a similar purpose and helps a soul to navigate between worlds. It is drawn to the source of life that water brings, as well as to the sound, though there are some necromancers who will argue that point. The mirror is used to capture the soul's aspect so that they cannot leave before bidden." He squinted at her. "I'm curious, if you did not use a mirror, what did you use to get your mother to stay? And you must have had a flame of some sort somewhere."

Hazel's mouth worked soundlessly a moment. She couldn't believe she was having this conversation. "Cake," she whispered. "I crumbled some cake. And lit a fire in the hearth."

Ash smiled. "Ah. A much gentler form of coercion. The dead are often drawn to objects that remind them of life, which could be any number of things. A favorite article of clothing, the smell of a certain flower. Or a particular food. Such coercive elements would never be strong enough to bind more willful souls, but for your mother and the connection you shared with her... yes, cake would work splendidly." He smiled again. "Well done."

Hazel looked away. She wanted to tell him she hadn't done it for him, that she didn't care for his opinion of her. But his words lit within her a spark of unexpected pride, and she realized that, even after all this time, after everything that had happened, she still cared what he thought of her. It made her ashamed, that deep-down spark of happiness she felt at pleasing him.

Silence lingered between them as Hazel stared at one of the bookshelves. Then she forced herself to look at him. She refused to let him see her shaken—to let him know the effect his words had on her. "Why am I here?"

"Given you've never employed a mirror in summoning the aspect of your mother, I can only assume you've not yet discovered the nuanced magic between summoning aspects and summoning visions."

Hazel frowned. "Visions?"

He nodded. "It's all very similar. The only practical difference between the two spells is the use of the tallow candle. While it could be said the flame represents the spark of a soul, it's the fat within the candle itself that we are in need of here. The fat represents substance, flesh, and serves as such in place of the person you are... ah... *compelling* to manifest visually. This vision can be observed in either the mirror or the basin. But I recommend the mirror, as I find looking upon visions in pools of water most tedious."

Hazel stared at him in open horror. "Compel? Do you mean to tell me that by simply using a tallow candle in your spell, you have power over living people? That you can coerce them into doing what you want just as you would the dead?"

Ash tilted his head. "Theoretically speaking, yes. But truthfully, it is more complicated than that. The living bear exceptionally strong wills that are not easily manipulated. Usually such spells will only cause nightmares for the person in question. In other cases the person will retaliate in the most remarkable and unexpected ways upon the spellcaster. There is a well-known anecdote of a man who cast such a spell upon his wife who had run away with another man and compelled her to return. His wife came back to him, burned down his house, stole his valuables and livestock, sold them at the local market for a hefty sum with which she purchased a respectable property for herself and her newfound lover." He chuckled. "It is a dark sort of magic that is best left well alone. This spell is only reliably used for visions, nothing else."

Hazel wrinkled her nose. "*Dark?* And what would you call necromancy? Slightly shady?"

"Necromancy is only dark in the way that sunlight produces shadows. It has dark elements, yes. But it also has light. This is what those in the Grove refuse to acknowledge, to everyone's detriment."

Hazel closed her eyes and forced herself to breathe. She didn't want to argue about this with him—she didn't want to waste what energy she had in trying to convince him to give up a belief he had held dear for so long. "What did you want to show me?" Maybe if she went along with him—for a little while at least—he'd be more willing to cooperate with her.

Ash worked a spell—was it a Hearth spell?—and lit the candle. He poured some water into the basin and, leaning over it, said, "Holly."

Hazel's chest tightened as the air seemed to thin. A mist passed across the surface of the mirror, though there was no mist in the room. Then the haze cleared, and she saw Holly riding in a carriage, her hair tousled and her rosy cheeks more flushed than usual from fatigue. Hazel bit her lip as tears stung her eyes. Part of her wished she had never left her sister, that she had never left home, that she had never once needed to know the burden of responsibility. She wished she could stand tall, convinced she had made the right decision, but she couldn't.

In a harsh tone, she said, "So you've been watching us then? All this time?"

"On occasion, yes. Just to see how you and your sister were doing. To see... how your mother was doing. That's how I knew she had fallen ill."

"And so you trapped her soul. Now you get to keep her forever, just like you wanted."

He looked away. Quietly he said, "It is a sort of living, isn't it? Isn't it better than the cold void of death? Isn't it better than being lost forever?"

"It's not right. And it's not what she wants."

A strange, soft expression fell over Ash's features. For a moment he looked on the verge of remorse, of letting go at last to shed long-suppressed tears. But then his expression hardened and he returned his gaze to Hazel. "Let us ask her ourselves what she wants."

Return to the Shrine

It was weird seeing the Shrine in the morning light, Holly thought. It looked like a normal building, old and unusually clean, perhaps, but not anything to be afraid of.

"Now, all of you keep your mouths shut," Elder said. "I will do the talking, and you will all stand there and nod and look sufficiently ignorant, suppliant, or pathetic, as the need arises. Do you understand?"

"Yes, sir," both Holly and Hemlock murmured.

Hawthorn said, "I'm sure I'm too pathetically ignorant to fully grasp your meaning."

"Good." Elder cleared his throat and fidgeted with his coat while casting a furtive glance at the Shrine's front door. "If we're lucky, we won't see anyone. Early morning at the Shrine isn't exactly a high hour." He poked at one of his coat buttons.

"You're stalling," Holly said. "Let's just go in and see what happens."

Elder nodded. "Yes, of course." He drew himself up a little. "Remember: ignorant and pathetic."

"A worthy mantra for any aspiring necromancer," Hawthorn said.

Elder shot him a sharp glare, then composed himself and marched up the steps, waved his hands as he worked a spell, then eased the heavy door open. He peeked inside. Then, relaxing a little, he signaled the others to follow him in.

They filed into a dark, windowless hallway. Gentle blue flames flickered behind glass sconces upon the walls that weakly illuminated the interior. Elder took a deep breath and exhaled slowly. He smiled. "There now, that's better. I don't know why I was so tense." He ambled down the hallway while the others trailed after him and stopped at a door. "Ah, here we are." He pushed it open and led them to a warm chamber furnished with plush sofas and chairs and polished tables. A few bookshelves lined the walls, but the most noteworthy feature was the great crackling fire and the man that sat on the sofa in front of it.

"Oh!" Elder said. "Beg your pardon, I thought the room would be empty at this hour. We'll find a different spot to, ah, hold our conversation." To Holly and the others, he said, "Come along then."

Elder turned to leave just as the man rose from the sofa. His gaze passed over them, fixing on Hemlock a bit longer than the others. "Aren't you the group that came here last night, looking for someone?"

Elder tried to chuckle but made a poor job of it. "What's that? Last night? No, no. You must be mistaken. These are associates of mine visiting from out of town. It is their first visit here." Elder made another strangled noise as he tried to laugh. "The first visit to the Shrine is always the most memorable, don't you think?"

The man continued to scrutinize them. "Yes. Of course. There's no need for you to go elsewhere. I was just leaving."

"Oh, no," Elder said. "I wouldn't think of it."

But the man made no indication of having heard Elder's continuing insistence that he stay and left the room.

Elder took a kerchief out of his pocket and mopped his brow. "Well then. I guess that's that." He turned to the others and tried to glower at them but only managed a menacing twitch of his eyebrows. "I do believe this concludes our business together. You asked me to get you in, and I did. What you do afterwards I'm sure is no concern of mine." He narrowed his eyes as he looked them up and down. "Yes, that's right. No concern of mine at all."

"Yes, yes," Hawthorn said. "You got us in. So thank you very much, but we'll be just fine now." He shooed at Elder with his hands. When Elder remained, Hawthorn shot Holly a warning glance.

She jolted herself into action and took Elder by the arm and led him to the door. "You did brilliantly well, Elder. Abby will be most pleased."

Elder's frown softened into a pleading stare. "Do you think so?"

"Oh, yes, absolutely. And when you get that orange tree, why, just imagine all that she'll do with it."

"You won't be the same man," Hawthorn said.

"That's right," Holly said. "I bet you'll be rejuvenated like you wouldn't believe, what with all the healing properties oranges have."

"Scurvy will be a scourge of the past," Hawthorn said.

Elder stared at him. "Scurvy?"

"Never mind him," Holly said and put on a fresh smile. She gave Elder a quick hug, but he just stood there like a sack of potatoes, his arms limp at his sides. Then she shoved him out the door and closed it behind him.

Hawthorn said, "I'm guessing we have about two minutes before that man comes back with a group of his colleagues and throws us out. And that's assuming we're lucky."

Holly nodded. "Agreed." She turned to Hemlock. "Please tell me you found something at Elder's house."

Hemlock fished around in his jacket pocket and pulled out a folded sheet of paper. "It's all I could find that looked remotely useful."

Holly snatched the paper and unfolded it. She wrinkled her nose. "What is this?"

"I think it's a picture Augustus drew."

She tilted her head and squinted at the paper. "But what *is* it?"

Hemlock stood next to her. "You're holding it wrong." He took the paper from her, turned it around, and handed it back. He pointed at a blotch of ink. "See? That winged thing there is Augustus. I think." He pointed at a pair of crooked scribblings. "And that might be Elder and Abby."

Holly screwed up her face. "Really? It looks like they've got three legs."

"Yes, well, I don't think Augustus is the most artistically capable creature."

"Fascinating," Hawthorn said. "But how does that even remotely help us?"

"Well," Hemlock said and moved his hand to the upper left corner of the paper. "Those jagged things there look like mountains. And see how they're surrounded by those inkblots? They kind of look like stars, don't you think?"

"I think it looks like he had a fit with his pen and scattered ink all over the paper," Holly said.

"I... I suppose that's a possible explanation. But I think they look like stars. The mountains... they look like they're surrounded by a... sea of stars."

"Are you saying this is a *map*?" Hawthorn said, incredulous.

"I... well..." Hemlock rubbed the back of his neck. He looked like he might be sick. Then he took a deep breath and adopted a look of resolve instead. "Yes, that's what I'm saying. This is a map."

"Um, guys...," Holly said.

Hawthorn held up a hand at her and, to Hemlock, said, "Now is not the time for false bravado. You have far more to lose than I do."

"You think I don't know that?"

"Guys...," Holly said again.

Still ignoring her, Hawthorn said, "To call that incomprehensible scratching a map is like putting a pig in a dress and calling it 'mother.'"

"You speak from experience?"

"Guys!" Holly shouted, and the brothers stopped bickering and turned to look at her. "Where's Tum? He was right behind me before, but now he's gone."

Before they had a chance to answer, the door opened and the man they had walked in on earlier stood in the doorway, backed by a pair of necromancers, one of whom looked much too muscular underneath his robe than was appropriate for a practitioner of a dark and creepy art.

"Well," Holly said as she tried to appear calm and not at all terrified. "This is awkward."

Reunions

"The moon is a week in its waxing cycle," Hazel said. "How can you summon Mother without a new moon?" She clung to a desperate hope her father wouldn't be able to summon Willow. The idea of it filled her with a peculiar dread she couldn't explain.

Ash smiled a patient, tolerant smile that grated against Hazel's nerves. "It's true that the cycle of the moon and the positioning of the sun and stars affects the magic we cast in different ways. But we are not beholden to those cycles. To have a command over necromancy is to have a command over ether—the very substance of creation. You will find that the moon holds very little power over you when you can master the substance that holds it in the sky."

He moved the candle further down the table, away from the mirror, then refreshed the basin with more water from the ewer. The surface of the mirror flickered as if with passing shadows. Ash stood before it, but it did not give him his reflection. Instead, the mirror stood dark, occasionally lightening beyond the glass as if clouds had departed from an unseen sun, to only become shadowed again the next moment.

Ash peered into the mirror and said, "Willow."

The hair on Hazel's neck prickled and she suppressed a shiver. The room darkened, matching the shifting shadows of the mirror so that Hazel was no longer certain she wasn't *in* the mirror. Her skin crawled in a way that made her feel like she was being watched. But she resisted the urge to turn around. She didn't want to acknowledge her father's magic—let it have any power of her.

The air in the room chilled—an unnatural kind of cold that Hazel knew all too well. She tensed and focused her attention on keeping her breathing steady and calm.

Ash turned away from the mirror and towards Hazel. "Willow," he said again.

A rustling sound came from behind, like a long skirt brushing over dried leaves. Hazel turned and found her mother, her skin pale and tinged slightly blue, just as it had been the last time Hazel had seen her. But she also exuded a gentle luminosity, as if she stood in sunlight even though there were no windows in the room.

Willow fixed her gaze on Ash. She hadn't seemed to notice that Hazel was there.

Ash extended a hand, and to Hazel's surprise, Willow took it. Her mother smiled at him as if they were enjoying an afternoon stroll.

"Mother," Hazel said.

Willow's gaze drifted over to Hazel. Her smiled wavered and her brow furrowed as if a distant, unpleasant thought had momentarily surfaced. But then it faded and she returned her attention to Ash.

"You see?" Ash said as he kept his gaze on Willow. "She is perfectly well. She is perfectly happy."

"No," Hazel said, "she is perfectly out of her mind."

Ash frowned at her. "What do you mean?"

Hazel thrust a hand towards her mother. "Look at her! She is not herself. She doesn't even recognize me. You've done something to her."

"I've given her a second chance. I've given her an existence she otherwise wouldn't have had. An existence that is arguably better than the one you and I continue to endure. Never again will she have to worry about growing old and feeble, of worrying about sickness and disease siphoning her strength. Now she is free to be whatever she wants."

"You mean she's free to be whatever *you* want. This is not who she is. This is not my mother."

"You've never truly known who she is. Not like I have. It does not surprise me that you do not recognize her as I have known her."

"You are deluding yourself. This is how you *want* her to be. It proves how wrong you were to bring her back. She can never truly be herself, not when a necromancer has full control over her like this. You need to undo it. Now."

Ash frowned, shook his head, and returned his gaze to Willow. "No. You do not yet understand. You always were a smart and clever girl, Hazel, but in this you are quite ignorant."

Hazel clenched her hands. She cast a Dissolving spell to release her mother's apparition, but nothing happened. She hadn't really thought it would work, but she needed to try something.

"Honestly, Hazel," Ash said. "Desperation does not suit you."

Willow remained silent, gazing upon Ash like a starving man might look upon a loaf of bread. It infuriated Hazel. This was *not* her mother. But she could do nothing to stop it.

With tears stinging her eyes, Hazel turned and hurried from the room.

∾

"It's quite a funny story, really," Holly said to the three necromancers that stood scowling in the doorway. Any minute now they were going to throw Holly and the brothers out of the Shrine. And who knew where Tum was. But Holly's mind went blank. How was she supposed to fix this?

She turned to Hawthorn. "Isn't it funny?"

Hawthorn stared blankly at her for one terrifying moment. Then he turned to the necromancers. "Oh, it's hilarious. It all started with an orange tree..."

"And a cellar gnome," Holly added.

"Disgusting creatures. But the oranges are lovely."

Holly nodded. "Oh yes, very delicious. Anyway, this cellar gnome... um..."

"Came here," Hemlock said, casting a sideways glance at Holly. "We think you might have an infestation."

"If you have an infestation," Hawthorn said, "the entire place will need to be emptied. Once they get in your walls..."—he made a dismissive wave of his hand—"it's all over."

One of the necromancers, the younger looking of the three, said, "What does this have to do with an orange tree?" The big, muscular necromancer standing next to him jabbed him with an elbow.

"I was getting to that," Holly said. She glanced at Hemlock and Hawthorn. "Right?"

Hawthorn drew himself up to his full height. "Of course everyone knows that orange trees are needed to get rid of cellar gnomes once they get dug in. They don't like the fruity aroma."

"Or the tartness," Hemlock said.

"Yes," said Hawthorn, "the tartness is most vile to those of a subterranean disposition. If you're going to rid yourself of this infestation, I dare say you'll have need of an entire orchard of orange trees."

"Oh my," the young necromancer breathed. The muscular one shoved him.

"Enough of this," said the necromancer that had been in the room when Holly and the others had walked in. He seemed to be in charge. "How stupid do you think we are to believe such nonsense?"

"He believes it," Holly said, pointing at the younger necromancer. His cheeks flared bright red, and he was unable to meet the other necromancers' gazes.

"You'd better believe it too," Hawthorn said. "We're not lying about the cellar gnome."

"I said enough!" the lead necromancer said. "You will explain yourselves. Immediately."

"But we *are* explaining ourselves," Holly said.

"You should really strive to listen when others speak," Hawthorn said.

The necromancer's face reddened almost as much as his younger companion. Holly tried to think of something to get them out of trouble. It was three against three. Maybe she and the brothers could club them over the head and steal their robes. Then maybe they could move around the Shrine without any problems. It was the sort of plan that was more likely to fail spectacularly than not, but even those dismal odds seemed more promising than their current situation.

As Holly tried to figure out how to convey to Hemlock and Hawthorn that they should all be clubbing the necromancers over the head, Tum came strolling by in the hallway.

He stopped behind the necromancers' legs. "What's all this then?" He had a portion of a great tapestry wound around him like a blanket, leaving the bulk of the fabric to drag along the floor behind him.

The necromancers turned. The younger one cried out in surprise.

"Great severed stars!" the lead necromancer said. "Is that our heraldry you're wearing?"

Tum glanced at the tapestry he had swaddled himself in. "Heraldry? Wouldn't know anything about that. But it is some nice and snug fabric, let me tell you. Thick and sturdy."

"You will unwind it from your person at once!"

Tum screwed up his face. "Unwind it from my what?"

"Give it to me," the necromancer said as he reached down towards Tum.

"Gotta go!" Tum said and ran down the hallway. The muscular necromancer grabbed hold of the tapestry as it swished along the stone floor behind Tum and stopped him short. Tum gave the fabric a quick tug back, realized it was a battle he was about to lose, then relinquished his prize and disappeared from sight.

The necromancer-in-charge took the tapestry from his colleague and petted it lovingly as he frowned at Holly and the others as if they had just inflicted the most grievous injury upon a loved one.

"In case you didn't realize," Hawthorn said, "*that* was a cellar gnome."

Holly couldn't help but grin. "And he's just getting started."

The lead necromancer took a moment longer to glare at them. Then he handed the tapestry to the younger necromancer behind him.

"Get that to the laundress. Keeper only knows what's been done to it." He turned to Holly and the others and thrust a finger at them. "You stay here." He and the other necromancers backed out of the room, and he slammed the door shut. There was a scratching sound near the knob, then a slight *click*.

Holly tested the door once the necromancers' footfalls had faded, but it was locked. "Well, now what?"

"Now I regret never having taken up Weaving magic," Hemlock said.

"Please," Hawthorn said. "Things are hardly as desperate as that."

Hemlock folded his arms and fixed his brother in a steady gaze. "How do you figure?"

"That we are standing here having this conversation proves that things aren't so dire."

"Somehow the notion of your being unable to speak doesn't strike me as a dire situation."

"Stop bickering, you two," Holly said. "Honestly, you're worse than Hazel and me."

Hemlock shuffled his feet. "Sorry," he murmured.

"You should be," Hawthorn said. "Weaving magic. I mean, really."

Holly pinched him, and he cried out.

"You knock it off and start looking for a way to get us out of here," she said.

Hawthorn lifted his chin and smoothed his hair. Then with an air suggesting it had been his intention all along, he walked over to the sofa and started poking around the cushions.

Holly tested the door again. Still locked. Not that she had expected a different result, but it would have been nice. She reached into her pocket and brushed her fingers against Chester's soft fur. She could send him out scouting; maybe he'd find something that could help them. Then again, what if he couldn't? Sending Chester out gathering in Zinnia's house was one thing, letting him loose in a necromancer lair was quite another.

Hemlock said, "You could always burn down the door."

Holly nodded without looking at him. "It's so unpredictable though, fire. Not that I'd care if we burned the place down. But... what if Hazel's in here somewhere? What if we couldn't find her before that happened?"

"Most of the building is stone, so I doubt that'd happen."

"There's the tapestries, though, and all the furniture. That'll go up fast. And then all the smoke it'll create. How are we supposed to find Hazel in a smoky building?" She rubbed her forehead and then took a deep breath. "I don't know. I'll do it if I have to. But I'd rather we find a different way first." She glanced over at Hawthorn rummaging around the sofa. "How's it going for you, Hawthorn?"

"Disgustingly abysmal, thank you for asking. You'd think these necromancers would animate a corpse or two to do the cleaning for them. But so far I've found a petrified biscuit, two copper pennies, and a note with sloppy handwriting making a dodgy attempt at poetry." He shivered as if spiders crawled up his spine. Then he looked at Holly with a pleading expression. "Don't make me go back."

Hemlock raised an eyebrow at her and nodded towards the fire burning in the hearth. Maybe he was right. Maybe burning the place down was their only option.

Just as Holly was about to pull fire from the hearth and hurl it at the door, a faint scratching sound came. Then the doorknob turned, the door swung open, and Tum stood on the other side, grinning.

"Well, well," he said as he rocked on his heels. "Look who's needing old Tum now."

"How'd you open the door?" Holly said.

Tum tossed up a key and caught it again. "Did you know that one key will open up all the doors in this place? Mighty handy, that. And they got keys all over. This one I got from a desk drawer that I convinced to open with a fire poker." He peered around. "You got a fire poker here?"

"I think so...," Holly said, then shook her head. "It doesn't matter. We don't need a poker. We need to find Hazel." She leaned out the door as Tum walked inside. The corridor was empty.

"What happened to the necromancers that were after you, Tum?"

Tum scampered over to the sofa and sniffed the stale biscuit Hawthorn had dropped. "What's that?"

"The necromancers. Where did they go?"

Tum waved a hand towards the door as he continued to scrutinize the biscuit. "They're a few corners back. Didn't see me dash under a table and into the linen closet. Was looking for the cellar, but I don't think they got a cellar here." He blinked at Holly. "What kind of people don't got a cellar?" He nibbled on the biscuit and winced.

"Did you see Hazel at all?"

Tum tossed the biscuit on the ground and started to root around the couch cushions. "Miss Hazel? No, no. Miss Hazel's not here." He found a penny and pocketed it.

"What? How do you know she's not here?"

"Heard one of the necromancers talking while hiding in the linen closet. Said something about a witch that had gone to some ocean. Figured it must've been Miss Hazel, right?"

It did sound like Hazel. "We need to check here anyway, just to be sure. And if she's not here, well, we need to find out how to get to this ocean."

"Whatever we're doing," Hawthorn said as he watched in horror as Tum rooted around the couch cushions, "we'd better do it quickly before the black-robed brutes return."

Holly nodded. "All right, let's go." Then an idea came to her. She turned to Tum. "Can you take us to the linen closet first?"

They all snuck down the dim hallway as they trailed after Tum. The gnome darted around corners and through chamber doors, giving no perceivable concern that they might run into necromancers who would be rather displeased to find them lurking where they didn't belong.

Holly got distracted by a shadow further down the hall when Tum darted around a corner and disappeared. She rounded the corner after him, but he was gone.

Hawthorn nudged her and nodded towards a door that had been left ajar. She snuck towards it, inched it open a touch more, revealing a spacious closet full of blankets and linen.

"This closet is bigger than my room at home," she said breathlessly.

"You and your sister should really find better living arrangements," Hawthorn said. "This closet isn't that remarkable."

Holly ignored him. It looked remarkable to her. All these towels and blankets, curtains, napkins, and... yes, there they were. Spare robes. Grinning, she grabbed an armful from the shelves and dumped them on the floor before she began sifting through them.

"What are you doing?" Hawthorn said.

She held up a robe, looked Hawthorn up and down a few times, then tossed the robe to him. "Give that one a go."

"This... this *sack*?" Hawthorn said, dropping the robe back onto the floor. "You've clearly lost your mind."

"You don't put that on, I'm going to lose it on *you*." She tossed a robe to Hemlock. He caught it and started unbuttoning his jacket to change. She sifted through the pile a bit more and found one that looked likely to fit her even though it *was* crudely made. These necromancers really needed better seamstresses.

When he saw the others ignoring him, Hawthorn reduced his protests to incoherent mutterings as he and Hemlock removed their jackets and pulled on the robes over their shirts and trousers.

Holly's dress was too full in the skirts to wear the robe over it, so she shooed the men out, took off her dress, and pulled the robe over her shift. She then took their discarded clothes and hid them behind stacks of towels and bedsheets.

When she walked out, the two men flanking the door in their black robes gave her a fright until she realized it was Hemlock and Hawthorn. She scrunched up her nose as she eyed the elder brother.

"What's that?" she said, pointing at a crudely fashioned white rosette pinned near Hawthorn's collar. "Is that *lace*? Where did you get lace?"

"He tore it off one of his handkerchiefs," Hemlock said.

"It's completely ruined now, I'll have you know. But it's worth it if it keeps me from looking like a rejected night soil shoveler, like the rest of this..."—he waggled his fingers towards the empty hallway—"necromantic rabble."

"I don't look like a night soiler!" Holly said as she looked down at herself. "Do I?"

"I'm pretty sure night soilers don't wear robes," Hemlock said. "It's far too impractical. And messy."

"Whatever they look like," Hawthorn said, "I will not be counted among them, you can be assured of that."

Holly felt a pang of envy at Hawthorn's rumpled rosette. Why did he always look so much better than her? It wasn't fair. She was about to ask him if he had any leftover lace when she remembered why they were there.

"Come on," she said. "Let's go see for ourselves if Hazel's really here or not." She headed down the hallway. Hemlock and Hawthorn trailed after her. Tum was, of course, still gone. But Holly couldn't be bothered about that; she needed to focus on finding her sister.

"Perhaps we should split up," Hawthorn said. "We'll cover more ground."

"No," Holly said. "Nobody's leaving anybody behind. We stay together."

They carefully navigated down the hallway, briefly checking rooms and chambers but found them all empty.

"This is entirely too convenient," Hawthorn said. "Where is everyone?"

"Perhaps they've all gone out," Holly said. "Do necromancers have picnics?"

"Or maybe they've all gone wherever Hazel's gone," Hemlock said.

Holly frowned. She didn't much like the sound of that. They continued on.

The Shrine had confusing, winding corridors. They didn't seem to have an end, and each hallway looked just like the next. Even the rooms they checked were starting to look the same.

"Are we going in circles?" Holly said. "I can't tell."

"This is ridiculous," Hawthorn muttered. "We're wasting time." He tried to cast a spell, but nothing happened.

Hemlock and Hawthorn both sucked in sharp breaths.

"What happened?" Holly said. "What did you do?"

"Nothing," Hawthorn said. "I can't do magic here."

"They must have wards in place," Hemlock said.

"We need to leave."

"Not without Hazel," Holly said.

"She's not here," Hawthorn said.

"You don't know that. Not for certain."

"We've checked everywhere. She's not here. Hemlock, tell her."

But before Hemlock could say anything, the blue flames in the sconces on the walls flickered and died, plunging the corridor in darkness. The air turned sharp and cold, as if they stood outside in the midst of winter.

"What's happening?" Holly whispered, but Hemlock and Hawthorn didn't reply.

The cold air coalesced around her, taking a shape she couldn't see— but she could feel it. It passed her right arm, making her skin tingle from the chill. Then it came and stood in front of her. Holly's eyes watered in the stinging, cold air. She reached out, and her hand passed through a cold so intense it almost felt like it had burned her. She yanked her hand away and stumbled back.

But the coldness was also behind her and then to her sides. It surrounded her, and Holly's heart hammered so hard it was all she could hear.

"Hawthorn?" she said, but there still was no reply.

Then a warm breeze fluttered by. It brushed against her face, smelling like sweet grass and sun-soaked pine. It made her relax, just for a moment, so that when the coldness consumed her, she didn't have time to scream.

Locks and Shadows

Hazel rushed down labyrinthine stone corridors as she fled from her father and the summoned aspect of her mother. She had no idea where she was going; she just needed to get away. A moment to breathe.

She should have never come here. She had known, deep down, that her father would refuse to release her mother. And yet Hazel had never come up with a plan on how she would stop him. That particular detail had always seemed so distant, caught in a hazy, nebulous future that had never felt pressing or urgent. But now that moment was here, and Hazel had no idea what to do.

She turned down one stone hallway and onto an identical one. She studied the doors, looking for a detail that would suggest she had passed this way with Verrin, but there was nothing. Eager to get out of the monotonous passageways, Hazel tested the doors until she found one unlocked. She passed through it and into a room with roughly hewn walls. The room was sparsely furnished though a fire blazed in the hearth. She wondered if there were servants who did nothing but go from room to room, lighting fires and tending to them throughout the day. If there were, why didn't she see any of them?

A painting hung over the mantle. At first it looked entirely black, but the longer Hazel studied it, the more details she was able to make out. Pale sloping hills stood out against a starless night sky. At the base of a hill stood a little cottage with a single thread of smoke curling from the low chimney. In front of the cottage stood a man or... something. It kind of looked like a rabbit, but it was tall like a man and it held a scythe so that the long, curving blade arced over its head.

"Those paintings have been known to drive men mad," came a man's voice from behind her. "So I wouldn't look at it too long."

Hazel turned and found Verrin standing in the doorway. She turned back around. "I'm not sure why you'd care whether I go mad or not."

"Someone should care since you don't seem to."

"Don't pretend to know my mind."

He came and stood next to her, his gaze on the painting. "Some say the picture is different for each person that looks at it. Others say that the picture will change, depending on the mood of the viewer."

"I think someone thought overly much of himself and used too much black paint to make the picture seem more mysterious than it really is."

Verrin smiled. "A distinct possibility." He glanced at Hazel. "He can help you, you know."

"Who?"

"Your father."

Hazel scoffed. "The only help I want from him is for him to undo his own mistake."

"And that is *your* mistake. Ash is brilliant. He's almost entirely self-taught. That alone is quite remarkable and nearly unheard of. He has enriched our Order beyond description. He could do the same for you, if you'd let him."

"Now I know why he favors you so much," she muttered.

"I beg your pardon?"

Hazel shook her head. "Nothing."

Verrin studied her a moment. "I'm to show you to your quarters. If you'll follow me, please."

He walked to the door, opened it, and waited for her.

Hazel glanced back at the painting, but whatever image she thought she had seen earlier was gone, and all she could make out were swirls of brush strokes, frozen in the black paint like forgotten tides.

Verrin led her through narrow, damp corridors that tunneled through the mountain. Rivulets of water sluiced down the rock while patches of moss and tiny, pale ferns grew from the cracks. Hazel felt as if the weight of the mountain pressed down on her. The cold from the stone seeped through her clothes and into her skin and bones, and by the time they stopped at a door that Verrin opened for her, she was shivering and her teeth chattered so loudly that the sound echoed down the hall.

Inside, a fire crackled in a spacious hearth while a long wooden table had been set with a cloche-covered tray, a stemmed crystal glass, and a bottle of wine. Hazel warmed her hands by the fire, relaxing as the cold ebbed from her bones. She yawned.

"You've traveled far," Verrin said. "I'll leave you to eat and rest. I'll see to it that you're brought sturdier clothing that is better suited to the climate here." He gave a slight bow and walked out.

Hazel looked around. The chamber was furnished much like her father's chamber had been. It was smaller and cozier, without an open wall that led to a balcony. But the quality of the furnishings looked the same, and she was glad to be in a snug little room warmed by the blazing fire.

She walked to the table and lifted the cloche from the tray. Some kind of roasted fowl—pigeon maybe—dressed with herbs, an onion-and-celery sauce, and greens Hazel had never seen before. They tasted bitter yet weren't unpleasant. She sat down, poured herself a glass of velvety red wine, and ate.

The meal was delicious, but she took little enjoyment in it. It felt strange eating alone, and the wine was strong and went to Hazel's head so that when she rose, she stumbled through the door that led to the bedchamber, collapsed on the bed, and promptly fell asleep.

When Hazel awoke, the air had cooled. The fire in the main room had died down to embers. This surprised her even though she was glad someone hadn't come in to poke at the fire as she slept. Then she noticed the tray had been removed, and in its place on the table stood a mirror, a silver basin, and matching ewer. Over the back of one of the chairs, a black robe had been draped. Hazel's contentment curdled into annoyance.

She ran a hand over the robe. It was softer than it looked and thick too. She supposed this was what Verrin had meant by warmer clothing, but it wasn't at all what Hazel had in mind. If they thought they would make her into one of them, they were sorely mistaken.

She moved over to the fire, making a point not to look at the ewer and basin. Who had left those there and why? At any other time in her life, Hazel would have assumed the items had been left there for her to clean herself up. But now she knew better. Now she knew exactly what kind of magic she could work with such tools—what kind of magic she *had* worked—and it made her uncomfortable.

As did the darkness in the room. There were no windows, and lamps that had been lit before now stood dark. The only light came from the dying embers that illuminated the room with a somber, eerie glow.

Hazel poked the embers into renewed life and looked for more wood, but there was none. She sighed. Whoever tended the fires must be too busy making sure all the empty rooms had blazing hearths while occupied rooms went cold. She went to the door, but it was locked.

Hazel stood there, staring at the black wood of the door as her hand lingered on the handle. Surely it wasn't locked. The door must be stuck. These mountain hallways were dreadfully damp, and she didn't care what kind of wood Verrin told her these doors were made of—they were wooden, and wood warped in dampness.

She tried the door again and pulled as hard as she could. Her arms shook, sweat broke across her brow, but the door did not budge.

"Unbelievable," she said, acutely aware of the oddness in speaking to herself. She banged on the door with her fist. "Hello? Anybody out there?" She banged until her hand throbbed with pain, so she kicked the door instead.

"Somebody! Let me out of here!"

But nobody came.

Hazel stopped kicking as she caught her breath, anger slowly rising in her in a way she had never felt. She grabbed the poker from near the hearth and struck the door handle with it. The impact jolted through her arm that rendered her bones into jelly. She struck again and again until pain radiated in her arm and up her neck, but the handle remained fixed in place, and the door still would not open.

She cried out and threw the poker across the room where it collided with a bookshelf and clattered to the floor. She clenched her hands as her breath came in deep, ragged breaths. This wasn't a mistake. The door wasn't warped.

They had locked her in. Her *father* had locked her in.

Hazel's mind went blank as she seethed in fury. She closed her eyes and forced herself to breathe. Throwing a fit wouldn't help her here; she needed to think.

When she had composed herself, Hazel opened her eyes. The room looked different now. Instead of a warm, comfortable space, it was now cramped and oppressive. And very, very dark. The coals in the hearth had died down again, and all she could see were the stones in the fireplace and the surrounding floor.

She summoned the little glowing moth Hemlock had showed her, swallowing the lump that rose in her throat when she thought of him. It felt like so long ago when she and Hemlock had stood on that hilltop together as he helped her learn her first Wyr magic spells. But it hadn't been long at all—a couple of months. It was nothing, all things considered, and now it was all over.

Hazel tightened her jaw and examined the handle on the door. It looked to be made of iron, but given the damp air and the absence of rust, it probably wasn't. Scratches and nicks marred the handle where she had taken the fire poker to it but otherwise looked to be in good condition.

She worked a Weaving spell that snaked into the lock, found the tumblers and levers, and manipulated and pushed them back so the door would unlock. Except nothing happened. She tried again. Through the spell she could sense the inner workings of the lock, the tiny little pieces that all worked together to determine if the bolt of the lock was thrown or not. But whenever she tried to manipulate a switch or a tumbler to do what she wanted, nothing happened. Her spell wasn't failing, it was working exactly as it should. It was the lock itself that wasn't responding.

Hazel closed her eyes and rested her forehead against the door. The lock must be enchanted though she didn't understand how. Any warding placed on the lock would be a Weaving spell, so she should be able to at least detect its presence, but there was nothing as far as Hazel could tell. Was it necromancy? Her father was a necromancer, so it stood to reason that would be the magic he'd employ, but she didn't understand how manipulating ether or spirits had anything to do with warding locks.

With her head still resting on the door, Hazel cleared her mind. She stopped trying to detect any magic or wards and instead let herself calm. When she turned her attention back to the lock, it had changed.

No, not changed—it was the same as it always had been. She had been too distracted to notice the slight darkness among the tiny crevices and sockets that clung to the inner workings of the lock like an oily film. Was that the ward? It wasn't like any ward Hazel had ever seen or heard of. It was more like a living veil, expanding and contracting as if breathing. It prevented the lock mechanisms from moving because, somehow, it had *become* the lock.

Hazel took a step back, unable to shake the feeling that the door had, at least partially, come to life. Necromancy was at play here. It was in the door in front of her, and its implements stood on the table behind her. She felt as if she had become entangled in a sticky web, and any attempt to free herself would only further enmesh her.

What was she supposed to do?

Necromancy, it would seem. It was no mistake that she found herself locked in her room with only a silver basin, ewer, and mirror for company. Her father wanted her to perform necromancy, though to what end, Hazel certainly didn't know.

But it was what he had always wanted, wasn't it? He had left a trail for her, somehow knowing she'd be able to use necromancy to find it. And she had. She had done everything he thought she would, without her ever realizing she was playing into somebody's plan.

What was his plan for her now? Apparently, it wasn't enough just to have her there. That notion could hurt Hazel, if she'd let it. But she hardened her heart. Ash hadn't been a father to her for a very long time. Nothing had changed.

She stared at the basin and ewer as the light from her moth gleamed off the polished silver surfaces. She didn't want anything to do with whatever game Ash was playing. She didn't want to do anything to encourage him. But what was the alternative? To sit and wait and slowly starve until Ash took pity on her and let her out? That wasn't an option, as far as Hazel was concerned.

She took a candle and lit it with the embers from the fire, then set it on the table next to the basin. Taking the ewer, she then poured a steady stream of water that glinted silvery white as the moth flitted around her head. Despite the lack of a reflection in the mirror, Hazel felt strangely calm as she peered into it. She thought of her sister, and in a voice barely above a whisper, she said, "Holly."

A mist collected over the glass. When it cleared, the mirror remained dark. Hazel frowned. Had the spell failed? She had worked the spell just as her father had done; she had done everything right, hadn't she?

"You're not a necromancer, Hazel," she said, no longer feeling so awkward with talking to herself. "What would you know about any of this?" She stared at the mirror a moment longer, then with a sigh she started to turn away.

An image flickered across the surface of the mirror. She turned back to it, but the mirror remained dark. Hazel released her moth and leaned in closer to the mirror—so much so that her breath began to fog the glass. The mirror remained shrouded in shadows, but the closer she looked, the more the shadows appeared to have... texture. It wasn't absolute darkness, there were variations in gloom that suggested that something was there, hiding in the shadows.

Then a flame alighted in the mirror. Startled, Hazel stumbled back. It was Holly, holding a little flame in her cupped hands that illuminated the worry on her pallid face. She lay in a cramped space, but that was all Hazel could make out.

With a shaking hand, Holly reached out—almost like she was about to touch the glass of the mirror—but instead pressed upon a surface that Hazel couldn't see. Holly's face went slack with fear. Then she started to scream. Hazel couldn't hear her, but she knew from the look of abject terror on her sister's face that she was screaming. It woke in Hazel a similar panic. Her heart racing, she pawed at the mirror, trying to reach Holly even though she knew it was impossible.

"Where are you?" Hazel whispered. Then the spell faded and Holly sank away into darkness, leaving the mirror to show only Hazel's distressed reflection.

She gripped the edge of the table as she tried to bring Holly back to the mirror, but nothing happened. She dumped the water from the bowl back into the ewer and then poured it back into the bowl and tried again, this time speaking Hemlock's name. Nothing.

Hazel cried out in frustration as she backed away from the table. She rubbed her forehead as she paced back and forth. She needed to keep calm. She needed to think.

She needed to get to Holly and help her.

Hazel rushed over to the door and tried to open it, but it was still locked. She cried out again as she slammed her hand against the door, ignoring the pain that pierced her palm. Did Ash know about this? Was he also watching Holly from his own silver bowl? Had he caused this? If so, what did he have to gain? Was it to get Hazel to cooperate with him?

She didn't know the answers to any of those questions, but at that moment, she didn't care. Hazel returned to the bowl, poured water from the ewer into it and then spoke her mother's name.

Her insides twisted at having to work the spell like this—the way her father had done it. But she didn't have any cake or food to crumble into the water, and so she didn't know of any other way.

"Hazel."

Hazel turned and found Willow standing near the dying coals in the hearth. Her mother's brow furrowed as she looked around, as if perplexed to be standing there.

"Do you know where you are?" Hazel said.

Willow lifted her chin. "What are you doing here?"

"You *know* what I'm doing here. I'm here to stop Father, just as I said I would. To make him undo what he did."

"I see," Willow said, her voice flat. "It seems to be going well."

Hazel narrowed her eyes. "You're different around him. What has he done to you?" When Willow said nothing, Hazel added, "Do you even remember it?"

"Why am I here, Hazel?"

Hazel was tempted to tell her she was there because Ash had trapped her soul. She wanted to shake Willow's shoulders until her mother showed some emotion other than this apathy. Instead, she said, "He's done something to Holly."

Willow's brow flickered into a frown. "What do you mean? What has he done?"

"He's trapped her somehow. She's alone in the dark somewhere. I don't know where."

Willow's frown deepened as her concern shifted to anger. "You left her alone? You let this happen to her?"

"I didn't *let* it. I came here alone to keep her safe."

"You should have never come here."

"I came here for you!"

"I never asked you to! I told you, time and again, the geas cannot be undone, but you refused to listen. You're just like him—you think only of yourself, of what *you* want—and now look what's happened!"

Hazel clenched her jaw as she struggled to get her breathing under control—as she struggled to keep her mother's words from hurting her. "You can hate me if you want, but help me find her."

Willow gave a hollow laugh. "What is it you expect me to do? You are not the only one trapped here, Hazel."

"Funny, you didn't look trapped the time last I saw you. You looked quite... content."

Willow's face darkened. She looked angry but also hurt, and Hazel regretted her words.

"Release me," Willow said.

"What?"

Her mother's face tightened. "I cannot leave unless you release me. I cannot help you; you need to find Holly on your own."

Hazel searched for something to say. She didn't want to leave things between her and her mother like this, but nothing came to mind. She released the spell, swallowing the lump in her throat as Willow faded into the darkness until she was gone.

Hazel stood in the shadows alone, staring at where her mother had been, letting the cold feeling gnawing at her gut spread throughout her body. She needed to find Holly and Hemlock. She needed to get out of this room. She needed to do whatever it took to make that happen.

She turned back towards the door, letting the coldness consume her until she no longer felt anything at all. She summoned a spell—it was like a Wyr conjuration only she twisted some of the words and turned them into something else—something dark and cold that matched the emptiness within her heart. The shadows around the door deepened and drew closer as the conjuration took shape. Every now and then the shadows would part and a gleam of light would lance into the room, leaving burned images on Hazel's vision. But as soon as a light would surface, the shadows would gather over it like clouds covering the sun, and the room would be made all the darker because of it.

"Unlock the door," Hazel said.

The shadowy form bobbed and weaved in what might have been a sign of acquiescence. It put its darkened hands—if they could be called that—to the door handle. The shadows sank into it, darkening the metal and sucking in what little light existed. Then the light was thrown back into the room in a blinding flash. Hazel put up her hands to cover her eyes. When she looked back, the shadowed creature was gone.

She walked to the door, almost afraid to try the handle. But she did, and a rush of relief came over her when the handle gave way and the door swung open.

Then she headed down the hallway in search of her father.

An Imparted Plea

Holly awoke in darkness. She tried to sit up but banged her head against a wooden plank.

"Ow!" She lay back down and rubbed her forehead. The air was warm and stifling; the room jostled to and fro. Where *was* she? She summoned a little flame into her cupped hands and sucked in a sharp breath.

She was in a wooden box.

The box was as long as she was tall but only about twice her width. Her heart floundered in her chest as she reached out and touched the wooden wall that loomed much too closely to her nose. She pressed against it—but the wood was solid and didn't budge. She pressed harder but still nothing.

A sharp, visceral fear unwound itself within her, and Holly screamed. The wood muffled her voice, warping it into something she didn't recognize. It fed into her fear, and she screamed even louder until her voice cracked.

Holly suddenly sobered, the skin on her neck prickling. She had an unsettling feeling that someone was watching her.

"Hello?" she said, but of course no one replied. She was panicking; she needed to calm down and get ahold of herself.

She extinguished the flame and put her hands to the wood and pressed against it with everything she was worth. When that did nothing, she kicked at it, but that only hurt her foot while the wood remained firmly in place. She summoned the little flame again and this time sent it against the wood. Heat licked at her face and singed her hair, and she coughed as smoke filled the cramped space. But the wood wouldn't burn.

"Stupid wood!" she yelled and extinguished the flame. "You're not natural!" The jostling of the box took a deep lunge, and Holly banged her head against the wood. Again.

She rubbed her head, biting her trembling lip to keep the tears away. She wouldn't cry. Whatever was happening—she refused to cry.

HAZEL MARCHED down the stone-encased hallway like she knew what she was about. Of course she had no idea, but she was too angry to care. Ash was here somewhere, and she'd find him sooner or later. Oh yes.

She passed through a smooth black door into a kind of atrium. The stone ceiling opened to the sunlit sky, while leafy shrubs and plants grew along the stony walls and in pots on the floor. A juniper tree in the middle of the room took up most of the space, filling the room with a clean, pleasant smell.

A man in a black robe trimmed the branches with a pair of shears and collected the little blue berries into a bowl.

Hazel marched up to him, and the man started. "Where's Ash?" she said.

"I... Well...," he said, scratching his head. "The dining chamber? Maybe."

"Take me there."

The man's mouth hung open as he stared at Hazel and the tree, then at the shears in his hand as if he couldn't account for all of these things demanding his time.

To help him out, Hazel took the shears and bowl from him and set them on the floor. "The dining chamber." In an attempt to be pleasant, she added, "Please."

"I... of course." He shuffled out of the room. Hazel followed.

They wound through more corridors lit by the flickering blue flames that the necromancers were so fond of. Every now and again gaps and crevices would appear in the walls to let in streams of sunlight that bathed Hazel in brief moments of blessed warmth. They passed black-robed necromancers in the halls, who did nothing to hinder them but would often stop and watch as they passed.

Eventually they came to a door. Hazel's guide stepped through it, and she followed him into a vast hall with a vaulted ceiling that disappeared into darkness. Polished black wooden tables and benches furnished the room, along with great iron braziers that bore blazing fires. Lines of men and women in hooded black robes sat at the tables, which were laden with bowls of fruit, baskets of bread, platters of meat, wedges of cheese, and crocks of honey and butter. Despite her sour mood, Hazel's mouth began to water at the sight of it all.

Her guide scurried away and disappeared among the other necromancers. She scanned the tables in search of her father, but everyone looked the same in their hooded black robes.

Hazel went up to a table and took a plate as if she had every right to be there. She took bread and cheese, and meat from a platter of glazed ham. She scanned the table as she did so, meeting the eyes of necromancers she did not recognize. Some of them spared her a brief glance before returning to their food. Others glanced off towards a corner of the great hall before quickly looking away again or returning to converse with a neighbor.

With her plate in hand, Hazel made her way to the far end of the chamber where the necromancers had looked and found Ash and Verrin sitting at a table.

Her father smiled. "Well done, daughter. Though you would have found me much more easily had you employed a familiar rather than conscripting poor Timmens into the job."

"He's a nervous fellow," Verrin said.

Ash nodded. "Gets more nervous by the year. I think he's harboring regrets in not pursuing botany instead."

"Do not give me advice on magic," Hazel said. "I am not your apprentice, and you are not my mentor."

Ash slathered some butter onto a warm roll. "Of course you are, and of course I am. Why else would you be here? Necromancy is in your blood, Hazel. Just as it's in mine. It won't do to deny it. Here, try this roll.

They're especially delicious today." He held out the buttered bread to her.

Hazel tightened her jaw and ignored his offering. "What have you done with Holly?"

Ash took a bite of the roll instead. "Holly? Why would you think I've done anything with her?"

"Don't act stupid. I saw her. She's trapped somewhere. You had a hand in it. I know you did."

A slow smile stretched across Ash's face. "You saw her? Well now. How did you manage that?"

Hazel glared at him. "You know how."

"Oh yes. I know very well how. I just want to make sure *you* know. You're a clever girl, Hazel, but this stubbornness of yours in refusing to accept the obvious does you no credit."

"Is that why you locked me in my room? To make me accept the obvious?"

"Of course. And it worked. You got out. You saw your sister. Just imagine what you could do with the proper knowledge and training."

She didn't want any of those things, but Ash refused to listen. "Where's Holly?"

Ash took another bite of the roll. "I'm sure if you apply yourself, you'll be able to figure it out."

Hazel slammed her plate on the table, and the sound echoed through the chamber. The room quieted, and everyone turned to look at her. "This isn't a game," she said, her voice low.

"Of course it isn't."

"Where is she?"

"You're wasting your time asking the wrong questions. I don't know where she is. What you should be asking is how to find her."

Hazel blinked several times. Despite his assurances, he was playing at something, and Hazel didn't want to get caught up in it. But she didn't know what else to do. Swallowing, she asked, "How do we find her?"

"Are you asking for my help?"

A long moment of silence passed.

"Yes."

Ash smiled and Hazel felt as if her heart would shrivel. "We'd better get started then."

Shadowed Depths

Hazel followed Ash through the long stone corridors, her mind racing as she tried to figure out what was coming next. That she had asked her father for help shouldn't have meant much of anything at all. But his smile had been entirely too smug, and the hush that had hung in the dining chamber too ominous.

What, exactly, had she done?

They passed through lengths of monotonous corridors, down flights of narrow stone stairs, and through countless nightwood doors. They descended until the gaps in the stone that showed glimpses of sunlight stopped and they were left with only the sconces of cold, flickering blue flames for light and the bone-chilling damp for comfort.

"Where are we going?" Hazel asked. She had hoped they would leave the mountain, but that possibility lessened with each downward step.

"You will see," Ash said.

Down and down they went. The sconces became fewer and far between. When they ended, Ash spoke a spell that made the lichen clinging to the stone walls glow. The light, though dim, was sterile and harsh—a dead kind of light in which nothing could grow. It turned Ash's skin pallid and the hollows of his eyes to shadows. Hazel must have looked as ghastly. The skin of her hands had turned pale and translucent, marbled with black veins like ink-stained webs.

They came to a narrow corridor with roughly hewn walls as if carved with a spoon. Then to a door—smooth and black just like all the others. They passed through it into an unlit chamber.

The air remained damp and cold, but it had turned fresher somehow, smelling like copper and salt and mulching leaves. The glowing lichen did not follow them here, so when Ash closed the door behind them, he and Hazel stood in complete darkness.

"You must create a light, Hazel," he said.

"Why me?"

"Because this is your journey."

"What are you talking about?"

But all Ash said was, "A light. Please."

Hazel took a deep breath and summoned a little glowing moth, but the light it emitted was feeble and strained. She held out her hand, and the moth fluttered to it, illuminating her fingers but nothing else.

"That is not the correct light," Ash said. "You know it is not."

Hazel supposed she did know. She let the moth linger on her fingers a moment. Then, closing her eyes, she uttered a different spell—one she had taught herself in the darkened depths of a basement not unlike this chamber.

A circle of blue flames flared alight before her, trembling in the shadows as if buffeted by a breeze. The flames flared outwards to illuminate a cavern with walls as roughly hewn as the passageway beyond the door. Nearby, a pool of water lay like a disc of blackened ice. All else remained shrouded in shadows.

Hazel edged her way over to the pool. The water remained still—no waves or ripples to indicate it was fluid. Perhaps it had frozen. She took care as she navigated across the stone floor, not wanting to slip on any patches of ice that might be lurking underfoot.

When she reached the water, she leaned over it, but it did not give her reflection. She tapped the tip of her foot against its surface and nearly lost her balance when the water gave way and its glassy surface broke into a languid ripple. After she removed her foot, the water stilled and regained its perfect placidity.

"What is this place?" Hazel asked.

"This place has no real name. People come here for different reasons and accomplish different things."

"People," Hazel said in a flat voice. "You mean necromancers."

"That is a distinction *you* draw, Hazel, not I."

"Why are we here?"

Ash fell silent a moment. "I suppose that will be for you to decide. I view this place as both a promise as well as its fulfillment. But what that promise is, and what it will fulfill, depends on the person in question. It depends on *you*, my daughter. I cannot say much more than that."

"Can't? Or won't?"

He tilted his head. "A measure of both, I suppose. This place defies description. Yet even if I could describe what you might expect within the pool, I don't think I would."

"Why?"

He smiled. "Where is the fun in that?"

Hazel scowled at him. "We're here to find Holly, not have fun."

"And you can use this place to find her, if that is what you desire. But the potential—both within you and within this chamber—is much, much greater than that. I hope you will not waste this opportunity. The times one is allowed to use this space is... limited."

"Limited? Why?"

"Because the power—the magic—that infuses this place has decreed it so. Most are only allowed one visit here—their first. After that, it is sometimes possible to use this chamber in times of great need, but that is not always the case. We do not truly understand it ourselves. But it is accurate to say that you will more than likely never get this opportunity again." He moved away into the shadows.

Hazel remained by the pool as her father's words floated in her mind. She didn't know what he expected of her—what he thought would happen here. She didn't even know what she expected of herself.

Hazel took a deep breath to clear her mind. None of that mattered. Whatever Ash expected or wanted to happen here didn't matter. She needed to help Holly and find out what had happened to Hemlock and Hawthorn.

She focused on the water—its smooth, glass-like surface reminded her of a mirror, especially since the water refused to give her reflection as Ash's mirrors had. She could probably use it like a mirror and view Holly through it, but Ash's words of wasted opportunity rang in her ears. Was she thinking too simply? She didn't need to *see* Holly, she needed to *help* her.

Hazel turned around and searched for her father in the shadows, but she couldn't see him. Was he still there or had he left?

"I don't know what I'm supposed to do," she called, but no reply came. Not even an echo. Her confusion dissolved into annoyance. She turned back towards the water and tapped her foot on the surface again, watching with a strange satisfaction at the way the water rippled from her foot. Its slow, easy movement had a look of thick cream rather than water.

She knelt down and put her fingers into the pool. The water was cool but not as frigid as she had expected. But it felt like water should and didn't cling to her fingers like a thick cream would. Small, gentle rings radiated from her fingertips, carrying across the entirety of the vast pool like wind over a grassy field.

In the wake of the ripple, a blue light appeared. Hazel looked up and there, in the dense shadows that served as a ceiling, floated one of the blue flames she had summoned. Yet in the water the reflection of the light gave off its own illumination. She could make out a silhouette of a tree and a rock, but then the water stilled and the reflection faded.

A few moments passed as she stared at the pool, thinking. Then she brought over all the lights she had summoned to join the single one above the water. They drifted on the air like cottonwood seeds, wayward and lazy.

She put her fingers in the pool and flicked the water. As the liquid rippled, the lights appeared in the water's reflection, illuminating a shadowed forest. Silhouettes of darkened trees plunged deeper into the shadowed depths of the water, reaching towards a sable sky with sapphire flames for stars.

As the water stilled, the scene faded. She flicked the water again, and the dark forest returned in sharp clarity. A curious thought entered her mind. This wasn't a reflection—this was real. At that moment, the world within the water looked more real to Hazel than the world in which she currently found herself. It filled her heart with an aching longing, soothed only by stepping into the water and allowing the cool liquid to lap at her ankles, her thighs, her waist, until finally it eclipsed her head.

Her booted feet scraped along the stony bottom of the pool. The shadowed forest stretched down around her from a watery sky, though they remained translucent. Impermanent, like coiling mist. Then her body became weightless as the floor fell out from under her, and the trees melted into the shadows of the pool. All became black; Hazel lost all sense of direction. Before she had time to orient herself or to panic, her head broke the water's surface, and she took in a deep, steadying breath.

A night sky loomed overhead, dotted with pale blue stars that floated lazily through the sky like candles on water. Tall pine trees surrounded a dark lake in which she found herself. The air smelled new, like rain before dawn.

Hazel swam to shore, her heart pounding as she worked against the heavy weight of her sodden dress with its ample skirts. She pulled herself atop a rock and lay there with her eyes closed as she caught her breath. The weight of her soaked dress pressed on her as if made out of iron. She needed to dry it, yet she couldn't bring herself to move.

A breeze brushed against Hazel's cheek, so warm that for a moment she believed a fire burned nearby. She opened her eyes. There was no fire, but her dress had dried.

She bolted upright as alarm mingled with curiosity. But as she ran a hand over her dry skirts, the sense faded. Everything was as it should be. She got to her feet and headed into the forest.

The stars followed her, bobbing and weaving around each other as if pulled along on invisible strings. When she stopped, the stars wavered and descended from the sky to float around her. One broke away from the others and led her out of the trees to a wide-open field washed in moonlight. A single road cleft the field in two, winding through it like a dried-up river.

Alongside the road stood Holly. She looked older, more severe. A wreath of ivy leaves crowned her brow, but when clouds passed over the moon, the wreath disappeared.

"Holly," Hazel said as she took her sister's hand and pressed it. "What's happened to you? Are you in trouble?"

Holly's gaze drifted down to her hand that Hazel held, but she said nothing.

Hazel pulled down one of the starlike orbs from the sky and sent it near Holly's head. The moon, clouds, and nearby trees vanished as walls of wood surrounded the sisters and enclosed them in a cramped space no larger than a broom closet.

A flame flared alight in Holly's cupped hands, and she glanced up and looked Hazel right in the eyes.

Hazel's heart floundered as her palms turned sweaty. No one had ever looked at her the way her sister did now. It was as if Holly looked into a part of her that Hazel had never known existed. All her strengths and weaknesses, her frailties and fears, the dreams she had dreamt in a lifetime of nights that had long since been forgotten. She felt as if Holly saw all of it, and Hazel couldn't bear the inadequacy of her own being before her sister's shrewd eyes.

Hazel stepped back and bumped into the wall. She pushed the darkness and the walls away from her, bringing back the star-studded sky and shadowed forest. In the moonlight, a wreath of oak and mistletoe crowned Holly's brow, even as she began to fade like morning mist. Hazel started to reach out to her but pulled back. Holly shouldn't be there. Neither of them should. And so, when Holly faded from the lonely, winding road, Hazel turned and headed back to the lake.

HOLLY TRIED to keep her breathing even and calm as she lay in the enclosed box. She wouldn't panic. If she panicked, she might suffocate, and Holly would rather that didn't happen. She clenched her eyes shut, bracing herself against the jostling to keep her head from getting any more lumps. Breathe in, breathe out. Nice and even, nice and slow.

Her thoughts turned to Hazel. Would she ever see her sister again? A lump formed in her throat that, in the close air, threatened to choke her. Holly tried to put the thoughts out of her mind, but panic and frustration flared up in her again. The air was too stifling and close. She needed to get out. Right now. She was about to kick at the box again for everything she was worth when a warm touch brushed against her hand.

She froze. Had she imagined it? She didn't think she had—it had been distinct enough to kill her outbreak of panic. But surely she must have imagined it. There was nobody here.

Was there?

The hair on Holly's neck stood on end. She couldn't explain it, but she suddenly felt like she was no longer alone. She summoned another flame in her cupped hands, relaxing with relief when the light showed that no one was there.

And yet...

The feeling stubbornly persisted. Holly's heart quickened, and her palms began to sweat. What was happening? Was she losing her mind? It was certainly starting to feel that way.

Extinguishing her flame, Holly clenched her eyes shut and forced herself to breathe, and as she calmed, her mind drifted back to Hazel.

Her sister stood in a moonlit field, silhouetted by the dark shadows of a distant forest. Pale blue orbs of light floated around her head, drifting away on their own courses only to return to her before drifting off yet again. One of the lights came close to Holly, and as it did, Hazel transformed.

Her hair grew long and wild, swinging past her waist in a wind Holly couldn't feel. Woven in her locks were shards of bones and broken raven's feathers and sprigs of yew with their bright red berries. Upon her head she wore a tall, jagged crown of blackthorn adorned with apple blossoms, wormwood, and broom. She wore a long black dress, full in the skirts and high in the neck, that had been sewn together with silver-spun thread. The material shifted in its darkness. One moment it looked gauzy and sheer, the next a mass of impenetrable shadows that even Hazel's light couldn't touch.

Neither sister said anything as they watched one another. Then Hazel frowned and took a step back, and a mist rose from the grass that shrouded the field in a murky haze.

Holly's box jolted, bringing her attention back to the present. Had she been dreaming? She hadn't realized she had fallen asleep. The box jolted again, violently, and Holly cried out as she braced herself against the box's walls. Then the box stilled.

Holly continued to brace herself against the wood as she caught her breath. When the wood cracked beneath her hands, Holly yanked them back. Then the entire box broke and shattered shards of wood fell on top of her.

Shaking, Holly pushed them aside and crawled away from the ruined box that lay in the middle of a wide dirt road that wound through a grassy field. A little further down was a crashed wagon, its axles broken. In the distance, a black-robed man chased a pair of horses as they bolted through the field. Holly pushed herself to her feet, dusted off her own robe, and looked back at the ruined box that had been solid and whole just a few minutes before.

"Stupid necromancers," she murmured. The day had faded, and the sinking sun captured a distant forest in a soft, golden light. Holly stared at the trees, remembering her odd dream about Hazel.

From the wagon came a pounding noise and distant, muffled shouting. Holly ran over and found a pair of long wooden crates still intact in the wagon's bed. From inside both of them, someone shouted and pounded.

"Hemlock? Hawthorn?" It had to be them. She hoped it was them.

"Yes!" came a muffled reply from one of the crates. Though whether it was Hemlock or Hawthorn, she couldn't tell. "Do you know what sap does to clothing? Get me out of here now!" Holly smiled. Hawthorn then.

She tried lifting the lid off the crate, but it wouldn't budge. She kicked at it, but that didn't do anything. "Hang on!" she said and cast a spell of fire against the wood. But just as before, the fire wouldn't take.

"Stupid necromancers!" Holly rubbed her forehead with the back of her hand as she looked around. In a corner of the wagon was an over-turned chest. She turned it over, unlatched the iron clasp, and found within a mess of tools. Among an array of loose nails, she found a hammer and chisel. She grinned and took the tools back to Hawthorn's crate.

It took a while, and Hawthorn's continual complaining didn't help, but Holly managed to wedge the chisel between the wooden slats and pry the crate apart. Thankfully, Hawthorn took over to let out Hemlock. By the time they were done, night had fallen.

"Where's Tum?" Holly said. "He wasn't in with you guys?"

"I should hope not," Hawthorn said.

"What happened to the driver?" Hemlock said. "And the horses?"

"I think they ran off that way," Holly said, pointing at the field.

"Unbelievable," Hawthorn said. "They box us up and cart us off to the middle of nowhere, then leave us to die on the side of the road." He tried to smooth his robe, made a face, then smoothed his hair instead. When he saw Holly and Hemlock watching him, he added, "It's rude."

"But what about Tum?" Holly said. "Something might have happened to him."

"We can't really worry about Tum right now, Holly," Hemlock said. "Hopefully, he got away. As for us, I think we need to work under the assumption that Hazel wasn't at the Shrine and has gone on to the Sea of Severed Stars instead. We need to figure out how to get there."

Holly pursed her lips and took a deep breath. She nodded. "All right. We'll look for Tum later." She peered towards the grassy field. "And I think I might know how to find the horses."

Cold, Quintessential Comfort

Hazel awoke on the stone floor of the dark cavern near the bank of the pond. Her head ached, and she rubbed it as she sat up and looked around. Ash stood nearby, watching her.

"What happened?" she said. "How did I get here?"

"You went into the pool, remained there for a while, then left and lay down there. I didn't want to disturb you."

"Where did I go? What was that place? How..." Her aching head increased to a steady pounding. She took a breath and tried to relax. "How did I get back?"

Ash considered her a moment. "You never left."

"What are you talking about? I went into the pool and... went *through* it to someplace else."

Ash continued to study her, putting Hazel's nerves on edge. Then a slow smile stretched across his face. "What did you see?"

"I... I saw Holly. What do you mean, I didn't leave?"

"Our realm and that of the Keeper of Stars are congruous and yet not. Her realm is meant for spirits and souls, and so only the spirit of your soul went there. The rest of you remained behind."

Hazel's body went cold. In a voice equally icy, she said, "What are you talking about?"

"You walked in the realm of Ether, Hazel. You saw the world through eyes of the dead yet while you are perfectly well and living." Ash beamed at her and gave a little laugh. "I wasn't sure if it would work. The only other living souls to have ever touched this pool had already formally dedicated themselves to the Keeper. One cannot even reach this location until one has done so. But I had my suspicions, and you've proven them correct." He let out a heavy breath and spread open his arms, as if inviting Hazel for a hug, but she remained still. "The Keeper has accepted you. You are well and truly one of us."

Hazel scrambled to her feet. "I am *not* one of you! You used me and lied to me. All to prove some theory? You didn't think it important to tell me what this pool was, of what would happen?"

"Would it have made any difference if I had?"

"Yes! I would have refused. I would have found another way."

"Is that so? What is this other way, Hazel? Why didn't you find another way to talk to your mother after she passed? Or to find the path that led you here? No one made you use necromancy to make a potion in the basement in the house in Sarnum or at the windmill in that backwater town. *You* made the decision to practice necromancy, Hazel. No one else. And you did this because you *know*, just as I do, that there is no other way."

"That was different. Those were just spells; they didn't mean anything. You didn't tell me that by using the pool here I'd be *dedicating* myself to your Keeper of Souls. Well, I refuse him, her, it, whatever!"

"You dedicated yourself to the Keeper from the first moment you cast a necromantic spell. The only thing that happened here was that the Keeper has accepted your dedication to her. *All* spells mean something, Hazel. Do you think our ability to cast magic is an accident? It is a gift from the gods themselves. Most people are completely cut off from doing any magic at all until they undergo a dedication ceremony. Haven't you ever wondered why everyone doesn't work magic? Why everyone's not a witch or a warlock?"

"Yes, but... the dedication ceremonies are just formalities."

Ash sighed and shook his head. "I see the Grove hasn't improved in its education. No, Hazel, they're not formalities. At least not for most. For *you*, however, they are and for others like you and me who are born with pure souls. For people such as us, dedication ceremonies are quite meaningless."

"Pure souls? What are you talking about?"

"We are the ones born with a connection to the Keeper. For us, magic comes naturally, without needing any ceremonies to appeal for a god's favor. Haven't you ever noticed you have a capability in schools of magic to which you have not dedicated yourself?"

"I... yes... but I didn't..."

"And how did you account for that?"

Hazel shook her head, trying to understand everything he was telling her. "I couldn't."

"Exactly. Do you understand now why I left? The people of the Grove, though well meaning, are too entrenched in their superstitious ignorance. They refuse to see the world as it is; anything that doesn't abide by their narrative, they ignore and forbid. And people like us are left to wither on their vine of mediocrity."

Hazel took a deep breath. "Let's suppose, for the moment, that you are right. What would my connection with this Keeper of yours have to do with my ability to cast Wyr magic or any other magic than necromancy?"

"Because, my dear daughter, all the other schools of magic are the foundation of necromancy. Wyr for Air, Wild for Earth, Hearth for Fire, Weaving for Water—these schools of magic are the bones of creation. Combine them all together, and you get something far greater than each discipline could achieve on its own—you get Ether, the *soul* of creation."

Hazel shook her head. "No. That's not possible."

"Do not fall back on your Grove upbringing and their propensity to outright ignore plain facts. Surely you must have noticed this yourself? What of the potion you created in Sarnum? There are many who would argue that potion-making is strictly a Hearth skill. And you are well familiar with Weaving magic, are you not? You must have noticed that some of the necromantic spells you cast are awfully similar, with only an altered pronunciation to separate them. How did you account for that, Hazel?"

Hazel closed her eyes and forced herself to breathe. She had noticed the similarities but had dismissed them. She hadn't ever wanted to dwell on why she had been able to work necromancy or what it had meant. "I didn't account for it," she whispered.

"This is who you are, Hazel—who you've always been from the day you were born. To deny yourself this is like denying yourself air to breathe, fire to warm your skin, water to drink, and food to eat. You are denying yourself the very essence of your existence. Surely you can see the folly in that?"

Hazel opened her mouth to protest, but the words wouldn't come. Her mind had numbed. She didn't know what to think anymore or what to believe.

Ash's expression softened, and he gently took her arm. "You are tired. We will return to your quarters."

Unable to bring herself to resist, she followed her father as he led her from the chamber.

Back at her quarters, the mirror, basin, and ewer were still on the table, just as she had left them. The poker she had thrown remained on the floor by the bookshelf. No one appeared to have been there.

"You should get some rest," Ash said. "I'll have someone bring you dinner when it's ready." He backed out of the door, closing it after him.

Hazel stood there. She felt as heavy as a rock and about as useless. She wanted to tell Ash he was mistaken; she wasn't at all meant for necromancy. It wasn't who she was. And yet deep down in her heart, his words sparked a warmth of calm assurance, a familiarity that brought her... comfort. That frightened her more than anything else. She didn't want to think about it—she couldn't. It was all too much. She went into the bedroom and lay down, hoping for dreams that would let her forget everything, if only for a little while.

Crossroads Conundrum

"Could we hurry this up?" Hawthorn said as he pulled off his necromancer's robe and dropped it on the ground. "There's a chill out, and I'm not dressed for cold weather."

"Well, you could start with keeping your robe on if you're so cold," Holly said.

He drew himself up and looked down the bridge of his nose at her. "That threadbare sack couldn't keep me warm in the middle of summer. If I'm going to die of exposure, I'd rather not do so in shabby raiments."

"It *is* cold out," Hemlock said and blew on his hands.

"Well, if you two would give me a chance to think, then I could do the spell." She picked up Hawthorn's discarded robe and thrust it at him. "And you keep that. You can bear looking shabby like the rest of us for a little while."

The brothers fell silent. Hemlock folded his arms and hunched his shoulders while Hawthorn frowned at the robe as he held it at arm's length.

"Right," Holly said. She cast a Calling spell, then waited, holding her breath as she listened.

"Well?" Hawthorn said. "Did it work?"

"I don't know. Animals have minds of their own. I can't *make* them come over. They have to *want* to, and I don't know if two necromancer horses will want to come over. Or even if they're close enough for the spell to work."

"So what are we supposed to do in the meantime? Stand here and freeze?"

"Good grief. I'll make a fire. Just help me with the wood."

They gathered some of the broken parts of the wagon and put them in a pile. Holly set the wood alight and into a crackling campfire.

Hawthorn warmed his hands by the flames. "I suppose we'll have to spend the night here."

"Don't start," Holly said.

Hemlock squinted as he peered down the road. "Is someone coming?"

"Hopefully someone with a carriage who's fond of making a little coin," Hawthorn said.

Holly looked down the road, but she couldn't see anything. She held her breath to listen and made out a faint thumping sound of galloping hooves. "It's the horses." She moved down the road. By the moonlight, she was able to make out the silhouettes of two horses, and...

"There's a man on one of them."

The brothers joined her. Hemlock summoned his fairy pocket watch light. Hawthorn conjured a goose with ivory feathers that glinted gold and silver.

"A goose?" Holly said.

"Geese are vicious," Hawthorn said.

"Hawthorn got bitten by one when he was a boy," Hemlock said. "He's never gotten over it."

"Yes, well, our friend approaching here isn't going to get over it either if he means to cause trouble."

Hemlock sent out his fairy, illuminating two black horses, upon one of which sat a rider tugging frantically on the reins.

"By the Nameless One, stop!" the rider cried as he and the horses drew closer. But the horses didn't stop until they reached Holly. One of them nudged her with its snout. She smiled and petted it.

The rider slid off the horse and ran a hand over his flushed face. He wore the black robe of a Shrine necromancer. He eyed the robes Hemlock and Holly still wore with a dubious expression. "Who—"

"Attack!" said Hawthorn, and the goose honked and pecked the necromancer on the thigh.

The necromancer cried out and tried to back away, but the goose had his robe in its beak. They fell into a bout of tug-of-war before he remembered himself and started a spell.

"No!" Holly said. One of the horses head-butted him and knocked him down. The goose honked again, flapped its broad wings, and pecked at him some more.

He curled into a ball as he covered his head with his arms. "Get it off me!"

"We need to tie him up or something," Holly said.

Hemlock ripped off the hem of the necromancer's robe. But between the goose's flapping wings and the necromancer rolling around, he couldn't do much else. "Could you ease up on your feathered terror?"

Hawthorn examined his fingernails for several moments before he released his spell. "Told you they were vicious."

With the goose gone, the necromancer scrambled to his feet and tried to run, but Holly tackled him to the ground. "Get him, Hemlock!"

Hemlock tied the necromancer's hands as Holly sat on his back. She got up, and Hemlock pulled the man to his feet.

"What did I ever do to you people?" the necromancer said.

"You put us in boxes!" Holly said.

"And left us here to die," Hawthorn said. "In the cold."

"Where's Hazel?" Hemlock said.

The man blinked. "Hazel? I don't know any Hazel. And I didn't put you in the boxes. I was told to deliver the crates to... well... somewhere. And so that's what I was doing." He sniffed. "It's a thankless job a man has when he finds himself attacked by wild animals."

"And tackled by young women," Hawthorn added. "Yes, you bear a heavy burden in life. Where is this 'somewhere' you were taking us?"

The necromancer lifted his chin. "I can't say."

"It wouldn't be the Sea of Severed Stars, by any chance?" said Hemlock.

The necromancer's brow furrowed for a moment before he composed himself. "No."

"You're a terrible liar," Hawthorn said. "Why were you taking us there?"

"I told you, I wasn't—"

"Yes, yes, you know nothing of the Sea of Severed Stars. If we must play this game, fine. Why were you delivering us to this *secret location* then?"

The man put on a defiant expression.

"Maybe you should bring the goose back," Holly said.

The necromancer flinched, but he remained silent.

"No," Hemlock said. "It doesn't matter why. If he was taking us to the sea, then we need to continue on and see if Hazel's there.

"But what about Tum?" Holly said.

"What about him?" said Hawthorn.

Holly ignored him and turned to the necromancer. "What did you do with Tum?"

"Tum?"

"Yes, Tum. Cellar gnome, about this tall. Kind of obnoxious."

The necromancer's mouth hung open as he stared at her. "What's a cellar gnome?"

Hawthorn snickered. "For once I envy a necromancer's ignorance."

Holly sighed. "Never mind. Let's just go."

She and Hemlock clambered atop one of the horses while Hawthorn and the necromancer shared the other. Despite her prodding the necromancer for his name, he refused to give it. So she called him Norman instead.

Hemlock's fairy lit the way down the long, flat road. Moonlight lit the surrounding grassy fields and, beyond those, shadowed forests that stretched towards the star-shrouded night. In the distance, a mountain range loomed on the horizon. Holly had never seen mountains like that before. She wanted to say they were beautiful—perhaps during the day they were. But now they looked like a portion of the night had been cut away, leaving only a deeper, starless darkness that the moonlight couldn't reach. Nobody spoke as they rode. The clip-clop of the horses' hooves, the wind stirring the grass, and the occasional hoot of a distant owl were the only sounds to accompany them.

They came to a crossroads. Hemlock and Hawthorn brought the horses to a stop.

"Well, which way is it?" Holly said. "Do you know, Norman?"

Norman sighed. "Would you please stop calling me that? It's a terrible name."

"Well, you won't tell me your real one. What else am I supposed to call you?"

He thought a moment. "Maldovar? That's a splendid name."

"No, you're definitely not a Maldovar."

Hemlock said, "We could split the difference and call him Malman."

"Maybe," Holly said.

"No!" Norman shrank within himself a little. "Norman's fine..."

Hawthorn said, "While it's very charming the two of you trying to name your pet necromancer, could we please choose a direction and get on with this journey? Riding a horse is terribly uncomfortable, smelly, and having to share the experience with Malman isn't helping at all."

"Norman," said the necromancer. "We decided the name is Norman."

"We might decide your name is Daisy unless you tell us which direction to take."

Norman set his jaw and straightened his back though his eyes didn't look as confident as his posture. "Do your worst."

"Maybe we should split up," Hemlock said. "Hawthorn and Norman will take one road. Holly and I will take another. As soon as one pair realizes they're on the right track, one from that pair can take the horse and ride back to find the others."

"That might work if we had two roads to choose from," Hawthorn said, "but we have three. Not to mention that I'm not at all encouraged by the prospect of teaming up with Malman here."

"Norman!"

Holly said, "I agree. I don't think we should split up. We need to pick a direction that we all agree on."

"Preferably before we all die in this cold," Hawthorn said.

Holly gave Norman a pointed look. "Well?"

Norman avoided her gaze a long while. "Left."

She blinked a few times. "Really?"

Hawthorn said, "If he said left, then we can assume that either the road straight ahead or to the right is the correct one, so that narrows it down."

"Unless he knew we'd think that," Hemlock said, "and it's actually the correct course."

"My head hurts," Holly said. "So which one do we take?"

Nobody said anything.

Her gaze returned to the mountains in the distance. "Which road will take us to those mountains over there?"

Norman frowned. "Why would you want to go to the mountains?"

"It seems as good a destination as any, don't you think?"

Norman shrugged and seemed bored with the question. "The road straight ahead looks like the most direct route."

"Where does the road to the right lead?"

"I couldn't say. I've never taken that road."

"Because you've only ever taken the one on the left."

"Yes. Exactly."

It made sense, what he was saying. Holly had no idea what a sea of stars or souls would look like, but whatever it was, a mountain didn't seem like it would fit. Of course, there was no telling what might lie beyond the mountain, but there was nothing to indicate that it was the right direction over any of the others.

"I think we should turn right," Hawthorn said. "*Norman* claims to not know what's in that direction, so obviously that's the one he's lying about."

"Unless he's lying about all of it," Hemlock said. "Or none of it. Either way, I think we should leave Norman's opinion on the matter out of it."

It wasn't supposed to be this hard. Choosing which road to take shouldn't be the deciding factor on whether or not they would find Hazel. What if they made the wrong choice? They would travel on, looking for something that wasn't there, possibly not ever realizing they had made the wrong decision. Not until it was too late, at least. The importance of this decision pressed on Holly. How would she ever be able to live with herself if she made the wrong choice?

She looked at Norman and found him staring at something further down the road ahead, his brow knitted and expression puzzled. She followed his gaze and, at first, saw nothing. Then just like the shadowed mountains looked like missing parts of night, a smaller shadow that looked like night itself bobbed along the road.

"What is that?" Holly said. When she turned back to Norman, his puzzlement had faded and he looked unconcerned.

"I believe it's a raven," he said.

"Raven?" Hawthorn said. "Wonderful. It probably means there's a corpse on the road ahead. More reason to turn right."

"There would be more than one raven if there was something dead on the road," Hemlock said as he squinted at the flitting shadow. "And I only see one. I think."

Holly didn't turn to see if it was actually a raven on the road or whether or not there was more than one or whether or not there was something dead their noses would have to contend with. She kept her gaze on Norman. The way he had placed his bound hands on the horse in front of him, the way he carried his shoulders, the expression that had settled over his features suggesting bored disdain looked, when Holly looked closely, a little too carefully placed. He looked like a man who didn't care—who wished to get on with the journey because sitting there was only growing increasingly intolerable. Yet his gaze, every now and again, would return to the raven on the road, as if his eyes had a will of their own. And at those fleeting moments, Norman looked... uncertain.

"I think we should go straight," Holly said.

Norman glanced at her but then quickly looked away.

"Are you certain?" Hemlock said.

Holly continued to study Norman, but he had fixed his gaze on a distant point and refused to look at her again.

"Yes," she said. "I'm certain of it."

"All right," Hemlock said, and he flicked the horse's reins, and the animal resumed walking.

Hawthorn brought up his and Norman's horse alongside them. "If there is a corpse on the road, then Norman has volunteered to clean it up." He clapped Norman on the back, and the necromancer flinched. "Right, Norman?"

Norman said nothing, keeping his gaze fixed ahead. Holly did the same.

A Star-Enshrined Heart

Hazel woke up and stared at the ceiling. A jagged crack seared across the stone surface to a corner where moss grew. She lay still a moment, savoring the softness of the bed before she realized a lamp had been lit in the room. Someone had been in her quarters. Again.

Annoyed, she got up from the bed and went into the main room. A fire had been lit in the hearth, and the poker that had been lying on the floor had been returned to its proper place. The basin, ewer, and mirror were all still on the table, along with a cloche-covered tray and lit tallow candles. Hazel continued to eye the room, but nothing else looked out of place, and the warmth from the fire helped ease her tension.

She walked to the door and tested the handle, but it was unlocked. She let out a breath, then went to the table and lifted the cloche. A bowl of pale, creamy soup lay on the tray along with an ample chunk of bread. The aroma wafting from the bowl smelled of herbs and wine. She picked up a spoon and tasted the soup, surprised at the lightness of the broth, and delighted to find salty pieces of cured fish. She ate the bowlful along with the bread and washed it down with water from the ewer.

After she had finished, Hazel remained at the table as she considered what to do. According to Ash, she had traveled in the realm of the dead and visited her sister. What did that mean? She had wanted to help Holly, but how could she be certain that she had? The entire experience felt unreal when she thought back on it.

Hazel poured water from the ewer into the basin and repeated the spell that had summoned the vision of Holly the day before. When she appeared in the mirror, Hazel let out a long, relieved breath to find her sister in the sunlight, her eyes no longer tinged with fear. Strangely, she wore a black robe and was riding a horse with... Hemlock.

Hazel stared at the mirror, uncertain how she should feel. Part of her felt relieved to find Hemlock well and happy to look upon his face again. But another part felt envious that her sister sat together so closely with him, that they shared experiences of which Hazel had no knowledge. It made her angry—at herself, mostly. She had chosen to leave them behind. Hazel wished she could feel confident in her choice. But of all the emotions that stirred within her, confidence was not among them.

She poured the water back into the ewer and turned the mirror away only to realize she had forgotten to look for Hawthorn. She didn't want to work the spell again—didn't want to keep looking back at what she had left behind. Hawthorn must be well—Hemlock and Holly would have made sure of it.

Her assurances took hold, and Hazel began to feel more composed. It was time to focus on what she had come here to do.

It had become clear that Ash had no intention of releasing her mother—Hazel would need to do that herself. Of course, she had no idea how to make that happen. This was her father's spell—it was possible that no one but him would be able to undo it.

Either way, she had to try, and she wouldn't be able to do anything from this room. She needed to find Ash's workshop or wherever he usually worked his magic, and she needed to find it on her own—preferably without him knowing. That meant she couldn't ask Timmens or anyone else for directions. Ash had told her before she should have summoned a familiar to help her find her way. And though the idea of it made her skin crawl, she conceded that, in this matter, he was right. Her father knew necromancy, and if Hazel wanted to undo the spell upon her mother, then she needed to know it too.

She walked to the hearth and warmed her hands by the flames. Closing her eyes, she took several deep and steady breaths. She wasn't like her father. No matter what he said or what he thought, they were different from each other.

Hazel turned her back to the fire and started a conjuration that brought to mind images of darkened nights with star-studded skies. Despite the warmth from the fire, the air turned cold, and the candles flickered and stuttered as shadows gathered in the room.

And from the shadows, a figure emerged.

Darkness shrouded it like a mourning veil. One moment the familiar would melt into the shadows and disappear, another moment it would catch the candlelight and its body would blush with a warm crystalline sheen.

The coldness in the room solidified as the familiar approached her, brushing against her cheek like feathered snowflakes. She steeled herself and in a voice barely above a whisper, said, "I need your help."

The presence moved away from her, and Hazel relaxed, just a little. "I need to find my father's quarters," she said. "I need to find where Ash does his magic."

The familiar disappeared within the shadows of the room, reappearing again as the candlelight glinted off its body like sun-soaked crystal. Then it moved away and passed through the door without opening it.

Heart pounding, Hazel followed the shadowy familiar as it moved down the hall. The corridors remained empty except for one necromancer. He turned his head to follow the familiar's passage but otherwise didn't seem to think much of it and walked past Hazel without sparing a glance for her.

Eventually they came to a nightwood door. The familiar lingered by it a moment before its shadows bled into the black wood and disappeared. Hazel opened the door and stepped inside her father's quarters—the uniquely wide room and open wall that led out onto a lush balcony. Sunlight spilled into the room. A breeze stirred, sweeping in scents of heather, rosemary, and sun-soaked stone. A fire blazed in the hearth that helped push back the chill in the air. The familiar stood beside her. In the daylight, its shadows had gone and its form had taken on a brilliance like crushed diamonds scattered over velvet cloth.

"Thank you," she said to the familiar. "Thank you for your help, but I don't need you anymore. You may return to... wherever you came from. To your own realm."

The air next to the familiar warmed, and the shimmering sparks of its body dissipated among the dust motes that danced in the sunlight.

Hazel crossed the room to the forest-scene tapestry, pushed it aside to expose the hidden door, and walked through it.

She navigated down the narrow dark hallway, still illuminated at the far end with a single blue light. At the end, she turned left and came to another door. She eased it open and peeked inside.

Ash's workroom looked just as it had before. The desktops and benches were still cluttered with papers, bookshelves still lined the walls, bowls and ewers still littered the room. But Ash wasn't there. Hazel stepped inside and closed the door behind her.

She went to a desk and sifted through a stack of papers. Her father's handwriting was at times graceful and even, harried and jagged at others. The former comprised journal-like entries that documented his daily events, what he had eaten, how he had felt. The latter leaned towards brief descriptions of spells to be tested at a later date and other scattered thoughts quickly penned so as not to be forgotten. She sifted through them all, looking for something to stand out, for some hint on how she could undo her mother's spell. But she found nothing.

Hazel pulled books from the shelves and looked at the empty spaces between them; she opened drawers and pushed around writing implements and more papers. One drawer was littered with small, broken bones. Disgusted, she was about to slam it shut but hesitated.

Perhaps a bone was what she should be looking for. Trapping a soul in a bone sounded like a distinct possibility, but it also sounded... disrespectful. If Ash truly still loved Willow like he claimed, he wouldn't trap her soul in something so crude. He would use something beautiful.

She continued to look around, but aside from the bookbindings and workmanship of the shelves and desks, there was nothing beautiful in the room. Everything held a purpose other than ornamentation. She needed to try something new.

Hazel walked over to a bench that bore a mortar and pestle weighing down a stack of papers. She fished her mother's lock of hair out from her pocket and put it in the mortar. Taking a moment to consider, she then retrieved a bone from the drawer and put it in the mortar along with the hair. Yet there was still something missing. The room lacked any plants or herbs, so she returned to her father's quarters and went out onto the balcony.

Sunlight warmed her skin, even though the breeze blew sharp and cold. She found a pot of flowering vervain, broke off a few of the purple blossoms, and headed back to the workshop to add the flowers to the mortar. Taking the pestle in hand, she ground up the ingredients as best she could though the hair was stubborn and wouldn't break down.

Hazel took another moment to consider. Taking a deep breath to steady her nerves, she returned once again to the main room, found a corked bottle of wine on one of the side tables, then lit a candle from the fire and headed back to the workshop. She pulled the cork out of the bottle, smelled the wine, and took a sip before pouring a small amount into the mortar. Then she tipped the candle to the sludgy mixture and stood back as it flared alight.

A thick, acrid column of smoke rose from the mortar. It smelled of burned hair and grass, stinging her eyes and making her cough. Yet underneath the unpleasant stench, a sweet aroma lingered like a half-remembered dream.

Hazel wiped her watering eyes, fighting the urge to double over in a fit of coughing. Had she done something wrong? There shouldn't be so much smoke, should there? She started for the door to get some fresh air when a light beyond the door stopped her.

She wiped her eyes again, convinced she was imagining it, but the light remained. A single orb, gentle and white, floated like a star that had been plucked from the sky. It shone through the smoky haze, through the doors and walls—it shone through all of it as if the light itself were the only true thing in a world built upon fragile illusions.

Hazel held her breath, transfixed by its gentle sway, marveling how the light flared a little brighter with each beat of her heart. Then the door to the workshop opened and her father stood in the doorway. The light shone upon his breast, through his clothes as if he had replaced his heart of flesh and blood for one of pure star shine. He stared at her, surprised, which quickly turned to anger.

"You shouldn't be here, Hazel."

Tears poured from her eyes so that she could no longer see, and the smoke had grown thick beyond bearing. She doubled over, coughing. And when icy tendrils snaked around her body, she was too weak and disoriented to stop it.

Of Mushrooms and Men

Holly gave silent thanks that they never found a corpse on the road. She had spent a fair amount of time holding her breath in anticipation, but nothing ever arose—either in the air or on the road ahead of them.

"Ravens aren't always a sign of death," Norman said, perhaps noticing her relief. "They are the world's oldest messengers, before pigeons and owls and other such birds became more fashionable. They are the eyes of the gods, keepers of gateways and of memories."

"Eyes of the gods?" Holly said. "Is that why you were so nervous when one appeared on the road? Do you think the gods are watching us?"

"The gods are always watching; we just do not always notice it."

"So what does it mean that we saw one? If it didn't mean there was something dead on the road?"

Norman looked her right in the eyes with an intensity that unsettled her. "It means that, for good or ill, something is about to change."

Creepy necromancers and their creepy omens. Holly turned back around and kept her gaze straight ahead.

Night had long since broken into day. They stopped from time to time to drink from a stream whenever they found one and to rest the horses. They didn't have any food though, and the pain in Holly's stomach grew sharper as the day wore on. She let Chester roam free during those moments, hoping he'd be able to find food for himself. Hawthorn complained frequently, of course. But both Holly and Hemlock refused to stop longer than necessary. They needed to find Hazel. After they did, then they could eat.

Day faded into night. The once-distant mountains now loomed closer—so close that Holly imagined she could feel the cold air rolling off their high peaks. The gibbous moon rose low in the sky, golden and swollen as if filled with honey. Stars sparked into the night above them, and in the surrounding field, stars bloomed in the grass like ghost-lit lanterns.

"Where are we?" Holly said, though she spoke so quietly she doubted anyone heard her. Nobody answered.

Had Hazel gone this way? Had she also seen this field that mistook itself for the night sky? Holly hoped so—not only because she hoped to find her sister—but because she hoped Hazel had gotten to see such beauty and wonder. Everyone should be able to see this.

A rider approached on the road ahead. An orb of blue flame followed him, illuminating his black robes and black horse far better than a plain lantern ever could. Hemlock and Hawthorn slowed the horses, and the rider stopped before them.

Silver embroidery adorned his sleeves and the hem of his robe. In the light of his orb, the thread almost looked alive, like snakes writhing in black soil.

The man pushed back the hood of his robe to show a young and handsome face. Yet his black robe declared him to be a necromancer. That didn't sit right with Holly—necromancers had no business being handsome.

He bowed from atop his horse. "I bid you good evening and hope you have had fair travels upon the road."

Holly didn't know how to react. His politeness unsettled her.

Silence lingered among the party until Hawthorn said, "If you don't account for us being boxed up, left for dead on a broken-down wagon, having to keep company with a truculent necromancer, and freezing atop a smelly horse while slowly starving to death, then our travels have been most pleasant, thank you for asking."

"I am sorry you've had troubles. It's why I'm here. I've come to escort you to safety and warmth, where you can avail yourself to as much food and rest as will please you."

"You're about fifteen hours late, by my reckoning, but better than never."

Hemlock said, "It's awfully convenient, your coming by with promises of food and safety, just as we need it. How did you know we were here?"

"It wasn't convenience. We share a common acquaintance, and it is by his request that I am here."

"Common acquaintance?" Holly said. "Who?"

"Your father, Ash."

Everyone turned silent.

"How...," Holly began, but her throat caught and she had to swallow. "How did he know we were here? Is Hazel with him?"

The young man smiled—kindly, not condescending as Holly would have preferred so she could have a reason to dislike him. "Your father is a great man. It would be best if he explained such things as I would not be able to do it proper justice. Please, the night grows colder as you've undoubtedly noticed. There will be mulled wine at home, and if we hurry, we might be able to get some while it's still hot."

"Home? Where's home?"

He smiled again and nodded towards the mountain, then turned his horse and started down the road at an easy pace.

Holly stared at the mountain shrouded in shadows. It didn't look at all homey. But then that was probably too much to ask for in a necromancer lair. "Well, I guess we're visiting the necromancers' home."

"As long as it's warm," Hawthorn muttered.

Once they caught up to the necromancer, they increased their pace. There was too much jostling and noise from the horses to have any real conversation, but Holly had managed to ask for his name and he had given it—Verrin.

The night wore on as they galloped down the road. Holly's muscles stiffened in the cold and turned achy from the horse. After a while, she no longer cared that they were headed towards a creepy black mountain. Well, not as much anyway.

Strangely, the closer they got to the mountain, the less scary it became. Lights shone in small square windows—*warm* lights from countless candles or fires in hearths. At least in some. Other openings emitted blue lights like the ones they had seen in the Shrine. Great pillars emerged from the mountain face, carved from the stone itself. They were rough, more utilitarian than decorative, but even those helped the formidable structure seem slightly less intimidating. Outside, paths of stairs switched back and forth up the mountain, illuminated by lanterns that cast a ghostly blue-green light.

Verrin stopped at a columned portal and dismounted from his horse. Holly and the others did the same while Hawthorn helped Norman down. Verrin noticed the necromancer's bound hands but said nothing about it. He led them down a dirt path overgrown with tall grass, lighting the way with his glowing orb.

They came to a black door set within the base of the mountain. Verrin pushed it open and stepped inside. Holly and the others followed.

The air within was thick and musty, smelling of earth and decaying leaves. The cramped room—little more than a cave—had solid stone walls and a ceiling so low that Holly could stand on her tiptoes and brush the cold rock with her fingertips. Boxes littered the bare earthen floor, all filled with soil, sawdust, and straw, within which different varieties of mushrooms grew.

Verrin extinguished his orb. But there was another light nearby—a lantern of golden, living flame that flickered near the feet of a man who knelt next to one of the boxes. He cut a mushroom with a small paring knife and placed his harvest in a nearby basket. Then he stood, stretched his back, and turned around.

Holly's breath caught. It was the same man she had seen in her vision when she drank Odd's potion. The man that looked an awful lot like Hazel. "Father?"

He smiled. "You remember. You don't know how much that pleases me."

Holly didn't remember him, she only guessed who he was by his strong resemblance to Hazel. But she remained quiet, not knowing what to do.

"Is Hazel here?" Hemlock said.

Ash's smile faded as he shifted his gaze to Hemlock. The two stared at each other a long while.

Holly glanced between them. "You two know each other, don't you?"

"More like a passing acquaintance, really," Hemlock said.

"You're Lupinus's boys, aren't you?" Ash said. "How is your father? I always found him a more reasonable man than most."

"Dead," Hemlock said.

Ash gave no reaction. "Pity."

"You didn't answer his question," Holly said. "Is Hazel here?"

"Are you familiar with cultivating mushrooms?" He waved a hand towards one of the boxes.

"They grow in filth," Hawthorn said. "Frightful things."

"True," Ash said. "Filth and darkness. But that is one of the things to be respected of mushrooms. People always go on about the sun and the life it brings to the world, but they rarely speak of the things that grow despite the sun's absence. Mushrooms are like sparks in the void, life out of lifelessness. That commands respect."

"I'm very fond of mushrooms," Holly said. "They're especially good on toast. But we need to talk about Hazel now. Is she here? Have you seen her?"

Ash walked over to a box filled with a mound of soil dotted with delicate mushrooms with stalks so long and thin that Holly wondered how they were able to hold up the papery, umbrella-like caps.

"Such wondrous things, mushrooms," Ash said. "With limitless possibilities. They provide everything from humble sustenance, like you said, to the most treacherous poisons. And there are more varieties than we can count." He turned towards Holly. "Did you know that mushrooms take well to magic?"

He looked at her in a way that suggested he expected an answer. She shook her head.

He returned his attention to the soil. "Some say that because mushrooms thrive in the dark, they belong to the realm of the Shapeless One, and that, due to this, they are especially receptive to magic. While the former could be debated among scholars, of the latter there is no doubt. Mushrooms thrive under careful ministrations tempered by magic, which can lead to new and fantastic varieties never before seen upon this earth. It's quite magnificent, don't you think?"

Holly didn't think it sounded magnificent—not if he was using necromancy to create new, freaky mushrooms that wouldn't at all taste good on toast. "Hazel," she said, trying to put a firmness in her voice but didn't quite succeed.

He kept his gaze on the mushrooms. "Your sister's a clever girl with great potential. But she is fragile. She has not yet found her way. And until she has, I'm afraid any distractions will likely prove harmful. I'm very sorry."

"Sorry? About what?"

Verrin extinguished the lamp and plunged them into darkness. From the boxes of earth, mushrooms glowed pale and blue like moonlight on ice.

Holly tensed, and behind her, Hemlock gasped. She tried to summon a flame, but before she could, a glittering blue dust fluttered through the darkness like wind-borne pollen. It floated around her head, tickling her nose and smelling oddly like sandalwood and fish. Holly sneezed, and then she knew no more.

Tormented Love

Hazel awoke on a cold stone floor with a pounding headache. She pushed herself upright and looked around, surprised to see she was still in her father's workshop. She must have fainted, probably from all the smoke. Had something gone wrong with her spell?

No, the spell had worked. There had been a bright light close to Ash's chest. That had meant something.

She got to her feet and started across the room, but it was like shadows had solidified around her, clinging like tar that made her movements heavy and strained. When she stopped, the shadows receded, but as soon as she tried to walk again, the shadows returned like night-tempered chains. Her father had done this. He had trapped her here.

Why? Of course he'd been displeased with her poking around where she didn't belong, but then why leave her there? Why not throw her out? Lock her in her room? Both seemed like more reasonable actions to take against a trespasser than leaving her exactly where she wasn't supposed to be.

Hazel conjured a beam of prismatic light and combined it with a sharp gust of air, but the shadows remained. Unsurprising, she supposed. She took a moment to think, then worked a corrupted version of a Weaving

Unraveling spell and tried to pull the shadows apart. But the shadows remained, as strong as ever. She tried corrupting the prismatic light and gust of wind, but that didn't work either. Hazel tightened her jaw as she pushed down her frustration. Should she try summoning a familiar again? She didn't know how that would help, but she was running out of ideas.

Before she had a chance to try, the door opened and her father stepped inside. Hazel eyed his chest, but the light that had been there before was gone.

Ash stood before her, his expression unreadable. He didn't look angry, but he didn't look pleased either.

"I don't really blame you," he said after a while. "I grew up in the Grove, just as you did. My mind was also filled with the ignorance and lies that pervade the region. I don't blame you for wanting to... undo what I've done. I don't blame you for not understanding. But I would be lying if I said your actions haven't wounded me. I had hoped..." He shook his head. "It doesn't matter. Perhaps I've been foolish in thinking it would be easier. That once you saw what I could offer, you would want my help."

"Help with what? Necromancy?"

"Realizing your true potential."

"I don't need your help. Not with that."

"We are so alike, Hazel. I was just as you are when I was your age. Gifted with certain talents, then crippled with the uncertainty that followed. What I struggled to find was that there is more in life than what the people in the Grove can offer. *You* don't have to struggle as I did. I can help you."

Hazel took a deep breath as she tried to keep calm. "I told you, I don't *need* your help."

Ash smiled and shook his head. "Even now, the similarities between us are striking. You are willful and stubborn, just like me. You refuse to compromise, just like me. You show an unflagging determination to reach a goal you have set for yourself—doing whatever it takes to succeed in it, for good or ill." He exhaled a short laugh and smiled again. "Just like me."

"I am nothing like you!"

His expression sobered, and he clasped his hands together and tilted his head as he regarded her. "Yes. Perhaps my own willfulness has prevented me from seeing that you are, in many ways, also like your mother.

You, like her, are much too quick to dismiss that which you don't understand. You put too much faith in the lies you have been raised with."

"What lies?"

"The lie that necromancy is a separate form of magic, one to be ignored and never discussed. That those who practice it are somehow... tainted. That is what you think, isn't it?"

Hazel said nothing.

Ash nodded as if she had answered. "What the people in the Grove don't understand is that necromancy is the *only* magic. Every other discipline, Wyr, Hearth, Weaving, and Wild, are all aspects of the same thing. Pieces of the same pie. The Lords of the Sun and Trees and the Ladies of the Sky and Sea are all aspects of the same being—the Shapeless One, the Keeper of Stars and Souls. Refusing to accept this is as absurd as refusing to accept that the sun is bright and the night dark."

"It sounds to me rather that someone thinks he's more important than he really is and extends that importance to his magical discipline of choice."

"This isn't about me, Hazel."

"Oh, I think it is. Because you keep ignoring what *I* want, choosing instead to believe whatever suits *you* best."

He remained quiet a moment. "You know, I sometimes wonder how I might have reacted if a mentor had come to me and offered to teach me of necromancy and all that I struggled to learn in my life. I wonder if I would have accepted such an offer. I've never much cared for accepting help from others. I've never liked the sense of obligation it gives me, the sense that I *owed* them something. You, perhaps, know what I mean?"

Hazel knew exactly what he meant, but she remained silent.

"But when I look back now," he continued, "I can see how much my life would have benefited from such a mentor. Much of what I've learned of necromancy, I learned on my own. I used to hold a sense of pride in that—not everyone could say the same. But now I wonder if that pride was misplaced. I can't help but wonder if I'd had some help, how much more I might have accomplished in my life, of what I might have accomplished for my family. Perhaps, if I'd learned more, I could have saved your mother from ever perishing in the first place."

Hazel tensed. She felt as if they had trod upon unsteady ground, and she needed to choose her words carefully. "People die. It's not your fault. It's not anyone's fault. It's just the way life is. You need to let her go."

"The way life is," Ash said, his voice dangerously flat. "You say that as if it's something we must accept. Life is malleable, as are the laws that dictate it. I refuse to bend to life's fickle whims. As should you."

"It's not fickle, it's just the way it is. Why can't you accept that?"

"And why can't you accept that life is what we *make* of it? We can manipulate souls and spirits, Hazel. The very essence of life! With enough time and practice, we could make life bend to *our* whims!"

"You've lost your mind. Do you hear yourself? Do you know what you sound like?"

"I hadn't wanted to do it like this. I had thought that with enough time, you would come to understand the world as I do, that you would see it as I do, because, given who you are, how could you see it any other way?"

"What are you talking about?"

His expression saddened. "You are right, in a way, about life. There is one aspect of it that is not malleable, that cannot be manipulated or changed or reversed. I've tried. But it inevitably binds us all, and eventually we all return to it."

Hazel's breathing turned heavy and ragged. Despite everything Ash had done to her and her mother, Hazel had never been frightened of him. Until now. "Father, what are you talking about?"

He fixed his gaze on her in a way that made Hazel wonder if he had ever truly seen her prior to that moment. It was like he saw straight to her heart—straight to her soul—and the tenderness he held in his gaze for her at that moment made her want to weep.

"I'm talking about love, daughter. It is life's greatest strength and greatest weakness. It hinders us as much as it bolsters us. But love's fire burns incredibly hot. Perhaps, within such a fire, a temperament for the greatest witch of our time might be forged."

Before she could say anything else, Ash returned to the door, opened it, and Hemlock and Verrin stepped inside.

Hazel cried out and clapped a hand over her mouth. Her outburst surprised her, as did the warmth and joy that filled her heart to look at Hemlock. He wasn't supposed to be there, and yet now that he was, she was grateful beyond words.

Hemlock remained quiet as his gaze met hers. He didn't look angry or disappointed, as she had expected. Instead, he looked tired, relieved, but also strangely enlivened. His eyes held a spark in them she hadn't noticed before, and it made her heart quicken to have such a gaze fall upon her.

Swallowing, she said, "You're not supposed to be here."

"Neither are you," he said.

Ash stood alongside Hemlock. "Perhaps your greatest failing, my daughter, is your continual misjudgment of a given situation. You insist on underestimating yourself and others. You choose to see things as you want them to be—or perhaps even believe them to be—instead of how things actually are." He placed a hand on Hemlock's shoulder, and Hemlock tensed as his expression tightened. "Take our mutual friend here. You chose to believe you could leave someone you love behind. That once you did, it would be the end of it. You would go your way, he would go his. That is what happened here, isn't it? I'll admit I've had to puzzle out a few of the gaps from what I've seen in the mirrors." He paused as he glanced between Hazel and Hemlock, but when neither said anything, he continued.

"Perhaps you chose to believe that you didn't love him, or he didn't love you. Or perhaps you underestimated the bond of love that ties you together. I've certainly made that mistake. Whatever you chose to believe, it put you at a disadvantage, and so now we find ourselves here, together, at a crossroads of sorts, don't you think?"

Hazel tried to walk towards Hemlock, but the shadows constricted and kept her from taking more than a step. Hemlock's face darkened, and he tried to go to her, but Ash tightened his grip on his shoulder, and Verrin summoned a tall, lanky woman with hair like midnight and crystalline skin. She put a bony hand on Hemlock's arm, causing him to wince as he paled, and he went still.

"What do you want?" Hazel said. "Why are you doing this?"

"I want what I've always wanted from the day you were born, Hazel. I want you to be true to yourself, without fear, without reservation. I want you to achieve your potential. I want you to recognize, as I do, how great your potential truly is."

"What does any of that have to do with Hemlock?"

He smiled as his brow furrowed in a quizzical manner. "Even now you refuse to see this situation for what it is. You underestimate the significance of this moment."

Hazel clenched her hands in an effort to keep calm. "Then why don't you tell me?"

"You have been holding yourself back, Hazel. You have preconceived notions of what it means to be a necromancer that don't sit well with your other preconceived notions of who you think you are. Perhaps you are afraid of what others will think of you. Perhaps you worry you will never be able to return home. Perhaps you worry about something else entirely. But one thing is clear: the right situation can push all that aside and force you to see yourself as you truly are. And there is no coming back from that."

A dreadful understanding unfolded itself for her, and Hazel's fear turned sharp and acrid. "Let him go."

"You've held me in such disdain for all of these years, accusing me of ruining your mother. But did you ever once put yourself in my shoes? Did you ever, just once, imagine what you would have done had you been in my situation?"

The conjured woman dug her pale fingers deeper into Hemlock's arm. His pallor turned waxy and his lips blue. The skin under his eyes darkened, and he would have fallen to the ground if not for the woman and Verrin holding him up.

"Let him go!"

"I never wanted this for you, daughter. I never wanted for you to witness what it's like to watch someone you love waste away before your eyes. I would have protected you from this, if you would have let me. But you *are* my daughter. I should have known you would choose the harder path, just as I always have. It was wrong of me to have expected anything different."

She fought against the shadows, but the harder she pushed, the harder they solidified around her. This couldn't be happening; never before had she felt so helpless. The woman tightened her hand again, and Hemlock's pallor worsened. Hazel hunched over and let out an enraged scream.

Familiar Fellowship

Holly jolted awake as a scream seared through her sleep-addled mind. Had she dreamt it? She must have, because everything now was so quiet except for the crackling of a fire in a nearby hearth and the gentle snoring of Hawthorn as he sat slumped in an armchair. She herself lay on a sofa. How had she gotten there?

She sat up and looked around the well-furnished room that she now found herself in. There were no windows in the stone walls, but the lavish curtains seemed to make up for it somehow. Plush carpets padded the stone floor, and the warm tones of the intricately carved wooden furniture added almost as much warmth as the fire that crackled so close to hand.

She got up and shook Hawthorn by the shoulder. "Wake up."

He opened his eyes and blinked at her, then scrambled to his feet. "Where are we? Where's Hemlock?"

Holly shook her head. "I don't know. I just woke up a minute ago, and we were here. I don't know where he's gone."

"That's some fine father you've got there. Who would've thought he'd poison his own daughter?"

"Well, I don't think we were *poisoned*...," Holly began but trailed off when Hawthorn's expression told her he didn't much care about that particular distinction. "Norman's gone too," she added, not knowing what else to say.

"Who cares about the necromancer!"

"His mother probably cares," Holly muttered.

"Good. She can shed an ocean of tears for him while we find Hemlock." He walked over to the door, but it was locked. He closed his eyes and let out a long, slow breath.

"Maybe he's with Hazel," Holly said, trying to sound hopeful.

Eyes still closed, Hawthorn said, "Why would he be with Hazel while we're left here?"

"I..." Holly tried to think of a reason that let her hold on to this thread of hope she had found, but nothing came to mind. She wrung her hands. "It's all ruined, isn't it? They're both gone. What are we going to do?"

"We're going to find them."

"How?"

"Well, an excellent start would be by getting out of this room, don't you think?"

Holly took a deep, shaking breath as she struggled to pull herself together. "Right." She smoothed her robe as if she might find some confidence hidden among the wrinkles and joined Hawthorn by the door. "Maybe we could burn it down."

"It's worth a try."

Holly pulled fire from the hearth and flung it at the smooth black door. Hawthorn winced and backed away from the heat. But once the fire died down, the door remained unscathed.

"Stupid necromancers!" Holly shouted.

Hawthorn cast spells of his own. There were bright flashes of brilliant, colorful light and powerful gusts of wind that threatened to knock Holly over. She took refuge behind the armchair. But after the onslaught of spells died out, Hawthorn stood there scowling and puffing at the door that remained locked.

"Damned necromancers," he muttered.

"Now what?"

Hawthorn said nothing.

His silence frightened her. There had to be a way out.

Holly reached into her pocket, relieved to feel the familiar, fuzzy little body curled up into a warm ball. She gently lifted Chester and petted his tiny head.

"Great," Hawthorn said. "Vermin."

Holly ignored him and lifted Chester up to her face. "We need your help again, Chester," she whispered. "We're stuck here. We need you to go find the key to the door or something that will let us out." She kissed Chester on the head, then put him on the ground. With a sharp squeak he scurried under the door and out of sight.

∾

HAZEL CLENCHED her eyes shut and shifted her focus to keeping her breathing steady and calm.

"Open your eyes, Hazel," Ash said. "You'll only add to his pain by hiding."

Hazel glared at her father. "*You're* doing this to him."

"And what are you doing to stop me? You don't get to choose to use necromancy as it suits you, Hazel. Everything you did to come here, everything that led you to me, you had to use necromancy to find. Are you really going to balk now, when so much is at stake?"

Frustrated, she cried out and tried work a conjuration, but her knowledge of such spells remained limited, and her distress scattered her thoughts. The conjuration took shape as a blackbird. When it flew towards the pale woman, she swatted at it and the spell unraveled.

"You can do better than that, Hazel."

"I don't know how! I don't know what I need to do!"

Ash considered her a moment, then nodded to Verrin. He gestured to his familiar, and the pale woman slackened her grip, allowing some color to return to Hemlock's haggard face.

Movement pulled Hazel's gaze to a corner of the room. A little brown mouse darted behind a desk leg. She never thought she'd be so glad to see a rodent in her entire life. Holly was nearby; she had to be.

"Your excuses grow wearisome, Hazel," Ash said. "But I am not an unreasonable man. I will give you time to reflect on the task at hand. Perhaps my absence will help you... focus." He started for the door.

Hazel, fearing he'd see Chester, who now nosed around one of the bookshelves, said, "Where's Holly?"

He turned back around. "Your sister is safe, if that's what you're worried about."

"And Hawthorn?"

"With Holly."

"Why don't you bring them here so we can all have this discussion together?"

"Because this doesn't concern them. They will only distract you."

"Or perhaps you're worried they will distract *you*."

"Your attempts at stalling are childish and unbecoming of you, Hazel."

Chester scurried from the bookshelf to underneath a table. The movement pulled Hazel's gaze before she could stop herself.

"Well, well," Ash said as he walked over to the table. "Looks like someone's come to join us after all." He crouched down just as Chester dashed underneath a pile of fallen papers. As Ash moved, a delicate silver chain poked out from underneath his robe around his neck. It gleamed in the light for the span of a breath, then he moved again and the collar of his robe shrouded it once more.

He put out his hand, and to Hazel's surprise, Chester scampered onto his upturned palm. He straightened and grinned while petting Chester's furry back. "I'd always thought there were never enough Wild witches and warlocks in the Grove. I was happy to learn Holly had become one."

"I wouldn't have thought you'd care for the discipline," Hazel said as she studied Ash's neck, trying to get another glimpse of the silver chain he wore.

"On the contrary, I care for all of them. Wild magic is the least pursued of all the disciplines. I've never understood why. Being able to interact with other living creatures is quite astounding. It's not to be underestimated." He brought up Chester near his face, angled so that both he and the mouse faced Hazel. "Why do you suppose this little fellow is here?"

"Perhaps you have an infestation."

He smiled. "Oh, I don't think so. Familiars of Wild practitioners never act quite the same as their cousins out in the natural world. This one belongs to Holly, and I think you know that."

Hazel said nothing.

Chester scurried up Ash's arm to his shoulders and went behind his neck. Just as Ash reached up to retrieve him...

"Ow!" he cried.

Chester leaped to the floor and hid underneath a gap in one of the bookshelves.

Ash put a hand to his neck. When he pulled away, one of his fingers was stained with a spot of blood. His previous good humor faded, and he scowled at Hazel. "Out of respect for your sister, I will overlook that particular trespass. But only this once." He walked out. Verrin, casting a single glance at Hazel, followed. The pale woman he had summoned faded, and Hemlock collapsed to the floor.

"Are you all right?" she said, but he never even looked at her. He stared at the floor as he took in slow, deliberate breaths. She tried to move towards him, but the shadows wouldn't let her. Instead, she crouched down and peered into the gap below the bookshelf where Chester had disappeared. She put out her hand, not really expecting the mouse to come out, but he did. The shadows didn't hinder his approach, and he scampered onto her palm. A fragment of black cloth had gotten snagged on his teeth. She pulled it free and let Chester run off again.

Hazel pinched the tiny bit of cloth between her fingertips, and they came away with a slight red smudge. A portion of her father's robe, stained with a drop of his blood.

With a Weaving spell, she altered the bit of fabric and made it grow larger and larger until it was almost the size of the palm of her hand. The bloodstain hadn't grown with it, and the mark was so small that, along with the dark color of the cloth, Hazel couldn't see where it was.

Knowing Ash, he had probably locked Holly up somewhere. It would explain why she had set Chester loose, not being able to get out herself. Maybe she could turn the fabric into a key somehow. Only problem was that she had no way of knowing how the key should be shaped, not to mention that changing cloth to metal would be exceedingly difficult. No, that wouldn't work.

She pursed her lips. She was still thinking like a Weaving witch. Her Weaving magic hadn't helped her when Ash had locked her up; she doubted it would help now.

Tired, she sat down on the floor and laid the fabric out in front of her. Then she got an idea.

She worked a spell similar to the one she had used to summon a familiar when her father had locked her in her room. But for this one, she wove elements of Weaving magic into it. She joined short words, lively and bright, with longer, complicated ones that lived in the shadows of her mind, bending under their own sorrows.

The patch of black fabric formed into the shape of a tiny little man. His body was entirely featureless except for the two bright eyes that peered at her like pinpricks in paper held up to the light.

"Hello," Hazel said, tremendously uncomfortable but hoping it didn't show on her face or come through in her voice.

The little man didn't respond. He teetered upon one stout leg, then the other. Chester came out from hiding and crept up to him. The mouse's whiskers twitched as he sniffed at the familiar, and the familiar touched Chester's nose with a tiny woolen finger. Hazel expected the mouse to run away, but he stayed put and began to wash his face with his paws while the little fabric man tottered in unsteady circles around him.

Hazel gently poked the familiar's chest. The fabric had gone cold, but it gave away at her touch far more easily than any stuffed doll she had ever put her hands on. It was like there was nothing inside but billowing air, cold headwinds whipped over star-soaked snow.

Hazel rubbed warmth back into her finger. "I need you to find Holly," she said to the familiar. It snapped to attention at her voice, though it still weaved back and forth as if unsteady on its legs. "Go with the mouse. He knows where she is. Do what you can to help her. Understand?"

The familiar put its tiny hands together, and its eyes flared bright before darkening and blending in with the surrounding fabric. It threw itself across Chester's back like a sack of grain, and the mouse scampered underneath the door with his burden.

Hazel took a deep breath. The familiar would help Holly—she needed to believe that. And now she needed to focus on Hemlock and figure out how to help him.

Stained Glass Memories

Holly sat on the floor in front of the fire. The flames warmed her back, and that warmth helped keep her fear under control. Everything would be fine—nothing could be so bad as long as you had clothes on your back and a fire to warm them. Right?

She needed to believe that.

Hawthorn remained in front of the creepy black door. He had rolled up the sleeves of his shirt, as if he intended to wrestle with the door if it didn't give way to his spells. Holly grinned a little. She'd like to see that.

"You should sit on a chair," he said without turning to look at her. "The floor is filthy."

"I like it here. It's warm, I can watch what you're doing, and it keeps me from wondering what necromancers stuff their chairs with."

He turned and arched an eyebrow at her. "The souls of laughing widows?"

"Or the bones of baby animals."

"The unwashed feet of wayward peddlers."

Holly giggled. "Exactly. So I'll stay right here."

Hawthorn turned back towards the door. But before he could work another spell, a faint scratching came from the other side. Holly scrambled to her feet. When Chester wriggled through the crack underneath the door, she scooped him up and gently rubbed the soft, furry mouse against her cheek.

But the scratching continued.

Both she and Hawthorn froze. In the same spot where Chester had squeezed through, a little woolen creature wriggled and writhed as it scrabbled at the floor with its little dark hands until finally it pulled free from the door and got to its little feet. It blinked up at Holly with tiny eyes that shone like glass beads.

"Wonderful," Hawthorn said. "Look at what your rat dragged in."

"He's not a rat," Holly said, half-distracted. Her heart wasn't in that particular argument. Her attention remained fixed on the creepy black woolen doll thing.

"How do we get rid of it?" He took a kerchief and waved it at the doll. "Shoo, shoo."

The doll remained unfazed by Hawthorn's flapping cloth. It stood on its tiptoes—well, what would have been the tips if it had any toes—and pointed up at the door.

"Yes, out," Hawthorn said. "That's where you should be going." He flapped his kerchief some more.

"No, wait," Holly said and picked up the doll before Hawthorn scared it away. It was cold in her hands, like frost-encrusted leaves.

"Ugh, don't *touch* it! You don't know where it's been."

"It's been with Chester."

"Hardly a redeeming factor."

"No, don't you see? I sent Chester to find something that will help us get out of here. This must be it."

Hawthorn frowned and wrinkled his nose, but he remained silent.

The little doll continued to point at the door, so Holly stepped closer to it. As she did, the doll flung itself from her hands and wrapped its arms around the glass knob.

"Agile little thing," she said.

The doll hung there a moment, then let go with one arm to reach for the keyhole.

"What's it doing?" Hawthorn said.

Holly shook her head—she had no idea.

Having hooked its hand—or whatever—into the keyhole, the doll let go of the knob. Holly jerked forward to catch it before it fell, but the doll had somehow managed to get its other arm in the keyhole and was now wriggling and writhing as it tried to work its way into the tiny slot.

"It looks like it's having a fit," Hawthorn said.

"It's not really going to get in there, is it? The keyhole's too tiny."

Yet somehow it did. It was as if the doll had collapsed in on itself, like a cake taken too early out of the oven. A lone, dark foot dangled momentarily from the keyhole before it, too, disappeared.

They stood in silence. Holly counted three steady breaths before a sharp *click* resonated from the door. Yet the little woolen man didn't come out. She took one more breath, then tested the knob, smiling as it gave way and the door swung open.

Hawthorn stepped into the hallway.

Holly leaned down and peered into the keyhole. "What do you think happened to the little guy? Is he still in there?"

"I don't know, and I don't care. We need to find Hemlock and Hazel, remember?"

"Wait." Holly squinted. A dark thread poked out of the keyhole. She pinched it between her fingers and eased out a swatch of black woolen cloth, a little smaller than her palm.

"Come on," Hawthorn said as he grabbed her hand and pulled her out the door, only to run into three necromancers backed by three tall familiars taking the form of pale men dressed in well-tailored, starched suits.

"Well, that's just great," Holly muttered.

~

THE SHADOWS surrounding Hazel had eased. Somewhat. Not enough to allow her to walk freely but enough that she could take a few steps before the shadows strengthened again and bound her. Unfortunately, it wasn't enough to reach Hemlock. But she had managed to reach a table with a mirror, basin, and ewer.

Hemlock sat limp and pale-faced upon the ground at the other end of the room. He watched her movements with dark-rimmed eyes. "Hazel," he rasped.

Was that a plea or a condemnation? She opened her mouth, wanting to say something, but Ash and Verrin returned.

Her father studied her and smiled. "I see you have regained some mobility. Splendid."

"Is that so?"

"Of course. I've only wanted what's best for you."

Hazel let out a short breath that was almost a laugh. "Obviously."

"Yet it is rather interesting, don't you think, that you've used your magic to help your sister—even after I assured you she was safe—but not the man you love?"

Hazel opened her mouth to reply, sharply, but before she could, Ash raised a finger and continued.

"You see, I believe I may have also misjudged the situation. I thought the others would distract you. But I see now that their continued absence is far more distracting than having them here. You seem to fear what you can't perceive, Hazel. So I'm here to alleviate that."

He opened the door, and Holly and Hawthorn stumbled inside, followed by a trio of necromancers.

"Hazel!" Holly said and tried to go to her, just as Hawthorn tried to go to his brother. Three pale men in impeccable suits came in from behind the necromancers, and two of them grabbed Holly and Hawthorn by the arms. It took Hazel a moment before she realized they were familiars.

"Don't move," she said.

Holly froze, fear etched on her face.

"This isn't how I imaged our reunion would go," Ash said. "But few things in life ever transpire as we would expect."

"It's not a reunion," Hazel said. "At least not yet." She poured some water from the nearby ewer into the basin and spoke her mother's name. The candle she had left on another table flickered, and Willow took shape in the mirror behind her.

Holly gasped and clapped a hand over her mouth. Ash's face tightened, then his expression turned sad and almost wistful. Hazel turned to face her mother.

Willow frowned, looking confused. Her gaze moved from Hazel to Ash and Holly, to Hemlock and Hawthorn, before finally settling on the collection of necromancers. Ash, following her gaze, sent them from the room, including the familiars. Hawthorn went to Hemlock's side, but Holly—at a warning glance from Hazel—remained fixed in place.

Ash took a step forward. "They are gone, love. Calm yourself."

Willow fixed him in a withering glare. "Do not tell me to calm down. And do not call me *love*."

Ash's expression turned troubled, but he quickly composed himself.

"She's different, isn't she?" Hazel said as she studied him. "When *you're* not the one summoning her, she's less under your control."

"She's agitated. When I summon her, she's calm."

"She's someone else."

Ash chuckled, dreadful and calm. "You have no idea who she is. You hold such loyalty to her. I wonder if you still would if you knew the truth."

"Shut up, Ash," Willow hissed.

"She left you, Hazel. Both you and your sister. Back when you were still children. Do you remember?"

"Of course I remember," Hazel said. "She came back."

"Oh, yes, she came back. The noble mother returning to her children after... what? A lovely little holiday? Did you ever ask her where she went?"

"Ash...," Willow said, her voice weaker though the harshness remained.

Hazel glanced at her mother before returning to her father. "She refused to say."

"Of course she did. How could she tell you, her beautiful daughters, that she had never intended to return? That she had intended to leave her little girls alone in the cold world and let them fend for themselves?"

"You're lying," Holly said.

"But even that's not the most interesting part," Ash said. "What's interesting is that she only returned when she found out that I intended to take you in. She came back to you, not out of love but out of *spite*."

"Ash!" Willow's voice boomed in the closed space, and everyone turned silent.

"It's not true," Holly said in a little voice. "Tell him it's not true, Mother."

Willow said nothing, her body shaking as she glared at Ash.

"She can't tell you that," he said, "because that would be a lie, which the geas will not permit."

Hazel said, "I don't believe you. If that were true, then you would've come back after she died. You wouldn't have cared about her wishes or whatever reason you gave for staying away."

"Yes," Ash said, his voice frighteningly calm. "I would have." He shifted his cool gaze over to Willow, and her mother stiffened her back and raised her chin, as if steeling herself for an onslaught. "I'm afraid I wasn't entirely honest with you earlier, Hazel. I had hoped to spare you some of the uglier truths. Though perhaps it would be better if your mother explained."

Willow continued to glare at him. Then to Hazel, she said, "You don't understand the situation. You don't know what *he* is capable of!"

"I have a fair idea," Hazel said. "But I still don't know what you're talking about."

"Tell her, Willow, of the spell you cast to keep me away."

"I cast no such spell."

Ash chuckled. "True. You found others to do it for you. Including a necromancer you hired from Sarnum. It seems your distaste for the discipline doesn't prevent you from employing it when the mood strikes you. How convenient."

To Hazel, Willow said, "I've made plenty of mistakes, many of which I regret. But protecting you and Holly from *him* wasn't one of them."

Hazel shook her head and, to her father, said, "I don't understand. You're a necromancer. How could a necromantic spell keep you away?"

"Because it wasn't just necromancy—it was all of them. Every discipline, each with its own corresponding spell, cast by a capable witch or warlock dedicated to that discipline. To be fair, the spell was genius. And though your mother didn't cast the spells herself, she still needed to orchestrate it, and that, perhaps, was the most impressive part of all."

"How?"

"How did it go, Willow? I'm not sure I recall all the details." When Willow said nothing, Ash continued. "Let's see... the Wyr spell made the wind turn foul should I approach the Grove, accompanied by illusions to lead me astray; Weaving magic rent my clothes and turned out my pockets and set whatever was in them to harass me." He chuckled. "That was a good one. Wild magic turned the trees to claw at me with their leafy branches while animals hunted me from among the shadows. Hearth magic turned the sun blinding, and fire would combust at inopportune moments that threatened to burn me alive." He grimaced. "Most unpleasant."

"And the necromancy?"

Ash fixed her in an intent gaze. "Necromancy is what held it all to-gether. It's what turned four disparate spells into a single cohesive one; it's what enabled her to bind the spell to me exclusively and, ultimately, what prevented me from undoing it."

"Why?"

"Without it I could have found others to undo the spells your mother had commissioned, but with it, even if I had managed to find someone willing, it wouldn't have mattered. The spell was bound to me, and so only I could undo it, but I lacked the knowledge."

"So you trapped her soul in a geas for... what? To get even with her? To lure me out?"

Ash shook his head. "I was truthful when I said I didn't do it for you. She got sick and... well..." His expression turned solemn as he fixed his gaze on Willow. Then, almost too quietly for Hazel to hear, he said, "It's a kind of life, isn't it? What I gave her? Isn't it better than nothing? Than the cold void of death?" He fell silent. Willow met his gaze though her expression remained unmoved.

He cleared his throat and returned his attention to Hazel. "But what your mother never accounted for was how much you would strive to seek me out."

"I only sought you out so you could undo what you did to her, which, you say, you didn't do for me. How do you account for that, if not by in-tention?"

He smiled. "I've found that the world often steers us on a path we are meant to walk. In this case, I played an unintended part—at first at least—on leading you down the path you now find yourself. But have you ever considered that, for you, there was never any alternative? That even if I hadn't trapped your mother's soul, you would still have found your way to necromancy some other way?"

"No, I hadn't considered that. Not once."

Holly, still on the other end of the room, rubbed her arms and looked uncomfortable as she averted her gaze. Ash walked over to her, studying her as he did.

"What do you think about all this, Holly?"

She pressed her lips together and shook her head.

Ash touched her chin and gently lifted her face. "You know other-wise, don't you, daughter?"

Holly looked at him, at Hazel, and back to Ash. She shook her head again, but the sadness in her eyes spoke of the truth in Ash's words.

Hazel's mouth fell open. She felt like she had just been slapped. "Holly?"

Holly squeezed her eyes shut. Then, clenching her hands, she looked right at Hazel. She stood tall with her shoulders squared—her stance spoke of defiance, yet her expression was more conspiratorial. It was like they shared a secret, and somehow that served to bolster Hazel rather than frighten her.

"Enough of this," Hazel said. "Undo what you've done. Release Mother from her geas. Now."

Ash gave her a severe look. "I love you, my daughter, but you are in no position to dictate my actions to me."

Hazel glanced at Hemlock. He remained on the ground, unresponsive as Hawthorn tried to revive him. She tightened her jaw, then grabbed hold of the mirror and smashed it on the tabletop. Willow's form faded into smoky translucence, but she still remained. Hazel took a shard from the mirror. Ash watched her as she picked it up, his eyes shining and expectant as she put the jagged glass to her palm.

Madness. This was madness. But she needed to give all of herself to this. She didn't know any other way. It was all or nothing.

She looked over at Holly. Her sister pursed her lips, her brow furrowed with worry. But she gave a slight nod, so Hazel sliced the glass into her palm.

She made a fist over the basin and let her blood drip into the crystalline water that bloomed like a drowned rose. Ash did nothing to stop her. Instead, he smiled a self-satisfied smirk, as if to say he never doubted this moment, as if to say *I told you so.*

Hazel clenched her hand, and the gentle drip-dropping of her blood turned into an irregular patter as it seeped between her fingers and stained her fist. Ash's smug complacency infuriated her. She would not be his pawn and play into whatever plan he had for her—she would find her own way.

Hazel grabbed the bowl and flung the bloody water out across the room. It splattered against books and shelves, tables and chairs, against unbound papers, bowls and ewers and flickering blue flames that hissed against the liquid but did not extinguish. Then she cast the same spell that had brought the swatch of fabric to life. Only this time she put all of herself into it; this time she gave it everything.

Wooden tables transformed into svelte horses and deer with long, arched necks and grain-marbled bodies. Books turned into ravens, peacocks, and swans, all with yellowing parchment feathers that rustled like blood-encrusted silk. Silver bowls turned into giant beetles with muted, tarnished carapaces and beveled legs that clicked and clacked against the cold stone floor. Mirrors grew into vast windows that looked onto a foreign night with stars that flitted like fireflies in a bruised plum sky among three golden moons. Bookshelves became broad-shouldered guardsmen in oaken armor bearing sheathed broadswords. Their faces were toothless and grim, yet they showed a careful tenderness among the aged vellum birds that flocked around them. Snakes of blue flames slithered from the sconces on the walls and gathered around Hazel's feet, pulsing with wavering light as they waited.

Ash smiled. "Finally. Now you see."

Hazel tightened her jaw. Attack, she thought, and without needing to utter the words, her creations turned upon her father. The oaken men unsheathed their swords, the snakes slithered forward, the deer and horses, beetles and birds all flapped and pranced and scurried towards him. The windows showed black expanses devoid of stars and moons.

Ash lifted his hands, and all of Hazel's creations froze in place.

"Your blood is my blood, daughter. Your magic is my magic." He waved his hands, and her creations returned to their original forms. Then he made the shadows pull themselves from the walls with long, sinuous arms that resembled rivulets of spilled ink.

If her magic was his magic, then his was hers. She worked a Dissolving spell, but nothing happened. She altered the spell, weaving warped and shadowed words into it, but still nothing.

Heart pounding, she took a labored step back. A shadow reached towards her, and its inky fingers brushed against her skin, cold and stinging. She didn't know how to undo her father's spells as easily as he had undone hers. And she couldn't think, not with shadows twining around her, smelling cold and crystalline like a frozen lake in a desolate winter's night.

A light erupted in the room, and the shadows momentarily paled. In the corner, Hawthorn stood and supported Hemlock as he leaned upon him. Hemlock's face remained pale and haggard, but he fixed Hazel in an intent gaze, his mouth moving as he spoke his spells.

Holly, staring wide-eyed as she clutched her robe with white-knuckled fists, jolted herself into action and worked a spell of her own. The cold blue flames in the sconces extinguished, replaced by warm, living flames of candlelight. This light, along with the light Hemlock created, washed out the shadows until they were nothing more than pale silhouettes.

Ash's mouth tightened. He walked over to the door and opened it, and the necromancers from earlier filed in, followed by their familiars.

"We've toyed around long enough," he said to Hazel. "We are not here to test our proficiencies in magic. You have made your choice. It's time to follow through on that."

"Follow through?"

Ash inclined his head. "To take up the robes of necromancy, as you were always meant to do. Before, you held yourself back. But now you have shown me you are ready. Do not refuse me this, Hazel. Not with your sister here and others you care about. Let us conduct ourselves civilly, for the good of all."

Hazel's stomach tightened until she felt sick. She had never wanted to involve the others in this; she had never wanted to put them in danger. And yet they were. Again. All because of poor decisions she had made. Again. For a moment Hazel was tempted to grant her father's request. To do whatever it took to send the others away and assure that they would be returned to the Grove, unharmed. But then Holly's intent stare caught her eye. Her sister didn't speak, but the deep furrow in her brow and the dark gleam in her eyes conveyed her meaning as well as words ever could. *Don't you dare.*

Hemlock and Hawthorn wore similar expressions, willing her to a course of action that went unuttered.

Don't you dare.

Swallowing the lump rising in her throat, she drew herself up and faced her father. "You don't get to decide what I'm meant to do. Just like you don't get to decide what to do with Mother's soul. She's not yours to keep. You need to let her go."

Ash's expression softened, and his gaze drifted over to Willow, where she stood in a corner of the room, her form translucent like a reflection on glass. "I've never gotten her to stay before, without the mirror." His voice was soft and distant, as if he spoke to himself. Then he sobered, and he returned his focus to Hazel. "Perhaps we are too alike, you and I. Just as you refuse my advice on your choice of actions, I must also follow my own heart. We must each choose our own path. I had only hoped that ours would converge even if only briefly."

Hazel winced inwardly. She wished his words hadn't caused a constricting pain in her heart; she wished that, deep down, she hadn't hoped for the same. But despite the similarities they shared, they were too different; the worlds they occupied too incompatible. "And they have, but that brief moment is over now. It needs to be over."

Ash nodded, his eyes sad. "And perhaps, under normal circumstances, it would have been. But now..." He shook his head. "It's quite impossible."

"What are you talking about?"

"You've come to the Sea of Severed Stars, Hazel. All of you. This is a hallowed place, where only dedicated necromancers are allowed to come. That you would formally dedicate yourself to necromancy, I held no doubt. It was a simple matter of time. But your refusal complicates that, as does the presence of your sister and your friends."

"You intended to trap me here?" Hazel wished that surprised her, but it didn't, and that broke her heart.

"I intended to set you free here."

"And Holly? Were you going to set her free as well?"

"She— *They*"—he flung a hand at Hemlock and Hawthorn—"weren't supposed to come here, but what choice did I have? What was I supposed to do? Ignore them? Let them inflict their damage and ruin my reputation? The others in Sarnum weren't at all pleased with their trespassing on the Shrine. If I hadn't stepped in and had them brought here, then who knows what would have happened to them."

"Yes, I'm sure they'd love to thank you for exchanging one prison for another."

"Damn it, Hazel! You don't get to judge me! Not after everything you've done to get here. Not after you've spilled your blood to make sure you get your own way. But it doesn't matter anymore. I know that had you been in my place, you would have done the exact same thing. That you refuse to acknowledge this doesn't change the truth of it. But I'm tired of arguing, and I learned long ago how to live with the consequences of my choices. It's about time you did the same." He extinguished the candle-light Holly had summoned, and the room plunged into darkness.

Before the Fall

In the darkness, the shadows constricting Hazel tightened their grip. The sound of soft, careful footfalls came to her ears. She held her breath, and her gut twisted in fear as the steps grew louder, closer.

She tried to move away, but her binds still anchored her. Heart pounding, she hunched over and managed to summon a feeble ball of blue flame in her cupped hands. It flickered into illumination just as a pale hand from one of the familiars grabbed her arm.

Startled, Hazel jerked back, but the familiar held on. His cold fingers dug into her skin, and it was like the blood cooled in her veins. Fatigue settled over her. Her mind clouded, and her eyelids grew heavy. For a moment she would have given anything to lie down and sleep. But she couldn't sleep. Not yet.

The fatigue deadened her fear, and for the first time in a long while, Hazel could think clearly. She grabbed hold of the familiar with both hands and worked a dispelling incantation, though she modified it with a spell she never thought it was within her to cast. It was like she *took* whatever essence the familiar had that gave him a semblance of life, and she used it to power another spell—one to undo her shadowy binds.

The pressure around her slackened, and she could finally move. She crouched low to the ground and crept through the darkness. Her light had extinguished in her encounter with the familiar, and she thought it best to go without. There were still two other familiars somewhere in the room—three if Verrin had summoned his pale woman again. If she kept still and focused, she could almost sense them—a faint chill in the air like winter seeping through a window crack. But she couldn't remain still, she needed to find Holly and Hemlock. Hawthorn too.

A scuffling sound came from nearby, then Holly's high-pitched voice as she cried out. Hazel started towards her, but a chill intensified near her hand and brushed against her skin. She reached out, trying to grab the familiar, but her hand only met cold, empty air.

"Come with me," Willow said as she took Hazel's arm.

Hazel resisted the urge to pull away and let her mother lead her through the darkness. "Where's Holly?" she whispered.

Willow tightened her grip, and the cold became so sharp that it felt like it would cut Hazel's skin. She stumbled over strewn books and papers as they moved across the room. When Willow let go, the mark left upon Hazel's arm felt hot by comparison.

"Holly?" Hazel whispered, but there was no reply.

"Do you think I can't see you, Hazel?" came Ash's voice from the darkness. "Do you think I can't see you scurrying around in the shadows like a rat in a cellar? Such feeble subterfuge does not become you."

He created an orb of light that revealed Holly standing about an arm's length away. She was shrouded in a filmy haze the color of cataracts. A great serpentine beast twined around her, with gnarled claws studded with onyx talons and wide, webbed wings that spanned between memory and sorrow. It... fed on Holly. Its claws and tail dug into her, and with a pulsating rhythm like a disembodied heart, its wings grew wider and darker, and the shroud around Holly turned more grey and opaque.

Before Hazel could move to help her, Ash created another light on the other end of the room. This one illuminated Hemlock and Hawthorn being circled by a pair of the serpentine creatures. They paced around a crystalline wall that the brothers had summoned around them. One creature swiped at it with a taloned claw, causing the wall to shiver. But it remained intact. For now.

"I admire your young man's tenacity," Ash said. "But it will do him little good in this case. Their wall will come down, and you, dear daughter, will need to make a decision."

Another swipe at the wall by one of the serpents, and this time it collapsed. Before Hemlock and Hawthorn could replace it—before they could move—the creatures were upon them and engulfed them in the same grey shroud as Holly.

"You would harm your youngest daughter, just to force me to choose between them?" Hazel said. "What kind of monster are you?"

Ash said nothing. He turned his back to her, whether out of disinterest or discomfort, Hazel couldn't tell. Not that it mattered. She wouldn't play his game.

She ran towards her father. One of the necromancers sent his familiar after her, but she returned one of the bookshelves into a sword-wielding warrior that blocked the familiar's path.

She grabbed Ash's arm and spoke a corrupted Weaving spell that broke his skin and drew blood. From his blood she conjured a trio of bats and sent them towards Holly, Hemlock, and Hawthorn. The serpents snapped at the bats and caught them in their blackened maws. As they swallowed their prey, their scaled, sinuous bodies melted like sealing wax. The grey shrouds fell away from Holly and the others and they stood there, blinking and befuddled, but unharmed.

Ash's mouth tightened. The other necromancers overcame Hazel's warrior and started towards her. But Ash held up a hand and they halted. He studied her a long moment, then smiled. "Exactly so, Hazel. Shall we continue?" He nodded to the necromancers, and they spoke in monotonous voices as they wove a spell in unison. All the mirrors in the room darkened to show a star-studded night sky. Verrin stepped forward, and the night within the mirrors leached into the room and twined around him while the stars wept luminous, mercurial tears.

He reached into a mirror and gathered the weeping starlight into his cupped hands, cradling the liquid with a careful tenderness that a mother might show her newborn child. He carried the light out of the mirrored otherworld and into the present, mundane one.

He brought his cupped hands to his face, and his features lit up as if with galvanized flame. For a moment he looked as if he meant to drink the light. Instead, he walked to the two familiars remaining to the necro-

Before the Fall

407

mancers. The third necromancer summoned a new one while casting a dark glance at Hazel. Verrin's own pale woman was gone.

He held out his hands, and each familiar drank the light. And as they drank, it was as if the light combusted within them. Their skin blackened and emitted ribbons of smoke that coiled and gathered near the ceiling like incense haze. The smoke tendrils hooked onto the familiars' skin and pulled at their charred flesh. They became like great marionettes, shuffling only because their unseen master didn't know how to make them dance.

Walking to each of their familiars, the necromancers pulled out short, curved knives from the wide sleeves of their robes and unceremoniously cut the familiars' throats. The shadows severed from the creatures as they crumpled to the ground, and the billowing darkness up in the rafters solidified. Scaled legs sprouted like eels from black mud. Sharp blue eyes winked open near the ankles, just behind long taloned claws that curved like onyx scythes. Black, gossamer wings webbed out from the amorphous body like wind-tattered sails rent from a storm. Then the body itself took shape—muscular underneath black scales studded with blinking blue crystals. The head of a dragon turned on a long serpentine neck and fixed Hazel in a star-studded black eye.

She stumbled back a few steps, unable to stop herself. Holly screamed, and horror gripped Hazel's own heart when the black dragon moved its serpentine head and fixed Holly in its blackened gaze.

"Hey!" Hazel shouted, but the dragon ignored her. Its talons scraped along the stone floor as it took one lumbering step, then another.

Holly ran behind a table, though judging by her stricken expression, she knew it was poor protection.

Hazel worked a spell of Dissolving, but nothing happened. She tried a corrupted version of it, twisting a conglomeration of a Weaving spell of Diminishing along with a Wyr spell of Prismatic Light into something else entirely, but it didn't have any effect.

Panicking, she hurried over to Ash. He watched the entire affair with bemused detachment.

"What's wrong with you?" she hissed at him. "You're just going to stand there and let that thing attack Holly?"

Ash fixed her in a level gaze. "'For beyond the veil of myth and memory, a deeper truth has always lain: we are all of us alone and yet not; the darkness consumes us even as it subsists us. And without this cold, dark, solitary oneness, we would all of us consume ourselves, cannibalizing our souls in a fruitless search for a glimpse of nonexistent light.'"

"What?"

But her father returned his attention to the black dragon with countless crystalline eyes as it advanced on Holly.

Enough. Hazel yanked Ash's collar, exposing a gleaming silver chain so delicate that it couldn't have possibly been made by human hands. She grabbed hold of it and pulled hard, expecting it to snap free, but instead her father stumbled forward and grabbed her wrist in a near-crushing grip. His eyes turned cold, and the dragon lost interest in Holly as it returned its gaze to her.

Ash pulled Hazel to a chair near a table laden with books and stray papers. He ran an arm over the table and sent everything crashing to the floor and pushed Hazel onto the seat.

"That got your attention," she said. "It's the geas, isn't it? It's how you've bound Mother to you."

"Enough of this, Hazel."

"Funny, I was thinking the same thing about you."

The dragon huffed out a stale breath that smelled of spoiled eggs and an unkempt cellar. It extended a tattered wing around her, like a mother swan protecting her cygnet. The air turned both stifling and cold, and sweat broke across Hazel's body even as she shivered.

A blinding white light seared across her vision, and the dragon reared up as the blue eyes studding its scales turned empty and white. In the corner of the room, Hemlock leaned against Hawthorn, his gaze fixed on Hazel while Hawthorn kept an eye on the dragon. Almost as soon as Hemlock began to work a spell, Hawthorn spoke one of his own. Pure white light flashed again through the dimly lit room, only this time it didn't sear Hazel's vision as before. This time it was like she stood within a shadow, and as the light flashed, the room around her changed.

The dragon diminished—reduced to nothing more than a shadow upon a whitewashed wall, cast by the three necromancers making shapes with their hands. Ash aged by twenty years, his back hunched beneath a weight that threatened to grind him into the earth. Willow stood beside him, offering him her arm, but she also stood next to Holly, a hand on her shoulder, though Holly didn't seem to notice she was there.

And from across the room, Hemlock stood proud and tall, no longer needing the assistance from his brother. He wore a jacket of finely tailored blackberry leaves, adorned with a cravat of woven nightshade and white carnations. He pricked his finger on a thorn of his coat, and as he studied the bead of impossibly red blood on his fingertip, a thin, silvery crown adorned his head, pale and translucent like moonlit wind.

One breath later, the light faded and everything returned as it was. Nobody else seemed to have noticed the brief change in the room. Except Hemlock. He still hung on his brother's arm, but his expression now held a degree of earnestness as he leaned forward as far as his strength, and his brother, would allow.

The dragon extended its wings again, but before they could wrap around Hazel, she spoke a corrupted Wyr spell and a sharp wind gusted through the room, blasting back the dragon's wings and allowing her to escape.

She ran over to Hemlock and Hawthorn.

"It's about time!" Hawthorn said. "What about Holly?"

"I don't know!" Everything had been happening so quickly she hadn't had any time to think.

Hawthorn made a disgusted sound and transferred Hemlock's arm over to her care. "Stay here while I go get her."

Hazel didn't like his insinuation that she had abandoned her sister, but she bit back the sharp remark that had settled on her tongue. If he could get to Holly, then that's all that mattered. She focused on Hemlock. He gripped her arm just as he had gripped his brother's and continued to look at her in that unsettling, insistent stare.

Hawthorn made to cross the room. The dragon turned and settled itself in his path. He cast a spell that started to make the light in the room grow blindingly bright, but then the necromancers all chanted in unison, and the dragon snapped its jaws and the room darkened again.

"He's going to get himself killed," Hazel muttered. She needed to help him, but she couldn't leave Hemlock.

"Hazel..." He held out a clenched hand. When he opened it, a shard of broken mirror lay on his palm. It had cut into his skin, and blood seeped from the wound and pattered to the stones below.

She gasped and gathered a handful of her skirts and tried to staunch the bleeding, but Hemlock jerked his hand away. He dropped the shard, and before she could stop him, he grabbed her hand in forceful, bloody grip.

"What are you doing?" This was unlike him. He must have lost his mind.

Hemlock brought his face close to hers. He closed his eyes and took a deep breath, as if savoring the moment, as if savoring *her*.

Then his expression turned sober and tired. He gave a feeble nod towards Ash. "Your blood is his blood," he rasped barely above a whisper. "It's the only way, and you know it." He let go of her hand and slumped onto the ground.

Hazel stared at her bloodied hand. *It wasn't supposed to happen like this.* The old thought floated into her mind, as stubborn and persistent as flowing water. But then a new thought occurred to her: maybe it *was* supposed to happen like this. Maybe everything was happening exactly as it should. Maybe she had always known what she was supposed to do.

She clenched her hand into a blood-soaked fist. She turned towards her father and, with a spell, unwound shadows from the dragon to take them as her own.

And she let the darkness consume her.

A Return to Light

Holly gripped the skirt of her robe so tightly that her hands had turned numb. Her whole body tensed; she wanted to run. But she couldn't—not with that dragon with its creepy, blinking scales and fetid breath blocking the way forward. Nor could she go back. Her mother stood right behind her, exuding a chill that made Holly's skin prick and the hair on her neck stand on end. It was too much, being wedged between a necromantic dragon and a dead mother. It was wrong, all of it.

From across the room, Hawthorn headed towards her. He had made it halfway across before the dragon put down a monstrous leg and blocked him from view. She needed to do something, but whenever she tried thinking of a spell, countless cold, otherworldly eyes across the dragon's flank would blink at her, and Holly's mind froze along with the rest of her body.

A chill gripped her shoulder, and her mother said, "Look." She extended an arm past Holly's cheek, pointing underneath the dragon's belly to Hazel on the other end of the room.

Her sister had grown taller. Hemlock, sitting on the floor, looked almost childlike next to her. Wisps of shadows arced from the dragon and twined around Hazel and flattened against her. They turned her dress an impossible black, and her skin had paled and faded, like she was becoming nothing. Like she no longer belonged to this world.

Hot panic seared through Holly's gut. She searched the room and found her father standing in an opposite corner from Hazel. She started towards him, but the dragon reared its head at her and expelled a plume of hot breath that smelled of spoiled eggs and ichor.

It opened its maw wide, exposing rows of jagged crystalline teeth as sharp as glass. Before Holly had a chance to move back, her mother stepped in front of her and pulled the dragon's attention.

"Go," she said without turning to look at Holly.

Heart pounding, she ran across the room and to her father. Verrin stood behind him, looking so smug that Holly wondered how she could have ever thought him handsome.

"What's happening to her?" she said.

Ash's gaze remained fixed on Hazel. "She is becoming her true self."

"What's that supposed to mean?"

Her father said nothing. He shifted his gaze over to Willow, who stood before the dragon with an upraised hand that, somehow, seemed to have enthralled the creature. Ash gave Verrin a pointed look, and Verrin barked orders in a harsh, guttural voice that made his words incoherent. At least for Holly.

But the necromancers wove their spells, and the dragon came out of its stupor and snapped its jaws at Willow before turning back towards Hazel.

Ash went up to Willow and took her by the arm. The determination she had held while facing the dragon faded, and she turned to look upon Ash as if nothing in the world existed except for him.

The necromancers continued chanting, and the dragon extended its wings, bringing night into the chamber. The bright blue scales blinking over its body became like stars.

The room faded away, and Holly found herself in a wide field dotted with purple cosmos flowers, underneath a pale golden sky with clouds like mother of pearl. A grey stone wall running alongside the field cast long, impossible shadows that stretched towards the setting sun and towards Holly's feet. She stepped back like she might step away from an encroaching mud puddle, but the shadows continued to creep and creep until they nipped at her toes.

A cry from Hazel rang into the air. The field faded, and Holly was back in the chamber. Yet the walls pulsed around her, as if they remembered the meadow and preferred to give way to it.

Hawthorn tried to run past the dragon, but it swiped a claw at him. He twisted out of the way, lost his balance, and fell.

As Holly ran over to him, twisting shadows passed overhead as they bled from the dragon to Hazel and the necromancers. Hazel never looked at Holly; she had taken on a distant look, as if watching something Holly couldn't see.

Then the shadows connecting the dragon to the necromancers severed, and they all cried out in surprise or maybe pain.

"I saw a room," Hawthorn murmured as Holly knelt next to him. "Paneled in stained walnut and... my father was there. Did that really happen?"

Holly tried to help him off the floor, but he just sat there like a sack of grain. She tapped his cheek. "Snap out of it, Hawthorn. I need your help."

One necromancer buckled to the ground and then another. The dragon, smaller than it had been but still imposing, lumbered towards the necromancers. Hazel watched its advance with apparent disinterest while Ash watched on with an expression that looked far too eager.

Holly pulled at Hawthorn one more time. "Get up," she said, then hurried over to Hazel now that the dragon had moved away. She grabbed her sister's arm but yanked her hand back when a shock of searing cold lanced through her bones.

"Stop this!" Holly shouted, as if Hazel stood across a great chasm and not right in front of her. She waved her arms, but Hazel's eyes had turned black and her gaze never moved from the dragon. She didn't even look at Hemlock, who still sat near her feet, looking much more ashen than a man ever should.

Hawthorn staggered upright, looking perplexed that Holly was no longer at his side. "I was coming to help you. Didn't you notice?"

"That's nice," Holly said as she looked around. She needed to bring Hazel back from... wherever she was. Holly didn't want to think about it too much. Hawthorn shuffled over to check on Hemlock just as Holly's gaze fell on a mirror on one of the tables. "Make sure she doesn't kill anyone."

"Right…"

Holly hurried over to the mirror, grabbed it, and returned to find Hawthorn waving a kerchief in front of Hazel's face. "What are you doing?"

"I don't know. Something reasonably inoffensive so she won't kill *me*. Have you seen her? She looks ill amused." He waved his kerchief some more, but Hazel never looked at him. "I don't think she even hears us. Or sees us." He stuffed the kerchief back in his pocket.

"Well, let's hope she can see something." Holly held up the mirror in front of Hazel. But her sister never blinked, just stared straight forward as if she could see through it.

Growing frustrated, Holly shouted, "Look at yourself!"

Hazel gave no reaction. The dragon reached one of the prone necromancers and stepped on his back with a scaled foot. The necromancer cried out. The other two worked a spell, but nothing happened.

"She's become the dragon," Hemlock rasped from where he sat on the floor. "Hazel, for the moment, is gone."

"The dragon?" Holly said. "How is that even possible?"

"I don't know. But judging by her behavior—and the dragon's—my guess is she's performed a variation of a keyhole illusion, only without the illusion."

"Impossible," Hawthorn muttered.

"Can you undo it?" Holly said to Hemlock. "You undid Hawthorn's keyhole spell. Can't you undo hers?"

Hemlock shook his head. "I've already tried; she won't let me in."

"That's because you can barely stand," Hawthorn said. He cast his own spell, then his face darkened.

"Well?" Holly said.

"Your sister's quite the stubborn girl."

The necromancer under the dragon's paw fell silent, and the dragon moved towards the remaining two. They tried to cast another spell, but when it failed, one ran out the door while the dragon trapped the other against a bookshelf.

Hemlock struggled to get to his feet, so Hawthorn helped him up. "Hold the mirror up again," Hemlock said.

Holly raised the mirror back in front of Hazel, but she still ignored it.

Hemlock lifted a hand, and a light shone from within the mirror.

"How did you—" Hawthorn began, but Holly shushed him.

This time Hazel's gaze moved towards the mirror. Her brow furrowed, and she reached towards the glass as if to try to pull out the light.

"Hazel," Holly said as she took her sister's hand. Her skin was painfully cold, but Holly endured it.

"Don't forget yourself," Holly whispered. "Don't forget why you're here. Don't forget... me."

Hazel's fingers tightened around Holly's, and she met her sister's gaze.

Holly bit the inside of her cheek to keep herself from gasping, for the eyes peering out from her sister's pale face were foreign. They were an eerie color—a mixture between charcoal and silver. And yet there was a gleam of familiarity deep within them, an indescribable aspect that could only belong to Hazel.

Her sister shifted her gaze back to the dragon and rasped whispered words that remained foreign to Holly's ears. The dragon started to unravel, but then Verrin stepped forward, lifted his arms, and worked a spell that kept the dragon bound.

It reared its head back towards Hazel and hissed a cloud of fetid breath.

Hawthorn coughed and lifted a kerchief to his nose, but Hazel cried out as if it had hurt her. She spoke a spell—deep and guttural—and the mirror Holly had brought over transformed into an eagle of spun glass.

The eagle veered over the dragon's head and pierced its scaly skin with its talons. The dragon snapped at the bird, but the eagle darted away. It soared across the room towards Ash and Willow. Willow took a step back, but Ash remained still. He cast a spell, but it must not have had the effect he wanted because his expression turned troubled, and then the eagle was upon him.

An Unadorned End

Hazel moved as if within a dark and disturbing dream. It was like she had become trapped in a net of ironbound mist. And she wasn't alone. There were others here with her, whispering against her skin, drawing long, shadowed fingers across her mind.

They desired things of her, wordless pleas that pulled on her thoughts and crawled over her skin. The men in black robes needed to die—they told her this. And they gave her a soulless dragon as her vessel.

Yet at the height of her fury, a light shone in the distance. It permeated the cloying whispers like sunlight spilling over a strawberry-strewn hill. She reached towards it, but then the warmth gathered around her hand as if she held the sun itself and it had refused to burn her.

Confused, Hazel stared at her hand. A faint light glimmered there. She focused her thoughts, pushed away the whispering voices, and before her stood a girl with golden hair and rosy cheeks.

The girl didn't belong here with the scratching whispers and worm-like fingers. She needed to leave, go someplace where her golden hair could shine in the golden sun. Hazel wanted to tell her, but the girl pressed her hand and told her to remember.

Remember what? Mountains grinding into sand that had been washed out to a long-forgotten sea? No, the sun. It must be the sun, shining and brilliant, warming her skin much like the girl's hand warmed hers.

Hazel squeezed her sister's fingers, for it was her sister. She remembered now. The wormlike fingers lacing through her mind eased, and the voices lessened. But shadows still connected her to the abominable dragon. She tried to send it back to its own realm, but before she could unravel it completely, Verrin severed the dragon's connection to her and took it as his own.

She cried out, mostly from the shock of no longer having its dark presence intertwined with hers. Then she pulled words from deep within her gut and turned a nearby mirror into a glass-wrought eagle. It dove at the dragon and pierced its scaly hide with crystalline talons. The dragon snapped at it, but the eagle soared out of the way and wheeled towards Ash.

He had been watching the unfolding events with an expression of smug amusement. Now as the eagle soared towards him on beveled wings, his smugness turned to annoyance. He took a few steps back as he cast a spell, but when the eagle still flew towards him, his annoyance gave way to shock as he put up his arms to ward off the eagle's outstretched talons.

The bird rent his arm, and he cried out. He worked another spell, and the eagle's glass feathers cracked, causing beads of broken glass to fall to the ground like crystallized blood.

Hazel put out her arm. The eagle gave a pathetic cry, but before it could return to her, the dragon crushed the bird in its jaws. The glass ground against its teeth, faintly tinkling like broken chimes.

The dragon headed towards Hazel and the others. She tried pulling control of the creature from Verrin, but his hold upon it was too strong.

"Are you going to let him keep control over you, Hazel?" Ash said.

She tried to sever his connection again, but failed.

Hemlock managed to summon a legion of fairies with ivory wings and set them upon the dragon. Holly patted her pockets, then frowned. "Stupid necromancer robes. I haven't any pinecones."

Hawthorn put out his hand and conjured a pinecone that took up his entire palm.

Holly's eyes widened, and she grinned. "Lob it at the dragon."

He did, and as the pinecone sailed through the air, Holly made it combust into flame. It struck the dragon in the neck and splintered into fiery shards.

Holly squeaked and giggled. "Again."

Hawthorn conjured another cone. But before he cast it, Hazel said, "Throw it at Verrin."

He did and Holly ignited it. The cone arced towards Verrin's head, and just before it struck him, he worked a spell that sent it veering off course. Yet in that moment, his concentration over the dragon had slackened. Hazel pulled the shadows from him. He resisted her and started to pull them back. Hemlock sent his fairies after him, and they flurried around his head, pulling at his hair and ears and poking his eyes.

Verrin's concentration shattered, and Hazel took control of the dragon. The beast reared around and swiped him with its tail. Verrin dodged out of the way, but the fairies poking at his eyes had blinded him, and he tripped over his feet. As he went down, the dragon breathed a cloud of its rancid breath into his face. Verrin coughed as his cheeks purpled. He tried to get up, but his arms turned wobbly, and he flopped back onto the floor like a land-bound fish. The dragon exhaled another breath, and Verrin, after a bout of fitful coughing, became still.

Hazel pushed the dragon's shadows away from her, back into the creature itself. She unwound the spell until the great serpentine beast dissipated into the shadows of the room and disappeared.

The sudden silence made Hazel's hammering heart deafening.

Until Ash said, "You understand now, don't you?"

His comment should have infuriated her. But the anger never came. At that moment, he was no longer her father—no longer the man that had broken her heart all those years ago when he walked out of her life. He was just a man, confused and afraid of his own frailty and ignorance, who tried his best to hide it. Just like her.

She crouched down and picked up a shard of broken glass and cut her hand anew.

"What are you doing?" Ash said. "Using your own blood against me won't work."

"My blood is your blood, Father. But I think you've forgotten that it's also hers."

Ash glanced at Willow who stood beside him, diaphanous and fading. "I think it's time she told you what she *really* thinks."

∽

HOLLY WATCHED as her sister cut her hand and angled the bloodied shard at their mother. The spell she spoke was frightening with its harsh vowels and angular words. But there was also a softness there, a delicate beauty that Hazel wove between the words that Holly hadn't ever noticed before.

Willow's form became solid, and her vacuous expression hardened into anger.

Ash reached out as if to touch her, then started to move away. But Willow grabbed hold of the silver chain around his neck and, grimacing, yanked it off. The chain bore a crystal amulet that shifted from black to blue to purple, depending on how the light hit it.

Ash held out his hand, palm up, as if expecting Willow to hand the amulet back. Instead, she clutched the crystal, as if trying to crush it in her pale hand, but the amulet didn't give way.

He gently took her hand and held it, and Willow's resolve seemed to waver as her expression slackened.

"Mother," Hazel said. "It's your choice to make. Don't let him make it for you."

Willow closed her eyes and stepped closer to Ash. She looked resigned, and Ash reached out to touch her hair. Her form faded into misty impermanence. The amulet fell to the ground, and before he could react, she thrust her fading hand into his chest.

The muscles in his neck tightened, his eyes bulged. His cheeks reddened, then paled, while his lips turned blue.

"Mother!" Hazel shouted.

Willow flinched and yanked her hand back, and Ash fell to the floor.

Holly gasped and ran over to him and put her hand on his forehead. "He's cold. Why is he so cold? He's not dead, is he?"

Nobody said anything. Willow stared at the amulet on the ground, keeping a distance between it and herself as if it were a poisonous viper.

Holly put her head against her father's chest. "He's breathing. Sort of. I don't think he's dead." She twisted her face up. "But you just can't tell anymore these days."

Hazel walked over and picked up the amulet from the floor. The silver chain dangled between her fingers, swaying back and forth like an errant pendulum. Willow licked her lips, opened her mouth as if to say something, but then closed it and remained silent.

Holly got to her feet. "What happens now?" She eyed the amulet in Hazel's hand.

"We came here to undo Father's spell," Hazel said. "Remember?"

Holly swallowed. "I remember."

But Hazel fell silent as she stared at the necklace. She thrust it at Holly. "You take it. You decide what to do with it."

Holly took a step back. "What? I don't want that thing."

"It holds Mother's soul. You should have it."

"I don't want it! Nobody should have it."

"Then destroy it."

"But won't that...?" Her eyes filled with tears. "She'll die if I do that."

"She's already dead, Holly."

"Then you do it. I can't."

Hazel swallowed as she fixed her gaze on the amulet. She closed her eyes and quietly said, "Neither can I." She thrust the amulet at Holly again. "Please, just take it. I can't have it. Do you understand me? I *can't* have it."

Holly didn't understand, but she understood the tremor in Hazel's voice. There was a warning there, danger. So with trembling fingers, Holly took the amulet from her sister's hand.

It was lighter than it looked. And cold, too, as if it had been buried in snow. Yet it warmed against her skin the longer she held it. Aside from the strange crystal, it almost seemed ordinary. Had she seen it at a market, she might have thought it lovely.

Willow walked up to her. Her form was more solid now, at least in the middle parts of her. On the outer edges of her hair, hands, legs, and feet, her form was still hazy and translucent. She took Holly's hand— the one that held the amulet—in a grip so cold that Holly gasped. But her mother's touch was gentle, and she tenderly wrapped Holly's fingers around the crystal of bruised twilight.

"Destroy it, Holly," her mother whispered.

Holly shook her head. "No, you'll die."

"It is too late for that."

Holly clenched her eyes shut against welling tears. "But isn't it better than nothing? Isn't it a kind of life, what you have? Isn't it enough?"

"It *is* nothing. It is not life. It is not death. It is being in between, for years on end, for no other reason than to satisfy the whims and desires of someone else. Let me go, daughter. Do not anchor me in a world in which I do not belong."

Holly shook her head again, and tears streamed down her face. "Aren't you afraid?"

Willow smiled and touched her hair. "The dead fear nothing, don't you know? Fear belongs to the living."

"But I'll miss you."

"We must all one day pass into the realm of memory. Who's to say that it isn't real, in its own way? Who's to say I won't live on there, more vibrant and vital than I ever was in this life? Who's to say that it is worse than what we cling to here? Who is to say we won't meet again? Somewhere, someday our paths will cross, and we will love each other all over again."

"I'd like that," Holly whispered. She looked down at the crystal that seemed to hold a turbulent night within its depths. She wasn't sure how to destroy it. The crystal was probably stronger than anything. It looked like the sort that would break rocks if one tried to smash it.

And yet...

It looked like it should be heavy, yet it wasn't. It had once been cold yet now held a warmth beyond what it could have absorbed from her skin. It was as though it was its own entity, abiding by its own set of rules.

She made a fist and squeezed the amulet against the palm of her hand. The crystal, though warm at first, grew colder and colder the harder she pressed. It grew so cold that her fingers began to tingle and her palm grew numb. But she kept pressing, watching her mother with tear-filled eyes, harboring a deep hope that it would remain unbreakable.

Then, like a thin layer of rime across chilled water, the crystal gave way and shattered. An intense cold engulfed Holly's hand, encasing it in pain before the numbness returned and she lost all feeling.

Willow's form began to unravel. The parts of her that had been solid now began to twine away in curls of smoke that dissipated in the air.

"I'm sorry!" Holly cried.

But her mother just smiled and put a fading hand to Holly's cheek.

She turned to Hazel, put a hand to her lips, and offered the hand to Hazel. One heartbeat later, Willow was gone.

Aggravated Acceptance

A chill settled in the room—wintery, just like the silence that accompanied it. Hazel didn't know what to say, and so she said nothing, standing stiff and unyielding like a frozen tree.

Holly fell to her knees and into tears. Hazel told herself to go to her, to comfort her, yet she couldn't bring herself to move. Instead, Hawthorn walked over and gave Holly a handkerchief, put an arm around her, whispered words that Hazel couldn't hear. They must have been comforting, for Holly nodded and gulped down gasps of air as her sobs lessened. She rested her head on his shoulder, so Hazel turned her attention to Hemlock.

He sat on the floor, cradling his head in his hands. Hazel knelt down next to him.

He looked up at her, then surveyed the room. Some of the color had come back to his face, though he still looked like he had been washed and wrung out by heavy, unforgiving hands. "So it's done then?"

Hazel swallowed and nodded, unable to say anything, even to him. Especially to him. After everything that had happened, after everything she'd done... It was all too much, so she fixed her gaze at a point beyond his shoulder. Looking near him but not at him. She couldn't bring herself to look at him, not anymore.

He put a hand to her cheek and pulled her gaze to him. He smiled. "You did it."

Hazel's lips trembled. How could he smile at her? How could he offer her kind words when she could find none for herself? Her body shook. She was tired, so unbearably tired. So she let herself rest against Hemlock, and she cried.

The room had warmed in the countless moments that had passed, though the silence lingered. Hazel sat next to Hemlock, across from Holly and Hawthorn. Between them lay Ash's prone body, unmoving yet alive, according to Holly.

Hawthorn spoke first. "You know I hate to be rude, but is it really necessary to sit here and stare at your father's prone form for an unbearable length of time? I know decorum calls for such things, but surely we've stared sufficiently long enough and can get on with the pressing business of leaving this place."

"We can't just leave him," Holly said.

"Why on earth not? You yourself said he's not dead. Leaving while he's still unconscious sounds like the perfect time for us to make an exit."

"I agree," Hemlock said. "Your father was rather adamant about us staying. We should go before he tries to stop us. Again."

"Yes," Hazel said, though she made no move to get up.

"But...," Holly said.

"But what?" said Hawthorn. "But you can't figure out the best way for us to get out of here? But you can't understand why you've all not been listening to me sooner? But my brilliance has not diminished for suggesting such a base and obvious idea? Surely that's what you meant to express."

Holly pursed her lips and fixed him in a level stare. "But we can't leave!" She got up and poked at a collection of jars scattered on one of the tables.

Hawthorn threw up his hands. Then he squinted at Hazel and thrust a finger at her. "She's becoming more like you every day!"

Hazel rolled her eyes.

They all remained sitting while Holly wandered around the room to examine whatever jars and bottles she could find. From time to time, Hawthorn would sigh, loudly, but when that didn't elicit whatever response he hoped for, he contented himself with poking at Ash's unresponsive face instead.

Holly returned with a few jars. "What are you doing?"

"There are different degrees of unconsciousness. I was wondering on which degree your father had settled."

"Well?" Holly said, then shook her head. "Never mind, it's not important. I found some tinctures that I think will help revive him."

"What?" Hawthorn said as he got to his feet. "You've lost your mind!"

"That's probably not a good idea, Holly," Hemlock said.

"No, but he's my father—our father—and I'm not leaving him like this." She raised her chin at Hazel, as if challenging her sister to stop her.

But Hazel just nodded. "Do it."

Hawthorn threw up his hands and moved away. He walked over to a bookshelf and pretended to examine the tomes but kept stealing glances over at Holly and the others.

Holly leaned down and unscrewed the lid on one of the jars and held it up to Ash's nose. His brow twitched, but he lay still. She removed the lid of another jar and held that up to his nose, and after a few seconds, Ash's eyes opened and he started coughing.

Holly helped him sit up as she patted his back. "That's some nasty smelling stuff you've got there. Would probably wake the dead..." She shifted her weight and looked uncomfortable. "Though I'm sure that's not why you have it..."

Ash rubbed his eyes, gave Holly a feeble smile, and put a hand on her shoulder. "Thank you, my dear." His gaze shifted over to Hazel and Hemlock, and his smile faded.

"I'm not staying," Hazel said before he could say anything. "So don't try to keep me here."

He winced and rubbed his chest as he looked around the room.

"She's gone," Hazel said.

Ash winced again, though Hazel was unsure if it was from pain in his chest or from a different kind of pain altogether.

"It's what she wanted," she said. "It's what was right."

He fixed her in a cool gaze. A long, tense moment passed between them before he said, "You should leave before the others get to talking.

I'll show you out of the mountain. Arrange a carriage." He tried to get up from the floor but couldn't manage it. Holly took his arm and helped him to his feet. He gave her another wan smile and patted her hand.

"Come," he said and shuffled out of the room.

Hazel helped Hemlock off the floor, and he leaned upon her as they followed Ash out.

Nobody said anything as they walked through the stone hallways. Occasionally they would meet another necromancer. Ash would nod and the necromancer, though eyeing Hazel and the others, would nod back and move on.

"Aren't you going to get in trouble?" Holly said after such an encounter. "You're not supposed to let us go, are you?"

"It could be argued I wasn't supposed to bring you here either. Yet I did, with no great harm to my reputation. There will be talk and complaints, but I doubt anything serious will come as a result. Besides, one can't live beholden to rules." He gave Hazel a knowing smile. She looked away.

They continued on, eventually following a set of stairs that led downwards into a stable. The air was sweet and cloying but not as unpleasant as an indoor stable could have been.

A black-robed acolyte came up to meet them while another one lingered behind near a table.

"Hitch up the carriage and prepare to take my daughters back to Sarnum."

The acolyte lingered as he eyed Hazel and Holly. "But, sir—"

"Now," Ash said, his voice turning harsh.

The acolyte clamped his mouth shut. Then he gave a slight nod, and he and the other acolyte got to work.

While they waited, Ash led them outside where the sun shone and gave a gentle warmth to the crisp, autumnal air.

"It would be best to leave the carriage at the Shrine," Ash said. "Not for me, but you'll provoke the others less this way." He gave Hazel a level look. "You don't want to give them more reasons to come after you."

"And what about you?" Hazel said. "You're really going to let us go? After everything? Just like that?"

He squinted against the sunlight towards a vast, flat field. "You made your choice, as did your mother. I will respect that."

"Is that so?"

He looked at her. "Just promise me one thing. Promise that you won't decide now how your life will always be. You are young, Hazel. Promise me you'll let your life be whatever it wants to be, no matter what anyone else thinks of it."

"Including you?"

He gave a half smile and exhaled a sharp, short breath. "Including me." He paused and his smile faded. "I couldn't go back, you know. Not after... this." He waved a hand towards the mountain. "I didn't fit anymore. But maybe you will be different. Perhaps... we are different."

Hazel swallowed. "Perhaps." She wanted it to be true, but at that moment, she felt more like her father than she ever had. After everything she'd done, how could she say she was different?

A gate opened from the nearby stables, and out rolled a black-lacquered carriage.

"Ah," Ash said. "Time to go then."

Hazel nodded. She wished she knew what to say to him. She wished she didn't feel so sad at this parting, especially when she thought she should be happy. She had done what she had set out to do. She should be happy, right?

Ash turned to Hemlock. "Sorry about that bit of business back there. Nothing personal. But I take the welfare of my daughters most seriously, however unconventional my approaches. I'm sure you understand."

Hemlock regarded Ash with a stony expression. "Of course."

Ash gave a tight smile. "Splendid."

Holly stood nearby, wringing her hands. Then she threw her arms around her father and gave him a quick hug before she ran into the carriage. Hawthorn held the door open, and Hazel helped Hemlock climb inside.

Before she could pull herself up, Ash said, "I will always be here, you know. Should you ever be in need."

Hazel froze in place for a moment. Then, without looking at him, she climbed inside and sat next to Hemlock. Hawthorn followed her, and the carriage pulled away.

A Future Found

The journey back to Sarnum was largely spent in tense, exhausted silence. When they weren't all sleeping, that is. Hemlock slept the most. Holly spent a good portion of her waking hours staring out the window, her expression pensive and distant. Hawthorn expended his energy avoiding Hazel's gaze. She couldn't really blame him, after all that had happened.

They reached Sarnum late the following day. The acolyte that served as their driver took them back to Sensi's Contemplation. Holly murmured her concerns over Tum having gone missing, while Hawthorn muttered his over his carriage that had undoubtedly been stolen. But all were too tired to do anything about those problems, so they all agreed to go back to the inn to figure out what to do next.

It was strange for Hazel, being back there. The three old women still sat on the sofa in the common room, knitting up a storm. That they had remained unchanged accentuated how much everything had changed for Hazel, that she no longer felt like the same person she had been before. She didn't know how to go back—she didn't know how to feel comfortable in her skin again.

They went upstairs to their respective rooms. Hazel escorted Hemlock to his door and had started to open it when Hawthorn cried out from his room nearby. She hurried over and found Tum and the driver inside while the entirety of Hawthorn's wardrobe had been strewn across the floor.

The driver's cheeks flushed red. He mumbled something incoherent and hurried out.

"What are you doing?" Hawthorn cried. He picked up one of his shirts between a pair of fingers, sniffed at it, then made a disgusted sound and dropped it back on the floor. "What *have* you been doing?"

Tum drew himself up. "Having a bit o' fun, that's what. You and Miss Holly all ran off to go spoiling without me, so I did some spoiling of my own."

Hawthorn's face turned an impressive shade of purple. He drew himself up and opened his mouth, but then Holly came up behind him. She squeaked when she saw Tum and ran inside and hugged him. Instead, Hawthorn clenched his eyes shut, took a deep breath, then turned and walked away.

Tum wriggled out of Holly's hug. "Oh, sure, it's all well and good once the spoiling's been done, but don't think I forgive you."

"They put us in boxes, Tum. I would've rather they didn't, and I would've rather you came with us, but we didn't have any choice."

Tum sniffed. "A likely excuse."

"It's probably good you weren't there. They didn't have any beer."

He looked at her out of the corner of his eye. "No?"

"No, none. They had these creepy mushrooms though."

Tum shook his head. "Nope, don't like mushrooms. Old Uncle Wirt kept some 'shrooms in his cellar, rather than beer like any decent gnome. They were a weird sort that stained his hands black and made you see odd sorts of things if you got too close to 'em." He sniffed. "Nobody liked Uncle Wirt."

"Um, yeah. See? It's good you stayed behind."

Tum nodded. "Suppose so." He looked her up and down. "So what'd you spoil?"

"I told you, nothing." Holly sighed. "Never mind. Let's just go find you some beer."

Tum perked up. "'Bout time." He ran from the room. Holly followed him out.

"At least some things haven't changed," Hemlock said as he leaned against the doorway. He smiled.

Hazel went over to him, and he took her arm. "Everything else has," she said as they walked back to his room.

"It always does, Hazel."

She helped him over to the bed, and he sat down.

"I'm sorry for what happened," she said, unable to look at him. "It was all my fault, Ash hurting you like that."

"From what I recall, he was the one who did the hurting, not you."

She shook her head. "If not for me, none of it would have happened. If I hadn't gone off alone... if I'd done something different... it never would have happened. It shouldn't have happened."

"You don't know what would have happened if you'd done things differently. Maybe things would have gone for the worse. Maybe not. Maybe if *I'd* done something differently..." He shook his head. "It's pointless wondering about such things. We are where we are. That's all we need to think about."

"And what are you thinking about?" She couldn't help but feel he must want to get away from her—away from the source of so much pain. How could he not? But she didn't have the courage to ask him directly.

Hemlock went quiet and stared at his hands a long while, and Hazel grew nervous.

Finally he looked up at her and said, "I'm thinking about whether or not it would be terribly inappropriate if I asked you to marry me."

Hazel's mouth fell open.

"Would it?" he said. "Be inappropriate?"

Stunned, all she could do was stand there and shake her head.

His brow knitted into a puzzled frown. "Is that 'no' it's inappropriate, or 'no' it's not inappropriate?"

"You don't want to marry me!" Hazel blurted out. She winced at how harsh she sounded.

Hemlock folded his hands and gave her a level look. "Oh? Would you care to tell me more about what I do and don't want? It sounds most enlightening."

Hazel tightened her jaw. "You saw what happened. You *know* what happened. You..." She took a deep breath and, calmer, said, "You should get as far away from me as possible."

"I see. And what would you say if I told you that I don't want to get as far away from you as possible? That I want the exact opposite of that. What would you say then?"

Hazel pressed her lips together to keep them from trembling. "Then I'd tell you you've lost your mind."

"Is that all?"

"I'm a necromancer, Hemlock! I can't deny it anymore. What's more, I'm not sure I *want* to deny it. I don't know what I want! I don't know if I'll be able to go home. I don't know if I can just start living my life the way I left it. I don't know if I even want to try. I don't know anything other than I'm confused and scared, and I know you can't possibly love someone like that because you deserve better. You... you deserve better, Hemlock." She covered her face with her hands and took a deep, ragged breath.

He was quiet a while. Hazel wondered if she should leave when he said, "Will you sit with me?"

She shouldn't sit down; she should leave. It would only be harder the longer she waited. But she didn't want to go, so she sat down on the bed next to him, though she kept her gaze fixed to the floor.

He turned so he could look at her and said, "You know, when you left, the only thing I could think about was how I needed to find you and stop you. I couldn't let you go through with it, and if you did, it would somehow be my fault. I would have failed."

"I know," Hazel murmured. "It's why I left like I did."

He gave her a half smile, though the other half looked sad. "Exactly. But looking back now, I don't know... it all seems kind of foolish."

Hazel frowned. "That you came after me?" Of course it was foolish, but hearing him say it still stung.

He shook his head. "No, I was foolish thinking I could keep you from doing something so important to you. Something that, I realize now, is a part of you."

Hazel stared at him; she didn't know what to say.

"Did Holly tell you we drank the potions?"

"What potions?" Then she remembered. "Odd's potions?"

He nodded. "Also probably not the smartest thing to do, but under the circumstances, it seemed worth the risk."

"What happened?"

He stared at the wall, looking thoughtful. "I saw a world in which you did not exist. Not even a little bit. It was like I had never known you. After I woke from that, I realized what a trivial thing it would be if you were a necromancer. What difference would any of it make, as long as you were in my life?" He took her hand and returned his gaze to her. "I don't want you to leave my world, Hazel."

"But what if I can't go back? What if the Grove won't take me back? What if... I don't *want* to go back?"

He smiled again, this time more happy than sad. "Then we'll live somewhere else. The Grove has never felt much like home to me anyway. We can figure it out, Hazel."

She wanted this—wanted it so much it almost hurt her. But she was afraid to say yes, afraid to look at this moment directly and frighten it away or break its delicateness with her clumsy, heavy way. So she said nothing, squeezing Hemlock's hand as if that would keep the tears from rolling down her cheeks. It didn't, but none of it mattered. It was as if he understood anyway. He took her in his arms and kissed her, and Hazel let him take some of her fear away.

Fastened Friendship

Tum toddled down to the common room as Holly trailed after him. Hawthorn sat at a table, sipping wine, and Tum clambered onto an empty chair beside him.

"Of all the empty tables," Hawthorn said, "you have to sit right there? Go find somewhere else."

"It's rude to let someone sit alone, you know. Tum's nothing if not polite."

"Oh, I can think of a few things that Tum is."

"Don't bicker," Holly said. "It's nice that we're all back together, isn't it?"

Hawthorn muttered something into his wine glass that Holly couldn't hear.

A willowy waitress came over, and Tum ordered beer while Holly ordered tea. When their drinks arrived, Tum took a sip of his beer and grimaced.

"When are we going home?" he said. "It's past time for a drink at the Green Man. This place doesn't measure up."

"I think we'll be heading home soon." Holly looked at Hawthorn. "Won't we?"

"Probably."

Tum eyed the three women knitting on the sofa near the fire. "What's going on there?" Beer in hand, he hopped off the chair and wandered over to them.

Hawthorn made a great effort of swirling and examining his wine. He didn't seem to notice that Tum had gone.

"It will be nice to go home, won't it?" Holly said.

"I suppose. I suppose everything will go back just as it was."

"That's good, isn't it?"

"Wonderful." Only he didn't sound at all pleased. He drank some wine.

"Except," Holly said after a while, "it probably won't *all* be the same."

"How so?"

"Well, Hazel and Hemlock are going to get married."

"What? They are?"

"Well, *probably*. I've kind of been assuming they would. That is, if Hazel doesn't ruin it."

Hawthorn grunted and nodded and drank more wine.

"And if they get married... well... I'm not sure what I'll do."

"Why would you need to do anything?"

"Well, they're not going to be the sort that live separately. I can tell. Plus Hazel's never liked that custom."

"So?"

"So... it just feels like it will be awfully crowded with me milling around while they start their new lives together."

He shrugged. "Come live with me then."

"What?"

"Have you not noticed? My house is huge. Hemlock and I will sometimes go days without seeing each other. You, too, could have that pleasure."

Holly stared at her tea as she pressed her lips together. "It's very nice of you, Hawthorn, and I am very fond of you, but..."

"But what? It solves all our problems."

"But I can't marry you!"

Hawthorn blanched. "Marry? I... What...?"

"Well, that is what you're asking, isn't it? You can't just ask a girl to move in with you without thinking that you... you know..."

Hawthorn's mouth hanging open as he dumbfoundedly stared at her suggested that he, in fact, did not know at all.

Growing flustered, Holly waved her hands. "Well, aren't you looking for a wife? Isn't that why you had that party all that time ago?"

Hawthorn winced and studied his wine. "Uh, yes. Yes, I was. But... to be compulsively honest... I don't want to marry. I never have. I was only looking because I felt it was my duty. You know, keeping up the family line and all that. I'm the eldest, and Hemlock was hopelessly reclusive, so that was never going to happen. It seemed necessary. But now... if Hemlock and Hazel, well... I'd happily hand over that responsibility to him." He took a deep breath. "You have no idea."

"It was quite an elaborate party for something you didn't want to do."

"One may as well have a little fun before one ruins one's life, don't you think?"

"Getting married wouldn't *really* ruin your life, would it?"

Hawthorn continued to stare deep into his wine glass. "Holly, me and women don't exactly get on." He looked up at her. "If you know what I mean."

"Well, if you scaled back on the sarcasm you might..." But then his words sank in as did his intent gaze, and her mouth fell open. "Oh." She blinked several times. "Well. Then I suppose in that case having a wife would not be ideal." She stared at her cup, unsure how she should act.

"I mean, women: they are soft and squeaky, and you never know which direction their moods will take. That party I threw was only the least bit fun because they were all appropriately adoring of me. The one true solace I found in the idea of taking a wife was the fact that I wouldn't have to live with her."

"You do know that I'm a woman, right?"

"Yes, which is why my affection for you is most puzzling. But there it is."

Holly couldn't help but smile. "You like me," she taunted and poked at his arm.

"Stop it, shrew."

She giggled. "Okay, so you don't want to get married. But what if I do?"

Hawthorn's expression turned slightly panicked.

"Not to you! But to... someone. I would like to get married someday, I think."

He shrugged. "Then I will be the first to offer you my best wishes." He sipped some wine. "After I kill the man."

Holly grinned, and Hawthorn smiled with her. He must have sensed her lingering hesitation though, because he said, "You don't have to move in. Just know that you have a home beyond Hazel and Hemlock's walls. If you want it."

She smiled and nodded. "Thanks, Hawthorn."

He cleared his throat. "Yes, well. That's quite enough of the unsightly baring of one's squishy heart for the afternoon. Don't you think?"

Holly giggled and sipped her tea. "Quite."

Tum waddled over, swathed in knitted scarves, mittens, and socks, all several sizes too large for him.

"Charming ladies!" His voice was muffled from layers of scarves. "I haven't been this warm since cousin Lur accidentally lit my pants on fire. The beer here might be unremarkable, but the hospitality is fantastic!" He started heading for the stairs, tripped on one of the trailing scarves, and tumbled down into a well-padded heap. "Marvelous!" came his muffled cry.

"I better go help him," Holly said. "Before, I don't know, he suffocates or something."

"No rush," Hawthorn said and took another sip of wine.

Heart Fire

They waited a few more days to allow Hemlock time to recover, then made the journey back to the Grove. Hazel had mixed feelings about it all. On the one hand she was glad to be returning home, but on the other she was afraid she wouldn't recognize it—or herself—once she got there. Other than undoing her mother's geas, nothing had gone the way she had expected. She hadn't ever thought she would turn to necromancy—she especially never thought she'd find beauty in what was supposed to be a grim, dreadful discipline. She didn't know what to think anymore, and so she didn't know what to expect when returning home.

Both she and Holly had their noses to the windows as the carriage rolled up in front of their cottage. They got out and remained on the road as the driver unloaded their luggage from the rack up top.

"It looks so small," Holly whispered. "Was it always so small?"

"I think so," Hazel replied.

Holly rubbed her arms. "I don't."

Tum hopped down from his perch next to the driver and bolted towards the cellar door.

Hemlock said, "Hawthorn and I are going to head home and take care of some affairs. We can stop by later if you'd like."

Hazel said, "That would be nice. Wouldn't it, Holly?"

Holly continued to stare at the cottage, but she nodded.

He smiled. "All right. Until later then." The carriage rolled away, and Holly, taking a deep breath, headed inside. Hazel followed.

The air inside was musty and stale, but everything looked as it should. Only dustier.

"Definitely smaller," Holly muttered and went into her room.

Hazel went to the kitchen. She had left a jar of flowers on the table that had since withered and browned. Purple columbines. Her mother's favorite. Hazel's too.

She put her hands over her face and cried.

The cottage was the same, yet different. It was as though ghosts had taken up residence while they were gone. So Hazel and Holly gathered all the candles they could find and lit them in an effort to keep the ghosts away.

"I bet Tum's got some candles stashed away," Holly said as Hazel tried to prod a fire to life in the hearth.

"More than likely."

"I'll go get them." Holly hustled outside.

Hazel blew on the feeble flames until they grew and caught the wood and burned on their own.

There was a commotion outside, then Tum came stumbling through the door, wearing red fuzzy pyjamas with matching cap and slippers. He scowled up at Holly, who followed him in, carrying a crate of mead and a few candles.

"Why do I need to come in here? I was perfectly comfortable where I was. Or hadn't you noticed?" Tum looked down at his body, as if to reassure himself of the obviousness of his comfort.

"It's our first night back," Holly said. "You shouldn't be spending it alone."

"But—"

"Nobody's spending it alone!" Holly took a deep breath, set down the crate, and took out a bottle of mead. She handed it to Tum. "Here. Drink this."

"I don't...," Tum began, but when he saw Holly's expression, he just said, "Right," took the mead, and sat on the sofa.

Despite the fire and candles, there was a gloom in the cottage the light couldn't dispel. Tum sniffed at the mead and grimaced and continued to stare into the fire while Holly poked around in the kitchen, looking for food.

"There's nothing here!" she called out. "Wait... Oh." She sounded disappointed. "A jar of green beans." She poked her head around the corner and held out the jar. "How old is this?"

"I don't know," Hazel said. "So probably pretty old."

Holly muttered something Hazel couldn't hear.

"We could go to the Green Man," Tum said. "I bet they got food."

"They don't have food," Holly said.

"But they got beer. That's a kind of food."

"I don't want—" Holly began but was interrupted by a knock at the door. She ran over and opened it. Hemlock and Hawthorn stood on the threshold. Hawthorn carried a crate while Hemlock carried a wide basket.

"Come in!" Holly grabbed Hawthorn by the jacket and pulled him inside. Hemlock followed.

"We brought refreshments," Hawthorn said and thrust the crate at Holly, undoubtedly to get her to unhand him.

"Oh?" Holly said. "What kind?" She lifted the lid to the crate and found several dark bottles nestled among handfuls of straw.

"Wine, of course."

"Oh."

"We also brought food," Hemlock said as he set down his basket and began to unpack it.

"Oooh!" Holly hustled over to help him. There was a braided loaf of bread, a roasted chicken, several apples, a wedge of cheese, a jar of brined olives, and two small honey cakes.

Holly ran into her room, pulled the blanket from her bed, and spread the blanket on the floor in front of the fire. She and Hemlock lay the food out on the blanket while Hawthorn rooted around in the kitchen and came back with four glasses.

"You didn't bring a glass for Tum," Holly said.

"Tum doesn't drink wine," Tum said and continued to stare forlornly at the fire.

"Exactly," Hawthorn said. He went over to the crate and pulled out a smaller, dustier bottle and handed it to Tum. "Besides, I figured he'd rather drink his beer from the bottle."

"Beer?!" Tum said. "You got beer?"

Hawthorn shrugged. "I found it in the cellar. Could be Merrick's. Or maybe it belonged to Father. Who knows? But I figured better to get it out of the house."

"And into old Tum's belly!" He grinned as he broke off the wax stopper and took a swig. He cackled. "Oh ho! It's horrible!" He took another drink.

"Where did all this food come from?" Hazel said.

"One of the many benefits of having a fully trained staff waiting for one's inevitable return," Hawthorn said as he looked around. "You should really consider hiring a maid."

Hemlock took the glasses and poured some wine, and everyone sat down on the blanket and started to eat.

"This is cozy," Holly said as she nibbled on an olive. "Don't you think, Hazel?"

It was. Somehow the tiny cottage had gotten too big for her and Holly, and they alone could no longer light its dark corners with the candles of their lives. Perhaps they never could, only Hazel had never realized it. She smiled and nodded and raised her tumbler of wine. "To family, new and old."

The others clinked their glasses to hers. Even Tum toddled over and clanked his dusty bottle against her glass.

And so they passed that first evening at home in the company of each other, making plans for the future and of the orange tree Holly planned to grow for Elder. As the candles burned down and the night grew darker, the room inside grew warmer as they all lay down on the floor, talking and telling stories before drifting off to sleep.

Hazel awoke in the night. She lay there listening to the breathing of the others as they slumbered. She clenched her eyes shut, telling herself to sleep as well. But sleep wouldn't come.

She got up, found a lamp, and lit it from the embers of the fire. Then she broke off a piece of honey cake, put it in her pocket, and walked outside.

The clear, crisp night smelled like rain and leaves and rotting wood. She shivered but dared not go back in for a shawl. She hurried down the road, the handle from the lantern slightly creaking as it swayed to and fro.

Barren, tangled vines webbed across the sterile stone of the cottage. She slipped past the waterlogged door, went to the hearth, and built a small fire from the pile of sticks and twigs in the corner. Rainwater that had leaked through the roof overflowed from the ewer. Hazel poured some of the water into the bowl, then took the cake from her pocket and crumbled it into the liquid.

She waited.

Hazel held her breath, listening, but there was only the cry of a distant owl and a scratching and rustling of leaves out in the brush. Everything else remained frightfully silent. Yet still she waited.

But Willow didn't come.

Hazel exhaled. Was she relieved? Disappointed? She didn't know. Part of her felt... empty. As if her heart had deflated and nothing had rushed in the void to fill it. Standing there, in the decaying cottage to which her mother would never return, she felt so very alone.

And yet she wasn't, was she? She had the love of her sister. Of Hemlock. After everything she'd done. Without them, she likely would have never been able to overcome her father. And that... warmed her. It helped push back some of the sadness shrouding her heart.

She didn't know what the future held, but she knew she didn't have to face it alone. That meant something. That gave her strength.

Hazel extinguished the fire with the cake water and tidied the ewer and basin on the table. She lingered a moment, not wanting to leave, feeling as though she would never return. But then, with a single look back, she left the cottage and returned to let the hearth fire of her home—of her family—warm her hollowed heart.

Dear Reader

Thanks for reading *Hazel and Holly*! If you enjoyed the story and have a few moments to spare, why not leave a short review? You'll help spread the word most fantastically, and you'll have my eternal gratitude to boot.

What's next for Hazel and Holly? I'm not sure. I have a couple of ideas, but I'd love to hear from you and what you'd like to see next. If you sign up for my mailing list, we can gab about the future of our two witch sisters. You'll also be the first to know about future releases, and get access to freebie stories too.

Sound good? Then head on over to: www.saracsnider.com/hazel-and-holly/signup

Aknowledgments

Those of you who read my blog know that *Hazel and Holly* originally started as a flash fiction story I wrote as part of a blogging challenge. You know that I decided to expand the story after some readers expressed a desire to read more, which resulted in my serializing the novel on the blog as I wrote it. But I'm not sure you know how grateful I am to you for that.

Hazel and Holly was, for the two years or so it took me to write it, a light in my life. It was my "fun project" (and then later my only project), that was very much like a little vacation every time I sat down to work on it. It was the story I gave myself permission to have fun with. To silence that inner-critic that likes to tell me what I've written is rubbish. And you, who read the installments each week and commented or mailed me with how much you were enjoying the story, helped me believe that not only could I do it, but that it was also worth doing.

If not for you, this story would not exist. These characters would not have found their way to my heart where they will undoubtedly stay for the rest of my life. And for that I am profoundly grateful. So thank you.

As always, many, many thanks and ridiculous amounts of gratitude goes to Anders Nyström, my partner in crime who not only puts up with me being a writer but actively supports me in it. Many thanks to the Stockholm Writers Group for their thoughtful and patient feedback and for helping me become a better writer. Thanks to Ray Rhamey for his thorough editing and Jennifer Zemanek for the beautiful cover and chapter artwork.

Lastly, thank you to every person I've talked or written to who's expressed their support and encouragement for this writing adventure I've undertaken. You all help make the road a little less bumpy.

About the Author

Sara C. Snider is a fantasy writer, cat wrangler, and multi-purpose nerd that likes to crochet and play video games. Originally from northern California, she now lives in Sweden where she is one step closer to fulfilling her childhood dream of becoming a forest hermit.

CPSIA information can be obtained
at www.ICGtesting.com
Printed in the USA
LVHW111602010519
616262LV00006B/827/P